INVISIBLE
GIRL

ALSO BY LISA JEWELL

The Family Upstairs

Watching You

Then She Was Gone

I Found You

The Girls in the Garden

The Third Wife

The House We Grew Up In

Before I Met You

The Making of Us

After the Party

The Truth About Melody Browne

31 Dream Street

A Friend of the Family

Vince & Joy

One-Hit Wonder

Thirtynothing

Ralph's Party

INVISIBLE GIRL

GIRL

— *A Novel* —

LISA JEWELL

ATRIA PAPERBACK

New York   London   Toronto   Sydney   New Delhi

ATRIA
PAPERBACK

An Imprint of Simon & Schuster, Inc.
1230 Avenue of the Americas
New York, NY 10020

This Atria Paperback Canadian export edition October 2020

ATRIA PAPERBACK and colophon are trademarks of Simon & Schuster, Inc.

For information about special discounts for bulk purchases, please contact Simon & Schuster Special Sales at 1-866-506-1949 or business@simonandschuster.com.

The Simon & Schuster Speakers Bureau can bring authors to your live event. For more information or to book an event, contact the Simon & Schuster Speakers Bureau at 1-866-248-3049 or visit our website at www.simonspeakers.com.

Interior design by Jill Putorti

Manufactured in the United States of America

1 3 5 7 9 10 8 6 4 2

Library of Congress Cataloging-in-Publication Data

ISBN 978-1-9821-6319-8
ISBN 978-1-9821-3735-9 (ebook)

To Jack, Sonny, Cocoa:
all the lovely animals I have loved and lost this year

INVISIBLE GIRL

Valentine's Night

11:59 p.m.

I DUCK DOWN and pull my hoodie close around my face. Ahead of me the girl with red hair is picking up speed; she knows she's being followed. I pick up my speed to match hers. I only want to talk to her, but I can tell from the way she's moving that she's terrified. I slow down at the sound of muffled footsteps behind me. I turn and see a figure coming after us.

I don't need to see their face to know who it is.

It's him.

My heart starts pounding beneath my ribs, pumping blood through my body so hard and fast that I can feel the cut on my leg begin to throb. I pull back, into the shadows, and wait for the man to pass. He turns the corner, and I see his body language change as he sees the woman ahead. I recognize the shape of him, the angles of his body, and I know exactly what he is planning to do.

I move from my hiding place in the shadows. I stride out, toward the man, toward danger, my actions my own but my fate left wide-open.

PART ONE

Before

1

Saffyre

MY NAME IS Saffyre Maddox. I am seventeen years old.

I am mostly Welsh on my dad's side and partly Trinidadian, partly Malaysian, and a tiny bit French from my mum. Sometimes people try to guess my heritage, but they always end up getting it wrong. If anyone asks I just say that I am a mixed bag and leave it at that. No reason for anyone to know who slept with who, you know. It's my business really, isn't it?

I'm in my first year of sixth form at a school in Chalk Farm, where I'm doing maths, physics, and biology because I'm a bit of a nerd. I don't really know what I want to do when I leave school; everyone expects me to go to university, but sometimes I think I'd just like to go and work in a zoo, maybe, or a dog groomer's.

I live in a two-bedroom flat on the eighth floor of a tower on Alfred Road, right opposite a school I don't go to, because they hadn't actually built it when I started secondary.

My grandma died shortly before I was born, my mum died shortly afterward, my dad didn't want to know, and my granddad died a few months ago. So I live alone with my uncle.

He's only ten years older than me, and his name is Aaron. He looks after me like a father. He works at a betting shop, nine to five, and does people's gardens on the weekends. He's probably the best human being in the world. I have another uncle, Lee, who lives in Essex with his wife and two tiny daughters. So there are finally some girls in the family, but it's a bit late for me now.

I grew up with two men, and, as a result, I'm not that great with girls. Or, more accurately, I'm better with boys. I used to hang out with the boys when I was a kid and got called a tomboy, which I don't think I ever was. But then I started to change and became "pretty" (and I do not think I'm pretty; I just know that everyone I meet tells me that I am), and boys stopped wanting to hang out as a mate and got all weird around me, and I could tell that I'd be better off if I could harvest some girls. So I harvested some girls, and we're not close—don't reckon I'll ever see any of them again once I've left school—but we get on OK just as something to do. We've all known each other a long, long time now. It's easy.

So that's the bare outline of me. I'm not a happy, happy kind of person. I don't have a big laugh, and I don't do that hugging thing that the other girls like to do. I have boring hobbies: I like to read, and I like to cook. I'm not big on going out. I like a bit of rum with my uncle on a Friday night while we're watching TV, but I don't smoke weed or take drugs or anything like that. It's amazing how boring you can get away with being when you're pretty. No one seems to notice. When you're pretty everyone just assumes you must have a great life. People are so short-sighted, sometimes. People are so stupid.

I have a dark past, and I have dark thoughts. I do dark things, and I scare myself sometimes. I wake in the middle of the night, and I've twisted myself into my bedsheets. Before I go to sleep, I tuck my bedsheet under the mattress, really hard, really firm, so the sheet is taut enough to bounce a coin off. The next morning all four corners are free; my sheet and I are entwined. I don't remember what happened. I don't remember my dreams. I don't feel rested.

When I was ten years old something really, really bad happened to me. Let's maybe not get into that too deep. But yes, I was a little girl, and it was a big bad thing that no little girl should have to experience, and it changed me. I started to hurt myself, on my ankles, inside my ankle socks, so no one would see the scratches. I knew what self-harming was—everyone knows these days—but I didn't know why I was doing it. I just knew that it stopped me thinking too hard about other things in my life.

Then when I was about twelve my uncle Aaron saw the scratches and the scars, put two and two together, and took me to my GP, who referred me to the Portman Children's Centre for therapy.

I was sent to a man called Roan Fours.

2

Cate

"MUM, CAN YOU talk to me?"

Cate's daughter sounds breathless and panicky.

"What?" says Cate. "What's wrong?"

"I'm walking back from the tube. And I feel . . ."

"What?"

"It's, like, there's this guy." Her daughter's voice lowers to a whisper. "He's walking really close."

"Just keep talking, G, just keep talking."

"I am," snaps Georgia. "I am talking. Listen."

Cate ignores the teenage attitude and says, "Where are you now?"

"Just coming up Tunley Terrace."

"Good," she says. "Good. Nearly here, then."

She pulls back the curtain and peers out to the street, into the blackness of the January night, waiting for the familiar outline of her daughter to appear.

"I can't see you," she says, starting to feel a little panicky herself.

"I'm here," says Georgia. "I can see you now."

As she says this, Cate sees her too. Her heart rate starts to slow.

She lets the curtain drop and goes to the front door. Folding her arms against the freezing cold, she waits for Georgia. Across the street a shape disappears into the driveway of the big house opposite. A man.

"Was that him?" she asks Georgia.

Georgia turns, her hands clasped into fists around the sleeves of her oversize Puffa coat. "Yes," she says. "That was him." She shivers as Cate closes the door behind her and bundles her into the warmth of the hallway. She throws her arms briefly around Cate and hugs her hard. Then she says, "Creep."

"What was he doing exactly?"

Georgia shrugs off her coat and throws it carelessly on the nearest chair. Cate picks it up and hangs it in the hallway.

"I don't know. Just being creepy."

"Creepy in what way?"

Cate follows Georgia into the kitchen and watches her open the fridge door, peer inside briefly, and then shut it again.

"I don't know," Georgia says again. "Just walking too close. Just being . . . *weird*."

"Did he say anything to you?"

"No. But he looked like he was going to." She opens the cupboard and pulls out a pack of Jaffa Cakes, opens it up, and puts one whole into her mouth. She chews and swallows, then shudders. "Just freaked me out," she says. Her eyes catch sight of Cate's white wine, and she says, "Can I have a sip? For my nerves?"

Cate rolls her eyes, then passes her daughter the glass. "Would you recognize him?" she asks. "If you saw him again?"

"Probably." Georgia is about to take a third sip from Cate's wine, and Cate snatches it back from her.

"That's enough," she says.

"But I've experienced a trauma!" Georgia says.

"Hardly," says Cate. "But it just goes to show. Even somewhere like this, somewhere supposedly 'safe,' you need to keep your wits about you."

"I hate it round here," says Georgia. "I don't know why anyone would want to live here if they didn't have to."

"I know," Cate agrees. "I can't wait to get home."

The house is a rental, a temporary accommodation after their home a mile away was damaged by land subsidence. They'd thought it would be an adventure to live somewhere "posh" for a while. They hadn't thought that posh areas were full of posh people who didn't really like the fact there were other people living in close proximity. They hadn't thought about the unfriendly security-gated houses and about how eerily quiet these leafy, mansion-lined streets would be compared with their bustling Kilburn terrace. It hadn't occurred to them that empty streets could be scarier than streets full of people.

A little while later Cate goes to the bay window in her bedroom at the front of the house and pulls back the curtain again. The shadows of bare trees whip across the high wall opposite. Beyond the high wall is an empty plot of land where an old house has been ripped down to make way for something new. Cate sometimes sees pickup trucks reverse through a gate between the wooden construction panels and then reappear an hour later filled with soil and rubble. They've been living here for a year and so far there has been no sign of a foundation being dug or a hard-hatted architect on-site. It is that rarest of things in central London: a space with no discernible function, a gap.

She thinks of her girl turning that corner, the fear in her voice, the footsteps too close behind her, the audible breath of a stranger. How easy it would be, she thinks, to break open those boards, to drag a girl from the street, to hurt her, kill her even, and hide her body in that dark, private void. And how long would it take for the body to be found?

3

"GEORGIA HAD A scare last night."

Roan looks up from his laptop. His pale blue eyes are immediately fearful. "What sort of scare?"

"She got a bit spooked walking back from the tube station. Thought someone was following her."

Roan had been out late the night before, and Cate had lain alone in bed, listening to foxes screaming in the wasteland opposite, watching the shapes of the branches outside waving like a crowd of zombies through the thin fabric of the curtains, overthinking everything.

"What did he look like, the man who followed you?" she'd asked Georgia earlier that night.

"Just normal."

"Normal, how? Was he tall? Fat? Thin? Black? White?"

"White," she said. "Normal height. Normal size. Boring clothes. Boring hair."

Somehow the blandness of this description had unnerved Cate more than if Georgia had said he was six feet seven with a face tattoo.

She can't work out why she feels so unsafe in this area. The insurance company offered to pay up to £1,200 a week for replacement accommodation while their house is being repaired. With that they could have found a nice house on their street, with a garden, but for some reason they'd decided to use it as a chance to have an adventure, to live a different kind of a life.

Flicking though a property supplement, Cate had seen an advert for a grand apartment in a grand house in Hampstead. Both the kids were at school in Swiss Cottage, and Roan worked in Belsize Park. Hampstead was closer to both places than their house in Kilburn, which meant they could walk instead of getting the tube.

"Look," she'd said, showing the advert to Roan. "Three-bed flat in Hampstead. With a terrace. Twelve-minute walk to the school. Five minutes to your clinic. And Sigmund Freud used to live up the road! Wouldn't it be fun," she'd said blithely, "to live in Hampstead for a little while?"

Neither Cate nor Roan is a native Londoner. Cate was born in Liverpool and raised in Hartlepool, while Roan was born and brought up in Rye, near the Sussex coast. They both discovered London as adults, without any innate sense of its demographic geography. A friend of Cate's who'd lived in north London all her life said of their temporary address, "Oh no, I'd hate to live round there. It's so anonymous." But Cate hadn't known that when she'd signed the contracts. She hadn't thought beyond the poetry of the postcode, the proximity to Hampstead's picturesque village center, the illustriousness of the blue plaque on Sigmund Freud's house around the corner.

"Maybe you should go and meet her from now on?" says Roan now. "When she's walking around at night?"

Cate imagines Georgia's reaction to being told that her mother would now be accompanying her on all nocturnal journeys outside the house. "Roan, she's fifteen! That's the last thing she'd want."

He throws her that look, the one he uses all the time, the look that says, "Well, since you have put me in the position of conceding all decision-making to you, you will therefore have to take full responsibility for any bad things that happen as a result of those decisions. Including the potential rape/attack/murder of our daughter."

Cate sighs and turns to the window, where she can see the reflection of her husband and herself, a hazy tableau of a marriage at its midpoint. Twenty-five years married, likely another twenty-five to come.

Beyond the reflection it's snowing; fat swirls of flakes like TV interference over their image. Upstairs she can hear the soft feet of their neighbors, an American Korean couple whose names she can't quite remember though they smile and greet one another profusely whenever their paths cross. Somewhere there is the distant whine of police sirens. But apart from that it is silent. This road is always so silent, and the snow has made it quieter still.

"Look," says Roan, turning the screen of his laptop slightly toward her.

Cate drops her reading glasses from her head to her nose.

WOMAN, 23, SEXUALLY ASSAULTED ON HAMPSTEAD HEATH.

She takes a breath. "Yes, well," she counters, "that's the Heath. I wouldn't want Georgia walking around the Heath alone at night. I wouldn't want *either* of the children walking alone on the Heath."

"Apparently it's the third attack in a month. The first was on Pond Street."

Cate closes her eyes briefly. "That's a mile away."

Roan says nothing.

"I'll tell Georgia to be careful," she says. "I'll tell her to call me when she's walking home at night."

"Good," says Roan. "Thank you."

4

"I KNOW WHO it was!" says Georgia, who has just burst into the kitchen, with Tilly in tow. It's just turned four thirty, and they're both in their school uniforms. They bring a blast of winter cold and an air of panic into the flat with them.

Cate turns and gazes at her daughter. "Who what was?" she says.

"The creepy guy!" she replies. "The one who followed me the other night. We saw him just now. He lives in that weird house across the street. You know, the one with the gross armchair in the driveway."

"How do you know it was him?"

"It just totally was. He was putting something out in the bins. And he looked at us."

"Looked at you how?"

"Like, weirdly."

Tilly stands behind Georgia, nodding her agreement.

"Hi, Tilly," says Cate belatedly.

"Hi."

Tilly is a tiny thing, with gobstopper eyes and shiny black hair; she looks like a Pixar girl. She and Georgia have only recently become friends, after being at the same school for nearly five years.

She is the first really decent friend Georgia has acquired since she left primary school, and while Cate can't quite work Tilly out, she is very keen for the friendship to flourish.

"He knew it was me," Georgia continues. "When he looked at me. I could tell he knew it was me, from the other night. It was a really dirty look."

"Did you see it?" Cate asks Tilly.

Tilly nods again. "Yeah. He was definitely not happy with Georgia. I could tell."

Georgia opens a brand-new packet of Leibniz biscuits, even though there's a half-empty packet in the cupboard, and offers it to Tilly. Tilly says, "No, thank you," and then they disappear to her bedroom.

The front door goes again, and Josh appears. Cate's heart lifts a little. While Georgia always arrives with news and moods and announcements and atmospheres, her little brother arrives as though he'd never left. He doesn't bring things in with him, his issues unfurl gently and in good time.

"Hello, darling."

"Hi, Mum." He crosses the kitchen and hugs her. Josh hugs her every time he comes home, before he goes to bed, when he sees her in the morning, and when he goes out for longer than a couple of hours. He's done this since he was a tiny boy, and she keeps expecting it to stop, or to peter out, but he's fourteen now and he shows no sign of abandoning the habit. In a strange way, Cate sometimes thinks, it's Josh who's kept her at home all these years, way beyond her children's need to have a stay-at-home mother. He still feels so vulnerable for some reason, still feels like the small boy crying into the heels of his hands on his first day of nursery school and still crying four hours later when she came to collect him.

"How was school?"

He shrugs and says, "It was good. I got my physics test back. I got sixty out of sixty-five. I was second top."

"Oh," she says, squeezing him again quickly. "Josh, that's amazing! Well done, you! Physics! Of all the things to be good at. I don't know where you get it from."

Josh helps himself to a banana and an apple and a glass of milk and sits with her for a while at the kitchen table.

"Are you OK?" he asks her after a short silence.

She looks at him with surprise. "Yes," she says.

"Are you sure you're OK?"

"Yes," she says again, with a laugh. "Why?"

He shrugs. "No reason." Then he picks up his milk and his schoolbag and heads to his room. "What's for dinner?" he says, turning back halfway down the hallway.

"Chicken curry," she says.

"Cool," he says. "I'm in the mood for something spicy."

And then it is quiet again, just Cate and the dark shadows through the window, her unfocused thoughts passing silently through the back tunnels of her mind.

5

LATER THAT NIGHT it happens. A sort of coalescence of all of Cate's weird, unformed fears about this place.

Georgia's friend Tilly is assaulted moments after leaving their flat.

Cate had invited Tilly to stay for supper, and she'd said, "No, thank you, Mum's expecting me," and Cate had thought, Maybe she just doesn't like curry. Then a few minutes after she left, there was a knock at the door and the doorbell rang, and Cate went to answer it, and there was Tilly, her face white, her huge eyes wide with shock, saying, "Someone touched me. He touched me."

Now Cate hustles her into the kitchen and pulls out a chair for her, gets her a glass of water, asks her exactly what happened.

"I'd just crossed the road. I was just over there. By the building site. And there was someone behind me. And he just sort of grabbed me. Here." She gestures at her hips. "And he was trying to pull me."

"Pull you where?"

"Not anywhere. Just kind of against him."

Georgia sits Tilly down at the table and holds her arm. "Oh my God, did you see him? Did you see his face?"

Tilly's hands tremble in her lap. "Not really. Sort of. I don't think . . . It was all just . . . quick. Really, really quick."

"Are you hurt?" says Georgia.

"No?" says Tilly, with a slight question mark, as though she might be.

"No," she says again. "I'm OK. I'm just . . ." She stares down at her hands. "Freaked out. He was . . . It was horrible."

"Age?" asks Cate. "Roughly?"

Tilly shrugs. "I don't know." She sniffs. "He was wearing a hood and had a scarf around his face."

"Height?"

"Kind of tall, I guess. And slim."

"Should I call the police?" asks Cate, and then wonders why she's asking a sixteen-year-old girl who's just been assaulted whether she should call the police.

"For fuck's sake," says Georgia. "Of course you should call them." Then before anyone else has a chance to pick up their phone, she's calling 999.

And then the police arrive, and Tilly's mum arrives, and the night takes a strange tangent off into a place that Cate has never been before, a place of policemen in her kitchen, and a tearful mother she's never met before, and a nervous energy that keeps her awake for hours after the police leave and Tilly and her mother disappear in an Uber, and the house is quiet yet she knows that no one can be sleeping peacefully because a bad thing happened and it is something to do with them and something to do with this place and something else, some indefinable thing to do with her, some badness, some mistake she's made because she's not a good person. She has been trying so hard to stop thinking of herself as a bad person, but as she lies in bed that night, the sudden awful knowledge of it gnaws at her consciousness until she feels raw and unpeeled.

———

Cate awakes just before her alarm goes off the following morning, having slept for only three and a half hours. She turns and looks at Roan, lying peacefully on his back, his arms tucked neatly under the duvet. He is a pleasant-looking man, her husband. He has lost most of his hair and shaves it now, revealing the strange contours of his skull that she had not known existed when she'd first met him thirty years ago. She'd presumed his skull to be a smooth thing, the underside of a pottery urn. Instead it is a landscape with hills and valleys, a tiny puckered scar. Raised veins run across his temples to his brow. His nose is large. His eyes are heavy-lidded. He is her husband. He hates her. She knows he does. And it's her fault.

She slips out of bed and goes to the front window, a large bay overlooking the street. The just-risen sun shines through the trees, onto the building site across the road. It looks innocuous. Then she looks farther to the right, to the house with the armchair on the driveway. She thinks of the man who lives there, the creepy man who'd followed Georgia home from the tube station, who'd thrown her and Tilly dirty looks last night as he put out his bins—the man who matches the description that Tilly gave of the man who assaulted her.

Cate locates the card the policeman gave her last night. Detective Inspector Robert Burdett. She calls him, but he doesn't answer, so she leaves a message for him.

"I'm calling about the assault on Tilly Krasniqi last night," she begins. "I don't know if it's anything, but there's a man, across the street. At number twelve. My daughter says he followed her home the other night. And she says he was staring at her and Tilly strangely on their way home from school last night. I don't know his name, I'm afraid. He's about thirty or forty. That's all I know. Sorry. Just a thought. Number twelve. Thank you."

———

"Have you spoken to Tilly today?" Cate asks Georgia as her daughter spins around the flat readying herself to leave for school later that morning.

"No," says Georgia. "She's not been answering my messages or taking my calls. I think maybe her phone's switched off."

"Oh God." Cate sighs. She can't bear the sense of guilt, the feeling that she somehow made this happen. She imagines Georgia, her beautiful guileless girl, a man's hands on her in the dark on her way home from a friend's house. It's unbearable. Then she imagines tiny Tilly, too traumatized even to take messages from her best friend. She finds the number that Tilly's mum put into her phone last night and presses it.

Tilly's mum finally answers her phone the sixth time Cate calls her.

"Oh, Elona, hi, it's Cate. How is she? How's Tilly?"

There is a long silence, then the sound of the phone being handled and muted voices in the background. Then a voice says, "Hello?"

"Elona?"

"No. It's Tilly."

"Oh," says Cate. "Tilly. Hello, sweetheart. How are you doing?"

There's another strange silence. Cate hears Elona's voice in the background. Then Tilly says, "I've got something to tell you."

"Oh?"

"About last night. The thing that happened."

"Yes."

"It didn't happen."

"What?"

"A man didn't touch me. He just walked quite close to me, and Georgia had got me so freaked out about that man who lives opposite you, you know, and I thought it was him, but it wasn't him, it was someone completely different and—and I came rushing back to yours and I . . ."

There're more shuffling sounds, and then Elona comes on the line again. "I'm so sorry," she says. "So, so sorry. I said she'd have to tell you herself. I just don't understand. I mean, I know they're all under a lot of stress, these girls, these days—exams, social media, everything, you know. But still, that's no excuse."

Cate blinks slowly. "So there was no assault?" This doesn't make any sense. Tilly's pale skin, her wide eyes, her shaking hands, her tears.

"There was no assault," Elona confirms in a flat tone, and Cate wonders if maybe she doesn't quite believe it either.

Outside Cate sees DI Robert Burdett climbing into a squad car parked across the street. She remembers the message she left on his phone early this morning, about the strange man across the road. A wave of guilt passes through her stomach.

"Have you told the police?" she asks Elona.

"Yes. Absolutely. Just now. Can't have them wasting their resources. Not with all these cuts they're having. But anyway, I'm sending her into school now. Tail between her legs. And again, I am so, so sorry."

Cate turns off her phone and watches the back end of DI Burdett's car as it reaches the junction at the bottom of the road.

Why would Tilly have lied? It makes no sense whatsoever.

―――――――

Cate works from home. She's a trained physiotherapist, but she gave up her practice fifteen years ago when Georgia was born and never really got back into treating patients. These days she occasionally writes about physiotherapy for medical publications and industry magazines, and every now and then she rents a room in her friend's practice in St John's Wood to treat people she knows, but most of the time she is at home, freelancing (or being "a housewife with a laptop" as Georgia puts it). In Kilburn she has a small office area on the mezzanine, but in this temporary setup she writes at the kitchen table; her paperwork sits in a filing tray by her laptop, and it's a struggle to keep everything organized and to stop her work stuff from being absorbed into the general family silt. She can never find a pen, and people scrawl things on the back of her business correspondence, yet another thing she hadn't thought through properly before making the move to a small flat.

Cate peers through the front window again at the house across the road. Then she goes back to her laptop and googles it.

She finds that the last time a flat was bought or sold at number twelve was ten years ago, which is extraordinary for an eminent address such as this. The freehold to the building is owned by a company in Scotland called BG Properties. She can find nothing else about the address or anyone who lives there. It is a house of mystery, she decides, a house where people come and never move out again, where people hang thick curtains and never open them and leave their furniture to rot on the driveway.

Then she googles ley lines at the address. She doesn't quite know what a ley line is, but she thinks there might be some strange ones at this junction, where there are no voices in the street late at night, where empty plots of land stay undeveloped, where the foxes scream every night, where teenage girls are followed home and assaulted in the dark, where she feels uncomfortable, where she does not belong.

6

IN THE WAKE of the events of the night that Tilly claimed to have been assaulted, Cate stops walking past the house with the armchair in the driveway.

The position of her house is such that she can turn either left or right to get to the main road or up into the village, and she chooses now to turn left. She does not want to risk crossing paths with the man she'd inadvertently sent the police to question three days ago about an attack on a young girl that apparently hadn't really happened. He wouldn't know it was her, but she would know it was him.

She tries not to even look in the direction of the man's house, but her eyes track quickly toward it now as she heads into the village with a bag full of mail order returns to drop at the post office. A woman, around Cate's age, maybe ten years older, is standing at a right angle to the front door. She is eye-catching in a long gray coat, a selection of patterned scarves, ankle boots, hair steely gray and held up in a bun very high on her head, almost to the point of tipping over her hairline onto her forehead. She wears black eyeliner under her eyes and is clutching a small suitcase and a selection of airport carrier bags. Cate watches her going through her handbag before removing a set of keys and turning to face the front door. Cate sees her stop for a moment in the hallway to riffle through some mail on a console table before the door closes behind her.

Cate realizes she is standing in the street staring at a closed door. She turns quickly and heads up the hill, up toward the village.

———

After dropping the parcels in at the post office, Cate takes the scenic route back to the flat. If she made a mistake choosing this location for her family's temporary accommodation, she wants to make up for it by enjoying Hampstead village as much as possible while she's here. Kilburn is bustling and loud and grimy and real, and Cate loves it with a passion. But Kilburn has no heart, no center; it's just a ladder of small roads set perpendicularly off a big road. Hampstead on the other hand has alleys and crannies and turnstiles and cottages and paths and hidden graveyards, and it spreads out this way in every direction for a mile or more, all the way to the Heath in the north and back down to the wide stately avenues in the south and west. It is the ultimate London village, and every new corner Cate discovers on her walks up here colors her day in some way.

Today Cate finds herself walking farther than before, across a small section of the Heath grooved with footpaths, through a whispering copse of trees and then down a winding lane lined with interesting old houses, mainly Georgian, until suddenly she finds herself in a different landscape altogether: flat and low, with white James Bond–style houses layered together like roof tiles, attached with concrete walkways and spiral staircases. Each house has a wide terrace overlooking the woods and the Heath beyond. She gets out her phone, and she does what she always does when she finds herself somewhere new in this village: she googles it. She discovers that she is in the most expensive council estate ever built, possibly anywhere in the world, part of an idealistic Labour Party experiment in the 1970s to house the poor as though they were rich. The land cost nearly half a million pounds to buy. Each house cost £72,000 to build. The project turned sour when the government tried to recoup their investment by charging tenants well over the odds for social housing. The experiment was a resounding failure.

Now these houses are an architect's delight. Cate finds a two-bedroom flat on an estate agent's website for over a million pounds. Who would have thought, she wonders, who would have guessed that this futuristic little world would be hidden away here behind an Edwardian mansion?

She looks behind her and is suddenly aware that she is entirely alone. There is not a soul around. She hears the wind talking to her through the leaves of the trees that surround this strange enclave. They are telling her to go. Now. That she should not be here. She walks faster, and then faster still, until she is almost running across the grassland, past the houses, down the hill, back to the high street, to the beauty salons and the boutiques and the shops that sell nonsense for far too much money.

As she passes the tube station her eye is caught by a poster for the local newssheet, the *Hampstead Voice*:

SEX ATTACK IN BROAD DAYLIGHT.

She stops, stares at the words, the adrenaline still fizzing through her veins. She wonders for a moment if the headline is from a parallel reality, where she stayed too long in the place that was telling her to go, whether if she reads the article she will discover that it was her, Cate Fours, fifty-year-old mother of two, brutalized on a desolate 1970s council estate, unable to explain what she had been doing wandering there alone in the middle of the day.

Then she thinks of Tilly again, as she has done nearly every minute of every day since she first saw her standing in her doorway four nights ago, and she wonders if there is maybe some connection between the spate of sex attacks in the local area and what Tilly claimed didn't really happen on Monday night.

Farther down the hill she passes the local newsagent. Here she buys a copy of the *Hampstead Voice* and heads back home.

———

Roan is late back again that night. Roan is a child psychologist and works at the Portman Centre in Belsize Park. Having a husband who is a child psychologist is not as useful as it sounds. Her husband is, it would seem, only capable of empathizing with children who have sociopathic tendencies (sociopathy in children is his specialism). Children like their own, who are a bit odd in some ways but perfectly and utterly normal in most of the other ways, seem to confound him entirely, and he reacts as though he has never before encountered a teenage child or, indeed, had any personal experience of being a teenager himself whenever either of them does something that could only be described as the stereotypical behavior of a teenager.

This infuriates Cate, who has never felt more in touch with her own teenage self than she has since her children became teenagers, as if she has walked through a door at the far end of parenting and somehow met herself coming the other way.

"How was your day?" she calls out to him now, in the tone of voice she uses to lay out her intent to be pleasant. If she can start the evening's discourse on a high note, then it can't possibly be her fault if it all goes down the hill later on. She has no idea if Roan can detect the hint of theater in this particular tone, but he responds from the hallway with a hearty:

"Not at all bad. How was yours?"

And then he is there, in the kitchen, her husband, his shaved head covered with a beanie, wrapped up against the January chill in a padded black jacket and gloves. He pulls off the beanie and puts it on the table. Then he pulls off his gloves, revealing long angular hands. He takes the cross-body bag off his chest and puts it on a chair. He doesn't look at her. They don't really look at each other anymore. It's fine. Cate isn't in great need of being seen by him.

His hand goes to the *Hampstead Voice* on the table. He looks at the headline. "Another one?"

"Another one," she replies. "Next road down this time."

He nods, just once, and carries on reading. Then he says, "Daylight."

"I know," she says. "Horrific. That poor woman. Just going about her business. Thought it was going to be a normal day. Some sick little fuck decides he can do what he wants, decides he has the right to touch her body." She shudders as she thinks again of tiny Tilly, her wide eyes on her doorstep.

Georgia walks in.

She's in her lounging gear: silky jersey shorts and a hoodie. Cate didn't have lounging gear when she was a teenager; she had her clothes and her pajamas and nothing in between.

Roan puts the *Hampstead Voice* in front of her. "Look, Georgie," he says. "A sex attacker in the area. Last attack was just down the road. In the middle of the day. Please, please keep your wits about you. And try not to stumble about with your earbuds in."

Georgia tuts. "My wits are totally about me," she says. "Remember my wits are young. Not old and shit like yours. And I bet you anything it's that guy." She taps the front page of the paper. "The one over the road. The creep. He looks totally rapey."

Cate shivers slightly at the mention of the man across the road, and she flushes with shame. She hasn't told Roan or the kids about calling the police and seeing them going to talk to him. She's too embarrassed. It was such a middle-class, meddling thing to have done.

"How's Tilly?" she asks, moving the subject along. "Has she said any more to you about Monday night?"

Georgia shakes her head. "Nope. I've tried talking to her about it, but she won't. She just says she's too embarrassed."

"And what do you think? Do you think she made it up?"

Her daughter considers the question. "In one way, yeah. I mean, it's kind of the sort of thing she'd do? If you see what I mean? She's lied about stuff before."

"What sort of stuff?"

"Oh, just small things, like saying she knows the name of some, like, rapper, or someone on YouTube, and then when you ask her who it is you realize she hasn't got a clue. So she says things sometimes just to fit in, to be one of the crowd. And she gets this, like, blind look in her eyes when she knows she's been rumbled, and then you feel really bad for putting her on the spot."

"But this—lying about something like this. Do you think she's capable of a lie that big?"

"I dunno," she says. Then she shrugs and says, "Yeah. Maybe. She overreacts to things. Maybe she just, you know, overreacted."

Cate nods. It's possible, she supposes. But then her eye is caught once more by the headline on the front page of the *Hampstead Voice*, and she feels a dark shadow of doubt passing through her head.

7

IT'S THE DAY before Valentine's Day, and Cate is in her local shopping center looking for a card for Roan. She won't get him anything romantic. Indeed, there have been at least a dozen years over the preceding thirty when she hasn't got him a card at all. Valentine's isn't really their scene. But something about the fact that they've made it to another Valentine's Day, still intact in spite of everything that happened last year, makes her think that a card might be in order.

She picks up a card that has a drawing on the front of two stick figures holding hands. The wording above their heads reads: "Yay! We still like each other!"

She puts it back on the shelf as though it has scalded her.

She is not sure that she and Roan do.

Eventually she picks up a card that simply reads, "I Love You Lots," with a big red heart. This is true. She does still love him. The love part is simple; it's everything else that's complicated.

It was this time, a year ago, Cate recalls, that she and Roan had nearly split up. It was just before the half term. They'd thought that they might have to cancel a seven-thousand-pound holiday, that's how bad it had been.

It was her fault.

All of it.

She'd thought Roan was having an affair. No, not thought, *believed*, with every fiber of her being, with no element of doubt, without having ever seen Roan with another woman, without having found texts from him to another woman, without having seen so much as a smudge of lipstick on a collar. She'd gone completely mad for a while.

For six months Cate had obsessively infiltrated all her husband's most private spaces: his email account, his text messages, his WhatsApp, his photos, even his work documents. She'd pored over the terrible details of a psychologically scarred but very beautiful young woman, looking for something to back up her belief that Roan was having sex with her, shamelessly breaching the privacy of a child who'd thought that everything she'd said to her psychologist was shared in the strictest confidence.

Roan had found out what she'd been doing in early February. Or, rather, she'd had to confess to what she'd been doing after he came home from work and told her that he thought his new assistant had been going through his patients' private records and even his email and his phone and that he was monitoring her and was prepared to report her if necessary.

She'd panicked at the thought of an official investigation and said, "It's me. It's me. It's me," and started crying and tried to explain but made no sense, no sense at all, because back then, for a few months, she'd been utterly, utterly mad.

She'd hoped for his arms around her after her confession, for his low, reassuring voice in her ear saying, "It's OK, it's OK, I understand, I forgive you, it's fine."

Instead he'd looked at her and said, "That is about the lowest thing I've ever heard of in my life."

Of course he had not been having an affair. He had just been working late, stressed, dealing with unimaginable horrors on a day-to-day basis, dealing with a new assistant who was not up to scratch, with a sick father. He'd also been trying to get fit by taking up jogging on an ad hoc basis, and was constantly frustrated that there was never enough time to get into a routine. He was just, as he'd said, struggling, struggling with it all. And there she'd been, idiot that she was, snuffling like a pig through his private affairs, breaching his professional security, endangering his job, imagining the very worst of him, the very worst.

"Why on earth," he'd said, looking at her imploringly, disbelievingly, "would I be having an affair?"

Such a simple question. She'd paused and taken a moment to think about it. Why would he be having an affair?

"Because I'm old," she'd said eventually.

"I'm old too."

"Yes, but you're a man. You don't have a sell-by date."

"Cate," he'd replied. "Neither do you. Not to me. You and me, for God's sake. We don't have sell-by dates. We're *us*. We're just . . . *us*."

He'd moved out for a few days after that. It had been her idea. She needed to clear her head. When he came back, he'd said, "I feel like we've lost our thread. Like we were in the zone and now we're out of the zone, and I don't know how to get back into it again."

And she'd said, "I feel the same way."

There'd followed a few days of existential drama and angst and many discussions about the cancellation of the extremely expensive skiing holiday and how the children might take it and looking at insurance policies (there was no special clause for "unexpected marital discord"). Then two days before they were due to fly, they'd shared a bottle of wine and had sex and decided just to go on the holiday and see if it fixed them.

And it had, to a certain extent. The kids had been on good form, full of laughter; the sun had shone all day, every day, and the hotel they'd chosen had been jolly and full of nice people. They'd returned home a week later and both decided, subliminally and without further discussion, just to get on with it and forget that it had ever happened.

But still, it had. She had crossed lines and boundaries, she'd broken the trust between them, and even now she still feels like a lesser person. Being a mother had given her so much command over the moral high ground, but in six crazy months she'd ceded her position entirely, and to this day she still flinches under Roan's gaze, scared that he'll see through her facade to the insecure, pathetic core of her. She feels safer now when he doesn't look at her, when he doesn't see her. Because if he can't see her then he can't hate her. And he hates her. She knows he does.

Saffyre, that was the name of the patient whose private records she'd read through. Saffyre Maddox. She was fifteen years old at the time and had been self-harming since the age of ten.

One day during the madness of last winter, Cate had actually gone to Saffyre's school and watched her through the railings. There she was, the girl Cate had been so sure was having an affair with her husband: tall, lean, flat-chested, her dark curls pulled back into a bun, her hands in the pockets of her black blazer, pale green eyes scanning the playground, almost regal. Not at all what Cate had expected. She'd watched as a boy approached the girl, playfully trying to engage her in some kind of banter. She'd seen Saffyre's eyes drift over his shoulder, and then she'd watched the boy fade away, go back to his friends, his good-natured demeanor that of someone who hadn't expected much more than he'd got.

Then two girls had walked toward Saffyre, and the three of them fell into step together, heading back to the school building.

Saffyre didn't look like a girl who cut herself with unfurled paper clips. She looked like the queen bee.

The last time Cate saw Saffyre was a couple of months after they'd moved to the flat in Hampstead. She'd been walking down the Finchley Road with an older man, and she was pulling a nylon shopping cart behind her.

Cate had followed them for a while, her heart racing lightly with fear of being caught. The older man had a pronounced limp, and Saffyre stopped every moment or so to allow him to catch up with her before they both turned into an estate at the Swiss Cottage end of the Finchley Road and disappeared through aluminum doors at the bottom of a tower block.

As the door closed behind them, Cate stopped and caught her breath, suddenly aware of what she was doing. She'd turned quickly and headed home at a brisk pace, trying to purge the wrongness from her psyche.

8

ROAN PASSES CATE a red envelope across the table the following morning with a shy smile. "Don't worry if you haven't," he says. "It was just a . . . you know . . ."

She smiles and takes her own red envelope from her handbag and hands it to him. "Go us," she says lightly.

They open their envelopes in tandem, slightly awkwardly. Roan's card to Cate is a Banksy. It's a Band-Aid-covered red-heart balloon from a wall in Brooklyn in New York. It's beyond apt.

She opens the card.

There, in his loose scrawl, are the words: "Are you ready to take off the plasters yet?"

She glances at him across the table. A small laugh escapes her mouth. Her stomach knots and unknots pleasantly. She says, "Are you?"

He drops his head into his chest and then lifts it again. He's smiling. "Totally," he says. "I have been for a long time. I just . . ." He glances down at the card she's just given him, with its bland inscription: "To my lovely husband, Happy V Day! Love, C x."

"I've been waiting," he says.

She nods. She's confused for a moment about who exactly has been wearing plasters on their heart, about who's been healing and who's been waiting. She'd thought it was the other way around. That she'd hurt him.

"Shall we go for a drink tonight?" he suggests. "Somewhere a bit shit maybe? Everything else'll be fully booked."

"Yes," she says. "Leave it with me. I'll think of somewhere a bit shit."

———

After Roan leaves, Cate opens her laptop and starts work. She's slightly unnerved by the interaction with her husband. Everything has felt so off-kilter since they moved here. Even her marital disharmony has changed somehow, shifted along a little to a place that she doesn't quite recognize. She almost misses how straightforward it had felt in the months after her confession to Roan. Roan good. Cate bad.

But since moving to Hampstead she's not so sure anymore. Roan's behavior *had* been strange. For months. He *had* come home late and been distracted and impatient with her and the children. He *had* canceled family plans at short notice, often without a reasonable explanation. He *had* taken whispered calls on his mobile phone behind locked doors and out on the street. There'd been something. Definitely. Something.

She picks up his card again, reads the words again. It's virtually an admission that she had reason to be hurt too. But by what? By his harsh response to her behavior? Or by something else? She closes the card and puts it upright on the table. As she works, her eye keeps being drawn back to it.

She's too unfocused to work, so she flicks screens to her browser and types in "pubs near me." As she scrolls through, she's aware of the clatter of the letter box in the communal front door, the thump of mail hitting the doormat. She jumps to her feet, glad of the distraction, and goes to the hallway to collect the post. She removes the letters for the other residents of the house and takes her pile through to the flat. Most of them sport large white postal redirection stickers, obscuring their address in Kilburn. But one is handwritten and addressed directly to Roan, at this address.

She stares at it for a moment. The handwriting is feminine, the postcode is incomplete, and the contents are stiff, clearly a card of some kind. It could be anything, she theorizes: a discounted promotion from the local dry cleaner's, some fancy window cleaner's business card. Anything.

She leaves it on top of the pile on the kitchen table and goes back to her internet search for local pubs.

A message arrives on her phone. It's from Georgia.

MUM. As if she was calling to her from down the hallway.

She sighs and replies. *Yes.*

Can you bring my form for the geography trip? Like, now.

Cate rolls her eyes. *Where is it?*

Don't know. Somewhere in kitchen.

Cate scours the kitchen, fans through piles of her own paperwork, finally finds it in the recycling bin. She smooths it out and replies to Georgia. *FFS. Got it. I'll bring it in now.*

In truth she's glad of the excuse to get out of the flat. It's sunny out, and she can pop to the shops on her way back. Plus she always gets a little thrill going through the door of her children's secondary school, infiltrating the mysterious world they inhabit for eight hours a day.

She passes the tower block on her way to school, the block she'd seen Saffyre entering all those months ago, pulling the wheeled shopper behind her. She slows for a moment and gazes up. The sunlight glitters off the windows, reaching high up into the sky. She thinks again about the card that arrived this morning, the feminine cursive addressed to Roan, and she can feel it bubbling to the surface once more, the itchy, discomfiting feeling that had plagued her into doing the unthinkable things she'd done a year ago.

Quickly, she picks up her pace and carries on briskly toward the burgundy-clad walls of her children's school where she's buzzed in by a young woman behind a desk who smiles encouragingly at her as though Cate might be about to ask her something awkward.

"For a student," she says, passing her the folded paper. "Georgia Fours in Eleven G."

"Oh, lovely, thank you. I'll make sure she gets it."

Cate's eyes scan the foyer, searching out a hint of a child she recognizes, a little something to take away with her. But it's lesson time, and there are no children around. She heads back out onto the street and breathes in deeply. She's conscious of her heart beating a little too fast. She's aware of everything feeling heightened and highly tuned as though there's a frequency in the air that she's only just become aware of.

In the supermarket she picks up avocados for Georgia, chicken strips and a baguette for Josh, a liter of apple and mango juice that will be gone within thirty seconds of the children getting home from school. She picks up stock cubes and salt in a rare moment of remembering to get stock cubes and salt. She picks up butter and milk and a box of chocolate-covered honeycomb and pays using the self-service checkout. There's no one behind her in the queue, so she scans slowly and calmly, her eyes going to the taxi rank outside; the same drivers are here every day, milling together on the pavement, a social scene of sorts. Then her gaze passes beyond the taxi drivers, toward the entrance to the tube station, where she sees a familiar figure heading inside. Tall, slim, a smooth dome of bare skull, a bag slung diagonally across his body, a pronounced ball-of-the-foot bounce in each step.

"Roan," she says quietly, under her breath.

There's her husband. In the shadowy secret moments of his life. It's similar to the feeling of being in her children's school. She pulls out her phone and calls him. It rings ten times and then cuts off. For some reason she pictures him pulling his phone from his pocket, seeing her name and putting it back in his pocket.

It's midday. As far as she's aware he doesn't undertake out-of-clinic appointments. Maybe he's meeting someone somewhere for lunch?

The fact that it is Valentine's Day passes fleetingly through her mind, and she finds herself picturing Roan in a trendy Soho restaurant, a single red rose on the table, a waiter pouring champagne into a flute for the beautiful young woman sitting opposite him.

She shakes her head to rid herself of the image.

She will not be that person again.

9

ROAN GETS HOME just before seven that night. Cate watches him flick through the letters on the kitchen table. He gets to the letter in the white envelope with the card in it and she sees it, a crackle of something passes through him, like a tiny pulse of electricity. His fingers stumble, vaguely, but he keeps flicking, then wordlessly puts the letters back down on the kitchen table.

"You still up for drinks tonight?" he asks.

"Definitely," she responds quickly. "I did have a look online, but I couldn't find anything that didn't need to be booked."

"Maybe we should just head into the village. Go to the least Valentiney-looking pub we can find?"

"That's fine with me. Eightish?"

Roan nods. "Eightish sounds good. I think I might just head out for a run, then. What time's dinner?"

She glances at the oven, where Josh's chicken strips are cooking. She hadn't thought about dinner for Roan. For her. "Are we not eating out tonight?"

"Can do. Fine with me. I'm not that hungry anyway."

She opens her mouth to say, "Oh, that'll be because you went

and had lunch in town somewhere, with someone, for some reason." But that's not how she wants the night to start. Instead she
smiles and says, "Great. Have a good run."

Georgia appears a moment later. She goes to the bread bin and
takes out the expensive rye and sourdough loaf that Cate buys especially for her. She puts it in the toaster and then goes to the fridge,
pulls open the vegetable drawer, rummages for a moment, emerges
with the fresh avocado in her hand, slices it over the sink, tugs out
the stone with the tip of the knife, drops the stone in the bin, mashes
the avocado in the same bowl in which she always mashes her avocado, grinds salt into it, smears it over the two large slices of toast,
sits it on the table with a large glass of apple and mango juice, and
bites into it.

Georgia sees Cate watching her. "You all right, Mum?" she says.

Cate nods, shaking herself out of her mild reverie. "I'm fine, yes."

Georgia picks up the Banksy Valentine's card with her spare
hand and examines it. "Aw," she says. "Sweet. Dad got you a card.
Bless. What's it mean?"

"It means . . ." She tugs a piece of kitchen towel from the roll and
uses it to mop up some spilled tea on the counter. "I don't know. I
think maybe he thinks I'm still a bit sensitive after what happened
last year."

"Oh, you mean your *crisis*?"

"Yes. Our crisis."

"That was so weird," Georgia says, her mouth full of food. "Just
so, so weird. What was it even about?"

They'd never told the children what it was about. They'd never
told the children how close they'd come to splitting up. They'd just
said they were having a bit of a crisis, totally normal after so many
years together, that they were going to spend a few days apart and

see how they felt after. And then there hadn't really been an after. Roan had moved back. They'd gone skiing. Life had continued.

Cate shakes her head. "I'm still not too sure," she says. "Just one of those things. Happens to every couple, I guess."

"But you're cool now? You and Dad?"

"Yes. We're cool now. In fact, we're going out to the pub tonight."

"Ooh, ooh, can I come too?"

Cate raises an eyebrow. "What on earth for?" She laughs.

"I like pubs."

"You're so strange."

"What's strange about liking pubs?"

"Nothing." Cate smiles. "Nothing." Then she says, "Get any cards today?"

"Mum, it is very old-fashioned of you to ask such a question. You should be asking me if I gave anyone a card. I'm not some passive blob, sitting round waiting for boys to do things to impress me."

"Good," she says. "Glad to hear it. So did you give anyone a card?"

"No way!" she says. "Have you seen the boys at my school?" She puts the Valentine's card down again. "Where's Dad?"

"Gone running."

"Freak."

Georgia and Cate share an anti-running sensibility. Neither of them is designed for running. They get stitches too easily and feel the ground hard and heavy beneath their feet. They also both think that Roan looks faintly ridiculous in his Lycra outfits.

Josh enters the kitchen in his shambling, slightly lost way, as though half-heartedly looking for something. He comes to Cate and hugs her. She smells school on him, and the deodorant he always wears. Then he reaches into his back pocket and pulls out a battered envelope.

"Happy Valentine's," he says.

She opens the envelope and finds a card he's made himself out of black paper with a red paper heart stuck on the front attached by a paper hinge. Inside it reads, "To the best mum in the world. I love you so much."

He's made her a Valentine's card every year since he was tiny. He's one of those boys: loves his mum more than anything in the world, puts her on a pedestal. In a way it's glorious. In another, she feels worried that she's only ever one bad decision or harsh word away from completely destroying him.

"Thank you, my lovely boy," she says, kissing him on the cheek.

"You're welcome," he says. Then, "What's for dinner?"

She switches off the oven and takes out his chicken and places the card next to the two already standing on the kitchen table. And as she does so, her heart jolts.

Georgia has opened the white envelope addressed to Roan; she has slid the card out and is about to open it.

"Oh my God, Georgia! What are you doing?" She snatches the card from Georgia's hand.

"God! Why are you overreacting? It's just a card."

"Yes, but it's addressed to Dad. You can't go around opening other people's mail."

"You open mine!"

"Yes, but you're a child! And I would never open something like that, that looks so personal." She picks up the envelope, hoping to slide the card back in, but in classic Georgia fashion, she's virtually torn the envelope clean in half to get the card out. "Oh, fuck. Georgia. I can't believe you did that. What were you thinking?"

Georgia shrugs. "I just wanted to see who was sending Dad Valentine's cards."

Cate forces the card roughly into the bottom half of the torn en-velope and shoves it in a drawer. She can't deal with this right now.

"Aren't you going to look? See who it's from?"

"No, I am not. It's none of my business."

"But how can you say that? He's your husband. Valentine's cards from strangers is, literally, one hundred percent your business."

"It's probably just one of his patients—i.e., none of my business whatsoever," Cate says.

"But if it's one of his patients, how the hell did they get this ad-dress?"

"No idea," Cate says. "Maybe it was written on something in his office. I don't know."

"Hm." Georgia raises her brow dramatically and puts a finger to her mouth. "Well, have a nice Valentine's night at the pub, then," she says facetiously. She takes her empty plate to the sink, letting it fall loudly as she always does. "Anything good for dessert?"

Cate passes her the box of chocolate-covered honeycomb, then turns to face the kitchen window, where she sees her face reflected back at her, the face of an older woman who looks just like her, a woman whose life, she feels very strongly, is heading down a dark, twisty path to somewhere she doesn't want to be.

Her fingers find the handle of the kitchen drawer, the one where Roan's mystery card is hidden. She pulls the drawer open, then shuts it again, very firmly, and leaves the room.

———

Roan doesn't get back until well after eight o'clock. Cate calls him three times between 8:05 and 8:15, but he doesn't answer his phone. When he finally appears in the hallway at 8:20, sweaty, almost gaunt-looking, he goes straight to the bedroom to shower in the en suite.

"I'll be five minutes," he shouts to her down the corridor.

Cate sighs and picks up her phone, passes a few moments mindlessly scrolling through Facebook. The card is still in the drawer. She still has not looked at it.

At 8:40, Roan is finally ready and waiting to go.

They say goodbye to the children, who are both in their rooms doing homework, or at least doing something on their laptops that they claim is homework.

The air is damp and cloying as they head up the hill into the village, and Cate feels her skin grow clammy. She thinks of reaching out to hold Roan's hand, but she can't bring herself to do it. These days, holding hands, like cuddling in bed or instigating sex or kissing on the lips, feels like an expression of approval, like stars on a reward chart, actions that need to have been deserved or earned in some way. To hold Roan's hand now would be to suggest that they were still the same people they'd been twenty-five, thirty years ago, that she still feels the way she felt about him then, about them, but she can't negate everything that has happened since. She can't pretend that none of it ever happened.

"So," she says, "long run today?"

"Yeah, well, I had a big lunch. I was making sure I had an appetite for dinner."

"Oh, what did you have for lunch?"

"Big bowl of pasta, with some kind of creamy sauce. I hadn't been expecting the creamy sauce but ate the whole lot anyway."

"At your desk?"

"No, no, I went into town."

His tone is light. There is no sign that there was anything untoward about his lunch in town, but her voice still comes out wrong, slightly high-pitched. "Oh, what was that for, then?"

"Just met up with Gerry. You know. From UCL? He wants me to run a first-year module for him next year in childhood psychoses. Three hours a week. A hundred an hour."

"Oh," she says, the strange darkness starting to lift slightly. "That's amazing! Are you going to do it?"

"Too right I am! Extra twelve hundred pounds a month. That'll pay for a decent holiday or two. A couple of new sofas when we move home. Plus I really like Gerry. And I got free pasta. So yeah. A no-brainer, really."

He glances down at her and he smiles, and it's a great, great smile, free of any editing or hidden agenda. He had a good lunch with a good person and now has a good job that will provide them with a good holiday and some good sofas. She cannot help but return the smile in the same spirit.

"That's brilliant," she says. "Really brilliant."

She wants to ask why he didn't mention the lunch when they were talking this morning. She would tell him if she was meeting someone for lunch to talk about a job. But she bats the complaint away and holds on to the good feeling.

They reach the top of the hill, and Hampstead village opens up to them like a dream or a film set as it always does. They find a pub down a cobbled alleyway with fires burning in the grates and dogs stretched out on gnarled old floorboards, and although they'd said it would be an anti-Valentine night, Roan comes back from the bar with a bottle of champagne and two chilled glasses and they toast his new job, and their faces fall in and out of shadow in the light of a dancing flame, and Roan's hand finds hers on the seat between them and he takes it in his and it feels nice, and for quite some time Cate forgets about the card in the drawer at home.

10

Saffyre

I WAS TWELVE and a half the first time I met Roan Fours.

I'd been cutting myself for more than two years by this stage.

I'd just started year eight; kids were turning from twelve to thirteen and boys were becoming a problem.

All the attention, the look in their eyes, the idea of the things they were thinking, of the things they were saying about me to each other—I'd spent most of my childhood hanging out with boys, so I knew what happened behind the scenes—was starting to make me feel tired, used, worn-down. I quite liked the idea of *therapy*, of being in a quiet room with a quiet man talking quietly about myself for an hour or so.

I'd been picturing a wild-haired guy in glasses, maybe a tweedy jacket, even a monocle. I had not been expecting a cool guy with eyes too blue and cheekbones too sharp and long, spidery legs in black denim that he crossed and uncrossed and crossed and uncrossed until you were almost dizzy with it. And hands that moved like some weird pale exotic birds whenever he wanted to describe something. And dope trainers. You know, really good ones, for an old guy. And a smell, of clean clothes, my favorite smell, but also of trees and grass and clouds and sunshine.

I didn't clock all of this the first time I met him, obviously. When I first met him I was still a child and just thought he was kind of cool-looking, in a Doctor Who kind of way.

He looked at a notebook for quite some time before he looked at me.

"Saffyre," he said. "That is a tremendously brilliant name."

I said, "Yeah. Thanks. My mum chose it."

It's totally a name a nineteen-year-old mum would choose for a baby, isn't it?

Then he said, "So, Saffyre, tell me about yourself."

"Like what?" Everyone knows you shouldn't ask kids open questions. They suck at answering them.

"Like, tell me about school. How are you getting on?"

"Good," I said. "I'm getting on good."

Here we go, I thought, some bloke ticking boxes, filling in forms, going home to watch *Game of Thrones* and eat quinoa or whatever with his wife. I thought: This is not going to work.

And then he said, "Tell me, Saffyre, what's the worst, worst thing that ever happened to you?"

And then I knew we were going to get somewhere. I didn't know where yet, I just knew that I was at a point in my life when I needed someone to ask me what the worst thing that ever happened to me was, rather than ask me if their eyebrows were on fleek or if I wanted chicken or fish for dinner.

I didn't answer him immediately. My head flooded. The obvious thing came first. The thing that happened when I was ten. But I didn't want to tell him that. Not yet. He waited, a good minute or so, for me to answer. Then I said, "All of it."

"All of it?"

"Yes. All of it. My mum died before I knew her. And my grandma.

My granddad was a single dad raising three children and a grand-child, then he got so ill that my uncle had to look after all of us from when he was, like, my age. So he had no proper life. Ever. We had a budgerigar. It died. The lady next door who used to fix my hair for me, her name was Joyce—she died. My favorite teacher at primary school, Miss Raymond, got cancer and died just after she got mar-ried. My granddad's got arthritis and is in pain nearly all the time."

I stopped abruptly, just short of the defining event of all the bad events, the event that had brought me to his door. I stared at him, at the blue, blue eyes that reminded me of one of those dogs that look like wolves. I wanted him to go, "Oh, poor you. No wonder you've been cutting yourself all these years."

Instead he said, "Now tell me the best thing that ever happened to you."

I was taken aback, to be honest; it was like nothing I'd just said meant anything. Like maybe he hadn't even been listening.

For a moment I didn't even want to answer him. I just sat there. But then something suddenly came into my head. There was a girl at primary school called Lexie. She was very popular, very kind; all the teachers loved her, and all the children loved her. She lived in a nice house on a nice street with crystal chandeliers and velvet sofas and she always invited the whole class to her birthday parties, even me, who wasn't really one of her proper friends.

One year she had an animal party. A man with white hair came with a van full of boxes and cages and in each box and cage was a different animal, and we were allowed to touch them. He brought a chinchilla, a snake, some stick insects, a vole, a ferret, some birds, a tarantula. He also brought a barn owl. It was called Harry.

The man with the white hair looked around at all the children and he saw me and he said, "How about you, would you like to hold Harry?"

He brought me to the front and gave me a big leather glove to wear, and then he put Harry the owl on my outstretched arm, and I stood there and Harry turned his big head and looked at me and I looked at him and my heart just blew up with something warm and velvety and deep and soothing. It was like I loved him, like I loved this owl. Which was just stupid because I didn't know him and he was an owl.

So I looked at Roan Fours and I said, "The time I held an owl at Lexie's birthday when I was nine years old."

And he said, "I love owls. They're extraordinary creatures."

I nodded.

He said, "What did it feel like when you held the owl?"

I said, "It felt like I loved him."

He wrote something down. He said, "Who else do you love?"

I thought, Hmmm, aren't we supposed to be talking about owls? Then I said, "I love my granddad. I love my uncles. I love my nieces."

"Friends?"

"I don't love my friends."

"What does love feel like?"

"It feels like . . . it feels like need."

"Like need?"

"Yeah, like you love someone because they give you what you need."

"And if they stop giving you what you need?"

"Then that's not love. That's something else."

"And the owl?"

I stopped. "What?"

"The owl. You said it felt like you loved the owl."

"Yes."

"But you didn't need the owl."

"No. I just loved him."

"Did it feel the same as the way you love your granddad?"

"No," I said. "It felt . . . pure." I realized that sounded wrong and corrected myself. "Not that there's anything not pure about the way I love my granddad. But I worry about him. I worry that he'll die. I worry that he won't be able to give me what I need. And that makes me feel bad. I didn't feel bad about the owl. I only felt good."

"Do you think both types of love are equal?"

"Yes." I nodded. "Yes, I do."

He stopped then and looked up at me, and he smiled. I hadn't been expecting him to smile. I thought that it was in his contract not to smile during therapy. But he did. And maybe it was because we'd just been talking about it, I don't know, but I got that feeling again, the soft, velvet-owl feeling.

So yeah, maybe I needed Roan Fours already, even before I knew it.

———

The first time I saw Roan outside of a therapy session at the Portman was about a year or so after our first session. I was walking home from school and he was just leaving an appointment at the school opposite my flat where one of his patients was a student. He was all smart and briefcasey, wearing a blue shirt, and he was talking to another man, also smart and briefcasey. Then they separated, and Roan turned to cross the street and he saw me looking at him.

I thought he might just wave and walk on. But he didn't. He crossed the road and came to stand with me.

"Well, hello," he said. He had his hands in his pockets and kind of rocked backward on his heels. It made him look like a teacher for some reason, and I had that really *eww* feeling you get when you see a teacher out of school, like they're naked or something. But at the same time I felt really pleased to see him.

I said hi and wondered what I looked like to him. I was wearing false eyelashes that day; this was early 2016—everyone was wearing false eyelashes. I didn't think I looked stupid at the time but I probably did.

"Finished school?" he said.

"Yeah. Just heading home." As I said this, I looked up at the tower, to the eighth floor. I always recognized my floor from the ground because of the ugly red-and-green-striped curtains in the window of flat thirty-five next door. It was like a marker.

"Up there?" he said.

"Yeah," I said. "Up there."

"Nice views, I bet?"

I shrugged. I'd happily forsake the views for a home with more rooms in it.

"So, our next appointment . . . ?"

"Wednesday," I said.

"Five thirty p.m.?"

"Yep."

"See you then."

"Yeah. See you then."

I headed toward the entrance to the flats. I turned around as I pulled the door open, because for some reason I expected Roan to still be standing there, to be watching me. But he wasn't. He was gone.

———

Roan and his family moved to a flat near the Portman Centre January last year. How do I know this? Because I saw them, literally on the day they moved in. I was walking to the village, up those big roads that go up the hill from my estate, those roads of mansions and Teslas and electronic gates.

And there was this van double-parked with hazards flashing and some young guys unloading boxes and lamps and chairs and whatnot. The door to the house was wide-open, and I always like to look inside an open door, and I saw a woman; she was thin and wearing jeans and a pink jumper and trainers. Her hair was blond and fine and shoulder-length. And there was a boy, a teenager, and they were carrying things through a door at the end of the hallway, and then a man appeared coming the other way and it was him. It was Roan. He was wearing a hoodie and jeans. He went to the back of the van and was saying something to one of the guys inside the van, and I almost walked on but I suddenly had this urge to let him know I'd seen him. I was about to cross over the street and say hello when the woman in the pink jumper appeared. I didn't know she was his wife then, but I assumed she must be.

They said something to each other and then both disappeared inside the van, and I caught my breath and carried on my way.

But before I left, my eye took in the number on their front door: seventeen.

I never told Roan I'd seen him move into his new home. We didn't talk about stuff like that. I'd never even really thought about where he might live or what his life might be like outside our room at the Portman. When we had our next session, about four days after I saw him moving house, we just went straight down to business as usual. He didn't tell me he'd moved and I didn't tell him I knew.

Then about two weeks later, Roan said that he thought we were ready to start thinking about terminating our therapy. He said this as though I should be pleased, as though I'd actually quite like to finish therapy, as if it were school or swimming lessons or something. He said he thought another two or three sessions should "bring us to where we need to be."

Strange, you know, because I'm not stupid but I'd been stupid enough to think that therapy would just keep on and on until I was ready to stop. Or maybe, you know, forever.

"How do you know?" I asked. "How do you know where we need to be?"

He smiled that weird, lazy smile of his, like he's not bothered but then thinks, Fuck it. "That's my job, Saffyre."

"Yeah, but don't I have some say?"

"Of course you do. Of course. What would your say be?"

I had to stop then and really think about my answer, because I didn't exactly know what I wanted. On a fundamental level I wanted the weekly punctuation marks of an hour in Roan's room; the familiarity of the suspended ceiling with the three halogen lights, one sickly yellow, two bright white; the double-glazed window with the view of a snapped branch on a tree that swung back and forth on winter nights when the wind blew, cutting shadows through the sodium glow of a streetlight beyond; the two red chairs with the nubby fabric; the low wooden table with the tissues and the little white lamp; the brown carpet with the crusty white patch near the foot of the armchair; the muted sounds of people walking past the door. I wanted to carry on seeing Roan's feet every week, in leather lace-up shoes, in his dope white trainers, in nasty strappy Velcro sandals, in snow boots. I wanted to hear his low, measured voice asking me questions, the slight clear of his throat as he waited for me to answer. And then after the session, I wanted to walk past the drama school, past the tube, past the farmers market, past the theater, feel the seasons changing in the textures beneath my feet: slippery wet leaves, hot paving stones, slimy snow, dirty puddles, whatever; all the months and months and now years and years of Roan Fours, how could it end? It was like telling me that day and night would no longer exist, that there would no longer be twenty-four hours in a day. It was that fundamental.

Eventually I said, "My say would be that I don't think I'm ready."

"In which ways, would you say, are you not ready?"

I shrugged. I said some bullshit about still thinking about hurting myself when I hadn't thought about hurting myself for over a year.

He gave me a look, calling me on my bullshit with his eyes. "Well," he said. "We're looking at another two or three weeks yet. I'll get the process in motion. We can always double back on it closer to the time if you still feel we need to. But genuinely I don't think you're going to feel the need to. You're amazing, Saffyre. The work we've done is incredible. You should be pleased."

I still hadn't told him about the bad thing that happened to me when I was ten. I wanted to say that to him, to shut him up. I wanted to say, *Someone did something unbearable to me when I was ten years old and you've been talking to me nonstop for more than three years and you still don't know that, so how can you say I should be pleased?* I wanted to say, *You're a shit psychologist.* I wanted to say all sorts of things. But I didn't. I just left.

Roan Fours signed me off three weeks later.

He tried to make a big, happy moment of it.

I pretended it was OK.

But it was not OK.

It was far from OK.

II

DID I TELL you that I am a trained killer? That I'm a ninja warrior?

Well, I'm not really. But I am a black belt in tae kwon do. There's a martial-arts school just over the road from me, in the sports center. It's what's known in the trade as a dojo, and I've been going there since I was about six years old. So you'd think I'd have been able to defend myself from a puny eleven-year-old boy with wandering hands and a sick mentality. But no, I was pathetic, let it happen, and then punished my own self for it for years afterward while Harrison John got to swan off to secondary school without a backward glance.

He would have said that I enjoyed it, because I was so passive. But I didn't.

At tae kwon do classes every week I kick and grunt and sweat, pretending every blow is on Harrison's head. I picture the walls splattered with his blood, bits of his tiny pea brain, fragments of his skull.

But at school, when I was a small child, I just let it happen.

I let it happen three times.

I still go to tae kwon do once a week; it's just habit really, but my skills have come in very useful the past few months. I'm not a small

person: I'm five feet eight, and when my hair is loose I look even
taller. I take up space in the world. People see me. But I can move
light on my feet; I really can. I can move about like a shadow if I
need to. I pull up my hoodie, keep my chin down, eyes up. I reckon
I could walk past my own uncle on the street and he wouldn't see
me, if I put my mind to it.

———

The first week that went by without me having a session with Roan
was OK. I'd missed the occasional session before if I'd been ill, or he'd
been on holiday or whatever. It was when the third week loomed up
that I suddenly felt this cold drip in the pit of my stomach, like icy
water. I imagined Roan sitting in our room, on our nubby chairs,
with some other kid, some kid with stupid annoying issues, and he'd
have to pretend to be as interested in theirs as he was in mine.

I was walking home from school one afternoon. It was about
twenty past five, and I remembered that this was the exact time I
would normally have been on my way to the Portman for my session with Roan.

Suddenly, I found myself turning right instead of left, walking
those familiar streets toward the Portman Centre. The sun was just
setting, and I was wearing a big black Puffa over my school uniform, black tights, black shoes, hair scraped back, hood up. I crept
between the trees in the parking area to the front and peered up at
his window.

Do you know how long I stood there for?

I stood there for nearly an hour.

It was March and it was cold. Really, really cold.

I saw occasional suggestions of movement, then I saw the lights
ping on in all the consulting rooms and I realized it had turned to

nighttime. My teeth were chattering, but I felt like I'd been there so long that I couldn't go now, that I couldn't go until I'd actually seen him.

He finally appeared about twenty minutes later. He was wearing a big black coat and a pull-on hat. I could see his breath even from a distance, the yellow cloud of it in the streetlight. He smiled then, and I thought for a moment that he'd seen me, but he hadn't—he was smiling at someone else, a girl coming behind him. She looked about eighteen, nineteen. He held the door for her, then the girl lit a cigarette and I watched them share it. I thought: You don't share a cigarette with someone unless you know them really well. I also thought that I'd never seen Roan smoke, not once in all the years I'd been his patient.

After they'd finished smoking the cigarette they went back into the building, Roan held the door for her again and he seemed to press himself against her as he followed her through. I saw her turn and smile at him.

I'd come to the Portman to sate some weird need for the familiarity of him, but I had set my eyes upon him and I had seen him as another person, a person who smoked, who stood too close to young women.

I was not sated. If anything, my appetite for seeing him was increased. I stood outside for another half an hour, until the car park began to empty out, the front door opening and shutting constantly as staff left for the day, calling out cheery goodbyes, talk of a quick one, comments about how cold it was. I recognized some of the people, the secretaries, receptionists, nurses I'd dealt with over the years. And then Roan reappeared. He was with the young girl again. Again, he held the door for her, chivalrously, and she exited beneath his outstretched arm, like a move in a dance, smiling at

him as she did so. I took a photo. Call me weird, but it just seemed
like something I needed to be able to study at my own leisure in
the privacy of my own room. I needed to analyze the girl's body
language and Roan's smile and work out what was happening, what
I'd seen.

I kind of expected them to go somewhere together, but they
didn't. They had a little hug, a kind of half embrace, where only
their shoulders and cheeks touched, then she hitched her bag up
on her shoulder and walked away in the direction of the tube station. Roan stopped for a moment, pulled out his phone, and tapped
his screen a few times. I saw his face in the glow of the screen; he
looked old. Then his face lifted and lightened, and he put his phone
away and he turned and caught up with the girl and they were close
enough now for me to hear him call out to her. "Wait, Anna, hold
up," he said.

She stopped and turned, and I could see the glitter of multiple
earrings in her ear.

"I've got half an hour," he said. "If you're not dashing home,
maybe we could have that coffee? Or something stronger?"

He sounded nervous, like a bit of an idiot.

But the young girl smiled and nodded. "Sure," she said. "Yes. I'm
not in a rush."

"Great," said Roan. "How about that new place that's just opened,
opposite the tube?"

"Fab," said Anna.

They fell into step, their footsteps ringing out in the cold dark
against the tarmac, and away onto the street, me still there, frozen
to the core, invisible between the trees.

12

Owen

THROUGH THE PLATE-GLASS window of the third-floor reception area, Owen watches flakes of snow tumble lazily from a heavy gray January sky. He hates London snow, the way it promises so much but delivers nothing but treacherous pavements, late trains, and chaos.

Owen teaches computer science to sixteen- to eighteen-year-olds at Ealing Tertiary College He's been teaching here for eight years. Right now, though, he is not teaching anyone. He is currently waiting to be called into the principal's office for some unspecified but rather ominous-feeling reason. His stomach roils unpleasantly at the prospect.

Finally, the principal's secretary calls him in. "Jed's ready for you," she says, putting down her phone.

In Jed's office, Owen is surprised to see Holly McKinley, the head of human resources, and Clarice Dewer, the student welfare officer. The atmosphere is weighty and murky. Clarice doesn't look at him as he enters, and he's always thought of Clarice as a friend, or at least as a person who sometimes talks to him.

Holly gets to her feet. "Thank you for coming in to see us, Owen."

She holds out her hand, and Owen shakes it, aware that his hands are damp, resisting the urge to apologize.

"Please, take a seat." Jed gestures at the empty chair before them.

Owen sits. He glances down at his shoes. They're quite new, and this is the first day since he bought them that they haven't hurt. They're not his usual style; they're brown leather, slightly pointy, kind of trendy. He keeps expecting someone to notice them, to say, "Nice shoes," but so far nobody has. Now he looks at them and wonders why he bought them.

"I'm afraid," Clarice begins, "that we've had a complaint. Well, in fact we've had two complaints. Both pertaining to the same incident."

Owen squints slightly. His brain scrolls through everything that's happened at work over the past few months for anything that could be described as an incident, but he finds nothing.

Clarice drops her gaze to her paperwork. "On December the fourteenth last year, at the Christmas party?"

Owen squints again. The Christmas party. He hadn't intended to go. He hadn't been for the two preceding years. As a member of staff at a students' party there was a sweet spot between being a dour observer and an overenthusiastic participant, and if you missed the spot it was no fun at all. But he'd bowed to pressure from two girls in his second-year class, Monique and Maisy.

"Come on, sir," they'd said (they insisted on calling him sir even though everyone else called him Owen). "We want to see your moves."

There was nothing new about this form of reverse sexual harassment. It happened all the time: because Owen was a quiet man who didn't like to reveal much about his private life, because he had a tendency to awkwardness and a need to maintain clear lines between his professional and personal personas, certain students made sport out of trying to breach his defenses. Usually girls, and usually using their sexuality to do so.

But they'd worn him down, Monique and Maisy—*Don't be so boring, sir, life's too short*—and he'd capitulated eventually.

He'd stayed until the end, in the event. He'd had shots. He'd danced. He'd raised a sweat—*Ew, sir, you're really sweaty!*—he'd taken a late tube home feeling a strange mixture of triumph and shame, and woken the next morning with a head like a wet tea towel. But he'd had fun, he'd felt, upon reflection. It had been a night worthy of its aftermath.

"Two female students maintain that you made"—Clarice refers to her paperwork again—"inappropriate comments regarding their sexual preferences."

Owen rocks slightly in his chair. "I made . . . ?"

Clarice cuts back in. "That you described your own sexual preferences in excessive detail. That you touched them inappropriately."

"I—"

"Around their shoulders and their hair. Apparently you also flicked some sweat from your forehead and hair onto the girls' faces, deliberately."

"No! I—"

"Not only that, Owen, but there was a more general suggestion of a certain way of talking to women in lessons, a *dismissive tone*."

Owen's hands are curled into fists on his lap. He looks up at Clarice and he says, "No. Absolutely not. I talk to all my students the same. One hundred percent. And as for the sweat, that was an accident! I was dancing, I spun round, some sweat flew off my head! It was absolutely not deliberate! And those girls, I know exactly which girls you're talking about, they've been pestering me, winding me up for months."

"I'm afraid, Owen, that we're going to have to launch an investigation into this. At the moment it's your word against theirs. The girls in question claim they have others willing to testify to your sexism in the classroom. And to your behavior at the Christmas party."

Owen feels a hard lump of fury pass through his consciousness. He wants to claw it out of his head and hurl it at the disciplinary panel, particularly at Clarice, who is staring at him with an antagonistic blend of pity and embarrassment.

"There *was* no 'behavior' at the Christmas party. I don't *do* behavior. I am utterly professional at all times and in every situation. In the classroom and out of it."

"Well, Owen, I'm terribly sorry, but we will be launching an investigation, and to that end, I'm afraid, we will have to suspend you from work while that is ongoing."

"What!"

"We cannot run a fair investigation while you're still in the classroom with your accusers. It's policy. I'm really, really sorry."

This came from Jed, who, to his credit, did at least look really, really sorry. Mainly, Owen suspected, because now he was going to have to rework all his timetables to ensure that his classes were covered, which, given that Ellie Brewer, Owen's counterpart, was about to go off on maternity leave, would prove very problematic.

"So, what . . . I mean, how long?"

"We'll start with two weeks and then be in touch. But I doubt it will be longer than a month. Assuming, of course, that the outcome is in your favor."

"And so do I just . . . ?"

"Yes, take what you need from your office and Holly will be waiting for you in the foyer to say goodbye."

Owen closes his eyes, then slowly opens them. He is to be escorted from the premises. Yet he has done nothing wrong. He wants to pick up the chair on which he's sitting and chuck it through the window behind Jed's head, watch it smash a hole through the plate glass, see the shards sparkling in the fallen snow in the car park below. He wants to walk into classroom 6D, where he knows that Monique and Maisy are currently halfway through a lecture in micro services, and stand before them mustering as much of his five feet nine and a half inches as possible and shout into their stupid faces. Instead he gets slowly to his feet, all his rage held tight inside his stomach, and he leaves the room.

———

It's stopped snowing when he leaves the tube station at Finchley Road an hour later. His rucksack weighs a ton on his back; it now contains the contents of his desk, including his lava rock lamp. He should have left it behind; he'll be back in a couple of weeks, but something had made him pick it up, a little voice saying, "What if they're right?"

There's a small and very steep hill leading from the Finchley Road to his street. At the top of this hill there are two private schools. He realizes as he starts his ascent that it is three thirty, that it's the end of the school day. The hill, consequently, is swarming with small, meandering children, mothers strolling behind clutching tiny rucksacks and brightly colored water bottles. While the snow on the ground has turned to slush it still lies in thick coats on cars and the children scoop off handfuls and hurl them at each other. They weave about and wander blindly into his path. He nearly loses his footing and has to grab hold of a wall to stay upright. The mothers are oblivious; Owen hates these mothers, these school mums with their weird leggings and blown-out hair, their fat winter coats with rabbit-fur hoods, their fading winter-holiday suntans, box-fresh trainers. What do women like this *think* about, he wonders, when it's just them, and the kids are in bed, and they've got one of those gigantic fishbowls of wine in their hands? What are they when they're not at the gym or collecting their children from school? Where do they exist on the scale of humanity? He cannot imagine. But then all women are an eternal mystery to him, even the ordinary ones.

Owen lives in a cavernous upper-ground-floor flat carved out of a grand mansion on one of the finest streets in Hampstead. In front of the house is a driveway, unkempt and unused, except as a storage area for bins and things the other residents of the house don't want in their homes. There has been an armchair sitting on the lawn in front of the house for almost a year now. No one complains because no one really cares; it's a building full of old people and recluses.

The flat is owned by his aunt, Tessie, and is the largest apartment in the building, boasting the highest ceilings, the tallest windows, solid four-panel doors with fanlight windows above that the other floors of the house don't have. Owen's bedroom is at the back-left corner of the flat, with a window overlooking the scruffy communal garden that no one takes responsibility for and a wasteland beyond a dividing wall where a grand mansion once stood. The house is an aberration on this street of glossy new apartment blocks and shiny mansions with security gates. The freeholder is a mysterious Scotsman known only as Mr. G, who appears to have washed his hands of his responsibility for the upkeep of this once-beautiful building. Tessie has tried writing to him but has received no response.

Tessie is currently away; she has a house in Tuscany, equally as run-down as her London apartment, and is there for substantial periods of time. When she's away she locks each door of her flat apart from the bathroom and kitchen. She says it's to keep her things safe from burglary, but Owen knows it's because she thinks he's going to go through her things. Even when she's here she locks doors behind her, and Owen has never, not even on special occasions, gone beyond the door of her elegant, high-ceilinged sitting room.

Now Owen lets himself into the apartment and breathes in the familiar, faintly toilety scent of the economy fabric conditioner Tessie uses on all her washing, the stale aroma of old cushions and dusty curtains, the sweet smoke of the dead ashes in her grate.

It's already starting to get dark at this, the bleakest time of the year, and Owen turns on lights, flicking the yellowed Bakelite switches that fizz alarmingly beneath his fingertip. Dirty light bulbs give off a sad, jaundiced light and it's freezing cold. Owen's room contains an electric storage heater, but Tessie doesn't run the heating when she's not here, and rarely even when she is, so he also has a plug-in blow heater hidden behind his wardrobe that Tessie would make him get rid of if she discovered it, convinced as she is that it would send her electric bill through the roof.

He drops his rucksack onto his bed and flops heavily into a small floral armchair. He reaches down to the blow heater and switches it on. Because of the height of his ceilings it takes a while for the room to heat up, but once it does, he kicks off his new shoes so that they disappear beneath his bed. He does not want to see the shoes again, let alone wear them. For some inexplicable reason he feels that the shoes are to blame for the events of the afternoon. They have made him someone that he is not: a man capable of inappropriate sexual comments to his students, a man in need of being walked off premises.

He pulls off his sweater and then runs his hands down his static-filled hair; Owen has fine hair. He tries to wear it in a side parting, but it always flops into a middle parting and he ends up looking as though he's deliberately chosen to wear his hair that way, like that tall bloke in *The Office*. Not that Owen looks like the bloke from *The Office*. Owen is much better-looking than him. No one's ever told him he's good-looking. But, then, no one's ever told him he's ugly either.

Through the window Owen can see another flurry of snow fill the tar-brown sky outside, each flake briefly lit on one side by light from the street. He starts to worry about it settling again, about struggling down the hill to the tube station the next morning, holding on to cars and walls to stop himself from falling. And then he remembers. There was an "incident." He is suspended. The contents of his office are currently in a bag on his bed. He has nowhere to go tomorrow. There is food in the fridge—enough for two days. The snow can fall and settle; he has no reason to care.

13

LATER THAT EVENING Owen opens up his laptop and types in "false accusations of sexual misconduct." He's looking for some online advice but instead finds himself reading a human-interest article in the *Guardian* about the impact on various men of being falsely accused of rape. The accusations leveled against him pale in comparison to what these men were told they'd done. The stories shock him at first, but then the shock recedes into a kind of numb acceptance, a sense that he'd always known this about women. Of course. Women lie. Women hate men and want to hurt them. And what easier way is there to hurt a man than to accuse him of rape?

He closes his eyes and pinches the bridge of his nose between his thumb and forefinger. He can feel the suppressed rage from his meeting earlier start to rise through his body like mercury. He thinks of Monique and Maisy; they're not even particularly good-looking, yet they act as though he should be so grateful to them for the warped attention they pay him. Maisy's actually fat (though no doubt thinks of herself as "curvy" in the modern parlance. A curve only exists where a body goes in at the middle, as far as Owen's concerned, not when it sticks out).

Then he thinks about the previous evening, about that stupid girl who'd got off the tube at the same time as him, who'd crossed the Finchley Road at the same time as him, who'd taken the same turning off the Finchley Road as him and then acted like he was about to jump on her just because he *dared* to live on the same street as her. He'd seen her take out her phone and call someone, the breathlessness of her voice, the little turns of her head over her shoulder every few minutes. She'd honestly thought he was deliberately following her. As if he'd have any interest in her. She was just a child. Owen has no interest in children. Owen likes proper women, mature women who grew up when he grew up, women who have good jobs and wear nice clothes and don't dress like vagrants as teenage girls seem to these days.

The girl's mother had been waiting in the doorway for her, her face all screwed up with nerves as she ushered her inside, safe and sound.

No nasty men in here, darling.

Owen feels his nails dig into the flesh of his palm and loosens his fist. He stares at the red half-moons and rubs them absentmindedly with his thumb. Then he turns his attention back to the screen and scrolls to the bottom of the article, to the comments. Owen loves the comments, the gray places where the dusty trolls live; he loves to see how low some people will stoop to get the endorphin rush of a reaction. He's been known to do it himself on occasion. It can feel like sport at the time, though afterward he feels a sort of pathetic remorse. What has he contributed to the great vibrant soup of humanity? Nothing whatsoever.

There are some angry men in the comments section of this particular article, but one in particular catches Owen's eye. His username is YourLoss and he seems articulate and well-informed. He has been through this himself, he says:

My colleague, who, might I say, was no oil painting, decided that my attempts to offer her advice about her love life (and I can tell you, all this woman ever talked about was her love life. I was locked in a small office with her and another woman who literally talked about men *all day long*) were actually meant as sexual overtures. And no, of course she did not say this to my face. Of course not, because that would just be civilised and human. No, Straight to Human Resources. They offered her counselling. They offered me nothing but dirty looks and assumptions of guilt. They never proved anything and I kept my job. But this woman asked to be moved to another area of the business, while her colleague swapped offices with someone across the landing and was replaced by a man. This man has a beard and looks at me in disdain. He puts soya milk in his coffee and refers to homosexuals as LGBTABCDXYZs or what the fuck EVER. He has clearly been radicalised by some rampant feminazi in his life. The stupid thing is that I genuinely believe in women's rights. I believe women should earn the same as men (providing they work as hard as men). I believe they should be allowed to go off and have babies and then come back to work (providing they don't keep taking time off to go and see little Sally in her nativity play leaving all their colleagues knee-deep in the shit). I believe they should be free to go out at night and get drunk and wear short skirts without being raped. So yeah, I'm a feminist too. But I'm also a realist. The pendulum has swung waaaay too far imo. It's time to throw a spanner into the pendulum, stop its trajectory, send it back a little our way. No wonder men want to be women these days. What teenage boy seeing what the future has in store for him wouldn't prefer to be a lady, to have all the rights and all the protection? Who's protecting the men? Nobody. Nobody gives a shit about us. It's time, people, it's time…

YourLoss's comment ends there, on something of a cliffhanger. Time for what? Owen wonders. Time for what?

Owen goes to the kitchen to get himself a cup of tea. He stands with his back against the counter as he waits for the kettle to boil.

The tiled floor is icy cold beneath his socked feet. There's a huge curtain of thick cobweb hanging across the top of the kitchen window. Tessie used to have a cleaner, but she died three years ago and was never replaced. Owen does what he can, but that doesn't extend to climbing up stepladders with a feather duster.

He thinks about YourLoss's post as he waits. He feels strangely energized by it. He senses a connection with the author: a man of a similar age to him, living somewhere bourgeois in the south, dealing with the aftermath of being wrongly and unfairly accused of sexual misconduct by a vile-sounding woman. The kettle clicks off, and he makes his tea. He opens a cupboard and takes out a packet of Tessie's special Italian almond biscuits. She's not due back for a week; they'll be stale by then. She'll probably have a little dig about it, but he doesn't care. He's got bigger things to worry about right now than Tessie's precious biscuits.

————

Early on Tuesday morning, five days after his suspension from work, a man appears at Owen's door.

He is tall, six feet four or so. He towers over Owen, and Owen immediately feels threatened.

"Good morning, sir, I'm DI Robert Burdett. I'm investigating an incident, last night."

An incident. That word again.

"Are you Mr. Owen . . ." He examines his notepad. "Pick?"

"Yes."

"Great, thank you. Yes. A young girl, a teenage girl, was sexually assaulted last night. Here." He turns and gestures toward the crossroads. "Just outside the wasteland. I wondered if you heard anything? Saw anything?"

Owen flushes red. He feels immediately guilty. Not because he's done anything, but because he might have done something. He's spent his whole life feeling like he might have done something wrong.

He breathes in hard to try to bring down the color in his cheeks, but it makes it worse. He blows the air back out and says, "No. No. I heard nothing."

"Your living room." The policeman nods his head toward the front window to the left of the door. "It overlooks the street. Maybe you noticed something without quite realizing what it was?"

"I wasn't in my living room last night. I mean, it's not even my living room."

"Ah, you live with someone else?"

"Yes. My aunt. Tessie McDonald. It's her living room. I never go in there."

"Might she have seen something?"

"No. She's in Tuscany. She has another property. She's often there. She's there now."

He's burbling. Tall men make him feel this way. Policemen make him feel this way.

"Right," says DI Burdett. "Anyway. It was at about eight thirty p.m. Maybe you were watching something on the TV about that time? Maybe that would jog your memory? Something untoward you noticed? A strange noise? Someone walking down the street who made you feel alarmed in some way?"

"No. Honestly. I was in my room all day yesterday. It's at the back of the house. I haven't seen anything or heard anything."

"A neighbor claims . . ." DI Burdett glances down at his notebook again, "to have seen you, on your driveway, at approximately four thirty p.m. yesterday."

Owen clamps his hand to his forehead. He has barely processed the accusations he's suffered at work, and now there are anonymous neighbors spying on him and reporting his movements to the police in relation to a sex attack.

"What?"

"Would that have been you? At four thirty p.m.?"

"I don't know," he says. Then he remembers that today is bin collection day and that yes, he had put the rubbish out yesterday. "I put the rubbish out at some point," he says. "But I can't tell you when." As he says this, he remembers the girls who had walked past. Two schoolgirls. One was the girl who'd acted like he was going to jump her when he was walking home from work the other night; the other was a tiny girl with black hair. They'd looked over at him and said something to each other; then they'd picked up their pace before disappearing into the house across the road.

He'd thought he was being paranoid at the time, that he'd imagined them talking about him. Now he can only assume that they had been. He sighs.

"But roughly?"

"Roughly the afternoon. It was dark, I remember."

"And you haven't left the house apart from that?"

"No. I have not."

DI Burdett folds his notepad in half and tucks it into his pocket. "Thank you, Mr. Pick. I appreciate your time."

"That's fine," he replies. And then, just as the policeman turns to leave, he adds, "Is she all right? The girl?"

DI Burdett smiles slightly. "She's fine," he says. "But thank you for asking."

"Good," says Owen. "Good."

14

OWEN HAD BEEN a beautiful child, oddly. His mother had put him in for modeling when he was about four. He hadn't been taken on because he was awkward in front of a camera. But he'd had a cherubic face: dark eyes, red lips, a dimple.

But the face that had looked so beautiful on a small child had not translated into a good face for a teenager, and he'd been a shockingly awkward-looking boy. To this day he cannot bear to look at photos of himself between the ages of eleven and eighteen.

But now, at thirty-three, he feels his features have settled again; he looks in the mirror, and a relatively handsome guy looks back at him. He particularly likes his eyes; they are so brown that they are almost black. He inherited them from his maternal grandmother who was half Moroccan.

He doesn't work out—that is true to say. He has little definition, but in clothes you wouldn't know that; you wouldn't know about the softness of the skin around his belly button, the slightly mammary sag around his pectorals. In carefully chosen clothes, he looks just like any average gymgoer.

Owen doesn't believe that he's being rejected by women on

the grounds of not having a "fit bod." This he could accept. But no woman has seen him undressed. Not once. Not ever. It appears that for some unexplained reason Owen fails to meet the criteria of every single woman in the land. And yet he sees men far worse-looking than himself, every single day, with women who appear to like them, or with children, proving that at some point a woman has liked them enough to let them do that to her; or wearing wedding rings, or with photos on their desks of nice-looking women or photos of the children who nice-looking women have let them make inside them, and really, it baffles him, it absolutely baffles him.

It's not as if Owen is fussy. He really isn't fussy; in fact he would probably say yes to 80 percent of adult women if they asked him out to dinner. Maybe even 90 percent.

In Tessie's bathroom, which is heated by an electric bar above the door that glows as red as a Saharan sunset, and which would probably fail a health and safety inspection, there is a full-length mirror opposite the toilet. Owen has no idea what would possess someone to put a full-length mirror opposite a toilet. But there it is, and over the years he's grown used to it. He ignores it most of the time. But sometimes he uses it to assess himself, physically. He needs to look upon himself at regular intervals, to see himself, because no one else sees him, and if he doesn't remind himself of his three dimensions, he might just dissolve and disappear. He looks at his penis. He has a nice penis. He's watched the dating show with the naked men standing in pods being scrutinized by fully clothed women and nearly every one of the men has had an ugly penis. But his penis is nice. He can see that objectively. Yet no woman has ever seen it.

He sighs, puts himself back into his underwear and zips up his trousers. He goes to his room and to YourLoss's blog, which he'd linked to on his comment on the newspaper article Owen had read the day before.

YourLoss's website is a portal into a world that Owen did not know existed.

He describes himself as an incel. The term is hyperlinked at the top of his website to a wiki page that describes incels thus:

> members of an online subculture who define themselves as unable to find a romantic or sexual partner despite desiring one, a state they describe as *inceldom*. Self-identified incels are largely white and are almost exclusively male heterosexuals. The term is a portmanteau of "involuntary celibates."

YourLoss is thirty-three, like Owen, and very open about the fact that he has not had sex since he was seventeen.

Owen, on the other hand, has never had sex.

He once had a girl touch him inside his trousers, when he was about nineteen. But it had ended badly and prematurely, with the girl withdrawing her hand rapidly and rushing to find a sink. It was one of the most embarrassing moments of his life. He'd replayed it in his head for years, over and over, like slicing himself over and over with a sharp knife. The more he thought about it, the scareder he'd become of ever putting himself in that position again, and he's blamed himself ever since for the lack of sex he's experienced, for the women who haven't looked at him or touched him. As far as he's concerned, it's his fault, entirely. But as he reads YourLoss's blog, he begins to wonder about this.

Because YourLoss doesn't blame himself. YourLoss blames everyone else, and he is really angry.

He's angry at people he calls "Chads." Chads are guys who get sex. According to YourLoss, Chads don't get sex because they're better than guys who don't get sex. They get sex because they're *looksmaxxing* and *mugging*. This means that they are pumping their bodies artificially to look more attractive than normal guys, that they are fake-tanning and tooth-whitening and getting plastic surgery and having things done to their eyebrows and their skin. They get sex because they are stacking the system unfairly against men like YourLoss. And, Owen suspects, men like him too. They are, apparently, cheating.

But mainly, he's angry at women. Stacys and Beckys as he refers to them. Stacys are the high-value women, the trophy women, the women who can have any man they want. These women sicken him because they know exactly what they're doing; they know their power and their worth and use it deliberately to make guys like YourLoss feel worthless. Beckys are the less-attractive women who still feel they have the right to reject men like YourLoss whom they deem to be not up to scratch.

YourLoss walks a lot. He walks and he sits on benches and in quiet corners of pubs and he looks and he reports what he sees; the injustices he perceives to be lurking in every corner of the nameless town in which he lives.

Owen clicks on an entry called "Snow Joke." He reads:

My town is white today. We're snowy. It makes me feel for a minute like anything is possible; everything hidden away, like the world's wearing a uniform. And everyone in their biggest, warmest, least attractive clothes, we're all equal now.

Except we're not, are we? Under the snow, that car there is still a Mercedes coupé and that car there is still a Ford Focus and you bloody well know it without having to scrape the snow away; there's that glint of red paintwork, that particular curve to the bumper, unmistakeable. So even though we're all wearing our worst clothes it's still plain to see who's winning and who's losing. There's the sad, sad Becky trailing her squashed old Uggs through the snow; doesn't she know they're not waterproof? Sheesh. No, she does not because she is stupid. And, look, there's a Stacy striding along in a pair of Hunter wellies—£100 a pair, don't you know? Ugly as all fuck. But at least they don't let in the water. And I'm sure there must be someone out there with a fetish for green rubber footwear… And she's in full makeup, of course, can't let a few frozen fractals stop you slapping on the slap. Can't let your standards drop completely.

This town, this fucking town. Full of poseurs. And if you're not a poseur you're a wannabe poseur. And if you're not a wannabe poseur then you're a loser, even when you're a winner.

I go to the gastropub just off the common. It's only been a gastropub for a few weeks. It was just a pub before that. Or actually an inn, to be precise. The Hunters' Inn as it was once known. It has lamps outside and a carriageway where horses would once have been tethered. In spite of its gentrification, in the snow, with its glowing lamps, it still looks vaguely Dickensian and for a minute I feel timeless and happy, as if I belong somehow. In the old days every man could find a woman. And if they couldn't make a woman fall in love with them, there were other ways of finding women and keeping them. Women needed us then, more than we needed them. What the hell happened to this world?

I buy a pint. I sit by the window. I watch the ducks skittering about on the frozen pond on the common. I watch the snow.

Tomorrow it will be gone.

15

OWEN PUTS ON a gray button-down shirt and dark jeans. He assesses himself in the mirror on the outside of his wardrobe. He looks fine. Possibly overdue for a haircut; his fringe hangs a little limply over his eyes. And he's very pale. But it is February, and he is always pale in February. He is due at a meeting at the college in an hour and a half. It will be the first time he's left the house for anything other than food shopping in over two weeks. His stomach churns slightly with nervous anticipation. Not just about the thought of going on the tube and sitting opposite people and walking through crowds of strangers, but also of what they are going to say to him. They have carried out a full investigation into the girls' allegations. They want him to "pop in for half an hour or so" so that they can give him an update.

"Can't you just tell me over the phone?" he asked.

"No," Holly had said. "I'm afraid not, Owen. It needs to be face-to-face."

He fishes the dreaded shoes out from under the bed, where they've been lurking ever since he kicked them under there two weeks ago. They appear, trailing a family of dust bunnies in their wake. He appraises them in the light of two weeks' absence. No, he decides, they are bad shoes. He will not wear them again. He puts on his comfy, rubber-soled black lace-ups instead, the ones he's had to glue the soles back on to twice.

He gets himself some breakfast in the kitchen: a slice of toast and a slice of cheese. Tessie appears as he's putting the butter back in the fridge. She is back from Italy and has been in a strange mood ever since she returned.

"Aren't you going to be late?" she says. "You know it's nearly ten o'clock."

"I'm not due in until eleven," he says.

He hasn't told her about his suspension. Why would he? She would just judge him, say something about his mother, make everything 10 percent worse than it already is.

"All right for some," she says, brushing past him to the sink where she takes an upturned teacup from the draining board and examines the inside of it before rinsing it and switching on the kettle.

Tessie is his mother's big sister. His mother is dead. She died when Owen was eighteen. Owen's father lives in south London with another wife and another son. Owen lived with them for a month after his mother died. It was the loneliest month of his life. He remembers Tessie, at his mother's funeral, touching his arm and saying, "Remember, I will always have a room for you if you need it."

Turns out she didn't really mean it. But now she's stuck with him, fifteen years later and counting. She was forty when Owen moved in. Now she is fifty-five, but she acts as though she is sixty-five. You wouldn't catch her in Lycra leggings and a hoodie. Her hair is steel gray and frothy, and she shops at odd boutiques in Hampstead that sell voluminous linen tunics and trousers with baggy crotches and floppy hats.

"I bumped into Ernesto last night," she says.

Owen nods. Ernesto is a single man of a certain age who lives in the flat above theirs.

"He said there was a visit from the police a couple of weeks back. Saw you talking to them on the front step. What was that all about?"

Owen breathes in hard. "Nothing," he says. "Some sort of attack in the area. They were doing door-to-doors."

"Attack," she says, narrowing her eyes. "What sort of attack?"

"I don't know." He throws his crusts in the bin. Thirty-three years old. He really should be able to eat crusts at his age. "An assault, something like that."

"Sexual?" she asks.

"Yes," he replies. "Probably."

There is a tiny but significant silence. Inside the silence he can hear the little intake of his aunt's breath; sees a thought passing through her mind so fast that it makes her head roll back slightly. Her eyes narrow again and then it passes.

"Well," she says. "I hope they caught whoever it was. I don't know what's happening to this area. It used to be so safe."

———

After a tense five-minute wait in the reception area at the college, Owen is shown into the same office he was shown to last time. Jed Bryant is there, once again, with Holly and Clarice. And there is another woman, small and sharp, who is introduced to him as Penelope Ofili. She is an adjudicator.

"Why do we need an adjudicator?" he asks.

"Just for transparency."

Transparency. Owen blinks slowly and sucks in his cheeks.

"Please," says Jed, "take a seat."

"How've you been?" asks Holly. "Hope you've had a chance to relax."

"Not really," he says. "No."

The smile freezes on Holly's lips and she turns away abruptly and says, "So, thank you so much for coming in again, Owen. As you know, we've been working very hard to investigate the claims made by two of your students regarding your behavior at the Christmas party last December."

Owen wriggles slightly in his chair, uncrosses his legs, crosses them again. He's been over the events of that night a hundred times since the allegations were made, and he still cannot find the point at which his behavior breached the line between jovial and abusive. Because that is the bottom line here: in order for all these people to be sitting in this room together, taking time out of their own days, calling in the services of an independent adjudicator, there must be some fundamental belief that abuse has taken place.

He uncrosses his legs for a third time and is aware that this will look edgy and uncomfortable, which is understandable but might also make it seem that he is feeling guilty. He should have spoken to someone; he realizes that now. Things have escalated rather than de-escalated since he last sat here.

"We've spoken to several people who were there on the night," Holly continues. "I'm afraid, Owen, that they all corroborate the original accusation."

He nods, his eyes cast downward.

"Several people saw you touch the girls in question. Several other people report being present when you splattered the girls with the sweat from your forehead. They all attest that it was a deliberate action and that you did it more than once when asked by the girls to stop.

"Furthermore, we've had several reports backing up the claims of inappropriate teaching: favoring boys, belittling girls, ignoring them, marking them more harshly in some cases or not prioritizing their work in others. Some usage of inappropriate language in the classroom."

He glances up. "Like what?"

"Well." Holly looks at her notes. "Using terms such as 'man up'. Referring to certain pieces of code as 'sexy'. Referring to female students as girls. Referring to other students as 'insane' and 'mental.'"

"But—"

"Making fun of students with food allergies."

"Intolerances . . ."

"And students who are vegans."

Owen closes his eyes and sighs. "For God's sake," he mutters under his breath.

Holly narrows her eyes at him, her finger on the last line of her notes, and says, "Also, excessive blasphemy."

"Blasphemy?" he says. "Really? Dear God."

He realizes his faux pas and shuts his eyes.

"So," he says, "what happens now?"

There is a brief silence. All three people in the room exchange a glance. Then Holly pulls a piece of paper from her folder and passes it across the table to him. "We would like you to attend this training course, Owen. It's a week long and addresses all the issues we've been discussing today. If at the end of the course it's felt that you've properly engaged with the training and have a clearer understanding of what's appropriate and inappropriate in a workplace with children, we can start talking a return to work. But you have to commit to it. One hundred percent. Have a read. Let me know what you think. You're a very valued member of staff here, Owen." A rictus smile. "We don't want to lose you."

Owen stares at the piece of paper for a while. The words swim and swirl before his eyes. The word "brainwashing" passes through his head. A week trapped in a room with a bunch of pedophiles being reprogrammed to think that vegans are superior beings and women can have penises.

No, he thinks. No, thank you. He pushes the paper back across the table toward Holly and says, "Thank you, but I'd rather be sacked."

Owen walks aimlessly for quite some time after he leaves Ealing College. He can't face the thought of the tube journey home. He can't face the thought of Tessie peering at him through her horn-rimmed glasses and saying, "What are you doing back so early?" And then sitting in his lumpy armchair for the rest of the day staring at a screen.

He could call the college, recant his resignation, agree to the training course. There are avenues still open to him. But if the best-case scenario is that he gets his job back and has to come into work every day and look at the faces of those two girls across his class-room and be surrounded by revolting teenagers who all think he is a pervy fascist then really, what is he fighting for?

Owen has savings. Tessie charges him what she charged him fifteen years ago when he was a newly bereaved teenager: twenty-five pounds a week. He has no social life, no expensive hobbies, and he certainly hasn't been spending his hard-earned money wining and dining a string of ladies over the years. He has thousands in the bank. Not enough to put down a deposit on a nice flat, but more than enough to live on for a few months. He does not want his job back. He does not want to fight for it.

He calls his father.

"Dad," he says, "it's me."

He hears the tiny pause, his father subconsciously recalibrating his mood to take his son into account.

"Oh, hi, Owen," he says, "how are you?"

"I haven't seen you for ages," Owen begins. "It's been, like, *months.*"

"I know," says his father apologetically. "I know. It's awful, isn't it, how the time just slips away."

"How was your Christmas?" Owen asks this sharply, not wanting to give his father any more opportunity to blame anything other than his own uninterest for their lack of communication.

"Oh, it was, you know, hectic. I'm sorry that—"

"It's fine," he interjects again. He doesn't want to go over it all again: the sick mother-in-law, the half brother having some kind of pathetic Generation Z crisis to do with drugs and gender dysphoria; *All a bit much this year, son, we're going to batten down the hatches.* The idea that his father *battening down the hatches* involved the exclusion of his firstborn son had been bad enough when it was first announced, and it hasn't improved with the passage of time.

"Did you . . . How was your . . . ?"

"I spent it alone," Owen says.

"Oh," says his father. "I assumed you'd be with Tessie, or . . . ?"

"No. Tessie went to Tuscany. I spent it alone. It was fine."

"Right," he says. "Good. Well, I'm sorry. And hopefully next Christmas will be a bit less . . ."

"Hectic?"

"Yes, a bit less hectic. And how's . . . how's work?"

"I resigned from my job today. They were accusing me of sexual misconduct."

"Ouf." He hears his father wince.

"Yes, apparently I stroked a girl's hair at the college disco, and apparently I use triggering language in lessons and apparently being a normal man is no longer an acceptable thing to be in the classroom. Apparently we all have to be like robots these days and think about every last word before it leaves our lips. Apparently modern women cannot cope with anything, with anything at all."

He's shouting. He knew he would shout. It was why he'd called his father. His father knows he's let Owen down, he knows he's been a shit, shit dad. He lets Owen shout at him from time to time. He takes it. He doesn't fix anything, but he takes it. And that'll do for now.

"Oh, Owen, it's all so bloody ridiculous, isn't it? Political correctness," he tuts. "It's madness; it really is. But do you think resigning was the right response, really? I mean, how will you get another job?"

Owen winces against the unpalatable question. Then he thinks of YourLoss, strolling around his pretentious little market town, writing his existential blog, doing his boring shitty office job. He seems happy enough. He seems to have it all under control.

"I'll get another job," he says. "It's all just so . . ."

"I know," says his father, "ridiculous. Absolutely ridiculous."

There's a significant pause. Owen feels the onus is on him to fill it somehow. But he can't, and he doesn't. Instead he leaves the way completely clear for his father to say, "Well, Owen, it's been good talking to you. I'm sorry to hear you're having a bad time of it. And we must get together soon. We really must. I mean, your birthday . . . ?"

"Next month."

"Yes. Next month. Let's do something."

"Yes. Let's."

"And, Owen?"

"Yes?"

"These allegations. The, you know, sexual impropriety. I mean, there's nothing to them. Is there?"

Owen sighs, lets himself sink to his haunches, his back against a wall. "No, Dad. No."

"Good. That's good. Bye, Owen."

"Bye, Dad."

Owen pulls himself back to standing. The anger that he transferred so very briefly onto his father has turned straight back onto himself, twice as hard and dark and sharp. He feels his veins fill with electricity. He walks fast now, toward the tube station. He's about to turn into the entrance when he sees across the road the rose-gold glow of a pub window. It's twenty to twelve.

Owen is not much of a drinker. He likes wine with a meal or on a night out with colleagues, but not drinking just for the sake of drinking. Then he thinks again of his cold bedroom, of Tessie bumping about resentfully, and he thinks of YourLoss with a pint in a quiet corner of a pub, watching, learning, thinking, being. He imagines him as a tall man, broad-shouldered, short hair, neatly cut, maybe even a short beard or mustache. He imagines him in a button-down shirt and worn jeans and walking boots. He imagines him wiping away a slick of foam from the tips of his mustache, placing his pint carefully back on the beer mat, centering it just so. Lifting his gaze. Watching, learning, thinking, being.

He turns away from the tube station, back to the pedestrian crossing, waits for the green man to flash, and heads into the warmth of the pub. He orders a pint. He finds a table for one. He sits at it.

16

A FEW HOURS later Owen pushes his way heavily through the door of the Oriental Star opposite his local tube station. He waits at the till for a special chow mein and a can of Tango and then takes them to the counter in the window, where he watches people pouring from the tube, wondering at the terrifying unknowability of strangers.

He uses the noodles to try to soak up the three pints of lager he had while he was in the pub by himself. Being drunk alone was an alarming experience. He'd gone to the toilet and pissed on his shoes, wobbled, laughed at his reflection in the mirror, and talked to himself, then bumped into a table on the way out, causing the wine in a woman's glass to slosh over the rim.

"I am so very sorry," he said. "Please don't report me to the authorities."

And she looked at him sideways, unsmilingly, and he said "Fucking bitch" under his breath, left the pub, and then immediately wished he hadn't said it.

After his noodles he ascends the steep hill to his road. The drunkenness is receding, dampened. He looks up and sees the moon shining down between two tall trees, against a navy-blue sky. He takes out his phone and tries to capture it, but the moon refuses to show off for him, imprinting itself as a vague white smudge on the image.

He puts his phone back in his pocket and then turns, and as he does so a thin figure comes hurtling toward him, shoulders him roughly, nearly knocks him backward.

The figure barely slows as it turns backward. "Sorry, mate. Sorry."

The figure then reverses and hurtles down to the end of the hill, runs on the spot, then turns and hurtles back up the hill, right up the middle of the road.

Owen stands and watches him.

He sees that it is a middle-aged man, wearing tight Lycra leggings and a zip-up jacket with strange black flaps over his ears and wires coming out of a tiny pocket in his jacket.

A jogger. He throws Owen a strange look before running back down again. The road is a dead end, separated from the six lanes of traffic on the Finchley Road by a set of stone steps. For a while it is just Owen and the jogger.

As the jogger reaches the top of the hill for the sixth time he stops and collapses into himself, breathing so loudly he sounds as though he might die. He glances up at Owen. "You all right, mate?" he asks.

Owen feels something stir deep inside himself, something dark. He looks at the jogger and he says, "Are you married?"

The jogger grimaces and says, "Eh?"

"Married?" says Owen. "Got a girlfriend?"

"What's it got to do with you?"

"Nothing," he replies. "I just wondered."

He starts to head around the corner to his street when the man catches up with him. "Do I know you?" he asks.

"I have no idea."

"Are we neighbors? I feel like I've seen you . . ."

"I live there. Number twelve." He points at Tessie's building and shrugs.

"Ah, yes. That's right. We live there." The man points at the house opposite, the one where the teenage girl lives, where the stupid mother with the concerned face lives.

Owen nods.

The man gives him a tight smile before jogging away from him. "See you around," he says.

"Yeah," says Owen. "See you around."

———

The TV in Tessie's sitting room rumbles through the closed door. She's watching the live feed from the Houses of Parliament. Something to do with Brexit. It sounds like a donkey compound.

He tiptoes past, gets himself a pint of water from the kitchen, and then locks himself away in his bedroom, where he undoes the top three buttons of his shirt, kicks off his scruffy shoes, and opens up YourLoss's blog. There's a new post up, but he doesn't read it. Instead he scrolls down the page to the link that reads *Contact. Hi,* he types in the contact form:

My name's Owen. I love your blog. Would love to chat sometime. I've just lost my job. Don't really know what my next steps are.

Yo, Owen, what's going down with you?

I'm a teacher. I was accused of "sweating on a student" and "taking the mick out of vegans." And I just turned down the chance to attend a "retraining course" and quit.

No way! Tell me more!

Owen replies succinctly. The outline of the thing. The party, the tequila shots, the girls, the meetings. The curl of distaste on the mouths of Clarice and Holly every time the word "sweat" was mentioned.

What's the deal with you? Are you celibate? Infrequent? Never? What?

Celibate. Never.

Do you like anyone? I mean, are you romantic?

Owen considers the question. He can't find an answer. Eventually he replies:

I don't know. I don't like anyone. But I have liked people.

Dated?

Kind of.

Dinner and flowers? The pub?

Dinner and flowers. Once.

And how did that go?

Shit. She left halfway through the date, said her mum was having an emergency.

LOL. Fuck that. What fucking bullshit. So, what are you going to do about your job?

I dunno. Going to take some time out. I've got savings.

And? What will you do with your time-out?

Haven't really thought about it. Maybe try to start something up, a company. Something like that.

You need a plan, mate. Otherwise you'll wake up one morning and your savings will be gone and you'll have put on twenty pounds and have nothing to show for any of it but a load of trousers that don't fit you anymore.

I'm not sure I'm ready for making a plan.

YourLoss doesn't reply for quite some time. Owen wriggles slightly and clears his throat, worried that he's said something to put him off. Then there's a plip and another message appears.

Where d'you live, Owen?

North London.

Righty-ho. Not far from me then.

Why, where do you live?

Just outside London. Look, here's my email address. Write to me. I've got a proposition for you. Bryn@hotmail.co.uk. Email me now, yeah?

Owen opens his email account, pastes Bryn's email address into the bar, and starts typing.

17

OWEN AND BRYN arrange to meet for a pint at a pub near Euston station.

Bryn has told Owen that he will be wearing a green jacket and has "a lot of hair" and wears glasses. Owen has told Bryn that he will be wearing a black jacket and jeans and then struggled to find any other identifying features to share with him.

He walks into the pub now; it's a scruffy mock-Tudor affair, set on a corner, with weather-beaten tables on the pavement and leaded windows. The air is thick with beer and dust. Lone men sit in corners. Owen's eyes scan the room until they come upon a man on the left, who is looking at him with some semblance of recognition. It doesn't somehow compute that this man might be Your-Loss, and Owen's gaze passes across him. But then the man is on his feet and coming toward him. He has a strange forward-leaning gait and is short. Very short. His hair explodes from his scalp and recedes halfway back like a clown wig. The bald part of his skull is shiny and raw-looking. His green zip-up jacket has a stain on it.

"Owen! Yes? Cool! Nice to see you, mate!" He grabs Owen's hand and pumps it up and down.

"Bryn," says Owen. "Great to meet you too. Can I get you . . . ?" He gestures toward the bar.

"No. No. I'm good."

Owen gets himself a glass of red wine and heads back to Bryn's table.

"Well, well, well," says Bryn. "This is a turnup for the books."

"It is a bit," Owen agrees.

The last thing he'd been expecting, in fact. Bryn had emailed him back the night before and asked him a bit more about his technical qualifications, abilities, interests, asked him about the circumstances around his resignation from the college. Owen hadn't quite been able to fathom his intent. Then Bryn had suddenly said: *This is kismet, karma, you and I were meant to meet. Drinks? Tomorrow? Euston way?*

"How's your day been?" he asks now.

Owen, who is unused to people asking him how his day has been, blanches slightly. "Good. It's been good." Then, checking himself, he adds, "Yours?"

"Oh, you know. Same old shit."

"Are you working right now?"

"Yeah. I am. Just come straight from the office in fact. Unlike you, you lucky bastard, you gentleman of leisure. How did you spend your day?"

He shrugs. "Slept late. Had a long bath. Watched a few episodes of a show. Ate a bowl of pasta."

"Oh, you lucky, lucky fucker. Fuck, I'd kill for a day like that. Anyway." He raises his pint of something murky-looking toward Owen's red wine and says, "Cheers."

He is absolutely nothing like Owen had imagined. But he has a certain charisma, a cartoonish charm. He has self-confidence, a touch of cockiness, which confounds Owen, as he'd always been under the impression that self-confidence was what attracted women to a man and that it was his own lack of confidence that was damaging his chances.

Owen's eye falls to the stain on Bryn's jacket; it's unidentifiable. It looks like it's been there for so long that Bryn no longer sees it. He pictures himself pulling Bryn's jacket off and shoving it in a washing machine on a hot setting. He pictures himself with a pair of shiny snip-snip scissors, chopping off the ludicrous curls, yanking off his unfashionable glasses, telling him to *stop smiling like that*. He's strangely furious with Bryn for sabotaging himself and then making himself the mouthpiece for men like Owen who try to do everything right; who don't have stains on their jackets and clown hair yet still can't get a woman to look them in the eye.

Bryn doesn't have a clue, Owen thinks. He doesn't have a clue what it feels like to be totally normal yet be overlooked by the world for no discernible reason. He seems to want to be despised by women. He thinks again of Bryn's comment under the article about being accused of sexual misconduct at work, and he thinks of the women in Bryn's office, and for a moment he feels sorry for them.

But he hides these misgivings from Bryn and smiles and says, "Cheers. It's great to meet you."

"So." Bryn rubs his hands together. "I suppose you're wondering what this is all about?"

Owen nods.

Bryn lowers his voice and glances around the pub. "I wanted to meet up, face-to-face, because what I want to discuss with you. It's kind of . . . sensitive. I don't want to leave anything in my trail. You know."

Owen nods again.

"So. You and me. I feel there's a kinship, yes?"

Owen nods for a third time.

"I'm looking at you, and I see a nice-looking fella. You're nicely dressed. But you're telling me that you've never, you know, you've never been with a woman."

Owen smiles apologetically.

"So, what does that tell you about the world?" Bryn doesn't wait for Owen to reply. "It tells you that the world is wrong. The world, Owen, is just totally fucking wrong. And why do you think that is?"

Again, he doesn't wait for an answer.

"It's a conspiracy. And I'm not some nutjob conspiracy theorist. I promise you that. But this, the shit that guys like you and me have to deal with. It's a conspiracy. Full-blown. End of. They call us 'incels.'" He makes the quotes with his fingers. "Like it's just bad luck. You know. Like there's nothing anyone can do about it. But that's the thing, Owen. They are doing this to us—deliberately. The media are doing this to us. And they've got the liberals and the feminists eating out of their hands. The world's collective brain is shrinking. People are becoming more and more stupid. More and more fixated on detail. Fucking eyebrows. There's a whole industry out there dedicated just to eyebrows. Did you know that? Multimillion-pound industry. And meanwhile the gene pool is shrinking and shrinking without men like you and me in it. Extrapolate another three generations into the future and what are we going to end up with? Nothing but a billion Stacys and Chads. And that's bad for the world, Owen. It's bad for the planet. We'll die out, the likes of us. It'll be a world full of people with shiny teeth and tattoos, all fucking each other and making more Stacys and Chads. In days gone by, there was a woman for every man, because women needed men. Now women think they rule the world. They get to pick and choose while men flail around waxing their eyebrows and pretending they're OK with their girl-friends calling them useless wankers. The world's destroyed, Owen, totally destroyed. And I've got a platform; I have over ten thousand subscribers to my blog. And it's building by the day, by the minute. I can use that platform, target people who might be on the same page as me. I mean, obviously we're all angry about the way we've been fucked over by the world. But it's a matter of targeting people who might be prepared to step out of their boxes and do something about it. Start a revolution."

Owen looks at Bryn questioningly.

"I'm talking about war, Owen. Are you in?"

———

Owen lies on his back on his single bed. He stares upward at the ceiling, eight feet overhead. Strands of cobweb dance about up there, blown by the draft from the window. It is midnight. He is tired, but he cannot sleep.

Every moment of his night out with Bryn is playing and replay-ing through his thoughts. Bryn's words roll about his mind like an upended bucket of marbles, skittering about deafeningly.

Even now, two hours after getting home, an hour after getting into bed, Owen cannot quite fathom the meaning behind Bryn's words. Bryn was unclear, his thought processes didn't seem to keep pace with his words, he seemed a bubbling geyser of ideas and anger and excitement and purpose, without any clear focus or intent. The one key thing he kept coming back to was the idea of a revolution.

Eventually he'd passed Owen a small pot of pills, with the words, "If you can't get it legally, then just fucking take it. While they're sleeping."

Owen had looked back at Bryn. "I don't understand," he said.

"Oh, you do understand," said Bryn. "You totally understand."

He sat back, his arms folded across his chest. He eyed Owen triumphantly for a second and then leaned in again. "Imagine," he said, "a whole army of us lot doing this. Hundreds of us. Do you see? Do you see?"

Owen felt his lunch rising gently up the back of his throat.

Bryn leaned in even closer and looked at him urgently. "This isn't about sex, you know that, don't you? This is about *us*. Fuck, if we were an endangered animal there'd be a charity out there doing everything they could to keep us alive. They'd be sending us every fucking fertile female animal they could throw our way to preserve our species. So why should we be any different? Why should we get a worse deal than a fucking animal, Owen?"

He steepled his fingers and looked at Owen across the tips.

They'd left the pub a minute or two later. "Think about it" had been Bryn's parting words. Owen had watched him leaping up the steps to Euston station, two at a time, quite nimble, his crazy curls bouncing up and down, the worn-down backs of his shoes flashing in and out of sight.

———

Owen sits up now and logs into one of the incel chat rooms that he's been frequenting since he started following Bryn's blog.

He found these forums reassuring at first. There has not been one day of Owen's life when he has woken up and felt OK about his aloneness. Not one day when he hasn't glanced at a couple on the street and wanted to scream in their faces about the unjustness of it all. And he was so relieved to find that he wasn't the only man in the world who felt the way he did.

But now Owen thinks of the stain on Bryn's coat, juxtaposed against the arrogance of what he thinks the world owes him, and he looks again at the forum and imagines, hiding behind the avatars and grandiose usernames, a sea of Bryns with stained jackets and unkempt hair and ridiculous rape fantasies, and he finds himself feeling sorry for these men; maybe, he thinks, they simply don't deserve nice women.

And now he wonders if maybe there's not anything wrong with him after all. That maybe he's just been in the wrong headspace, that he's just been overthinking it all these years. The answer, he suddenly realizes, is not Bryn's pathetic war against the world; the answer is making peace with himself.

He reaches down to the floor by his bed for his phone. He switches it on and swipes the screen, looking for the little red flame logo of the Tinder app.

18

IT'S 7:00 P.M. on Valentine's Day, and Owen puts on a dark-navy crew-neck sweater with a white shirt underneath. He can't quite get the collar to sit right, and it looks a little scruffy, but he's running out of time so it will have to do. His hair is all wrong, but that's par for the course. He wears a smart blazer over his sweater and chinos, mainly to try to camouflage his wide hips.

Owen is taking a woman out for dinner. A woman he met on Tinder three nights ago. He's tried the Tinder approach to meeting women before, but it never worked out for him, nothing more than a run of excruciating exchanges with women who weren't even particularly good-looking, and which he handled, he felt in retrospect, quite badly.

But he was a different person then, more brittle, less world-weary. He'd pinned too much on each encounter, set his hopes way too high. If his weird interlude with Bryn had done one thing for him, it was to reset his idea of romance. Anything that wasn't date-rape now seemed like a good thing.

The woman is called Deanna. She's thirty-eight, lives in Colin-dale, and works in marketing for a direct-mail company. She has a ten-year-old son and a face like a sincere apology for something that really isn't her fault. None of her photos show her body from the shoulders down, which suggests that she might be overweight. But that's fine. Owen doesn't mind.

He crosses paths with one of Tessie's friends as he exits his bedroom, a man called Barry who sometimes stays the night but often doesn't. Barry reeks of very strong aftershave and is wearing a handkerchief in the top pocket of an expensive-looking gray woolen jacket.

"Good evening, Owen," he says gruffly.

"Hello, Barry," he replies.

Tessie appears from the sitting room and looks strangely at Owen. "You look very smart," she says suspiciously. "Where are you off to?"

Owen reaches for his coat and pushes his arms into the sleeves. "I'm going to meet a friend."

Tessie pulls a mustard-colored scarf from the hook in the hallway and starts wrapping it around her neck. Her demeanor softens. "Oh," she says. "A friend. A red-roses-and-chocolates kind of a friend?"

"No," he says firmly, not wanting to give anything of his private life to Tessie that she might one day throw back at him. "Nothing like that. Just a friend."

She sighs. Then she says, "Owen. Are you . . . well, do you have any interest in women? Or men? I mean, I'm sorry if that seems intrusive, but you're—what are you now? Thirty-five?"

"I'm thirty-three."

"You're thirty-three. You've lived here since you were eighteen. And in all that time . . ." She leaves the end of the thought hanging, like a loose thread.

Owen decides to pretend that it wasn't said. He picks up an umbrella and says, "You going out too?"

"Yes, Barry's taking me to Villa Bianca. Have fun with your friend."

She pulls a lipstick from a drawer in the console, twists it up, and puckers in the mirror. He hears the lipstick smack of her lips as he pulls the door closed behind him.

On the tube Owen tries to stifle his nerves. He can feel damp patches developing in the armpits of his shirt, his forehead feels clammy, and he suspects he looks quite shiny. He exits the tube at Covent Garden and greedily breathes in the cold, damp night air. Glancing at his phone he sees a message from Deanna.

It reads: *Here early! At a table near the back!*

Owen gulps.

Why is she early? Who on earth turns up early for a date with someone they met on Tinder? He picks up his pace, annoyed that now he is going to get even hotter and arrive even more flustered and unkempt than he already feels. People get in his way as he tries to negotiate Neal Street, and he tuts at them and shoulders past them.

Then he is there: a jolly Italian restaurant, lots of red and white, walls hung with black-and-white photos of dead Italian film stars eating spaghetti. It's full. The woman at the desk says, "Have you made a reservation?" and he says, "Yes, Pick, eight p.m."

"Ah, yes, your companion is already here."

Owen clears his throat, touches his hair again, straightens his jacket, follows the woman through the winding path between the tables until he is there. In front of her.

Owen says, "Hi. Deanna?"

And she immediately says, "It's De-ahna. Not De-anna."

He says, "Oh. Sorry." Then he says, "I'm Owen."

"I guessed," she says. She's smiling, but Owen can't work out if she's being facetious or not.

"Shall I sit down?" he asks.

She nods and rubs awkwardly at the tips of her elbows.

He realizes he should have kissed her, or shaken hands with her, or something like that, but she threw him off completely with her correction of the pronunciation of her name and now he feels as though he's fallen off the tracks and can't get back on them. It has been at least ten seconds since either he or Deanna said something, and he sees Deanna staring at him strangely.

"Are you OK," she says, "or . . . ?"

Her eyes go to the door, and he thinks that she is suggesting that they should maybe cut the date short, that it has already gone so wrong, in under a minute, that they should end it now. He sighs and lets his shoulders drop. And then he does something quite out of character, because he feels so very much like he has nothing left to lose.

From a soft, open part of his psyche that he barely knew existed, he says, "I'm really sorry. I'm a bit . . . *nervous.*"

She smiles encouragingly.

He says, "In fact, I'm very nervous. Unbelievably nervous."

Her face softens completely now, and she says, "Well, then, that makes two of us."

And now Owen looks at her, properly, for the first time since he walked into the restaurant, and he sees a pleasant-looking woman, possibly not as smooth-skinned as the woman in the photographs on the screen of his phone, eyes possibly not as bright or quite as blue, jawline a little less sculpted. But it is her, recognizably her, and she is looking at him playfully, as though wanting him to say something else. His mind immediately empties and he blanches, but she laughs and it's not a laugh of derision or humiliation; it's a laugh of kindness, a laugh that says, "Look at us, on a Tinder date, isn't this nuts?"

A waiter arrives to take an order for drinks.

Owen thinks of the money sitting in his bank account, the money he never spends, and while Deanna peruses the wine list he looks at her and says, "Champagne?"

He sees immediately that he has hit a jackpot of some description, that Deanna is the type of woman to respond very positively to the suggestion of champagne. She opens her mouth to say something, and he opens his mouth and finds himself saying, "My treat."

She smiles and says, "Well, in that case, then," and closes her wine list.

They spend some time discussing what to eat, and then Deanna looks up at Owen and says, "You know, you look better in real life than you do in your online pics."

Owen smiles, almost laughs, and says, "Wow, thank you. That photo was probably the best photo I've ever seen of myself, so . . ."

There's a short silence, and Owen realizes what he's supposed to do. He clears his throat, and he says, "You look much prettier, too."

It's not entirely true; she doesn't. But she's certainly far from ugly. Her photos were not dishonest.

"Thank you," she says.

"Your hair is a lovely color."

It *is* a lovely color, a kind of brittle toffee shade, with blonder bits at the ends.

"Takes three hours in the salon," she says, touching the tips. "I'm naturally mousey."

"Mice are good, too," he says. And she tips her head back and laughs.

A waiter appears with their champagne and makes them feel suitably special as he arranges an ice bucket and chilled, misted glasses in front of them. He shows Owen the bottle, and Owen knows that he is to nod, just once, and say, "That's good," even though he can't remember the last time he had champagne.

When the champagne is poured, they touch their glasses together and Deanna says, "Cheers. Here's to Tinder sometimes getting it right."

Owen blinks. Then he smiles. "To Tinder, sometimes getting it right."

He glances about himself briefly. All around are couples. He wonders how many are on first dates. He wonders how many met on Tinder. He wonders how many are virgins. She sees him looking and says, "Nice restaurant. Well chosen."

"Thanks," he says. "It's just a chain, but you know, Valentine's night, beggars can't be—"

"Choosers." She completes his sentence for him, and they catch each other's eyes and smile again.

"So," she says, "how's your day been?"

"Oh, pretty boring really. Got up late. Mooched about. I'm just kind of enjoying my freedom for now."

He explained his current work situation to Deanna during one of their online chats, veering away from the aspects that reflect badly on him and playing up the aspects that made her say, *Oh, honestly, you can't say anything these days, can you?*

"I don't blame you," says Deanna now. "That's exactly what I'd be doing in your position. I am so tightly strapped to the treadmill that it's not even funny. Up at six every day, on the bus with Sam to breakfast club—he's usually the first one there, poor soul—another bus to the tube station, desk by eight thirty, eight hours of utter tedium, tube, bus, collect Sam from after-school club, bus home, cook dinner, homework, housework, bed. Every single day. I would give anything for a break. For a chance to jump off the treadmill for a while. See what else life might be able to offer me. I mean, I know it's shitty that your employers have let you go without a fight, but wow, just some time to breathe, some time to be yourself."

Owen says, "What about your son's father? Does he never help out?"

"He's dead," she says, her voice catching.

Owen gulps. Not the feckless undeserving bastard he'd assumed but a dead man. "I'm really sorry," he says. "Really, really sorry."

"Yeah, well, you know. It's been way longer that he's been dead than that I knew him. We were only together for a couple of years. He died nine years ago. It's a strange statistic. Hard to know how to feel about it really. And what about you? Have you ever been married? Anything like that?"

He shakes his head. "No," he says. "Nothing like that."

She smiles at him, knowingly, as though she sees him and his loneliness and his desperation but is not put off by it. As though she has met someone like him before.

Their food arrives: tagliatelle al ragù for Owen, a seafood risotto for Deanna.

"I'm having a really nice time," she says.

Owen pauses, his fork halfway to his mouth. He puts down the fork, and he looks at Deanna, and with a hint of wonder in his voice, he says, "Yes. Me too."

19

ON THE TUBE on the way home, Owen feels a plume of pleasure rising through his physiology; he pictures it as pink ink blooming over wet cartridge paper. He is being reconstituted somehow, and all because a nice, slightly overweight lady from Colindale talked to him as though he was a human being for an evening.

He's a little drunk too, which is adding to his sense of well-being. Deanna, it transpired, was a fast drinker, faster than him, and he'd had to race to keep up with her. The champagne had disappeared in under forty minutes, after which they'd shared a bottle of wine, and when that had gone, before their desserts arrived, they'd each ordered a cocktail. Owen can't remember now what his was called, but it had tequila in it and tasted like smoke.

He's drunk enough and happy enough not to feel other people's eyes upon him on the strip-lit tube carriage. He doesn't feel jealous of the loved-up couples clutching single red roses swarming the streets. He doesn't feel angry when people walk across him or fail to let him through. He doesn't care if they can see him or not, because, for a full three hours this evening, he has been seen.

Owen replays the night over and over in his head: the easy exchanges, the kind look in Deanna's eye, the way she kept touching her hair, nodding encouragingly at him when he was talking about himself, the slowness at the end of the night, as though she was trying to delay its finale.

As he climbs the hill back to his house the air is icy sharp. A couple passes by, holding hands, the woman clutching a posy of red flowers. They smell of wine. Owen almost says something to them—something like "Happy Valentine's, fellow lovers!"—but thinks better of it and stops himself with just a second to spare.

Owen stifles a laugh and turns left. He passes a man walking a small white dog. The man says, "Good evening," making Owen jump slightly.

"Oh," he manages to toss over his shoulder, just a beat too slow, "evening." He's walked past this man and his dog a hundred times over the years, and this is the first time he's ever said hello. Owen smiles to himself.

Around the next corner he sees a woman. She has hair the color of sand and wears a brown coat that ties up at the waist. She's looking at her phone. As he gets closer, he can see that she's pretty, very, very pretty. Probably pretty enough to be a model. Owen's defenses automatically go up, as they always do when he is confronted with extreme female beauty. He averts his gaze and veers across the pavement, trying to clear her a path, but she is too busy looking at her phone to notice and wanders straight toward him. He tries to make room for her by moving the other way, but she moves too, and suddenly they are standing face-to-face only a foot or so apart, and she looks up from her phone and straight at him and he sees it there, utter, utter fear.

"Oh," she says.

Owen moves again so she can pass. Yet again she moves in the same direction. He sees her eyes fall to her phone, the edge of her thumb touching the emergency icon on her screen.

He gestures her past with his arms and says, with some indignation, "Maybe you could try not looking at your phone for five minutes. You might find it easier not to walk into people." He turns and starts to walk away but then:

"Fuck you, creep."

He stops. "What?"

"I said, *Fuck you, creep.*"

He rocks slightly.

He closes his eyes and draws in his breath. He pictures himself turning now, turning and running at her and pushing her over. He exhales, counts to three. He carries on walking.

"Bitch," he calls out over his shoulder as he walks.

He hears her call something out to him, the fading urgent echo of her heels against the paving stones, the ringing in his ears of adrenaline pumping through his system; he feels the wine in his stomach curdle slightly and his legs turn to jelly. He stops for a moment and holds a wall to steady himself. His head spins, and for a moment he thinks he might be about to throw up.

And then he feels his phone vibrate, and he takes it out of his pocket and there is a message from Deanna.

Dear Owen, I really enjoyed myself tonight. Thank you for being such good company and making me feel good about myself for the first time in a very long time. I hope you sleep well and I look forward to seeing you next week. My treat this time! Deanna x.

All the rage and nervous energy leaves his body immediately.

Smiling, he turns the last corner of the block and arrives outside his house. The lights are all off, and the moon shines blue off the lead on the roof. He stops to peer through the hole carved into the wooden gate of the building site next door where he sees two amber dots glowing in the dark. A fox, staring at him.

"Hello, foxy," he says into the darkness. "Hello, beautiful!"

He glances across the street. There is a light still shining in one of the windows. He sees the suggestion of movement behind it. He hears raised voices coming from somewhere out of sight. Then he sees a person standing outside the house: tall, slender, in a black hoodie, tips of angular elbows protruding from their sides like wings. The person stands for just a moment, watching the light in the window, just as he does. Then the person turns and in profile he can see it is a young girl, her hands stuffed into the pockets of the hoodie, her jaw set hard.

As he watches her, she turns and looks at him.

I know you, he thinks, *I know you.*

PART TWO

After

20

Cate

CATE SPOTS IT late in the day, a small piece in a copy of the *Times* she picked up for free in the supermarket the day before. She often picks up the complimentary paper but rarely reads it, and she only reads it today because she's looking for an article advertised on the front page about how to have sex in your fifties.

She turns the pages quickly, but her eye is caught first by the word "Camden" halfway down page eight.

The headline reads: "CAMDEN SCHOOLGIRL STILL MISSING. POLICE QUESTIONING LOCALS."

And there, beneath the headline, is a photo of a young girl with exquisite, symmetrical features, an enigmatic smile, large hoop earrings, dark curly hair held back on one side in a single tight braid, pale green eyes. Cate doesn't immediately recognize her. But then she reads on and her eye is drawn back to the girl in the photograph and then she knows it is her.

Camden schoolgirl Saffyre Maddox, 17, has not been seen since she left home on the evening of 14 February to visit a friend in Hampstead. Saffyre, who lives with her uncle, Aaron Maddox, 27, in Alfred Road NW3, is studying for A levels at Havelock School, NW3. Teachers at her school describe her as a good student and a sociable member of the school community. According to Aaron Maddox, she left home at roughly eleven o'clock on the night of her disappearance, wearing dark jogging bottoms, a black hoodie, and white trainers.

Cate gasps and looks around her as though there might be someone here to share this with. The children are both off school for the half-term holiday, but neither of them is in, and Roan is at work.

She picks up her phone, photographs the story, and before she's had a chance to think about what she's doing has WhatsApped it to Roan.

For obvious reasons, Saffyre's name has not been mentioned for months, but there's no reason why Cate shouldn't still recognize it when she sees it printed in a national newspaper.

The tick remains gray. Roan always has his phone in flight mode when he's with patients. That was one of the (many) things that had fanned the flames of her madness the year before: that he always forgot to take it out of flight mode afterward, would walk around completely uncontactable, long into the evening. She'd never been able to work out how he could go around with a dead phone without automatically feeling the need to turn it back on.

She reads through the article again.

Six days ago. Valentine's night. The night she and Roan walked into Hampstead and had champagne in a murky, fire-crackly pub and then shared a red beef curry at a Thai restaurant on the way home, the night they'd got on really well and found lots to talk about and laugh about and been not like one of those long-married couples trying to hold it together in public on Valentine's night, but like a real, compatible, happy couple.

And meanwhile Saffyre had been somewhere between Swiss Cottage and Hampstead wearing not enough clothes for what was a very cold night. Maybe they'd walked past her? Maybe they'd even seen something? Was it possible?

She shakes the thought from her head. Of course it wasn't possible. There would have been thousands of people between Swiss Cottage and Hampstead on Valentine's night, thousands of places she could have been. And maybe Saffyre hadn't been going to Hampstead at all, had just said that to cover her tracks, had left her home and walked in totally the opposite direction, her uncle none the wiser.

Cate pulls open her laptop and googles "Saffyre Maddox."

The papers all run a story about her disappearance; they all use the same photograph of her. None of them has any extra detail.

At around 2:00 p.m. she gets a reply from Roan.

It reads, simply: *Oh my God.*

She replies: *I know.*

But the ticks remain gray.

He's gone already.

———

The card that arrived on Valentine's Day for Roan still sits in the kitchen drawer in its ripped envelope. Cate had tucked it firmly away between a pile of tea towels, hidden from prying teenage fingers. She had categorically not looked at it after their lovely Valentine's night in Hampstead, and then not the following day either. Then it had been the weekend, and now it was the half-term holiday and, strange as it sounds, she has stopped thinking about the card. It bears no relationship to the harmonious atmosphere in their home, to the soft exchanges between them, the sex they've had twice since then, both times initiated by her. The card has become metaphorical dust, of no consequence or interest to her.

But now.

She claps her hands to her ears as something passes through her thoughts, a high-speed train of a notion. The feeling takes her back to last year, to when her whole life had felt like this, when every minute of every day had been spent potholing through doubt and paranoia and distrust. She had not been happy in that place and she does not want to go back there. She is happy here, right here, in this rose-hued world of Valentine's cards and snatched hugs.

She decides to strip the beds. Cate is not usually the type of person to use domestic drudgery to take her mind off things, but now she sweeps through the three bedrooms of the flat, trying to put as much space between herself and the drawer in the kitchen as possible.

In Georgia's room she pulls off the crystal-white sheets that her daughter insists upon; long gone are the days of pink and lilac fairies. White sheets, white lamps, white sheepskin rug. When Georgia was younger, thirteen, fourteen, Cate would find it virtually impossible not to rifle though her daughter's things when she was in her bedroom, desperate for clues to the person she was turning into. Now she has no need; Georgia shows herself to Cate crystal clear, every minute of every day. She hides nothing.

Cate moves efficiently around her bed, balls the sheets together, and leaves them on the floor in the hallway. Then she goes to Josh's room.

Josh is a tidy boy; he always has been. She pulls the blue chambray sheets from his bed, then puts on a fresh green sheet. His laptop is tucked underneath his bed, plugged in and charging. She is half tempted to open it, to see what her mysterious son does when he's alone in here, but for some reason her son's privacy seems more sacred, more fragile than her daughter's. She doesn't ponder for too long on why she might feel like this; she just does.

Then she goes to her bedroom, her marital quarters, where, for the last five days at least, marital things have been happening. She snatches up the gray bedding and creates another ball, adds it to the pile in the hallway, stretches a pale blue sheet over their mattress, puffs up the duvet inside a fresh cover.

The curtains in here are still drawn; at this time of the year it sometimes seems futile to open the curtains in a room that was dark when you awoke and will be dark once more when you return.

She pulls them apart and is startled by the reminder of the world beyond. There is her street, there is the man with the white dog, there is the bin on the corner that only gets emptied once a fortnight when its contents are spilling onto the street, there is a Sainsbury's delivery van, an Amazon delivery van, there is the house across the street with the armchair on the driveway and . . .

She stops. She remembers. Remembers standing right here. It was nighttime. There was something . . . What was it? When?

She shakes her head slightly, trying to locate the source of the half-formed memory.

Was it that night? Was it Valentine's night? Drawing the curtains, readying herself for the possibility of sex with Roan, a figure, out there? Movement. Muted voices. A sense of being under surveillance? Or was she imagining that?

She had not been sober, after all. There had been champagne, followed by beer, followed by more beer in the Thai restaurant. No, she had not been sober, not at all.

She turns, as if someone has just called her name.

But they haven't of course; she is alone.

It's the card in the kitchen drawer calling her. The card telling her that there is something she's not seeing, that maybe she's not mad or bad or wrong.

Before she can check herself or think herself down, she strides back into the kitchen, pulls open the drawer, flips through the tea towels, and pulls it out.

Her hands shake as she takes the card from the envelope.

The card has a pink bird of some description on the front, a watercolor, rather insipid. Inside, in a very childish script, are the words:

Dear Roan

Thank You for being my therpist.

Please be my Valntine.

Love

Molly

xxx

She shuts the card and collapses against the edge of the kitchen counter.

A card from a child.

Molly.

Little Molly who still writes phonetically.

Little Molly who wants a bald fifty-year-old man to be her Valentine.

Little Molly who knows his home address.

She stuffs the card back into the envelope and tucks it inside the tea towels again, her heart racing lightly.

———

A couple of hours later Georgia appears with Tilly.

"Oh," says Cate, looking up from her work. "Hello, Tilly. Haven't seen you for ages."

It's the first time Tilly's been here since the night back in January when she claimed to have been sexually accosted.

"How are you?" asks Cate.

"Good," says Tilly, eyeing her own feet awkwardly. "I'm good."

Georgia is plundering the drawers and cupboards for food. She is starving, apparently, having not eaten breakfast and only having had "like, a few nuggets" for lunch. She finds some sweet-and-salty popcorn and pours herself and Tilly each a large glass of juice, then they disappear.

"Thanks for changing my bedding!" Cate hears her daughter call from down the hallway.

"You're welcome!" she calls back.

Cate sits down again and tries to focus on her work but finds there are now too many other things needing to be put in order in her head: the card from a child (whose handwriting is that on the envelope? Who bought and licked the stamp? Who put it in a letter box?); the lingering strangeness of Tilly lying about being accosted that night (something must have instigated it, surely?); the disappearance of Saffyre Maddox (somewhere between her own home and here); the figure outside the window on Valentine's night (or was it a figment of her drunken imagination?); the weird guy across the road (every time she sees him, he gives her an odd look that chills her to the bone); the increasing number of daylight sexual assaults in the vicinity.

But they refuse to be put into any sort of order; they refuse to line up and make sense of themselves.

Tilly leaves a couple of hours later.

Georgia appears in the kitchen.

"How's Tilly?" asks Cate.

"She's all right."

"Did you ever . . . Has she ever explained? About that night?"

"Kind of. Not really."

"Meaning?"

"Meaning, I think something did happen. But it wasn't what she said it was."

"So, something like what?"

"Don't know. She wouldn't tell me."

"What do you think it might have been?"

"Don't know."

"But—"

"Really, really don't know, OK? You'll have to ask her yourself."

"I—"

"Look, Tilly's just weird, all right. She's weird. Whatever it was, it was probably something really boring." She pauses for a second, then looks at Cate curiously. "If she says anything, I'll tell you. OK?"

"OK," says Cate. "Thank you."

21

Saffyre

EVERYONE NEEDS A hobby, don't they?

Well, for pretty much the whole of last year, my hobby was watching Roan.

I didn't have anything else to do. I had no real friends. No boyfriend. I did my homework late, when I was in bed. I was never mentally ready to start it before eleven o'clock, never in the right headspace. I'm a night owl. So, after school I'd wander across to the Portman Centre most days, see what Roan was up to. The thing with the young woman fizzled out pretty quickly. I saw her a lot: because she was a smoker she spent a lot of time outdoors. I think she was a secretary. She wore a lanyard but looked too young to be a clinician. But I never saw her and Roan share a cigarette again; I didn't see them swan off for drinks or whatever. I think maybe she went off him after their little rendezvous that first evening. Maybe she realized she was way too young for him. Or maybe he was inappropriate in some way.

And that's the weird thing, because all those months and years I spent with Roan as a patient I never got anything sexual off him, not ever. He was, well, not quite avuncular, not fatherly, but sort of matey. Like one of those teachers at school who you feel you can be yourself with, yet you still respect them.

But outside of that room with its halogens and its nubby chairs, I saw another side of him. He didn't seem to be able to have a conversation with another woman without some kind of physical contact with them: hugs, squeezed arms, doors held open but not leaving enough room for the woman to get through without pressing against him, shared umbrellas, linked arms. His eyes were always on a woman. If he couldn't find a woman to look at, he looked lost.

The days started getting longer, and at some point it was still light when I came after school, and I realized I couldn't hide in the trees in broad daylight; I needed to be more mobile, to keep moving. So I started to wait across the street, pretending to look at my phone, and then I'd follow him wherever he went. And it was surprising how infrequently he went straight home. He often joined people for drinks at the scruffy pub on the corner of College Crescent, or for coffee at the place opposite the tube station.

I had my hair braided about this time. The braids were pale pink. It wasn't meant as a disguise, per se, but he hadn't seen me for a while: I'd grown; I was different. I followed him into the pub one night last summer. We'd had a nonuniform day at school, and I wore a crop top, baggy bottoms, a camo jacket, all in dark colors, my hair under a baseball cap. I ordered a lemonade and took it out into the beer garden. The football was showing on a big sports screen. There were loads of guys out there. Only two other women apart from me. I sat under a canvas canopy on a metal chair, with my back mostly turned toward him.

He was with a woman and two men. It was loud in the garden, men cheering at the football match, the animal sound of the crowd pumping out through two huge speakers. I couldn't hear what they were saying.

The woman with them was about thirty. She had soft red hair tied into a long plait that sat over her shoulder. She wore no makeup and smiled a lot. At first the conversation was between all four members of the group, but then the other two guys started watching the football match more seriously, turning their backs slightly to Roan and the girl, leaving them to talk between themselves.

I played with my phone on my lap, turning every now and then to watch Roan and the woman. They were engrossed. I could have stood square in front of them and blown a raspberry and they wouldn't have noticed. I took a picture of the two of them. I turned away again.

The match finished and the volume in the beer garden went down. I heard one of the guys with Roan offer to go to the bar for more drinks. There was a pause; then Roan said to the girl, "Want another drink? Or we could maybe go on somewhere else?"

"I don't mind," said the girl. "Whatever you want to do."

"I dunno," said Roan. "I mean, we could wander up the road a bit maybe, grab something to eat?"

"Yeah," said the girl. "Yeah. Why not?"

I drained my lemonade superfast. I waited till they'd passed by me and then followed them a few steps behind. They turned left and wandered aimlessly for a moment, peering at menus in restaurant windows. They settled on a Chinese restaurant with shiny ducks hanging in the window.

I sat at a bus stop across the road. They sat at a window table. He was all over her. He cupped her face with his hand. He stroked her plait. He stared and stared at her. He was creepy as fuck. But she seemed to like it. She took mouthfuls of food from him like a baby. She kept the eye contact. She held his hand across the table. She threw her head back with laughter.

They were in there for an hour. Then the bill came and I saw him insist on paying. I thought, That's nice, you, with a family at home, buying noodles for some girl young enough to be your daughter. I thought, You total wanker.

He walked her to the tube station afterward. They did a sort of hand-squeezing thing, a quick hug, no kissing, too close to home, I guess, too close to work.

I saw his face as he turned back to cross the road, the sly little smile on his face. I thought of his skinny blond wife back at their posh Hampstead flat, probably putting some freshly cooked meal in the refrigerator because her husband had eaten his dinner out tonight. I wondered what he'd told her. *Just a bite with colleagues.*

I watched him cross the Finchley Road, sprinting through a break in the traffic when the red man was up. He took his phone out at the other side, no doubt texting his skinny wife: *On my way home now!*

It was starting to get dark; the sky was a kind of chalky lilac, and cars had started to put on their headlights. I was hungry, and I knew Aaron had cooked something good for dinner. Part of me just wanted to go home, get rid of my heavy rucksack of books, eat something good in front of the TV. Another part of me wanted to find out what Roan Fours looked like walking into his house after taking a woman out for dinner.

I waited for the red man to turn green; then I sprinted across the road and caught up with him just as he turned the corner to the stone steps up to the steep hill. He'd put his earphones in now. I could hear him humming very quietly under his breath. He walked fast, and I was out of breath by the time we got to his street. I didn't realize how fit he was.

Then he was outside his house, looking for his keys, opening the door, closing it behind him. He had a certain swagger to his entrance, like he was lord of the manor.

I was standing outside a kind of empty building plot; it had a big wooden gate across it and high brick walls overhung with flowering foliage. I peered through a hole in the gate and saw a huge piece of empty land covered in flowers and rubble; it didn't look quite real, like a secret park or fairyland. I could see the foundations where a big house had been. The land must have covered at least an acre, maybe even more. Above it the sky had turned violet and gold. There was a notice taped to the gate. Apparently they were going to build some flats here. The notice was dated three years ago and the planning permission would expire next summer. I hoped that no one would ever build flats here, that it would just stay like this, hidden away, growing layers and layers, getting denser and denser.

I saw a movement to one side. Something fleeting and shiny. A fox.

It stopped for a moment and stared at me. Right at me.

My stomach rumbled. I hitched my schoolbag up on my shoulder and headed home.

22

Owen

ONE MORNING, ABOUT a week after Valentine's night, Owen's doorbell rings. He waits for Tessie to answer it, but she appears to be out.

After the second ring, he goes to the intercom and says hello.

A female voice responds. "Hello. Is this Owen Pick?"

"Yes."

"Good morning, I'm Detective Inspector Angela Currie. We're making door-to-door inquiries about a missing person. Could I ask you to spare a minute to answer a few questions?"

"Erm . . ." He peers at himself quickly in the mirror by the front door. He hasn't shaved for three days, and his hair is in dire need of a wash. He looks dreadful. "Yes, sorry, sure. Come in."

Angela Currie is a heavy-set young woman, short and broad, with disproportionately small feet. She has what looks like naturally blond hair braided across her hairline and tucked into a bun at the back. She has a nice face and is wearing a flick of black eyeliner across each eyelid.

Behind her is an equally young man, introduced as Police Constable Rodrigues.

"Could we come in?"

"Er . . ." Owen looks behind him at the open door to Tessie's flat. How to explain that there is nowhere to sit in his own home, as his aunt won't let him in her living room? "Is it OK if we talk out here?" he says.

He is aware that this makes it sound as if he is trying to hide something.

"It's my aunt's flat," he explains. "She's a bit funny about letting people in."

DI Currie tips her chin to look into the space visible through the crack of the apartment door. "No problem," she says.

They settle themselves on the small bench next to the stairs leading to the two upper-floor flats. It wobbles precariously, not really designed for sitting on but for resting parcels and such on. DI Currie has to sit with her head bent slightly forward to avoid the mail baskets nailed to the wall above.

"So," she begins, "we're investigating the disappearance of a local girl. I wonder if I could show you some photographs?"

Blood rushes to Owen's head. He doesn't know why. He nods and tries to cover the hot parts of his face with his fingers.

DI Currie pulls a printout from an envelope and passes it to him.

It's a photo of a pretty girl, mixed race by the looks of it, though hard to ascertain precisely her ancestry. She's wearing large hoop earrings, and her hair is worn in a similar style to DI Currie's, a kind of tight plait close to the skull holding it to one side. She's wearing what looks like a school uniform and is smiling.

He passes the sheet back to the detective and awaits another question.

"Have you ever seen this girl before?"

"No," he says, his hand moving from his face to the back of his neck, which he can feel growing blotchy and hot. "Not that I'm aware of."

"Where were you on the night of February the fourteenth, Mr. Pick?"

He starts to shrug; then DI Currie says, "It was Valentine's night. That might make it easier to recall."

He sucks in his breath, covers his mouth with his hand. Yes. He knows what he was doing on Valentine's night.

"Were you home? Or out in the local area? Might you have seen anything?"

"No," he says. "No. I was out. I went for a dinner. With a friend."

"Ah. OK. And what time did you get home? If you can remember?"

"Eleven thirtyish. Maybe midnight."

"And how did you get home that night?"

"I got the tube. From Covent Garden to Finchley Road."

"And did you maybe see anything strange walking back from the tube station? Anything untoward?"

He draws his hand across his mouth and shakes his head. He thinks back to the strange episode on the street, when that pretty girl had called him a creep and he'd called her a bitch. It feels like the twisted remnant of a strange dream when he thinks about it now, as if it didn't really happen. Everything about that night now feels dreamlike, faded in parts like an old photograph.

"No." He shakes his head slowly. "No. Nothing."

He sounds like he's lying, because in a way he is.

"And you said you live with your aunt? Is that . . ." She looks at a list on a clipboard. "Tessa McDonald?"

He nods.

"And where is Ms. McDonald?"

"I don't know. She's probably in the village. Shopping."

"Great, well, we'll be back again, I'm sure, once we've built up a better picture of the situation. In the meantime, maybe you could pass my card on to your aunt when she gets home, ask her to give me a call if she can remember anything about that night." She peers up the staircase. "Anyone else in, do you know?"

He shakes his head. "No idea. You can ring on their doorbells, if you like."

She smiles, clicks her ballpoint pen shut, slides it into her pocket, and says, "No. I'm sure that will be fine. Maybe I could leave some more of these here?" She points a couple of printouts toward the mailboxes above the bench. "And some more of my cards?"

"Yes," he says, getting to his feet. "Yes, of course."

"Well," she says, hitching her leather bag up higher onto her shoulder, "thank you, Mr. Pick, for your time. I really appreciate it. I'm just at the end of a line if you, or anyone else, remembers anything."

"You know," he says, his eyes feeling suddenly too big for his head as a buried memory bursts through the clouds, "I did see something that night. I saw someone. Out there." He points through the front door to the house opposite. "Standing outside that house, in the dark, just sort of looking in. I thought it was a man at first. And then they turned around and it was a girl."

"A girl?"

"Well, at least I think so. It was hard to tell, because they had a hood up."

His eyes drop to the page in his hand; he reads the description of what the missing girl was wearing just as DI Currie says, "What sort of hood?"

"Like, a hoodie? I think?"

"How tall was this girl?"

"It might not have been a girl. It might have been . . . I wasn't sober. I'd had some wine. Quite a lot of wine. I can't be sure."

"This person, how tall? Roughly."

"I genuinely can't remember."

"And roughly what time was this?"

"Just as I got to my front door. Midnight. Ish. Maybe later."

"And it wasn't"—she taps the printout with her fingertip—"it wasn't this girl?"

"I really, really don't . . . It was dark and, like I say, I'd had some wine. I really don't . . ." He's started to talk very fast and he's aware that he sounds panicked. He's wishing he hadn't said anything now about the strange girl in the hoodie. The police would be gone now, and he could be safely back in his room.

"Well, actually, that's very useful, thank you so much. I'm glad you were able to remember that for us. And if you don't mind, we'd like to be in touch again. Once we've had a chance to talk to people who live across the street."

The people across the street.

The people who give him dirty looks whenever they pass.

The skinny blond woman with the annoying face.

Her thunder-thighed daughter.

The ridiculous father with the leggings, running up and down that hill in the dark as though seeking oblivion.

23

Cate

CATE HAS HER bag on her shoulder and is opening her front door, about to head to her borrowed room in St John's Wood to treat a patient, when she jumps at the sight of a small blond woman dressed in black, accompanied by a man in police uniform. She stops and stares at them for a moment. Immediately she knows that they are here to talk about Saffyre Maddox.

"Hi," she says. "Sorry. I was just on my way out."

"That's OK. We can come back."

"Oh," she says. "No. It's fine. I can spare a few minutes."

"If you're sure?"

She shows them into the living room, freshly tidied, thank goodness, cushions all in a neat row.

"Nice flat," says the woman.

"Oh," says Cate. "It's not mine. I mean, it's a rental. Just temporary."

"Well, it's lovely. I love the high ceilings. DI Currie." She extends a small hand. "And PC Rodrigues."

"Can I get you anything?"

"No, we're fine. But thank you."

They all sit down, and DI Currie takes out a notepad and sheaf of paper.

. "We're looking into the disappearance of a local schoolgirl." She passes a sheet of paper to Cate, who stares blankly at the familiar photograph of Saffyre Maddox.

"Ah," she says. "Yes. I saw this in the papers."

"Good, then you know a little about the case?"

Cate nods. She waits for the DI to say something about Roan, about his connection to Saffyre Maddox, but is surprised when the DI says, "Valentine's night. Can you remember where you were?"

"Oh," she says. "Right. Yes. I was in Hampstead, having drinks and dinner with my husband."

"And what time did you get home?"

"Roughly eleven thirty."

"And did you see anything? Anyone? When you returned?"

Cate stops. She's about to say something about the figure she glimpsed through the curtains. But something stops her. "Not that I can remember," she says.

"Around midnight? Maybe?"

"No." She shakes her head. "No. I was in bed by midnight."

"And your husband?"

"My husband?"

"Was he also in bed? At midnight?"

She can't remember. She cannot remember. "Yes," Cate replies firmly. "I'm pretty sure he was." She looks at the time on her phone. "I'm really sorry," she says. "I'm going to have to go now. I have a patient in St John's Wood in twenty minutes."

"Oh, a patient. Are you a doctor?"

"No. I'm a physiotherapist."

"Oh. I'm so sorry," says DI Currie, getting to her feet. "Please don't let us keep you another minute."

They all leave together in a slightly awkward huddle. DI Currie and PC Rodrigues stand by the front door and examine the doorbells. "Anyone else in?" DI Currie asks.

"Sorry, no idea." Cate smiles at them apologetically. "Bye, then," she says, and turns and heads down the street, her heart racing painfully hard under her ribs.

———

Roan did have an affair once. It was in the very early days of their marriage, when they were still very young and getting used to the fact of being married when none of their friends were.

Cate had kind of guessed it was happening. Roan had been pretty bad at covering his steps. Condoms had started disappearing at a rate that was incommensurate with the amount of sex that they'd been having— still quite a lot back then, pre-babies. Cate had been responsible for picking up the condoms from the family-planning clinic, so she was more aware than most women about how many condoms should be in the box.

Roan had still been a student then, that had been part of the problem, while Cate had graduated three years earlier and was working full-time at a sports rehab gym. There'd been a disconnect for a year or two; Cate was bringing in money, spending her days with people older than her, tired by ten o'clock. Roan was bringing in no money, spending his days with other students and usually in the pub at 10:00 p.m.

He'd been having sex with another student. Her name was Marie; she was the same age as Cate, and she had very long hair. Roan ended the affair—though refused to acknowledge that it was an affair, said it was just "basic sex"—the moment Cate confronted him with her suspicions. Marie came to their flat an hour later, and Cate ended up holding her on the pavement outside while she cried and rocked and wailed.

When Cate went back indoors a moment later, she found one of Marie's hairs on her cardigan. She pulled it off and stared at it for a moment before discarding it on the floor. Roan sat with his head hanging, his shoulder blades two pointed peaks of contrition, sniffing in some kind of approximation of tears.

"Has she gone?" he said.

She nodded and poured herself a glass of wine.

"Are we over?"

"Over?" she asked facetiously. "We're married. What do you mean, over?"

"I mean, is that the end of our marriage?"

She remembers staring at Marie's solitary hair, no longer a part of Marie, a foot and a half long, an S-shape on the carpet. *S* for "sex." *S* for "shame." *S* for "slut." She remembers imagining Roan's fist around her hair in bed while they did "basic sex." She'd had to stifle a laugh. The whole thing was so pathetic.

"I can't live without you. You know that, don't you? I can't live without *us*." Then he'd started to cry, properly, contrite shoulder blades heaving up and down like pistons.

The horror of it, she recalled now, the shock. For a moment she'd wondered if she even loved him, if she'd *ever* loved him.

"I'd die without you," he'd said as she passed him a tissue. "I'd literally just die."

———

Roan had graduated a year later, quickly found his way to the Portman and become a serious, grown-up man, widely respected, superb at his job. They'd even been able to crack a joke about Marie eventually, about her appearing with her red-rimmed eyes that evening, ending up in Cate's arms on the pavement. The fact they'd been able to joke about it had put a stake in its path, a definitive sign that what had happened had been an aberration, a one-off, something unconnected to them and the couple they were to become, the parents they were to become, the life they would go on to build for themselves.

Nobody knew about it.

Cate hadn't even told her closest friends.

It was theirs and theirs alone.

So she hadn't been totally mad to think the worst a year ago. She'd said as much to Roan. "It's not as if," she said, "it hasn't happened before."

He'd scoffed at that, as if it was somehow irrelevant. And she'd allowed him to scoff because she'd been so ashamed of her own actions.

But in retrospect she could see that he'd been clawing back the moral high ground from her after twenty-five years, expunging his own memories of the crying, pathetic, desperate man in the scruffy flat in Kilburn claiming he'd kill himself if she left him. Maybe he'd known that Cate had questioned her own love for him in that moment. Maybe he'd been waiting for a moment to suggest that he too was capable of questioning his. Redressing the balance.

Theirs is a strong marriage. It has survived a lot. And still they are able to find a way to feel good about each other.

But as Cate walks to her patient appointment that morning, a watery sun playing on the flush on her skin, she thinks of DI Currie's very particular question, and she thinks again of the figure outside her window, and she wonders again where Roan was and what he was doing at midnight on Valentine's night.

24

"THE POLICE CAME this morning," Cate tells Roan that evening. "They were asking about Saffyre Maddox."

Roan's phone has been switched off all day, and this is the first chance she's had to discuss the day's events with him.

"Oh," he says. "What did they say?"

"Said they were doing door-to-door. But I didn't see them going to anyone else's door. Just ours. I suspect they'll probably be on your trail soon, too."

"Oh," he says. "Yes. They came to see me this morning."

He says this nonchalantly, as though the police coming to talk to him about a missing girl was a day-to-day occurrence. Cate almost gets the feeling that if she hadn't asked him about it, he wouldn't have brought it up.

"What did they say?"

He shrugs, goes through the mail on the kitchen table, unties his woolen scarf. "They wanted an insight, I suppose. An idea of what sort of person she is, why she might have run away."

"Run away?"

"Yes. Although I had to tell them that I haven't seen her for months. So I'm not sure really what sort of state she'll have been in recently."

"But I thought she was missing. Not run away?"

He looks at her blankly. "Well, it's kind of the same thing really, isn't it? Until you know what's happened."

"But a runaway would take a bag, surely?"

He shrugs. "Maybe she did?"

"She did. But there was nothing in it. Look." Cate points firmly at the flyer. "That's exactly what it says. Surely that's what they said to you?"

She's being overzealous, but she's feeling some kind of bizarre complicity with the whole thing, as if it is oddly connected to her in some way.

"They didn't say, no. They gave me very little information at all. They were much keener to understand her condition while she was under my care."

"And what was it? What was her condition?"

He looks at her again. "You know I can't tell you that."

"But she's not even your patient anymore, surely you can—"

"No," he snaps. "You know I can't. I can't believe you're asking me."

And there he is again, that man from last year, the brittle, righteous man she'd nearly left because of all her misgivings about him. The man who'd made her feel mad and bad and toxic. But this time round it's different; this isn't her feeling that something's amiss and hunting desperately for evidence to back up her feelings; this time something *is* amiss: a young girl is missing.

"But was it something that could make her behave like this? I mean, you don't have to tell me exactly what it was, but do you think she was unstable?"

She's pushing him, but she doesn't care.

He puts his hands palm down on the kitchen table, raises his eyes to her, and says, "I signed her off because she was doing well. She'd stopped certain harmful patterns of behavior. Beyond that I have no idea. I don't know what was happening in her life before she disappeared."

"You didn't see her again?"

He sighs, audibly, for her benefit, so she can see how far she is pushing him. "No. I didn't see her again."

"So, what's your theory? What do you think's happened to her?"

"I have absolutely no idea. She's seventeen. Rocky upbringing. Buried trauma. Who knows?"

He sounds as if he finds the whole concept of Saffyre's disappearance bothersome in some way. He sounds almost glib.

She looks at him and says, "You sound like you don't care."

He rolls his eyes. "Of course I care."

"But you don't sound like you do."

"My professional duty of care is one thing, and Saffyre no longer comes under that. But of course I care about her and her outcome. Of course I care that she's disappeared. I just don't really see what I can do about it."

Cate pauses. She collects two used mugs from the table and slowly takes them to the sink. She rests her hands on the edge of the counter and stares out of the window. "They asked what we were doing at midnight that night," she says. "You know, Valentine's."

He doesn't respond.

"I said we were in bed."

"Well, we were, weren't we?"

"Well, *I* was. You were . . . I don't know. I lay there for quite some time waiting for you to come. And when you did, I asked you what you'd been doing and you said you hadn't been doing anything and then we had sex."

"And?"

"Well, what had you been doing?"

And there it is. A question too far. Immediately they are back in the same place where they'd spent all those hellish weeks last year.

"Cate," he says, in that tone of voice she'd got so used to back then, that patient, do-I-really-have-to-put-up-with-this-nonsense tone of voice, "what on earth are you talking about?"

She unpeels her fingers from the kitchen counter and turns again, puts a smile on her face. She doesn't want to go there.

"Nothing," she says lightly. "Absolutely nothing."

25

Saffyre

I WATCHED ROAN Fours's adulterous affair with the girl with the red hair unfurl over the summer months.

Her name was Alicia. I knew that from overhearing him calling to her across the car park at the clinic. They went to the scruffy pub on the corner quite a lot. They'd press themselves into the tightest corners of the beer garden and talk like they were gonna die of each other. They looked quite good together, despite the age gap. A better match than him and his wife, in some ways. His wife looked like life had got to her, whereas Roan had this box-fresh look about him; he never looked tired or worn down, always looked like he'd just had a shower, just had a holiday, was ready to get up and go. He had a glow. I don't know how old he was, but around fifty I'd say. Alicia was much younger, but somehow they matched.

I did some googling and found a junior psychotherapist at the Portman called Alicia Mathers. There was a biography for her on the website. She had a degree and a masters in psychology from UCL and a PhD. Clever girl. I followed Alicia home one night after one of their early evening dates (they rarely said goodbye to each other later than about eight, nine o'clock). She lived in a flat in a small apartment block off Willesden Lane. Kind of nondescript. I saw a light go on on the fourth floor after she got home. So that was where she lived, then. Useful to know. I took some photos, and I found my way home.

Of course, Granddad and Aaron were getting a bit worried about the amount of time I was spending away from home. I just said vague things like: I'm seventeen now, I'm nearly an adult, give me some space. I could tell Aaron was particularly worried about me. He even said at one point, "You seem anxious, Saff, maybe I should get in touch with Dr. Fours?" (Aaron *loved* Roan, was virtually reverential toward him. If Aaron had had a cap, he'd have doffed it, that sort of thing.)

I said, "Don't be stupid. What for?"

"I don't know," he said, "maybe you're stressed about your exams? Maybe there's something else going on in your life. I mean, is there a . . . like a boy?"

I laughed. There'd never been a boy, and I couldn't imagine for a moment there ever would be. That part of me had shriveled and died when Harrison John did what he did to me when I was ten years old. I could look at a boy and see nice eyes, or a good face, or even a fit body, but that never translated to feelings. I never *wanted* them or their attention. I said, "No, there's no boy. I'm just walking a lot. Clearing my head. You know."

Sometimes if I had a free period during the day I might come down and look at Roan's wife. I felt so bad for her. There she was in her FatFace jeans and her flowery tops, trundling about the place, obliviously buying stuff to cook for her family, fluffing out duvets, filling in forms, clearing out the fridge, wiping down floors, all that stuff I imagine middle-class housewives do. And for what? For her husband to walk through the door one day and say, "I've met someone. She's younger than you and prettier, and I want to have sex with her whenever I like."

And then what? What happens to a woman like that with a pretend job and children just about to leave home? Where would Cate Fours end up? I honestly really ached for her. I truly did. It's horrible when you know something that someone else doesn't know; it makes you feel somehow responsible for their predicament.

Then, toward the end of that summer, the day after I got my GCSE results in fact (I got nine, in case you were wondering), a strange thing happened.

It was late on a Friday night; I'd been at my friend Jasmin's for a takeout and to listen to music. She was getting ready to go out to a club or something. I didn't want to go. Not my scene, not my thing. But I like watching my friends get ready, I like listening to music, I like chicken tikka and paratha, I like Jasmin, so you know, I hung out for a while.

It was about nine o'clock when I left Jasmin's. The sky was darkening, but it was still warm, so I decided to walk home via Roan's house. I wasn't intending to hang around, just pass by, take a look, carry on home. It was such a part of my makeup by this point; I was like a dog or a sheep or a pigeon: it was like a homing thing.

I came from the other direction because of being at Jasmin's, past the side of the building site that backs onto another road. Even before I got to the site, I could smell it, the sickly strong smell of weed. I stuck my head through a gap in the foliage and peered around the plot. Couldn't see anything at first, but then I saw the glow of a phone and the burning red tip of a fat zoot. I saw a face, a boy's face. He was alone. He looked young. The red tip grew bigger and brighter as he inhaled. The light of the phone died when he switched it off. And then I saw him turn and look behind him. I heard him make a noise under his breath and saw him put his hand into his pocket. He brought something out of his pocket and then turned again, making the same noise.

And then there he was: the fox. He stopped for a moment and just stared at the boy. I thought he would just run away eventually, like every fox I'd ever met on the street always did. But this fox did not. This fox started to creep forward, very slowly, an inch at a time, his head down, his shoulders back. He looked behind himself every few seconds. But eventually he was side by side with the boy. I heard the boy say, "Good evening, sir," to the fox, and I saw him hand the fox something to eat. The fox took it a few feet from the boy, let it drop from his mouth, and ate it slowly and methodically from the ground. The boy held out another piece of food, between his finger and thumb. The fox came back and took it gently.

Then, crazily, the boy touched the fox's head and the fox let him.

My jaw fell open. I had never seen such a thing in my life. I took a photo: boy and fox, side by side. I took it just as the fox turned to look up at the boy. Almost like a faithful dog looking at his master.

The boy finished smoking his zoot and ground it out at his feet. The fox heard a sound from somewhere far distant and scampered away from him. I saw the boy get to his feet, pick up a schoolbag, wipe down his trouser legs and backside with his hand. I turned away sharply so he wouldn't see me. I got out my phone and pretended like I was just standing about looking at Snapchat and then he peered out of the foliage by the corner, climbed up on the top of the wall, and jumped down onto the pavement. He turned the corner, and I saw him saunter toward Roan's house, and it was only then that I clocked who it was: it was Roan's boy. Old gangly legs.

And I thought: Every family has its black sheep, its shady character. I'm that one in my family—that's without a doubt. Now it looked like I'd found the shady one in Roan's family. Who was this young boy picking up his weed from? Why was he smoking it all alone on a building site? And how was he hanging out with a fox? What kind of Dr. Dolittle weirdness was that?

I zoomed in on that photo when I got home. I loved it. The boy had a good face, like his dad's but not quite formed. In the dark, colorless shadows of the photograph, with his harsh haircut, his raw, overdeveloped features, his earnest expression, he looked almost Victorian. And then I zoomed in on the fox, its eyes fixed on the boy, the light from the street just glinting off one white whisker. So beautiful. So calm. It was a photo that could have won a prize in a competition.

I saved it into my favorites.

Then I put down my phone, closed my laptop, and, while Jasmin headed into town with her boobs popping out of her Boohoo top and a hip flask of vodka in her tiny bag, while Roan did whatever Roan did with that beautiful pre-Raphaelite girl with the PhD after work on a Friday, while his son sat in his room stoned and with his pockets full of meat, I sat on my bed and opened a book.

26

Cate

THE MORNING AFTER the visit from the female detective, Cate's road is cordoned off. Two squad cars are parked diagonally across the street, their blue lights slowly revolving, casting patterns across the walls of Cate's bedroom. There's an unmarked van parked in the middle of the road and two uniformed policemen standing by the ribbon telling people to go the other way. Across the road, curtains are twitching, people are peering through front doors in their dressing gowns.

Georgia appears behind Cate and says, "What the hell is going on?"

"I have no idea. I assume it must be something to do with that girl. Saffyre Maddox."

"Oh my God." Georgia claps her hands to her cheeks. "Do you think they've found her? Her body?"

"Oh, God, Georgia. Don't. That's . . ." Cate trails off, but it had already occurred to her. The big wooden gate into the building site across the road is wide-open and there are plainclothes officers going in and out.

"I'm going to ask," says Georgia, turning on her heel and leaving the room.

"Georgia, don't," says Cate. "Leave them, they're trying to get on with their . . ."

She hears the front door go, then sees Georgia, still in her pajamas with her hoodie thrown on over the top and just the fronts of her feet wedged into trainers, which she is still trying to put on properly as she hops along toward the uniformed policemen. Cate watches through the curtains as her daughter stands in front of them, her hands in the front pocket of her hoodie, nodding, shaking her head, pointing to the building site, pointing back toward their house. After a moment she turns and heads back. Cate meets her at the front door.

"What did they say?"

Georgia kicks off the unfastened trainers and heads into the kitchen, talking to Cate over her shoulder. "They said they've found something in that building site. They've got forensics in there. I asked if it was a body. They said no, it wasn't a body. I asked if it was to do with Saffyre Maddox. They said they weren't at liberty to tell us. They said they're going to be in there all day, maybe tomorrow too."

Cate nods. Her stomach turns. She looks at the time; it's just after 9:00 a.m. Roan had left early for work this morning at seven. She wonders if the police were already here when he left. She wonders how that would have made him feel. She sends him a WhatsApp message: *Police cordon on our street, forensics in the building site over the road. Any idea what's happening?*

The tick stays gray. She puts down her phone and fills the kettle. "Want a cup of tea?" she asks Georgia.

Georgia is halfway through a Cadbury Mini Roll. She says, "No, thank you, I'm going back to bed," then tugs off her hoodie and drapes it over the back of a chair. She drops the Mini Roll wrapper in the vague area of the bin, but it misses and lands on the floor. Cate is about to call her back to pick it up, but she can't find the will, so she sighs and picks it up herself.

Tiny shocks pass through her nervous system as she moves.

She goes to the drawer where the tea towels live and pulls out Roan's mysterious Valentine's card again.

As she does so, something occurs to her: Molly's card is not the same shape as the envelope. It is slightly too tall, not quite wide enough. The card did not come with this envelope. She pulls it out again, opens it, reads it. Little Molly. What a strange little girl she must be, sending Valentine's cards to old men.

She turns the card over in her hands, examining it for something, some tiny thing that might make more sense of it. But there's nothing. Roan's job, after all, is the care of strange children; why should she be surprised that one would behave strangely toward him?

She sighs and puts the card back in the drawer.

Then she turns and jumps. Josh is standing in the doorway. He is wrapped up in a toweling dressing gown; his hair is rumpled. "Why are there loads of police outside?" he says.

"Don't really know," she replies. "Something to do with that missing girl, maybe? They've found something in the building site, got forensics in there."

"Really?" he says, wandering back to the hallway, into Cate's room, peering through the window. She follows him. The back of his neck is raw from a fearsome haircut the day before, the *Peaky Blinders* haircut all the boys seem to be getting these days that makes their heads look too big for their bodies.

She stands behind him at the window. They both watch as a man and woman in plain clothes exit the entrance to the site holding plastic boxes. The police manning the cordon pull it back for another police vehicle to pull in. Two more people get out. One of them Cate immediately recognizes as the detective who'd sat on her sofa the day before, the one who'd asked so very specifically about where she'd been at midnight on Valentine's night. There are fifty streets between Alfred Road, where Saffyre lives, and the village, where she told her family she was going. A thousand houses. Tens of thousands of people. Yet the police chose her doorbell to ring, her sofa to sit on, her whereabouts to ask after, and now the building site opposite her house to investigate. Not to mention the fact of her husband's relationship to the girl they're trying to find.

She and Josh both crane their heads upward as the sound of helicopter blades starts to rumble and boom overhead.

"Reporters," says Josh. "I wonder how they found out?"

"It only takes one phone call," says Cate. "It's not as if the police are doing anything to hide what's going on here."

Cate sees a movement across the road, and the front door of the house opposite swings open. There's the man, the weird man. She ducks slightly so she's not visible.

Behind him is the woman he appears to live with, the statuesque silver-haired woman she'd seen looking for her keys in her bag that morning weeks ago. And behind the silver-haired woman is a very tall gentleman with gray slicked-back hair.

Slowly they emerge. The older man looks upward at the sky for the helicopter he can hear. The woman walks to the police by the cordon, and Cate watches her ask them questions. The older man and the younger man stand side by side, a few feet away. Suddenly it occurs to Cate that maybe the weird man has something to do with all of this, that maybe the police coming to her house to ask about midnight on Valentine's night was nothing to do with her and everything to do with him.

She stares at him now, overriding her physical discomfort. He has his fingers over his mouth, one arm wrapped around his waist. He keeps turning to look at the building site. After a minute he leaves the older couple standing on the front drive and heads back into the house.

She sees the female detective talking to the two people who have just walked out of the building site with plastic boxes. She asks them something. One of them nods. One of them shakes their head. They all turn to look at the building site. Then the female detective turns and looks directly at Cate's house, at Cate herself. It looks exactly as though they have been talking about her, about her family.

"Come on," she says to Josh, who has barely breathed for the past two minutes. "Let's leave them all to it."

She touches his shoulder and he recoils, almost imperceptibly. "No," he says. "I want to stay here and watch."

She sighs. "OK," she says lightly. "Do you want a cup of tea?"

"Yes, please," he says. "Thank you. Love you."

"Love you, too," she replies. Her heart aches a tiny bit at the thought of him. Her soft boy with his endless love and his raw, shaved neck.

27

OWEN HEARS HELICOPTER blades breaking apart the air above the house. He opens his bedroom window and peers out as far as he is able. At this time of year, before the trees come back into leaf, he can see parts of the big empty space next to their house.

There used to be a mansion there called Winterham House. For decades it had sat with broken windows and ivy climbing up to precarious balconies, toppled chimney pots, graffitied walls, and overgrown grass. When Owen first moved into Tessie's flat it was two months away from a demolition order. He'd watched in fascination as the whole building was dismantled and demolished, brick by brick, all the finery being taken away in vans to be sold as reclaim at vastly inflated prices, the bricks taken away to be put back into stock, everything else being broken down into components small enough to fit in the back of a pickup. It took about three months, and then the demolition people left and suddenly the dust stopped, the noise stopped, there was light through the trees and into Owen's room, birdsong and foxes, meadow flowers every summer. Occasionally on warm nights Owen can hear teenagers in there and the smell of skunk wafts into his room.

One day a notice went up outside to say that someone had applied for planning permission to build a development of five luxury town houses on the site. Of course the whole neighborhood joined together to try to block it. In the end the house builder who had bought the site compromised with plans for a small block of flats, thus maintaining the maximum amount of greenery and space. That had been approved four years ago, but since then, nothing.

The open, verdant aspect from his bedroom has made Owen feel rather as though he lives alone, in a wilderness; the view from his room is nothing but trees; there is no sign of urban life to be seen.

But as he peers from his bedroom window now, he sees that that silent oasis is teeming with people. Voices call out to one another; radios crackle. He sees the suggestion of bodies moving across the open space while the boom of the helicopters overhead fades in and out. He assumes this is something to do with the missing girl, the one the police asked him about yesterday. He assumes it is his fault they are here, because it was he who stupidly mentioned the girl in the hoodie outside the house opposite on Valentine's night. And he's not even particularly sure what he saw. The night is a blur, a sped-up film that stops occasionally on a random still and then moves on again at high speed. He can barely remember getting into bed that night and had woken up wearing his shirt and one sock.

He heads out into the hallway. Tessie and Barry are already there, standing in the front door, watching the activity.

"They've found something," she says. "Something to do with that girl they were asking you about, the one on the flyer."

"What have they found?"

"They wouldn't tell me. But they're going to be keeping the road closed off all day. And they asked for access to the outside areas."

"Of what?"

"Of here. Of the house. I said of course."

Owen blinks.

"You don't mind, do you?" she asks, her eyes narrowed.

"No," he says. "Why would I mind?"

"I don't know. You might feel it was a breach of your privacy. Or something like that."

"Well, it's not my garden, is it? It's everyone's garden."

"Yes," says Tessie, "yes. That's right."

There are police in their back garden now, picking through the undergrowth, over the piles of rusty old gardening equipment that no one ever uses. He watches them for a while, trying to hear what they're saying. He catches the occasional word but not enough to form any idea what they might be talking about.

There appears to be a smaller group of detectives searching in the vicinity of his bedroom window, at the back of the house. A flash of anxiety passes though Owen's gut, and he heads back to his bedroom and closes the door behind him.

He hears a voice, close to his window, a man calling to someone else. "Here, look. Bring the flashlight."

He catches his breath, stands to one side of the window, his back pressed against the wall, listening.

"Get DI Currie," says the man.

He hears someone run off through the grass and across the graveled drive, calling out for the detective.

A moment later he hears a woman's voice. "What have you got?"

Owen peers cautiously around the window frame. He looks down and sees the tops of three heads, a light being shone into the grass, a suggestion of rose gold glinting in the beam. He sees gloved hands gently parting the blades of grass. He can see the phone case being plucked from the grass and dropped into an outstretched plastic bag.

The air feels electric. Something is about to happen. Something extraordinary. Something appalling.

The helicopter blades spinning overhead sound like herds of heavy-footed animals through thick black dust.

Owen turns away from his window and collapses against the wall.

28

Saffyre

ROAN'S SON'S NAME is Josh. Joshua Fours. You almost have to say it posh, otherwise it doesn't sound right. He goes to the school opposite my flat. I saw him from time to time that autumn term. I would never have picked him out in the crowd before, just your typical gangly white dude in a North Face jacket and black trainers. He had a friend; weirdly this friend had red hair and a pointy face, and it was almost as though the friend and the fox were somehow interchangeable, like maybe Josh only liked things that resembled foxes.

I followed him home a few times that autumn. He walked so slowly, like a tortoise. If he wanted to look at something on his phone he'd literally just stop in the middle of the pavement, oblivious to whoever was behind him or near him. Sometimes he'd cross the street for no good reason, then cross back again. He'd stop and look into shop windows that didn't look like the sort of shop he would even care about. It was as if, I sometimes thought, he was just trying to drag it out. Like maybe he didn't even want to go home.

He slipped through the bushes into the empty plot quite often, to smoke weed. One night he went in with the boy with the red hair. I heard them laughing a lot, and I was pleased that he had a friend to laugh with.

Then one day, late September, during my first few weeks in the sixth form, I went to my Thursday class at the dojo, and there he was, all green and nervous, doing a trial class. I was a few minutes early for my class, so I sat and watched him finish his. He was a foot taller than everyone else; it was a beginner class—so mainly kids. I couldn't work out what he was doing there, this shambling, weed-smoking, fox-chatting boy. He did not seem the type.

He'd been paired with a small girl for the last exercises. He looked embarrassed. She looked resigned.

Then it was over and they were taught how to end the class:

"*Kahm sa hamnida.*"

"*Ee sahn.*"

He shuffled into the changing rooms and reappeared a moment later in his school uniform, his North Face coat, his schoolbag. He caught me staring at him, and I nodded. He flushed and turned away.

It seemed like it meant something, that this boy was there, at my dojo. I wondered for a moment if he'd seen me following him and was trying to turn the tables on me; you know, like letting me know that he knew what I was up to. But he never seemed to notice me there; he didn't have a vibe about him as if he was aware of my presence.

The third time he was there I arrived late and I was in the changing area with him. The curtain was pulled across. Two small boys sat cross-legged on the floor tying up the laces on their school shoes. I took off my coat and my hoodie and hung them from a peg. I turned to Josh and I said, "How are you finding it?"

He looked at me as if I were the first person who had spoken to him ever in his whole life. "What?"

"I said, how are you finding it? You're new, yeah?"

He nodded and said, "It's OK."

"What's your objective?"

"Sorry?"

"What's your objective? I've been at this since I was six. Did it so that no one on the street could scare me, intimidate me, you know. Just wondered what you were getting out of it?"

"Same, I guess."

"Self-defense?" I asked.

"Yeah," he said. "Kind of. I was mugged."

"Oh my God," I said. "When?"

"Like, a few weeks ago."

"Shit. That's bad." I glanced down at the small boys on the floor and said, "Sorry." Then to Josh: "Did they hurt you?"

He shrugged. "No. Not really. I didn't put up much of a fight, so, you know."

I did know. I really, really did know. "Any idea who it was?"

"No. Just a white guy, with a hood."

"Scary," I said.

"Yeah," he said. Then he picked up his bag and left without saying goodbye.

He never came back again.

———

One night at around the same time I first saw Josh at the dojo, I got home and found my granddad flopped in the armchair; his skin looked gray. I said, "Granddad, are you OK?"

He said, "I think so. I'm not sure." He said he had indigestion, so I got him some medicine. He rubbed his chest a lot and grimaced.

Aaron got home an hour after me and called an ambulance.

Shortly after that I was in a squeaky plastic chair at the Royal Free holding my granddad's hand and telling him that everything was going to be all right.

But it wasn't.

It was all wrong.

Granddad spent three days on the ward having various tests. He was finally diagnosed with angina and then, after more tests and more scans, with coronary artery disease. He was sent home with a long list of new ways in which to live his life, things he should be eating, medicines he needed to take. I could tell he had no intention of doing any of it. He'd lost his wife and his daughter, he'd been in pain for years, he had no social life and no job, and now that I was nearly grown, nearly an adult, he could not see the point in changing everything just so he could be around in twenty years' time still being a problem for us all to deal with.

So he pushed away all the healthy food that Aaron bought and cooked for him, and he left the pills sitting on the table next to his chair, and he refused to go out for nice walks with me, and then, before we'd even really started trying to save his life, he had a massive heart attack and died. He was only fifty-nine when he passed away. Sounds so much younger than sixty when you're talking about dying.

So, there I was. No mum, no dad, no grandparents, just two uncles and two little cousins. Not enough.

I couldn't get out of bed for a week after Granddad's funeral. I felt hollow, like you could just blow me away or crush me under your thumb.

For the first time in my school career, I fell behind with my coursework.

Aaron went to talk to my teachers, and they sent this woman over, something to do with safeguarding or pastoral care or whatever, I'd never seen her before in my life. She was grumpy, with a face like a lump of pastry—it's not like the movies y'know, where Sandra Bullock or someone like that comes over and turns your life around—and she sat on the other side of our little dining table from me, both of us with our fingers wrapped around blue mugs of tea made by Aaron, and she said stuff to me and there were words, a lot of words, and she meant well and she was nice and all, but the minute she left I just went straight back to bed.

It was Bonfire Night that got me out of the slump. Sitting on the back of the sofa with Aaron and pulling open the curtains and watching the sky explode into all those different colors. It was weird, Granddad not being there, but it also reminded me that life goes on, as mundane as that sounds, life just goes on; fireworks still pop, people still watch in wide-eyed wonder, children still hold sparklers, foxes still skulk through urban blackness looking for chicken bones.

I put on my Puffa coat, and I told Aaron I was going to get lemonade from the shop downstairs. Instead I bought a packet of *Fridge Raider* chicken bites and headed up toward Hampstead, through the leafy avenues where the fireworks exploded privately in people's back gardens, smudges of glitter just visible above ancient trees. On the corner of Roan's road, I sneaked through the same gap I'd seen Josh using to access the empty plot. It wasn't cold, and I took off my Puffa and used it as a blanket.

I opened the packet of Fridge Raiders and sat it on the damp gravel next to me, hoping that the smell would wend its way across the open space. I switched on my phone and messaged Aaron. *I'm going over Jasmin's place. See u laters.*

He replied, *Everything OK?*

I started to type my response, and then I stopped at the sound of rustling behind me. It was him; it was the fox. I rested my phone on my lap and held my breath. I could hear his little paws, pad-padding across the gravel, closer and closer to me. I put my hand inside the Fridge Raiders packet and pulled out a nugget of whatever in hell that stuff actually is, held it between my forefinger and thumb, just out by my side. I still didn't turn and look. I could hear the fox's breathing, an anxious, active sound. I felt him stop, and I could tell he was inches away from me. And then I felt the warmth of his breath against the skin of my hand. I dropped the meat and heard him snaffle it up. But he didn't move. So I pushed the bag forward a few inches to see if he'd follow it. And then there he was, standing by my side, looking down at the bag expectantly, like a pet dog.

"Want another one?" I said.

He didn't look at me, just stared intently at the bag, his little gingerbread eyes totally fixed on the spot. "OK, then," I said, taking one out. "Here you go."

A huge firework exploded overhead and for a moment the fox looked like he was going to scamper away. But he held his ground, and his snout appeared in my peripheral vision and then there he was, taking the snack from between my fingers. I inhaled so hard I heard my own breath catch.

And here I was, I realized, back in the same place I'd found my-self that time at Lexie's animal party, when the guy gave me the owl called Harry. All the black inside me turned silver and gold. I felt the punch of a connection with the ground, the sky, the trees, the air, so strong that it almost winded me. Butterflies whipped through my stomach. I stifled a giggle and covered my mouth with the back of my hand. I looked up into the gunpowder-stained night sky, and I searched with my eyes until I found a star—muted and grubby, but there—and I clasped my hands together in a prayer and said, "I love you, Granddad. I love you, Grandma. I love you, Mum."

I picked up my phone and replied to Aaron's message.

I'm all good! with a smiley-face emoji.

And still the fox stood by my side.

I passed him more snacks and laughed out loud.

I thought, Ha, see, Roan Fours, I didn't need you after all. I only needed nature. I only needed owls and foxes and stars and fireworks.

I was fixed.

Or so I thought.

29

Cate

THE POLICE CORDON has been stretched across Cate's street for two days. The helicopters are back. But there's nothing on the news. Clearly they haven't found anything yet. Clearly there's no body in there. If there was, Cate thinks, surely they'd have found it by now?

Roan is eating a bowl of cereal, standing up. He's making annoying eating noises, scarfing it down for some reason, as though he's late for something.

"Are you in a hurry?" asks Cate.

"Yeah, a bit. I want to be at work early."

"You went in early yesterday."

"Yes. Lots on. Two other clinicians on holiday—you know, half term. Need to catch up with myself."

"You could do that here," she says, gesturing at the kitchen table.

"This is your zone," he says.

"Not at seven in the morning it's not. I'm about to have a shower and get ready, why don't you stay here awhile and catch up?"

He scrapes the bowl for the last spoonful of cereal and swallows it down. "I need to be at work," he says, taking the bowl to the sink. "I need access to things there. Why are you so keen to keep me here?"

She shrugs. "All this, I suppose." She points upward in the direction of the helicopters. "And that." She points toward the front of the house. "It's unsettling. I mean, if something did happen to that girl, right here, right over the road, then maybe it's not safe. I mean, do you think we should be thinking about keeping Georgia in at the moment?"

Roan stops, his back curved over the sink. He sighs, then turns. "Maybe ask the police about that? See what they say."

She nods. "Yes," she says, "maybe."

He moves toward her, puts a hand on her arm. "It'll be fine, whatever it is. I'm sure we're safe." He picks up his bag, his coat, his scarf. "I will see you later. I'll try and get back early tonight. Maybe we could even do something."

She forces a smile. "Yes," she says. And then, before he disappears from view, she says, "Roan? Who's Molly?"

He stops. Then he turns and looks at her. "Molly?"

"Yes. I kept meaning to say. You got a card from her. Valentine's Day. Georgia opened it by mistake and I put it away because I knew you'd be cross about her opening your stuff. Then I forgot about it." She goes to the drawer and pulls it out. "Here," she says. "Sorry."

Roan walks toward her and takes the card from her hand. She watches him open it and read it. He smiles.

"Oh," he says. "*Molly!* Yes. I know Molly. She's a patient. Or at least, she was. I don't see her anymore."

"And she has your address?" She shows him the envelope.

He looks slightly confused. "She does appear to, yes."

"How?"

He takes the envelope from her hand and stares at it for a moment. "I literally have no idea," he says. "I mean, maybe it was in my office, on a letter or something?"

Cate takes the card from him and puts it back in the drawer. "Well," she says, "you should be more careful."

He gives her a strange look. "Yes," he says. "You're right."

He kisses her briefly on the cheek, and then he goes.

She grips the back of a chair, feeling her heart racing in her chest, the sickening rush of adrenaline caused by the confrontation. She hears the front door slam, but almost immediately she hears it open again. She hears Roan's voice in the hallway and then a female voice.

The door to the apartment opens, and Roan walks back in, with DI Angela Currie following behind.

"No problem," he's saying to her. "No problem at all." He catches Cate's eye. "This is DI Currie. She just wants to ask us a few questions."

Cate touches her collarbone. "Me too?"

"Yes, please. If you have the time?" says the detective.

"Sure. Yes. Can I get you anything? A tea? Coffee?"

DI Currie taps a plastic bottle of water in her hand and says, "Thanks, but I'm fine."

Roan leads her into the living room. She sits on the armchair. Cate and Roan sit side by side on the sofa.

"So," DI Currie begins, "sorry to bother you this early in the morning, but it literally just came to our attention, and I have to be honest, I don't really know how we missed this before, but having interviewed you both separately regarding this missing person case—Mrs. Fours as a potential witness and Dr. Fours as someone who worked closely with Saffyre—it has only just come to our attention that you both live here. And obviously that throws a very different complexion on things; opens up a whole new angle. So I hope you don't mind if I ask you both a few more questions?"

She smiles, and then she looks upward and says, "Bloody helicopters. I'm so sorry. It must be a nightmare. But we're nearly done now. They'll be gone soon. I promise."

She pulls a ballpoint pen and notebook from her shoulder bag.

"Dr. Fours, we spoke a couple of days ago about Saffyre coming under your care for a while and you confirmed that you stopped your sessions with her roughly a year ago?"

"That's right."

"And you didn't see her again after that?"

"No. Or, as I told you yesterday, I saw her around the area a couple of times, but not to stop and talk to."

"So after you signed her off from treatment, that was the end of your relationship with her?"

"Yes. That's correct."

"Great," says DI Currie, "thank you for clarifying that for me. And then, on the night of February the fourteenth, Valentine's night, it was the two of you that had dinner together, in the village?"

They both nod.

"And you both returned home at around eleven thirty p.m.?"

They nod again. Cate says, "Roughly."

"And you were both in bed by midnight?"

Cate and Roan exchange a look. Cate says, "Yes, thereabouts."

Roan nods, and then he turns to the detective and says, "Well, I might have been a bit later than that. I seem to recall going outside for some reason."

Cate stares at him.

"I mean, it's not particularly fresh in my mind, it was over a week ago, I wasn't sober, but I do remember coming outside—I think I was putting some rubbish out. And I heard something. And I looked over the road and that guy, the one from the house opposite, he was just standing there."

"Standing there?"

"Yes."

"Did he see you?"

"No. I was in the front garden, by the bins. I was out of view. I could see him through a gap in the hedge."

"And what was he doing, this man?"

"Just standing, staring. He looked drunk. I've had run-ins with him before when he's drunk. He stared at me once when I was out running, around the corner. Stood and stared for quite some time. When I asked him what his problem was, he just asked me if I was married. I thought it was . . . odd. And then there was that other time." He turns to Cate and gives her a complicitous look. "Remember, earlier this year, when Georgia was walking home in the dark and he got really close to her and was freaking her out?"

Cate stiffens slightly. She's not completely comfortable with what Roan's implying. "Yes," she says, "that is true. And he is a bit odd, but that doesn't mean—"

"No," DI Currie cuts in. "No, you're right, Mrs. Fours. It doesn't mean anything. Obviously. But it's all worth making a note of." She turns back to Roan. "So this happened at roughly midnight?"

"Yes, roughly midnight."

"And then you came back inside and went to bed?"

"Yes. That's right."

"And when you were out there, putting out the rubbish at midnight, apart from the man across the street, did you see anything else? Anyone else?"

"No. That was all. The man across the street."

"Is it possible," she continues, "that he might not have been staring at you, that he might have been staring at someone else?"

Roan wrinkles his brow. "I don't know what you—"

DI Currie closes her notepad. "Would it be possible, do you think, for you to show me exactly where you were standing that night, when you saw your neighbor staring toward you?"

"Sure," says Roan.

They all get to their feet.

Cate throws on one of Josh's hoodies from the hallway and follows Roan. DI Currie follows Cate, and they head out to the little wooden-covered area in the front garden where the communal bins are located.

"I was standing here," says Roan. "I put the bag in the bin. I'd just closed the lid, and I saw him through here." He points out a gap in the hedge that grows in front of a low brick wall.

DI Currie stands in Roan's place and peers through the gap. She stands back and peers around the corner to the front path and the metal gate at the bottom. Then she peers once more through the gap in the hedge. She writes something down in her notebook, and then she shuts it.

"Wonderful," she says, "thank you so much. I think that'll be all we need from you both for now. But a last question, Dr. Fours. I know you say that you hadn't seen Saffyre since your final appointment with her back in March 2018, but can you think of any reason, any reason at all why she might have been in the vicinity of your house on the night she went missing?"

"So, she was—" Cate begins.

"We don't know anything for sure yet. We're looking at dozens of possibilities. But that is one possibility, yes. So, Dr. Fours, can you . . . ?"

Cate looks at Roan. Roan shakes his head firmly. "No," he says. "No. There is absolutely no reason I can think of why she would have been here. None."

"And you definitely didn't see her?"

"I definitely didn't see her."

There is a long pause, as though DI Currie is hoping that Roan might say something else. When he doesn't, she smiles again, that unnerving smile of hers that is half Clinique consultant and half twisted primary school teacher.

"Thank you again, so much, both of you. And as I say, we're nearly done here. I reckon the cordon will come down in the next hour or two. You can get your street back!"

She puts her hands into the pockets of a very nice green woolen coat with big buttons, smiles one more time, and then she is gone.

Cate and Roan look at each other. He takes his phone out of his pocket and checks the time. "Fuck," he says, "I really need to get going." He drops another perfunctory kiss on Cate's cheek and, moving very quickly, strides away from her, down the garden path, and onto the pavement.

30

Saffyre

LAST DECEMBER WAS cold. Do you remember it? So cold. Or maybe I remember it that way because I spent so much of it outdoors.

It's odd, I know. I had a home, a warm home—almost too warm, you know the way they heat these council buildings, no thermostat, central settings. I had Aaron taking care of me and nice food and a nice bedroom and yet . . . for some reason I really did not want to be there. Maybe it was because my granddad wasn't there anymore. Maybe it was that simple. But it felt more complicated than that to me, like I was turning into something else, something not entirely human.

I don't know, maybe I read too much Harry Potter growing up, but I didn't feel grounded up there on the eighth floor; I felt untethered, like there was no gravity up there. I needed my feet on solid ground. I needed the air on my skin. I needed trees and soil and damp and moonlight and daylight and sun and wind and pigeons and foxes. It was like I was becoming feral.

That's an exaggeration. Obviously. I was still going to school every day. I was still showering, still making my hair look nice, wearing eyeliner, wearing clean underwear, you know; I wasn't *dirty* feral. I was just outdoorsy. Anytime I could be outdoors I took the opportunity.

I spent a lot of time in the building plot opposite Roan's house. It was cool there. I could see all the comings and goings through the gaps in the hedges without any risk of being spotted. The fox came to see me often. I brought him other processed meat gifts, and he was always very grateful to me. And then there was the guy whose bedroom window faced out onto the land. I don't know what his name was, but I called him Clive. I don't know why, he just looked like a Clive.

He was kind of odd. And I say that as someone who is also kind of odd. If I stood on top of the digger that was parked on the plot I could see right into his room through the gap in his curtains; it was like an old lady's bedroom. He had this nylon counterpane thing over his lumpy little bed, and one of those clunky antique wooden wardrobes like they have in bad B and Bs with a mirror on the outside door and his sad little stripy dressing gown hanging off the back of his door and a painting of a rugged landscape in a crap frame. The room looked cold. He sat in it every night in an armchair with his headphones on and a laptop on a cardboard box in front of him, and he looked at his stuff—I don't know what stuff, I couldn't see the screen. Not porn though, I know that, because I never saw him doing what men do when they look at porn.

Sometimes the woman would come in, the gray-haired woman he lived with. I always saw him sigh and roll his eyes before he opened the door to her. She would have her arms wrapped round her waist and a sour look on her face and say something to him, and he would say something to her, and she would look even more sour, then go.

I felt sorry for him. I couldn't imagine what it must be like to be him. He looked old enough to be married with a kid or two. He was clearly doing something wrong to be living as he was living. I wondered if he was cross about being so lonely. I wondered about Clive a lot.

Our paths crossed about a week before Christmas. He was walking up the little hill that joins Roan's road to the Finchley Road. It was late, about eleven o'clock. He looked a state. His hair was all over the place; his work bag was hanging off his shoulder, pulling his jacket down on one side. His shirt had a big stain on it, and he was kind of stumbling along. He glanced at me, and I saw that he was drunk. He smiled then, and as we passed each other he said, "Merry Christmas!" and I said, "And a Merry Christmas to you too, Clive."

He stopped and said, "Clive?"

I smiled and said, "Nothing. Just kidding. Merry Christmas."

"Owen," he said. "My name's Owen."

"Owen," I said. "I'm Jane."

"Merry Christmas, Jane."

We shook hands. His was clammy and sticky.

"Sorry," he said, "bit sweaty. Been dancing. A school disco. I'm a teacher though. Not a student. Obviously."

He laughed. I laughed.

"Night night, Jane."

"Night night, Owen."

Then he went and I went, and I thought, Owen, his name's Owen.

———

Roan took Alicia out for dinner just before Christmas. He took her to the nice little French restaurant nestled below my block of flats.

I'd followed them from the clinic, watched them go in. I took my paparazzi-style photos: *click, click.*

Alicia looked beautiful. She was beautiful. Much more beautiful than Roan's wife. And she was getting more beautiful the longer her affair with Roan went on, like he was pumping her full of some magic elixir. She had her red hair down in long waves and was wearing a black coat and red Chelsea boots and a pink scarf and red lips and black tights. She couldn't stop smiling. He looked more circumspect, held the door for her, as was his way, quick look over his shoulder as he went in.

I watched them being led to a table right at the back of the restaurant.

I wouldn't be able to see them from where I was standing, so I put my phone back in my pocket and went home.

Aaron was there. He'd bought a Christmas tree, and that cheered me up. One good thing about Granddad going was that Aaron got to sleep in the bedroom now, not in the living room, and we could have a proper Christmas tree, not the funny little skinny space-saving one we'd been using for years, which sat on a tabletop. The tree smelled so good. I stood with my face buried inside its branches and breathed it in.

Aaron passed me the box of decorations from the cupboard in the hallway. "There you go," he said. "Girls' work." He winked and I gave him a shove. Aaron's not exactly a feminist, but he's no chauvinist either. He likes the idea of the world being run by women. He likes women.

I dressed the tree and stared out the window every now and then, down to the plaza below where the posh little restaurant was, and as I stared I found myself wondering what I was doing, following Roan about the way I did, taking pictures of everything he did. I wondered where it was all heading. I wondered if I was mad, maybe. But I didn't feel mad. I felt totally fine.

Aaron put our dinner on the table. He said, "It's nice to have you here. For once."

He said this with a smile because he wasn't having a go at me. He meant it as it sounded.

"You know," he said, spooning yellow rice onto his plate, glancing over my shoulder at the twinkling tree, "it feels kind of strange. First Christmas without my dad. If you want to talk about it . . ."

I just smiled and shook my head and said, "I'm fine. Really."

"I do worry about you, Saff. We all do."

I threw him a questioning look.

"The family. Me. Lee. Tana. The girls."

"Not much of a family really, is it?" I said.

"Oh. That's harsh." He smiled. "It's quality, not quantity, yeah?"

I smiled too. "Yeah," I said.

"Just keep us in the loop, Saff, OK? Whatever it is that's bothering you. *Who*ever it is that's bothering you. We're all here for you. Yeah?"

I looked up at him. "But what about you?" I said. "Who's here for you?"

He looked kind of abashed. "What do you mean?"

I said, "You're nearly thirty. You work two jobs. You haven't had a girlfriend since you were like twenty-four or something. Who's worrying about you?"

Aaron put down his knife and fork and looked at me very sternly. Aaron looking stern, I should add, is not very stern at all. He has the face of an angel.

"Saff," he said, "I don't need worrying about, OK? Please, God, don't worry about me. Just focus on yourself. Focus on school, on these A levels. Then focus on getting into university. Then focus on getting a good degree. And then, maybe then, I'll let you worry about me. But until then, we're good here, OK?"

I nodded, but I felt a lurch in the pit of my stomach. Aaron would be thirty-one by the time I left university. And then what? I thought of Clive—or Owen, or whatever his name was— and his sad little bedroom and his sad little stripy dressing gown and I thought he looked like he was probably about thirty-one, and I didn't want that for Aaron.

"I might not even go to university," I said.

"'Course you will," he said.

"Why? Just because I'm clever, there's no law about it. I can do whatever I want to after I've left school. I could get a job and get my own place, and then you could have this flat to yourself."

He laughed. "I don't want this flat to myself! Why would I want this flat to myself?"

"So you can start a family."

He laughed again, loud and hard. "I don't want a family, fam! You're my family!"

I laughed too, but inside I was starting to feel panicky. Aaron was such a good man. He'd worked hard at school, like me, and got good exam results, but here he was working in a betting shop and doing people's gardens and then coming home and having to worry about me, wasting the prime years of his life, and I thought, You know, maybe it would be better if I wasn't there.

After dinner I told Aaron I was going to Jasmin's and he said *Have fun* and I said *Will do*, and I headed out with a heart full of strangeness about everything. I sat on one of the outdoor gym bikes on the plaza and idly wheeled the pedals round and round with my hands inside my pockets, my hood up against the chill night air. I put some music on my phone and listened for a while, watching people come and go. No one looked at me. No one saw me. When you wear a hood, you're invisible.

And then after a while Roan and Alicia left the restaurant, and I waited to see what they would do, and you want to know what they did? Those dirty devils? They checked into a hotel, the Best Western by the drama school.

My jaw fell open. I don't know why I was surprised. It had all been leading to this moment. But it still shocked me. Roan was going to have sex with a woman he wasn't married to. About half a mile away from the woman he was married to. He was going to lay Alicia down on a bed and do things to her.

I shuddered slightly, pulled down my hood, showing my pink hair to the world, and I went to see Jasmin.

31

Owen

OWEN AND DEANNA had spent two hours messaging the night before. She'd been trying to persuade him to think about getting his job back at the college. She'd made some good points, some compelling points. Mostly to do with the fact that the girls who'd reported him would be gone in a few months, there'd be a whole new intake, no one to remember what had happened: he could have a clean slate. Also to do with the fact that he'd quite enjoyed his job. And the longer he left it without having a job, the harder it would be to explain to a potential employer what he'd been doing.

Her concern had made him realize that up until now he'd not had one person in his life to offer him proper, empathetic, sensible, caring advice about his life, his choices, not ever. Not since his mother had died.

They'd said good night at eleven o'clock; Owen could have gone on talking for hours, but Deanna of course had to be up early for work. Owen had fallen asleep with his phone on his chest, a smile on his face.

He gets out of bed now and goes to his bedroom window. The police are back. They're still picking around in the back garden.

They'd cordoned the whole garden off last night before they left, spoken to all the residents, asked them not to cross the cordons. There'd been a solitary policeman stationed outside the building site all night long.

Owen peers down to the spot in the grass that the police had been examining yesterday, where they'd found the phone case. Something flashes through his thoughts as he stares at the grass.

A movement of some kind, a cry of pain.

He shakes the thought from his head and goes to the bathroom, where he showers and washes his hair. In the mirror he looks at his hair and decides that it is now officially too long. He's not sure he can be bothered to go the hairdresser's just for a trim, so he takes a pair of scissors from the bathroom cabinet, smooths his hair down onto his forehead with his fingers, then trims it across the line of his eyebrows. He starts at the left side and watches the dark fronds fall into the sink, where they look like tiny discarded mustaches. He is about to trim from the right-hand side and back to the middle when there is a loud, insistent thumping at the door. He jumps slightly, and the tip of the scissors nicks his skin. A bead of blood appears, and he rubs at it roughly and shouts out, "What!"

"Owen," says Tessie. "The police are here. They need you to come out."

He sighs. "I'll be a few minutes."

"Sir"—he hears a male voice—"we need you to come out now. Please."

"I just got out of the shower. You'll have to wait."

"Sir, please just come out."

"Fuck's sake," Owen mutters under his breath. He dries himself roughly with his towel and pulls on his old dressing gown. He opens the door and sees Tessie recoil slightly at the sight of him.

"Can I at least get dressed?" he says to the uniformed officer standing beside her.

The officer turns to a woman standing behind him. It's DI Currie, the female detective. She nods. "But I'll need PC Rodrigues to go in with you, I'm afraid."

"What?"

"I'm so sorry. It's just procedure."

"But what's the issue here? What's the urgency?"

"The urgency, Mr. Pick, is that we need to bring you into the station to question you regarding the disappearance of Saffyre Maddox. We also have a warrant to search your room." She holds up a piece of paper. Owen blinks at it. "I'm afraid that means that we need to ensure that you don't touch anything in your room. I'm so sorry." She smiles at him. It's an unnerving smile. It looks almost soft, but there's something cold and hard at the very far corners of it.

He starts to say something, but then realizes he can't find any words. He's also aware on some level that whatever is going on here is something that he could make infinitely worse by saying or doing the wrong thing. So he nods, firmly, and heads for his room, the male PC following close behind. His eye goes around his room as he dresses; he tries to think what might be here, what they might find that could connect him in any way to the disappearance of a girl he'd never heard of until two days ago, a girl he may have imagined seeing entirely.

"Faster, Mr. Pick, if you wouldn't mind."

He throws on yesterday's outfit. He'd put it on his washing pile, intending to wear something fresh today, but he can't think straight enough now to put together another outfit. He pulls on his old, glued-together shoes and runs his fingers through his wet hair. Something on his forehead comes away under his fingertip; it's the dried blood from the nick from the scissors. Blood follows and he goes to pull a tissue from the box by his bedside table but the PC says, "Sir. Please do not touch anything."

"But I'm bleeding."

"We can sort you out once we have you in the car. Just leave that for now. Please, sir."

Owen tuts. Then he takes one more look around the bedroom, grabs his jacket from the hook on the back of the door, and follows the policeman back down the hallway.

Tessie stands by the door. She is wearing a silk kimono over green pajamas. Her hair is down. She looks tired and sad. As Owen passes her, she touches his arm and says, "What did you do, Owen? What did you do?"

"I didn't do anything, for God's sake. You know I didn't do anything."

Tessie turns and walks away.

"For God's sake, Tessie," he shouts after her. "You know I didn't!"

She walks into her bedroom and pulls the door quietly shut behind her.

He feels a hand on his shoulder. "Mr. Pick, please, we need to leave."

He shrugs the hand off, anger beginning to replace the shock and awe. "I'm coming," he says. "I'm coming, OK?"

As he leaves the house, he is suddenly aware that the proportions of the street outside are all off, that there's something not right, a feeling of impending chaos, and then they appear: a flock, a pack; a dozen men and women with cameras, with microphones, pressing toward them. The PC and the detective both cover him instinctively with their arms and hustle him onward, through the throng.

"Mr. Pick, Mr. Pick!"

They know his name. How do they know his name? How did they know this was going to happen? How did they know?

He glances up and straight into the lens of a camera. He opens his eyes wide and is dazzled by a burning white flash. Something forces his head down again. He is in a car. The car door is closed. There are faces at the window, faces and lenses. The car moves quickly; people touch it; they are so close Owen doesn't understand why their feet aren't being crushed by the tires. And then he is not on his street anymore, he is on the main road and there are no more people with cameras, just normal people going about their business. Owen sits back in the seat. He exhales.

"Who told them?" he asks the backs of the heads of the two people sitting in the front.

"The press?" says the woman.

"Yes. Who told them you were coming to get me?"

"I'm afraid I have no idea. They knew we'd been searching the area. People talk. I'm sorry you had to experience that."

"But . . . it'll be in the papers," he says. "People will think I did it."

"Did what, Mr. Pick?"

He peers at her face in the rearview mirror. She's looking right at him. There's that chilling smile again.

"The thing!" he says. "Whatever the thing is that you're arresting me for."

"You're not under arrest, Mr. Pick. Not yet."

"Then why?" He stares out of the window, watches a small girl from a dog-walking company trying to load a giant bloodhound into the back of a van. "Why am I here?"

He looks at himself in the rearview mirror. His hair has started to dry. It's shorter on one side than the other and sticking up on the top. The blood from his cut has dried into a kind of huge tear shape, dripping into his eyebrow. He looks horrendous. Absolutely horrendous. And the nation's press has just photographed him like this, being placed into the back of a police car to be questioned about a missing teenage girl. He doesn't even like teenage girls. And he's not even under arrest. He's left his phone at home. What if Deanna is trying to message him? What if she thinks he's ignoring her?

And then an even worse thought hits him. What if he's in the papers tomorrow? With his crooked hair and blood-encrusted eyebrow and yesterday's clothes looking like a horrible pervert, with a headline screeching something like "IS THIS SAFFYRE'S KILLER?" He groans out loud.

"Are you OK, Mr. Pick?"

"No!" he replies. "God. No. Of course I'm not OK. I'm going to be in the papers, and I'm not even under arrest! Is that even legal?"

"Yes, I'm afraid it is legal, Mr. Pick. I'm afraid it is."

"But everyone will have seen my face, and then you'll let me go and no one will care that I didn't do it; they'll just remember my face. I'll never get a job, I'll—" He envisages Deanna peeling open the *Evening Standard* on the tube tonight. "Oh God!"

"Mr. Pick. Let's just take this one step at a time, shall we. Hopefully we'll be able to let you go within an hour or two. We'll notify the press. They'll have no interest in running the story if there's nothing to it. So let's just see how we get on, shall we?" She smiles again.

Owen sits back, folds his arms around his stomach, and rocks slightly. The world feels like a straitjacket, sucking all the air out of his chest cavity, squeezing his bones. He looks at people out the window: normal people doing normal things. Walking to the shops. Going to work. Being normal suddenly looks like the most alien concept in the world, something he can barely conceive of.

"Do I need a lawyer?" he asks.

"That'll be up to you. Do you have one?"

Tessie's friend Barry is a lawyer. But he's not Owen's lawyer. "No," he says.

"Well, we can assign you one if necessary."

"No," he says. "No. I'm sure I'll be fine."

"Let's see how we go, shall we?"

Owen nods.

And then, like a house falling on him from the sky, its shadow getting bigger and bigger, faster and faster, he suddenly remembers something.

In his underwear drawer. Shoved to the back in a slightly shameful rush after his night out with Bryn, with the intention of putting them in the public bin on the street corner next time he was out, and then completely forgotten about.

The date-rape drugs.

A terrible overdose of adrenaline hits the pit of Owen's stomach. His head spins. His heart stops and then races, sickeningly. "Oh my God," he whispers.

"Everything OK?" says DI Currie, peering at him in her mirror.

"I think I'm going to . . ." He puts his hand over his mouth. He suddenly realizes he's going to be sick. "I'm going to . . ."

DI Currie tells the PC to stop the car. They pull over by a grass verge, the PC jumps out to open Owen's door and Owen tips forward and throws up, noisily, painfully. His skin ripples with goose bumps, and his head throbs with the force of it. He gasps and throws up again. DI Currie appears in front of him, a tissue in her hand. She looks down at him. Owen can't tell if it's pity in her face, or disgust. He takes the tissue and dabs his mouth with it.

"All OK?" she asks him.

He nods.

"Ready to keep going?"

He nods again.

She smiles and waits for him to put his legs back into the car before closing the door and going back to the passenger seat.

"Something you ate?" she asks a moment later, looking at him in the mirror.

He nods, his fist balled against his mouth. "Yes," he says. "Must be."

She smiles, but she doesn't look as though she believes him.

32

Cate

"MUM," SAYS GEORGIA, walking into the bathroom without knocking. "They just arrested him!"

"Who?"

"The policewoman detective person. She just went into the house over the road with another cop. Came out with the creepy guy. Put him in a car and drove him away! There's journalists and all sorts out there, taking pictures! Come and see!"

Cate dries her hands on the backs of her jeans. It's been two hours since DI Currie was here talking to them, since Roan left for work. She'd thought things might be winding down, but apparently not. She goes to the front door with Georgia.

There are people hanging around, a couple of small film crews packing their things away. Cate goes outside and wanders over to a young woman in a yellow anorak with a furry hood and says, "What's been going on? Where have they taken that guy?"

"Owen Pick, you mean?" The woman, whom Cate assumes to be a journalist, shoves some wires into a black bag and zips it up.

"I don't know his name—the guy who lives in that house? Youngish, with dark hair?"

"Yeah. Owen Pick. They've taken him in for questioning."

"About Saffyre Maddox?"

"Yes. Apparently they found some of her stuff outside his bedroom window and traces of blood on the wall and in the grass."

"Oh my God." Cate brings her hands to her mouth. She hears Georgia gasping beside her.

"Oh my God, is she dead?" asks Georgia.

The woman shrugs. "No body found yet, but it's looking increasingly likely."

"God, that's so sad," says Georgia. Then she says, "That guy is weird. It doesn't surprise me much that he could do something like that."

The journalist stops and looks at Georgia. "They don't know for sure yet that he did. So probably best not to start spreading that about." She pauses, looks at Owen Pick's house and then back at Georgia, and says, "Although, you know . . ."

Cate follows her gaze toward the house. She thinks about that night weeks ago when Georgia thought she'd been followed home by Owen Pick. She thinks about that night a few days later when Tilly appeared on her doorstep to say she'd been accosted on the other side of the street. She thinks of the string of sex attacks in the area. She thinks about Roan seeing Owen Pick that night, staring at their house.

She feels a weight lift from her gut, a weight she had barely acknowledged until now: the weight of doubt, the weight of suspicion, of thinking that at any moment now the world could collapse on her head.

––––––

She and Georgia make a cake. It's nearly the end of the school holiday. Georgia's been studying all week, or out with friends, and Cate's barely seen her. It's one of those gray, muffled days where everything feels fuzzy and unformed. The focus of weighing and measuring and counting and stirring is exactly what the day calls for.

Georgia has one of her playlists on Spotify, a mixture of music that Cate once danced to in nightclubs and modern music that sounds meaningless and empty to her ears. They're making something they found on the internet called a choca-mocha cake. Cate gets an espresso from the coffee maker and leaves it on the side to cool. Georgia is creaming sugar and butter together. The oven hums as it heats up.

Owen Pick's face keeps passing in and out of Cate's consciousness. That vaguely displeased look he has about him, as though he's constantly thinking about unsavory things. His hair with that slightly defeated, secondhand look about it. The worn-down shoes, incongruous in contrast with strangely smart clothes that look as though they don't come naturally to him. He looks the type, she thinks. He seems the type: a single guy, living alone with an eccentric aunt in a grubby-looking house with tatty curtains at the windows.

And now there is blood under his bedroom window.

She glances up at Georgia. Georgia's cheeks are pink from the heat of the oven, from the effort of getting the butter and sugar to combine. She has a hank of hair hanging across her face that she blows out of the way from the side of her mouth.

Cate leans toward her and pushes the hair behind her ear for her. Georgia drops a kiss onto Cate's hand and says, "Thank you, Mum."

They exchange a look. Cate knows they're both thinking the same thing.

Saffyre Maddox might be dead and their neighbor, who might have killed her, could have killed Georgia, too.

But now the police have him in custody and they are safe: they are making a cake.

33

Saffyre

CHRISTMAS DAY LAST year was good.

Lee came over with the family, Aaron cooked amazing food, a mix of British Christmas fare and things I've been told my grandma used to cook for Christmas lunch: baked macaroni, sweet potato pie. We drank rum punch with umbrellas and tinsel in it and did karaoke with the machine Lee brought over and the tree looked amazing and we put a fake fire on the plasma screen and it really was, in spite of Granddad not being there, a proper Christmas Day.

I was so fat and tipsy and sleepy after that I didn't even really want to go outdoors. I felt quite grounded that evening with my big belly in my comfy chair on the eighth floor. I just sat and rubbed my stomach and watched my little cousins playing with their new things. I'd spent months and months by then following Roan and his family and his lover around, and to spend a day connecting to people in a real and proper way felt like magic. Maybe if I could have held on to that feeling, the sense that I belonged in that world, that I was meant to be there and not somewhere else, then maybe everything else would have been different.

But for one day at least, I was chilled, I was present. It was nice.

The day after Boxing Day I started getting really antsy again. The flat was so hot and there was this awful feeling of confinement in the building, like we were all gerbils locked up in tiny boxes. The sun was out, and I put on my snow boots with my pajama bottoms, tied back my hair, and threw on my Puffa. I looked rough, but I didn't care; I just needed to get out.

I called in on Jasmin. She looked rough too. We both laughed about how shit we looked, how fat we were. She came out for a walk with me, and we went to Starbucks on the Finchley Road and sat on the sofa there just chatting. I had half an eye out the big plate-glass window, onto the street, just in case I saw anyone I knew walk past. Then she said she had to get back because she had family staying and she was supposed to be around, and I walked her home and then it was already starting to get dark, that stupid moment in the middle of winter when you've only been awake a few hours and the sky suddenly turns dirty yellow and the bare trees turn into black skeletons and nighttime lands bang slap middle of the day.

I turned and looked back at the estate, at the top floors of my block. All the windows glowed different colors and flashed with Christmas lights. It looked warm up there. It looked pretty.

I shivered slightly and, instead of going home, I turned and walked up the hill toward the village.

———

Hampstead village looked like a life-size snow globe at that time of year with all the trees wrapped up in white lights. I liked walking up there for the exercise really; it's uphill the whole way from my flat, so it's good aerobically. After two days sitting in my flat eating

Ferrero Rocher it felt great to have the cold air passing in and out of my lungs, to feel my blood whooshing through my veins. I should have run it really, but I'm built for many things and running is not one of them.

It was busy in the village: the sales had started already, and the shoppers were out in force. I peered into shop windows at things I couldn't afford and didn't need. The shop for yoga mummies with the hundred-pound leggings. Designer tile shops, designer paint shops, a shop selling just one brand of cooking pan in about twenty different colors: Le Creuset. I didn't quite understand Hampstead, but I liked it.

I was about to head right up to the other end of the village, to the very top of the hill where the air is thinner, where the Heath begins with its raggedy entryways and endless vistas and its futuristic view of the pointy glass towers all the way over the other side of London, and I turned, and as I turned I saw that I was face-to-face with a man and that that man was Roan.

I wasn't wearing my hood up, so he recognized me immediately, and for a tiny beat it was a bit awkward. He was wearing a cloth cap and a padded coat and was carrying a huge Reiss carrier bag with the word "Sale" printed on it in red. He hadn't shaved and looked kind of bizarre.

He said, "Hi, Saffyre. Wow, how are you?"

"I'm good. I'm good," I said. "How are you?"

He glanced down at his big bag. "I'm great. Just exchanging a gift that didn't fit."

"From your wife?" I said, before I could check myself.

"Yes," he said, and I noticed his smile set like cement. "Yes. Too big. Unfortunately."

I nodded encouragingly and smiled.

"And you?" he said. "You're OK?"

"Yeah. Well, my granddad died." I shrugged. "A couple of months ago. So that was bad."

"Oh, Saffyre, I'm really sorry to hear that."

"You know," I said. "One of those things, isn't it? People die."

He nodded. "Yes, people die, that is true. But it is horrible. I'm very sorry for your loss. I know how close you all were. How are you coping?"

"Well, you know, in some ways it's easier? Because Aaron doesn't have to do so much cooking and caring and stuff. But in other ways, it's shit really, because my family is just too small now. It's too, too small."

I said this lightly, like maybe it was a joke, but I think it came out more emotional than I intended because Roan put his hand on my arm and looked at me with great concern and said, "Do you think you need to talk this through with someone?"

I thought, Ha, yeah, right, because you did such a good job of fixing me last time I came to you broken, didn't you?

But I kind of laughed it off. "No, honestly. It's all good. Just takes a bit of getting used to." Then there was a brief pause and I said, "How's the family?"

He made a weird shape with his mouth and nodded. "Good," he said. "We're all good."

And then—and there's no point telling me that I shouldn't have done this because it's too late now, I did it, it's done—I looked him hard in the eye and I said, "How's Alicia?"

Strike me down dead. Whatever. He deserved it. Standing there in his daft cap, with a coat in a bag that his wife bought him because she stupidly thought he was her loyal husband, not some horny sex beast.

"Sorry?" he said, and I could see the panic swimming about in his eyes, like tiny tadpoles.

"How's Alicia?" I asked again, and then I got the adrenaline rush to my heart as my brain finally caught up with what my mouth was doing. "Your colleague."

He nodded, then shook his head and said, "Sorry? But how do you know Alicia? Have you been back to the clinic?"

I just shook my head and smiled at him.

I could see him scrambling for the next thing to say or do, and I decided that now was the time to step away from the hand grenade I'd just unpinned. I said, "Anyway, nice seeing you, Roan. Have a happy holiday."

He turned as I left and said, "But, Saffyre—what did you mean by that?"

"Can't stop. Must dash."

I walked that last leg of the hill at about a hundred miles an hour. Dainty trees full of twinkly white pom-poms. Restaurants full of rich people. I passed art galleries, estate agents, nail bars with pink chandeliers. It was properly dark by the time I got to the top. I stood with my hands on my hips and looked down, my breath coming in and out of me so loudly I could hear it.

34

Owen

OWEN IS IN a room with pale blue walls, a plate-glass window on one side, a tall thin window on the other with opaque, textured glass and three vertical white metal bars.

In front of him are DI Currie and another detective, a man called DI Jack Henry. He's wearing a really nice blue suit with a tight white shirt underneath. He has blond hair, like DI Currie, and is about the same age as her; they look strangely like a couple, as if they've just ordered pizzas in a branch of Zizzi's and are trying to think of something to talk about.

"So, Owen." DI Currie smiles at him, running a fingertip over her paperwork. "I'm really grateful to you for agreeing to come at such short notice and for being so cooperative. Thank you."

Owen says, "That's OK."

"We'll try to keep this as short as possible. I'm sure you've got things you need to be getting on with. But we do, just for your information, have a warrant to keep you for questioning for twenty-four hours. So if there's anyone you need to talk to, just let us know and we can contact them for you. OK?"

She smiles again.

Owen nods.

"So," she begins, after setting the machine to record. "Owen. Let's go back to the night of February the fourteenth, if you don't mind. I know we've already spoken about this, but just for the sake of our recordings, so we have it on record. You went out that evening?"

"Yes."

"And where did you go?"

"I went to an Italian restaurant. On Shaftesbury Avenue."

"And who were you with?"

"I was with a woman called Deanna Wurth. On a date."

"So, you had a drink?"

"I had a few drinks."

"How many, would you say, roughly?"

"We shared a bottle of champagne and then a bottle of red wine. And a cocktail. I'm not really a big drinker, so that was quite a lot for me."

"Gosh," says DI Currie. "I'd say that was quite a lot for anyone!" She exchanges a look with DI Henry, who shakes his head and smiles.

"So," she continues. "You weren't sober when you got home?"

"No. I was really quite drunk."

"And this was what time?"

"Roughly eleven thirty. Maybe later."

"And what did you do when you got home? Could you talk us through that again, please? How did you get home?"

"I got the tube to Finchley Road. Then I walked to my house, via Winterham Gardens."

"And then?"

"I saw the person in the hoodie outside the house opposite. I went indoors. I went to bed."

"And just going back, if you don't mind, to your walk from the tube station that night?"

Owen blanches slightly at the hazy memory of a woman, her fearful gaze on him, her finger over the emergency icon on her phone screen.

"Did you perhaps see anyone when you were walking home?"

He shakes his head.

"Yes or no, please, Mr. Pick."

"No," he says. "No, I didn't see anyone."

"What about this lady?"

DI Currie passes him a photograph. It's an attractive young woman in what looks like an official company portrait. She has long blond hair and is wearing a red blouse.

He shakes his head, rubs his chin nervously. "No," he says. "I don't know her."

"Well, this lady lives two doors down from you. And she says on the night in question that you physically threatened her at around midnight. That you attempted to block her path. That you called her a 'bitch.' She says she felt very, very intimidated by you and nearly called the police."

Owen inhales deeply. "That's not what happened."

"OK, so you do remember this lady."

"Well, I do now. I just didn't recognize her from that photo. But I remember her being there. She was staring at her phone. She didn't see me coming. And it was her who got in *my* way. She was rude to *me*. I was just defending myself. Reacting to her rudeness. For God's sake." He tuts and folds his arms petulantly.

"OK, so you're heading home. You have a contretemps with this lady. You see the young girl outside your neighbor's house at about midnight. Can you describe it for us now? Whatever you can remember about that?"

He sighs. "I mean, I don't even know anymore. It was late. It was dark. I was still quite drunk. It could have been anything."

"Just try, Owen, please. Thank you."

"I saw . . ." He pauses, tries his hardest to put himself back there, outside his house, the chill air of his breath around him. "A figure. With a hood. Slim. Not tall. Not short. I thought it was a man at first. They were staring ahead, at the top of the footpath, by the gate. They had their hands in their pockets so their elbows were sticking out like this." He makes pointy wings of his own elbows. "And then, after about a minute—less, half a minute—they turned and walked away, and I saw then that it was probably a girl. With kind of . . ." He searches for the right word. "Puffy hair."

"Puffy? You mean like Afro-Caribbean type of hair?"

"I don't know," he says. "I don't really know what that means."

"OK. So you saw this figure. And then what happened?"

Owen shakes his head gently, searching his memory for the moment that came after the girl's eyes met his. But there's nothing there.

He shakes his head properly. "Nothing happened. I saw her, and then I went straight indoors."

"And then?"

"I got into bed and I fell asleep."

"Did anyone see you coming back in?"

"No, not that I'm aware of."

"We've asked the neighbors in your building and none of them recall hearing the door close at that time of night."

He blinks. "I don't see . . . ," he begins. "They were probably all asleep. Why would they hear the door go?"

"I don't know, Mr. Pick. But it's a big heavy door. And it does make quite a loud bang when it's shut."

He blinks again and shakes his head. "Not really," he says.

"Well," says DI Currie, "I suppose that's a matter of opinion." She glances at the other detective. "OK, I think DI Henry has a few questions too. Are you OK? Can I get you some more water? A hot drink? Anything to eat?"

He shakes his head. "No, thank you."

DI Henry opens his notes. He clears his throat and he says, "So, your neighbors across the street, the, er, the Fours?"

Owen shakes his head.

"Cate and Roan Fours."

"No, I don't know who they are."

"OK, well, they live in the house across the street where you say you saw a figure on the night of the fourteenth."

He nods. "Right." He knows who they're talking about now. That family. The Lycra dad and the nervous wife and the overconfident daughter and the gangly boy. "The ones with the kids?"

"Yes, the ones with the kids; that is correct. How would you say your relationship with them is?"

"I don't have a relationship with them."

"Dr. Fours says that you once accosted him in the street when he was out for a run; he said you were rather drunk and asking him strange questions."

Owen repositions himself in his chair. "What has this got to do with . . . ?"

"Well, nothing directly, Mr. Pick. But tangentially, we are forming a picture here."

Owen breathes in sharply as he realizes what is happening. He is being led by this pair of bland, blond, cookie-cutter human beings down an opaque, twisting path toward incriminating himself.

"You know what," he says. "I think maybe if you're not going to be asking me anything to do with actual evidence of me having done anything wrong and you're just going to talk about things I may or may not have said to my neighbors three weeks ago, then maybe I should have a lawyer. Please."

The blond twins look at each other and then back at him. "Of course, Owen. Absolutely. Do you have a number I could call?"

"Mr. Barrington Blair. Barry. I think he works in the West End somewhere. Soho, that sort of area."

"Great, we'll get someone to call him now. In the meantime, maybe we'll take a short break."

They shuffle their papers together. DI Henry straightens his jacket, his collar. DI Currie touches the back of her complicated hairstyle, pressing a loose strand into place. Owen wonders if they're real people or very sophisticated androids.

"Someone will bring you something to eat, Owen. Just hold tight."

And then Owen is alone. He stretches his legs out and crosses them at the ankle. He scrapes a piece of encrusted food off the cuff of his sweater. He suddenly thinks that there may be a row of police officers and detectives sitting on the other side of the plate glass watching him, so he decides to move about as little as he possibly can.

A moment later a young uniformed policeman comes in with a couple of sandwiches and a paper cup of tea.

"Tuna," he says. "Or chicken Caesar wrap?"

"I'm not hungry," Owen replies.

"I'll leave both," he says. And then he gives him the tea and leaves the room.

"How long?" Owen calls toward him through the crack in the door.

The boy reappears. "No idea," he says chirpily. "Sorry."

There's nothing in this room to look at. Nothing to distract him. He looks at his fingernails; he fiddles with his hair, tries to straighten his stupid asymmetric fringe. He touches the scab on his forehead. He crosses and uncrosses his legs. Time passes in long, hollow moments, stretched out of all shape by the weirdness of the scenario.

He pulls one of the sandwiches toward him. Tuna mayo and cucumber. He hates tuna and he hates cucumber, and it's brown bread, which he's never actually eaten. He doesn't even look at the other one; he knows he won't like it.

He sips the scalding tea gingerly. His heart jumps about again at the thought of the police rifling through his bedroom, the pills in his sock drawer. He tries to work out what he's going to say about the pills when they inevitably find them. How will he explain Bryn? How will he explain his relationship with an insane incel who wants to incite mass rape of women?

Owen taps his fingertips against the tabletop and tries to control his breathing. He can feel a red ball of panic hurtling toward him, threatening to swallow him up. He pictures the police behind the reflecting glass again. He cannot freak out, he cannot. Barry will be here soon. Barry will tell him what to do.

He takes another sip of tea, too quickly, feels it scald the inside of his mouth, winces, and says *fuck* under his breath.

Finally the door opens again and the two detectives return. The woman says, "We've contacted Mr. Blair. He's on his way. We can carry on talking while we wait—that could get you home quicker? Or you can wait until he's here. It's up to you."

He thinks again of the pills in his underwear drawer.

He says, "I think I'll wait."

35

ROAN COMES BACK from work early that evening.

Cate glances up at him from the screen of her laptop when he walks into the kitchen. "Oh!" she says. "You're back early."

He walks past her and directly to the fridge and starts pouring himself a glass of wine before he's even taken off his coat. He holds the bottle aloft and says, "Want one?"

It's barely 6:00 p.m., but she nods.

"How was your day?" she asks.

"Pretty grim," he says, unzipping his coat and taking it off. "Pretty bloody grim."

She knows there's no point expecting him to expand. It usually means a suicidal patient, or some violence or something appalling involving bodily fluids. It also sometimes means a set-to with a colleague or a superior. Whichever is the case in this instance, Cate doesn't ask. She merely raises her wineglass to his and says, "Here's to Friday night."

He returns the gesture drily and gets out his phone, starts scrolling through something on his screen. Then he turns it to face her. "Have you seen this?"

She takes the phone, puts on her reading glasses, and looks at the screen.

"Oh my God."

It's a photo of the guy from across the street. His mouth is open, and you can see his fillings and a gray tongue. He has blood encrusted on his forehead, and his hair is greasy and slightly brutal-looking. It's a shocking photograph. The headline above it says: "Is this Saffyre's killer? Man taken in for questioning after 'blood and phone case' found on his property."

"Did you see this happening?" he asks her.

"I didn't, no. But Georgia did."

"Did you know about the blood the detectives found?"

"Yes. A journalist told us. Who told you?" she asks.

"A colleague. Well, many colleagues. It's all anyone's talked about today. It's . . . fuck. It's just awful."

She looks at the page on Roan's phone again. She imagines a million phones in a million hands, a million people looking at this man's face, right now. This man who lives across the road from her.

She reads the story beneath:

Earlier today, Owen Pick, a 33-year-old college lecturer, was brought in by north London police for questioning regarding the disappearance of 17-year-old Saffyre Maddox. Pick, who lives in Hampstead with his aunt, Tessa McDonald, was recently suspended from his job as a computer science lecturer at Ealing Tertiary College, after allegations of sexual misconduct from several students. One student, Maisy Driscoll, told reporters that Pick had a reputation among the female students at her college for "being creepy." She said that he had stroked her hair at a college party and shaken sweat into her face a number of times. The college would give no comment about Mr. Pick's employment with them.

Neighbors in his leafy Hampstead avenue describe Mr. Pick as "odd," "a loner," and, one woman, Nancy Wade, 25, recalls being accosted by him on the street just before midnight on the night of Saffyre Maddox's disappearance. She told reporters that Mr. Pick "deliberately blocked my path. When I asked him to move out of my way, he turned nasty and abused me verbally. I was genuinely scared for my life."

Ernesto Bianco, 73, who lives in the flat above Mr. Pick and Ms. McDonald, told reporters that this is not the first time Mr. Pick has been questioned by the police in recent weeks. According to Mr. Bianco, Mr. Pick had previously been visited by the police in relation to a string of serious sexual assaults in the area, including two in the immediate vicinity of his property. No one has yet been found or charged with these attacks. It is thought he will be questioned about these events too.

Unsubstantiated reports suggest that while searching the area beneath Pick's bedroom window, police officers uncovered possessions, including a phone case, that are suspected to belong to the missing teenager. It is also thought that they discovered bloodstains on the brickwork close to Pick's bedroom and in the grass below. Forensic officers are still on-site and the case is ongoing. No body has yet been found, and the search for Saffyre Maddox continues.

Cate hands the phone back to Roan. She thinks about how guilty she'd felt after sending the police to Owen Pick's door those weeks earlier. But she'd been right, she thinks to herself now, she'd followed her instincts and her instincts had been absolutely spot-on.

"Did you read that bit?" she asks him. "About the sexual misconduct at work. I mean, it looks pretty clear, doesn't it? It must be him."

Roan takes his phone from her outstretched hand. "Looks like it. Yes."

Cate takes a sip of wine and looks at Roan thoughtfully. "But it's still so odd, isn't it? That she was here? On our street? I mean, why here? Of all the places? And why him and why her? It's just . . ." She shivers. "It's unsettling."

Roan shrugs. "I guess she didn't live that far from here. And this is one of the roads you'd walk up to get to the village. Maybe it's not that weird after all."

"But where was she really going? No one says they'd made arrangements to meet her?"

"I don't know," says Roan, spreading his arms. "I don't know anything about her or her private life."

She sighs. "Just to think," she says, "that time he was following Georgia last month . . ."

"Well, thank God she had the common sense to call you."

"Yes. Absolutely. I can't even . . ."

"No," Roan says, shaking his head gently. "No. Neither can I."

————

Cate watches from her bedroom window that night, to see if the police bring Owen Pick home. But the street is quiet. A fine drizzle falls from a black, clouded sky. She can see the silky filaments of it through the yellow streetlights. The police ribbon has gone from the road but is still taped across the gate into the building site. It's the weekend tomorrow. Do police carry out forensic searches of crime scenes at the weekend? She has no idea. She hears a sound behind her and turns, expecting to see Roan, but it's not, it's Josh.

"What're you doing?" he says.

"Just seeing what's happening over there."

He puts a hand onto her shoulder, and she covers it with hers.

"I feel sorry for him," he says.

She turns and looks at him.

"Who?"

"Him," he says. "The guy over there. I feel bad. Everyone will just think he did it, whether he did or not."

"What makes you think he didn't?"

"I didn't say that," he says. "It's just, innocent until proven guilty and all that. But people, you know, they like having someone to blame, don't they? They like knowing who the bad person is. Who to throw the eggs at. The rocks. I feel bad for him."

Cate turns and looks at her boy. She puts a hand to the side of his face and cups his cheeks, feels the suggestion of three-day-old boy-stubble, soft as summer grass. "You're such a lovely boy," she says. "Such a lovely boy."

He smiles and rubs his face against her palm, then draws her toward him for a hug. She feels the bones of him, the sinew and the tendon. He smells of the fabric conditioner she uses. He smells of something else, too, a slightly tobaccoey smell. She wonders if he smokes. And if he does, she wonders if she minds. She smoked at fourteen. In fields and by railway tracks and behind walls and hedges. She smoked Silk Cuts. She stole them from her mother and then when her mother found out and started hiding her Silk Cuts, she smoked roll-ups instead. Can she be angry with him for doing what she herself had done?

She feels that in the current climate of murder and blood she does not mind that her son might be smoking. Maybe she will mind later on. She lets him go and smiles.

"I'm sure justice will be served," she says reassuringly. "I'm sure the right person will be punished."

36

Owen

IT IS NEARLY midnight. Owen is still sitting in a pale blue room with a long narrow window and a two-way mirror. DIs Currie and Henry are still sitting facing him. On the table in front of them are two empty paper cups, the wrappings of three Kit Kat bars, four empty sugar packets, and three wooden stirrers. Owen drags his finger through the edges of a small puddle of tea and makes a tentacle out of it. He does this seven more times, until it is an octopus.

Apparently they are awaiting a report from the guys who've been ransacking his bedroom all day. Barry sits next to Owen, picking at his cuticles. He wears cuff links with green stones in them and a lilac-and-green checked shirt. He looks incongruous in this room with the bland detectives, the peeling walls, and Owen himself, who is starting to feel very stale and unfragrant.

Owen hasn't told Barry about the Rohypnol in his sock drawer. When Barry walked in four hours ago Owen had taken one look at him and realized the only reason he was here was to get paid. There was no smile of recognition or of empathy, no suggestion that Barry had ever seen Owen before in his life. He'd been businesslike to the point of cruelty.

The door opens and two more policemen enter. They look at Owen strangely as they walk in, and Owen feels his stomach curl at the edges. He knows what that look means.

They take DI Currie out of the room for a few minutes; then she returns alone. She spreads some new paperwork on the table in front of her, clears her throat, says something into DI Henry's ear, stares straight at Owen, and says, "Well. Mr. Pick. I think . . ." She moves the paperwork around again. She's clearly working out her next move, wants to make sure she pitches it just right. "I think, maybe, we need to back up a little here. I think we need to discuss, maybe, your activities over the past few weeks—since, in fact, the date of your suspension from Ealing College. Would you say, Mr. Pick, that that experience has changed you at all? Made you view life differently?"

Barry leans forward, runs a finger down his exquisite silk tie, and says, "Don't answer that, Owen. It's a ridiculous question."

Owen closes his mouth.

DI Currie inhales and starts again. "Mr. Pick, we have been through the browsing history of your laptop. We've found some quite disturbing entries in a number of what I believe are known as *incel* forums. Mr. Blair, do you know what an incel forum is?"

"Indeed I do," says Barry, taking Owen somewhat by surprise. Barry looks as though he came straight from 1960; Owen cannot imagine him owning a computer, let alone knowing what an incel forum is.

"You have been frequenting these forums quite a lot lately, Mr. Pick, would you say?"

He shrugs and says, "No. Not really."

"Well, I can tell you exactly how much time you've spent fre-quenting these forums, Mr. Pick, because we have the data right here. Since Thursday, January the seventeenth, the day you were suspended from your job at Ealing College, you have spent roughly four hours a day on these forums."

"Owen, you still don't need to say anything. This is all complete nonsense."

"Owen, you've said some pretty dreadful things on these forums. You've joined in discussions on how to rape women, which sort of women deserve to be raped, and why. And you've referred to women in such derogatory terms that I can barely bring myself to repeat the terminology. You sit here, looking like butter wouldn't melt in your mouth, with your big, sad eyes, while thinking these things, expressing these vile, vile opinions about women."

Her voice is raised, her eyes flash. For the first time since Owen first set eyes on Angela Currie, she is showing some genuine personality. She turns the papers around so he can see the words he typed in a frenzy of euphoria from meeting people he could relate to.

The words swim in front of his eyes.

> ... Slag ... Mouth ...
> ... Fist ...
> ... Whore ... Hard ... Face ...
> ... Slut ...
> ... Bitch ... Bleed ... Hole ...

He closes his eyes.

He didn't mean any of those words.

He'd just been joining in. The new boy. Getting carried away.

"Can you confirm that these were written by you?"

He looks at Barry.

Barry just blinks at him. He is disgusted.

Owen nods his head.

"Please affirm verbally, Mr. Pick."

"Yes. I wrote these words. But I didn't mean them."

"You didn't mean them?"

"No. Not really. I mean, I am, I *was* cross about a lot of things. I was cross about being reported for things I hadn't done at work . . ."

"Hadn't done?"

"Hadn't done in the way those girls *said* I'd done them."

"You mean they misread your intentions?"

"Yes. No. Yes. I don't have the slightest interest in teenage girls. Not in that way. They look like children to me. So whatever it was they thought I'd done, it had to have been done entirely innocently, unintentionally."

DI Currie nods. "So you were cross about that, and you went to these places on the internet"—she stabs a piece of paper with her fingertip—"and you said disgusting, violent things about women, because you were angry?"

Owen nods. "Yes. That's right. But I didn't mean any of it."

"Just like you didn't mean to flick sweat on those girls or ask them if they liked girls or boys?"

"What? I didn't say that . . ."

"They say you did, Mr. Pick. Nancy Wade says you made her fear for her life while she walked alone in the dark. Your neighbors identified you as a potential sex threat when their daughter's friend said she'd been accosted close to their home last month and a police officer was sent to ask you about that. You have spent dozens of hours in chat rooms and on forums discussing the best way to rape women, and we have found traces of Saffyre Maddox's blood on the wall and in the grass beneath your bedroom window, Saffyre Maddox's phone case also beneath your bedroom window, and now,

Mr. Pick, we have been told of the existence of a large amount of the prohibited drug Rohypnol in one of your bedroom drawers—Rohypnol being, as I'm sure we're all aware, a very well-known example of what is a date-rape drug.

"The time is currently twelve-oh-three a.m., the day is Saturday the twenty-third of February. Owen Michael Pick, I am placing you under arrest for the abduction of Saffyre Maddox. You do not have to say anything, but it may harm your defense if you do not mention when questioned something which you later rely on in court. Anything you do say may be given in evidence. Do you understand?"

Owen looks at Barry as if there is something he should be saying or doing that could make this go away.

But Barry just closes his eyes and nods.

37

Saffyre

A FEW DAYS before New Year's Eve, I found Aaron standing at the door of our flat looking edgy and bouncy. I'd just got out of the lift. I said, "What's up with you?"

"I've got a surprise for you."

I smiled suspiciously at him. "Oh yeah?"

"Take your coat off," he said. He took it from me as I slipped my arms out of the sleeves and hung it up for me. "Come. But be quiet. OK? Take your shoes off."

I kicked off my trainers and looked at him questioningly.

Then I followed him into the living room. He led me toward the Christmas tree and said, "Oh, look! There's another present under the tree! Santa must have come back because you have been such a good girl!"

I frowned at him and then knelt down next to the parcel. It was more of a box than a parcel, a shiny red box with a lid and a golden bow.

"You'd better open it, don't you think?"

I slowly pulled the lid up. I looked in the box. And then I

gasped. My hands went straight to my mouth. I looked at Aaron and I said, "No!"

"Actually, yes." He smiled hard.

Inside the box was a tiny cream kitten. It was like the sort of kitten you see on Instagram: big blue eyes, so much fluff. It opened its mouth like a lion about to roar and made a tiny, pathetic mewling sound. I laughed and put my hands into the box to scoop it out. It barely weighed anything; it was all fluff and no physical mass, just a tiny breath of a thing. "Is it ours?" I asked Aaron.

He shook his head. "No," he said. "He's yours. He's your cat."

I made some weird noise, like a squeal mixed with a groan. All my life, all my life I'd been asking for a pet, and all my life I'd been told no, that it was too much work, we didn't have enough space, that Granddad had allergies, too expensive, too much. And I'd finally given up asking a couple of years back, and now here was my pet. Here he was. In my hands. I kissed his head and said, "For real?"

And Aaron said, "Yes. For real."

"Oh my God. Oh my actual God. I can't believe it. I really can't believe it."

I put the kitten down on the floor and let him explore. He stood on his back legs and pawed at a low-hanging bauble. Aaron and I looked at each other and laughed.

He said, "What are you going to call him?"

"Gosh, I don't know. What do you think?"

"I dunno. I mean, the blue eyes—Frank Sinatra?"

"Who?"

"Frank Sinatra. He's a singer from the old days. Called Ol' Blue Eyes. Because of his blue eyes. How do you not know this?"

"Why should I know this? I'm young. I'm not old like you."

"But Frank would be a cool name for him, don't you think?"

I picked up the kitten and looked at his big blue eyes. He did the tiny noise thing again. I thought, No, he doesn't look like a Frank. He looks like an angel. I said, "Angelo. I'm going to call him Angelo."

———

I know why Aaron bought me the kitten. I'm not stupid, and it was pretty obvious. He bought me the kitten to make me want to stay home. I knew he was uncomfortable about the amount of time I was spending outside the flat, and he's not stupid either. It was kind of genius. Because how could I want to be hanging round outside on my own in the dark and the cold and the wet when I could be cuddled up with Angelo, the kitten of my dreams?

But it didn't really work. It was kind of out of sight, out of mind. When I was home with Angelo, I was obsessed with him. I stared at him; I watched him like he was the best TV show ever made. Everything he did enchanted me. In the mornings he'd wake me up by walking across my face with his little needle claws out, and I didn't even mind. He smelled like a cloud, like a pool of fresh water, like the top of a mountain. I picked him up sometimes just so I could smell him. I loved him. I really, really did love him.

But he wasn't enough, not enough to stop me wanting to go out, pull up my hood, and disappear in plain sight.

———

The first time I spent the whole night outdoors was New Year's Eve.

I told Aaron I was going to a party at Jasmin's and spending the night. Aaron had a job behind a bar in Kilburn for the night, double hourly rate and massive tips; he did it every year, usually came home with a couple hundred pounds for one night's work. I said I'd be home early on New Year's Day to take care of Angelo, and Aaron said he'd take me out for a late Nando's if I was up for it.

I packed up my overnight bag, and got my sleeping bag out of the top of my wardrobe (bought for and not used since my year-six camping trip. It was bright pink with hearts on it). I packed some food, some meat for the fox, a hot-water bottle in a furry cover, a portable charger for my phone, a toilet roll, and some hand sanitizer. I wore lots of clothes even though it wasn't that cold. I picked up Angelo and kissed him and pulled his claws out of my clothes and smelled him and left him in the kitchen with some newspaper down and some food in his little bowl.

The last thing I heard before I left was the sound of his little teeth crunching up his food.

I did show up at Jasmin's. She was having what she kept calling a soirée. Rolling the *r*. A swor-r-r-ay. I don't even know where she got the word from. She looked appalled when I took off my coat and she saw me all layered up in hoodies and fleeces and my worst joggers.

"Are you even trying anymore?" she asked.

I said, "I've got plans. I need to be warm."

"Tell me you've got some cute little bralette on underneath that or something?"

I said, "No. I look shit. Deal with it."

I stayed till about eleven o'clock. It was fine. It was the girls from school, a couple of their boyfriends. I had a glass of red wine. I figured it would help me sleep. There was music and chatting, and then some of Jasmin's aunties turned up drunk from the pub and they were really loud and funny, and then there was louder music and some dancing and it was nice. I knew everyone would make a fuss about me disappearing before midnight, that they'd all try to persuade me to stay. So I didn't say I was going. I just picked up my rucksack and the end of a bottle of wine and I went.

———

I peered into Roan's windows from the street. They were a little steamed up, so I figured they were home. I wondered what people like Roan and his wife did on New Year's Eve. Did they go out for posh dinners? Or get drunk and dance in their mates' houses? Or did they just sit and drink wine on the sofa?

I climbed over the wall into the empty plot and set up my little sleeping area behind the digger. No one would see me there if they happened to wander in. It also protected me from the wind. I put a blanket down on the ground, after moving a few chips of rock out of the way. I took off my top hoodie and rolled it up into a pillow shape. I put my Puffa coat back on and pulled a beanie down over my ears. I sat with my back against the digger and I drank the wine from the bottle. I'd never had more than one glass of wine before, and I was pleasantly surprised by how good it felt, what a difference it made to everything. I looked at my phone: Jasmin was posting endless films of everyone dancing and screeching and leering into the camera. I didn't feel like I was missing out. I was where I wanted to be.

I checked the time: 11:28 p.m.

I messaged Jasmin and told her I'd gone home because I was tired and wished her a happy New Year, and she didn't reply, which meant she was still having fun. I didn't want her to worry about me.

I finished the wine and felt a blanket of gooey drunkenness envelop me.

At midnight the sky filled with fireworks. I thought of Aaron behind the bar in Kilburn, loading a dishwasher with glasses, surrounded by drunk people. I thought of Granddad up in the sky doing whatever dead people do in the sky.

And then I heard a door open and close, and the sound of a man coughing. I went to the front wall and peered through the trees and saw Roan shrugging on a coat, leaving his house. I tiptoed round the perimeter and watched him as he turned the corner and pulled his phone from his pocket.

"Hi," I heard him say. "It's me. Happy New Year."

I heard a tinny woman's voice in the background.

"Are you OK? Are you . . . ? Oh, OK. Yeah. Good. No, I can't talk for long. I just said I was putting some rubbish out. Yeah, we're all just, you know, hanging out. Having champagne. Nothing special. You know. No. Nothing like that. Quite quiet. Yes. I know, I wish that too. Fuck, yes, of course I wish it. You know I do. I wish it so much. Alicia. Fuck, I love you so much. Yes. Yes. This time next year, I swear. I swear. This time next year it will be you and me, the Maldives, maybe, the Seychelles, yes! Better food! God, yes! Just us. I promise. I swear. I love you so much. I love you so much. Fuck. Alicia. I need to go back in now. Keep the faith, my beautiful girl. Just keep the faith. Yes. Yes. You too. Happy New Year. I'll see you in three days! I love you. I love you. Bye. Bye."

And then, silence.

I went back to the front of the plot and looked toward Roan's house. The wife was there, in the doorway, in a sparkly jumper and jeans, socked feet, a glass of champagne in her hand.

"Where've you been?" she called out to Roan as he turned the corner.

"Nowhere," he said. "Just thought I heard something."

"Heard something?"

"Yeah. Shouting. I was just being nosy. Think it was just merry-makers."

I didn't hear what the wife said in reply because another load of fireworks went off. But my heart raced. Roan Fours, the man I'd sat in a room with every week for more than three years while he un-peeled the layers of my psyche so gently and skillfully: here he was, making plans to leave his family for some titian-haired temptress. *This time next year.*

This time next year the skinny wife would be living in some shit flat somewhere because it would be all she could afford, and his kids would have to shuttle back and forth between two shit flats and sit making awkward conversation with Alicia, and look-ing after their mum because her heart would be broken and she wouldn't be the mum they knew anymore, she'd be a new mum, and their childhoods would be shattered and changed. And how did I know all this? I just did. I could see it in the skulking form of the son with his spliff and his fox, who already knew that life was going to be hard, and in the confident swagger of the big-boned daughter with the booming voice who thought that life was always going to be this easy. And I saw it in the nervous elbow-rubbing of the wife who'd built her life around a man she thought would never let her down, while knowing all along that he would. I knew it because I could see it. With my own eyes. Because, as I keep telling you, I'm not stupid.

I felt the red wine start to sour in my stomach.

And then I moved back into the shadows again at the sound of the front door opening and closing once more. I heard soft foot-steps approach and then turn the corner.

A male voice. "Flynn. Mate. Over here."

"Yo."

"Happy New Year and all that."

"Yeah."

"Man. 2019."

"Fuck. Yeah."

"Hope it's not as shit as 2018."

"All years are shit."

"True. Very true."

I could see the shadowy outline of the two boys fist-bumping each other through the hedges. Then I saw them turn the corner and head toward the gap between the trees. I flattened myself into the farthest corner. Another load of fireworks went off, and I used the noise to cover the sound of me burrowing my way into the undergrowth.

"Whoa," I heard one of the boys say. "Look. Rough sleepers."

I saw the light from a phone arcing across my little campsite.

I felt a burst of territorialism and had to stop myself from storming over and telling them to leave my shit alone.

"Wonder who it is?" said one of the boys.

"Looks like a girl," said the other. "Look. Pink sleeping bag."

"God, that's really sad. Fancy having to sleep rough when you're a girl."

"Got wine though," said one of them, holding up my empty bottle.

I saw them both stop then and look around the plot. And once they were reassured that the mysterious rough sleeper wasn't about to jump out at them, they sat down and built themselves a zoot.

I was close to "Clive's" bedroom window in my little hidden corner. I glanced up at the muted light seeping from his curtains and wondered what he was doing in there. Poor old Clive and his nylon counterpane.

The smell of weed reached me a minute later. Their voices drifted slowly across with their exhaled smoke. "Things are going to be different this year."

I couldn't tell which boy was speaking; they both sounded the same to me.

"Oh yeah. You mean . . . ?"

"Yeah. The mask's coming off."

One of them laughed. Then the other one joined in.

"No more Mr. Nice Guy?"

"No more Mr. Nice Guy. Fuck that. Fuck it hard."

More laughter.

"This time next year."

"Yeah, this time next year."

"Maybe we'll be famous."

"Infamous."

"Yeah . . ."

More fireworks obliterated the rest of that particular conversation.

After a few minutes they packed their stuff away and got to their feet.

"No fox tonight?" said one of them.

"Probably scared by the fireworks," said the other.

They both paused and looked down at my little pile of possessions. "I wonder if the homeless girl will turn up."

"Maybe she's already here."

"Ooooh, scary!"

"Shall we leave her something?"

"Like what?"

"I dunno. The rest of this champagne?"

I noticed for the first time that one of them was holding a bottle by the neck.

"Yeah. Why not, I don't want it."

They planted the bottle carefully on the ground by my things. Then one of them said, "Happy New Year, homeless girl."

And then the other one said, "Hope your year gets better, homeless girl."

And then they disappeared again.

I watched them part ways on the street outside. I saw Joshua walk slowly across the street to his house and his equally lanky friend walk the other way, down the hill.

And then the fireworks stopped; the sky cleared; it fell silent. I took off my trainers and put on the big fluffy socks I'd packed. I tucked myself inside my sleeping bag. I sniffed the rim of the half-drunk bottle of champagne and thought better of it. I switched on my phone and replied to some messages, including one from Aaron saying he was on his way home and he'd see me in the morning. I stared up at the sky, the fresh 2019 sky. Black, new, unwritten-on.

38

Cate

CATE GOES TO see her house in Kilburn on Sunday. She doesn't like going during the week when the builders are there and she gets in the way and they look at her curiously as if she has somehow caught them in the act of doing something bad.

It's early when she leaves the flat; the children are still asleep, and Roan is in bed, propped up on pillows with his laptop, catching up on some work. She decides to walk; it'll take thirty minutes, and it's a pleasant morning. She crosses the street and peers into the empty plot through the foliage. You would never know, she thinks to herself, you would never know about the detectives and the police cars and the helicopters; it was as if none of it had ever happened. Then she walks past Owen Pick's house, not avoiding it for once. All is quiet. Curtains are drawn. The morning has only just come.

In her empty house in Kilburn, she can see her breath. Her footsteps ring off the bare floorboards; carpets will be coming, tiles will be coming, curtains and furniture and wallpaper and cushions will be coming. The bare bones are in place now, and she can almost picture it as her home again. She stares from the window on the mezzanine level, out into their wrecked back garden. It's full of bags of cement and lengths of wood and the grass is obliterated by builders' debris. She pictures herself out there, in a few months' time: it will be high summer, the sky will be acid blue, they will have some nice new garden furniture—she's already picked out the things she wants from the IKEA catalog—and maybe there will be a barbecue going. She will no longer have to see Owen Pick's house every time she leaves her front door. No longer have to pass by the scary empty plot with its screaming foxes.

She inhales deeply and holds on to the quiet thrill that passes through her, the anticipation of it all. She passes up the staircase to the room that is very near to being her bedroom again; it overlooks the street, out toward a row of unthreatening terraced houses, just like hers. No sinister empty spaces, no ancient, creaking trees throwing shadows across her bed, no sex pests lurking behind heavy doors and grubby curtains. Just normal houses filled with normal people. She will never take Kilburn for granted again.

She takes some photos of the progress for Roan to look at later and then she locks the door behind her, lays the palm of her hand briefly, affectionately, against the outside wall of the house and heads back to the flat.

———

Roan is in the kitchen making toast when she gets in.

He says, "Want some? I can put another slice in?"

She says, "No, thank you, I had breakfast already."

He looks strangely perky, she thinks. Upbeat. "Have you seen that?" he says, pointing at the screen of his laptop. She touches it and she sees the BBC home page. The headline reads: "COLLEGE LECTURER ARRESTED FOR THE ABDUCTION OF SAFFYRE MADDOX."

"Oh my God," she says. "They've arrested him!"

"I know," says Roan. "I'm so relieved."

She glances up from the screen. "Relieved?" It strikes her as a strange choice of word.

"Yes," he says. "Now maybe we'll find out where she is."

She drops her eyes again and reads the story.

Former college lecturer Owen Pick, 33, has been formally arrested and is being held at Kentish Town police station charged with the abduction of missing teenager Saffyre Maddox. Miss Maddox, 17, was last seen nine days ago on Valentine's night heading into Hampstead village after telling family she was going to meet a friend. Police sources say that Pick, who is unmarried and lives with his aunt in her flat in Hampstead, has provided no explanation for blood traces found at his property. He has also been found to be active on a number of what are known as "incel forums," internet websites where men who identify as "involuntary celibates," unable to form sexual relationships with women despite a desire to do so, come together to share their frustrations. It is theorized that the abduction of Miss Maddox might have been the result of the online radicalization of Pick by other forum users. Many recent mass shootings in the USA have been attributed to the influence of radical elements on such sites.

Pick's family have been unavailable for comment. It is believed that his bail has been set at one million pounds.

"Incel forums?" says Cate, her stomach churning at the concept. She'd seen a documentary about incels once that had chilled her to her core. The hatred and the bile and the bitterness. "Christ."

"I know," says Roan. "Kind of adds up though, doesn't it? When you look at him, when you see where he lives. I mean, you can tell, just by looking at him, that no one gives a shit about him."

"Have you ever treated a patient like that?" she asks a moment later. "You know, someone who hates girls because girls don't like them?"

"God yes," says Roan. "Little boys who will totally grow up to be on incel forums talking about the best way to rape women. I certainly have. I had an eleven-year-old boy once, a few years ago; he'd been caught at school writing elaborate and very violent rape fantasies."

Cate shakes her head, slowly, wondering not for the first time about the grueling nature of her husband's job. "Doesn't it ever, just, you know, get to you? Dealing with kids like that?"

He stops buttering his toast and turns to look at Cate. "Of course it does," he says. "Christ. Of course it does."

———

It's the Sunday before the children go back to school after the February half-term, which means that Georgia will spend the whole day in her pajamas angrily finishing her homework, shouting at junctures about how much she hates school and hates exams and hates Cate for making her go to school and hates the government for making her go to school and hates life and hates everybody and doesn't care about her GCSEs anyway. Until finally the homework will be done and she will make herself something sugary to eat and have it in front of the television which she will feel she has totally worked for and deserves and enjoy all the more for it. It will be a high-drama day, a draining day and Cate is ready for it from the moment she hears Georgia's bedroom door opening at eleven thirty that morning.

"Hello, angel."

"Urgh," says Georgia. "I woke up at, like, eight o'clock or something and I couldn't get back to sleep."

"Well," says Cate, "I came in and looked at you at about ten thirty and you were out cold."

"Yeah, well, I was kind of drifting in and out."

"Want something to eat?"

Georgia yawns and shakes her head. "It's nearly lunchtime. I'll wait."

"I went to see the house earlier," Cate says, turning on her phone and bringing it to Georgia.

"Oh," says Georgia, brightening. "House! House! Let me see!"

Cate shows her the photos and then heads down the hallway to Josh's bedroom to check in on him. He's normally up earlier than Georgia. She would have heard the shower going by now, the sound through the wall of music coming from his phone which he props up against the tooth mug. But there'd been nothing.

She knocks gently. "Joshy?"

There's no response.

"Josh?"

She pushes the door open.

Josh's bed is empty.

She goes to the bathroom and finds Roan sitting on the toilet with his trousers round his ankles playing Candy Crush.

"Seen Josh?"

"No," he says. "He's still in bed, isn't he?"

"No," she says. "He's not. He must have gone out somewhere."

She goes into the kitchen and takes her phone back from Georgia. "Any idea where Josh is?" she asks her.

Georgia shakes her head. "I think I heard the front door go half an hour ago?"

Cate composes a message to Josh and sends it. *Where are u?* She watches the tick double but not turn blue. She sighs.

The ticks stay gray for another hour. She calls him. The call goes through to his voice mail. She leaves him a message. They have lunch—spaghetti with chili and garlic and prawns. She scoops out the last portion into a bowl, covers it with cling film, and puts it in the fridge.

At two o'clock Georgia finally settles down at the kitchen table to do her homework. Roan and Cate sit side by side in the living room and try to watch a film on TV, but Cate can't concentrate. The room grows gloomy as the sun starts to slide down the horizon and Cate checks her phone every thirty seconds. She sends Josh five more messages and calls him three more times. As the credits roll on the film she turns to Roan and says, "I think we should call the police."

"What!"

"It's nearly four. He's been gone about five hours."

"Cate. He's fourteen years old. It's daytime."

"I know," she says. "But he's not the sort of fourteen-year-old to just disappear. He always tells me when he's going out. And why isn't he answering his phone?"

"Probably run out of charge, or maybe he's on the tube."

"Josh doesn't *go* on the tube," she replies with exasperation. Really, sometimes it felt like Roan didn't actually know his children. "He gets panic attacks, remember?"

"Well, whatever, I really think calling the police would be a bit over the top."

"But how long are we going to wait?"

"Dinnertime?" says Roan. "But even then, it won't even have been twelve hours." He stands up and stretches. "I think," he says, "that I might just go for a run. I can keep an eye out for him on the way."

"Yes," says Cate. "Yes. Brilliant. You do that. I'm going to try and find a number for Flynn."

Flynn is Josh's only known friend.

He's never been inside their house; he skulks outside and texts Josh if they're going out together. He has never been more than a flash of red hair and a name to Cate.

"Georgia," she says, coming into the kitchen. "You don't happen to have a number for Flynn, do you?"

"Flynn?"

"Yes, you know, Josh's friend. With the red hair?"

"Why on earth would I have a number for *Flynn*?"

"I don't know, darling. I just thought maybe you might. I mean, is he on any social media with you?"

"*Of course* he isn't. God."

"Do you know his surname?"

"Oh my God, no. Of course I don't. I don't even know him. He's just . . . he's just Josh's friend. He's nothing to do with me."

"Do you . . . ?" Cate starts cautiously. "Do you have any theories about where Josh might be? He's not answering his phone."

Georgia exhales heavily. "Mum," she says, "I'm trying to do my homework and you're really not helping right now."

"No, no, I'm sorry. You're right. But I'm worried about him . . . it's getting dark . . ."

"He's fourteen years old, Mum. He's fine. Try looking in the plot across the road."

Cate stiffens. "What?"

"The building plot. You know. Where the police were. He used to hang out a lot there last summer. Him and Flynn sometimes too."

"Hang out doing what?"

"How am I supposed to know? Do you think I care?"

"No. But . . ."

"Look, he's your son. Your guess is as good as mine. He's a mystery to me. All I know is that he used to hang out across the road sometimes."

"But how did he get in?"

"There's a gap," Georgia says dismissively, as if everyone should already know about the gap. "Around the corner. Where the wall is low."

Georgia turns her attention back to the schoolbook in front of her, and Cate heads down the hallway. She picks up her coat and her door keys and heads outside.

The sky is turning from gray to black in petrol tones. She switches on the light on her phone and feels her way along the foliage around the corner until she locates the point where the trees are wide enough apart to allow her to squeeze through. She lands on the other side, on a patch of ragged grass. The plot looks vast from this angle. She throws the light from her phone across the space.

"Josh," she calls out. "Josh?"

She shines her light into corners and behind machinery. There is nobody there.

Across the space she peers through the trees and into the back garden of Owen Pick's house. There, facing the plot, is a sash window with drawn curtains. His bedroom. She pictures him there behind it, his face lit by the glow of his laptop, writing depraved things on incel forums, plotting his abduction of a beautiful, troubled young girl, fantasizing about what he was going to do to her when he finally had her in his disgusting clutches.

She glances around as though maybe she is here, Saffyre Maddox, as though the dozen police officers who spent three days combing every inch of this space might just have missed her, that she might just rise up from the ground and walk toward her.

She feels her phone buzz inside her hand and switches it on. It's a text from Josh.

On my way home, Mum. See u soon x.

Where've you been? she replies hastily.

Cinema, he replies. *Phone on silent. Soz.*

She turns off the phone and clutches it to her heart, gazing upward into the oily sky. *On his way home.* Her heart loosens. Her breathing steadies. The cinema. Her baby boy had been at the cinema.

She clambers back through the gap between the tree and lands in front of a surprised dog walker.

"Oh," says the woman, clutching her heart.

"Sorry," says Cate. "I was looking for my son. But now I've found him."

The dog walker looks behind her as if the son might be about to appear.

"He was at the cinema," she says breathlessly. "Not in there."

The woman nods and carries on her way, the small dog skittering along behind her, throwing Cate a few bemused looks over his tail as he goes.

"What did you see?" she asks Josh when he walks in a few minutes later, cheeks red with the night cold.

"That thing with Dwayne Johnson," he says. "About wrestlers. Can't remember what it was called."

"Oh," she says, wondering at her son's choice of film. "Was it any good?"

Josh shrugs. "It was OK. Can I eat something?"

She pulls the pasta from the fridge and puts it in the microwave.

"Why didn't you tell me?" she asks. "That you were going to the cinema? How come you just disappeared?"

He shrugs. "Just a bit last-minute."

"But I was in here." She points at the ground. "Like literally, standing right here. You could have just popped your head around the door and said goodbye."

He shrugs again. "I'm sorry. I didn't think."

She's been using her phone as she talks, to google the film her son says he's just been to see. She finds something called *Fighting with My Family*. She turns the screen of her phone toward him and shows him the picture. "This?" she says. "You went to see this?"

He nods.

"Have you been out on a date?" she says, a smile forming on her lips, a warm glow going through her at the thought of her funny, lonely boy, sitting in the back row of the movies, watching a quirky comedy about female wrestlers with his arm around a girl.

"No," he says.

She thinks he's lying.

If it were Georgia standing in front of her blatantly lying, she would not waste a second before calling her out on it. She would say, "Bullshit, tell me what really happened," and Georgia would smile that smile she smiles when she knows she's been backed into a corner and then tell her the truth.

But she can't bear to put her boy on the spot, to make him squirm, to make him suffer. He wouldn't smile a smile. He would just look pained. So she just says, "OK," and takes his pasta out of the microwave.

39

Owen

Owen sits up with a start. It's been three hours since his last interview with the detectives, and he's been sitting in his cell with no idea what's happening next. He was given lunch in his cell: some kind of meat in bread crumbs with potatoes and green beans. And then a beige pudding with a jam sauce. He's almost embarrassed by how much he enjoyed it; it's the sort of meal his mother used to cook for him, bland and salty and safe. He scraped his tray absolutely clean.

"Who is it?" he asks now.

"I have no idea," says the police officer drily.

"Am I going to them, or are they . . . ?"

"I'm taking you to an interview room. Can you stand back from the cell door, please?"

He stands back from the cell door, and the officer opens it and leads him through three sets of locked gates to a small blue room. Tessie is sitting there, wearing a green velvet wrap around her shoulders and huge silver earrings with matching green stones at their centers. Her mouth is already pursed with disapproval.

She starts talking before he's even sat down. "I'm not staying long, Owen. But I brought you some things. Your phone. Though you're probably not allowed it. And some underwear and a change of clothing, etc. I bought it new. I didn't want to go rifling through your things. Especially not after what the police found in your drawers. Good God, Owen. And that girl, Owen! What on earth has happened to that lovely girl?"

Tessie covers her face with her fingers, mismatched rings overlapping into a kind of armor. She stares down at the table for a long moment and then looks up, and her eyes are full of tears.

"Owen. Please. You can tell me. Where is she? What have you done with her?"

Owen smiles. He can't help it. It's just too ridiculous.

"Tessie," he says, his hands clutching the edge of the table. "Really? You really think I had something to do with it?"

"Well, what on earth else do you expect me to think? Her blood! Outside your wall! Her phone cover outside your bedroom window. Date-rape drugs in your sock drawer. And all those things, those terrible things you wrote on the internet. My goodness, Owen. You don't have to be Miss Marple to work it out. But for the sake of that poor girl's family, you have to tell the police what happened."

"Oh my God!" Owen tugs at his hair and then bangs the table. "I did not do anything to that girl! I'm not even sure I saw that girl! I just saw *a* girl! And it might not even have *been* a girl. It might have been a boy. And the only reason, literally the *only* reason I said anything was because I was trying to be helpful. I mean, Tessie, seriously, if I had killed that girl or done something dreadful to her, why would I have told the police that I'd seen her? Why? Think about it, for God's sake. Just think about it. It doesn't make any sense!"

Tessie pushes down her lower lip and shrugs. "No," she says. "It does not make sense. But then, Owen, nothing about you makes any sense. Nothing. I mean, what are you, thirty-four . . . ?"

Owen sighs. "I'm thirty-three, Tessie. Thirty-three."

She continues. "Thirty-three, yet you've never had a girlfriend. You rarely go out. You dress like . . ." She gestures at him vaguely. "Well, you dress very strangely for a man of your age. You only eat white food. I mean, Owen, let's face it, you're very odd."

"And that means I killed a teenage girl, does it?"

She narrows her eyes at him. But she doesn't reply. Instead she says, "I've spoken to your father. He's very worried."

Owen rolls his eyes. "I'm sure he is."

"Yes," she says firmly. "He is. I suggested he come and see you, but he'll need some persuading, he's slightly . . . overwhelmed."

"Don't bother, please, Tessie. I have no desire whatsoever to see him. Certainly not in these circumstances." Owen lets his head drop so that his gaze falls between his kneecaps to the scuffed linoleum on the floor. He's tired. He has had two nights on a horrible bed in a cell. He has had hours in the interview room with a rotating group of detectives trying harder and harder to get him to tell them where Saffyre Maddox is, and Owen has seen enough police dramas to know how these things are orchestrated, layering on different approaches until the interviewee doesn't know their left from their right. But it doesn't matter how much they try to befuddle and confound him, the one constant, the one thing he knows for sure, is that he has nothing to do with Saffyre Maddox or her disappearance.

Barry told him something interesting yesterday.

Apparently Saffyre Maddox was once under the professional care of the Lycra man across the road, the jogger. Apparently Lycra

Man is a child psychologist at the Portman. Apparently Saffyre Maddox was under his care for over three years, and apparently Lycra Man has a rock-solid alibi. He was in bed with his wife.

Owen can hardly believe that the police would take such a flimsy alibi on face value. It's typical of course, typical to give credence to married people, to assume that of course married people would be in bed together on Valentine's night, that married people would have no reason to lie about their whereabouts.

He'd told the police yesterday about Bryn. He'd been unable to think of any other reasonable explanation to offer them for the presence of Rohypnol in his bedroom.

"Bryn who?" they'd asked.

"I don't know his surname."

"Address?"

"I don't know where he lives. Somewhere just outside London. His train comes into Euston, that's all I know. And he's thirty-three. Like me. Oh. He's got a website! It's www.yourloss.net."

"Bryn someone. Outside London. Thirty-three. Got a website."

Skeptical was an understatement. But they'd gone away and looked for Bryn and come to Owen this morning and told him that no such person existed. That his website didn't exist, that the only people in the UK who were thirty-three and called Bryn lived in Chester, Aberdeen, Cardigan, Cardiff, London, Bangor, Newport, and Dartmouth. There was, apparently, nobody in the Home Counties called Bryn who was currently thirty-three years old.

"Well," Owen said. "There you go. Thanks to the British press and my face plastered all over the papers, he's had time to disappear. But he's there, in all the forums you found me on. Run searches for him, for YourLoss. You'll see. He's a leader. An influencer. People kind of look up to him."

"And you?" said a detective whose name Owen hadn't quite caught. "Did you look up to him?"

"Yes," he said. "In a way. But not," he quickly countered, "not in *that* way. When he gave me those drugs, when he told me what he wanted me to do, what he wanted *all of us* to do . . ."

"All of us?"

"Yes, us on the forums."

"Incels, you mean?"

He hadn't liked the sound of that. It had made them sound like Masons or Ku Klux Klan, giraffes, even, something other. Something not quite human.

"So you would call yourself an incel, would you, Owen?"

He shook his head. "No," he said firmly. "No. Going on those forums—it was a phase. It was a response to what happened with my job. I was cross and frustrated. I felt impotent. I needed to vent and the forums gave me a place to vent. But I never thought I was one of them. I never felt I belonged. And Bryn . . ."

"Yes, tell us about *Bryn*." They'd said his name as if it were in italics, as if he were a character in a book.

"Bryn was just funny, I suppose. A lot of those guys on the forums were really dark and humorless, took it all so seriously. Bryn was funny. And charismatic. People liked him. *I* liked him. But then when I finally met him in person, I saw him for what he really was."

"And what was that, Owen?"

"Well," he said, after a moment's consideration. "Mad. I suppose."

But now as he sits opposite his aunt and thinks about the cruel injustices being played out against him as a single man, an "odd" man, a lonely man, a man who is clearly not decent or honest enough to have found a mate to give him alibis for his heinous crimes against young girls, he feels a yearning for Bryn and his view of the world. Not the stuff about impregnating women against their will, but the stuff about how imbalanced the world was, how it was all geared toward favoring the wrong people for the wrong reasons. He would like to discuss that now with someone who saw the truth. But Bryn has gone—Bryn, or whatever his real name was. He's disappeared like one of those little felt rabbits in a sleight-of-hand trick. Pouf! And now no one will ever believe him about how he ended up with date-rape drugs in his drawer, that he'd never had any intention of using them.

He looks back up at Tessie. She's staring at the top of his head.

She says, "Do they let you wash in here?"

He nods.

"Do you want me to bring you some soap? Some nice shampoo?"

He nods again. "Yes," he says in a small voice. "Please. And, Tessie, can you do something else for me? Please. Can you contact someone for me? The woman I went out with on Valentine's night? We'd been chatting a lot since. Messaging. And we were supposed to be going out again next week. I just don't want her to think, you know, that I've forgotten about her."

"Oh Owen. Dear Owen. You're all over the papers, all over the news. I can guarantee she knows why you haven't been in touch."

He swallows down another burst of anger, closes his eyes, and then slowly opens them. "Please, though, Tessie. Would you mind? Whether she knows where I am or not, I'd like her to know that I'm thinking about her. That I wish . . . I wish I wasn't here, that this wasn't happening, that things were just . . . you know. Please, Tessie."

She rolls her eyes and takes a notepad from her bag and a pen.

He gives her Deanna's email address, as it's the only one of her contact details he can remember off by heart.

"Tell her I think she's amazing, please, Tessie. Tell her I'm not that person, the person in the papers. Tell her that if she comes to see me, I can explain everything. Tell her to come and see me, Tessie. Please. If you don't do anything else. Just that one thing. Yes?"

He watches her close her eyes; he sees the hollows of her cheek form and then disappear again. "Fine," she says. "Fine. Though I'm not lying on your behalf, Owen. I'm not going to say anything I don't believe is true."

"No." He shakes his head. "Don't say anything apart from just what I said. Promise me."

She sighs and says, "Yes. Yes, fine." Then she glances at her wristwatch and sighs again. "I have to go. It's my afternoon at the shop. Good God"—she gets to her feet and grinds her jaw—"what on earth am I going to say to people? Because they'll ask, Owen, they'll ask."

Tessie works one afternoon a week at the Oxfam bookshop in the village. It makes her feel good about herself and her indulgent life. He watches her leave. She doesn't touch him or attempt any sort of farewell. She just goes.

The police officer standing in the corner opens the door and leads her out.

The other police officer, sitting at the end of the table, clears her throat.

"Ready?" she says to Owen.

He gets to his feet and follows her to the door.

The room still smells of Tessie, of dusty velvet and cheap fabric conditioner and Penhaligon's iris perfume.

40

Saffyre

I GOT HOME at 6:00 a.m. on New Year's Day. Aaron was asleep, and Angelo was in the little bed I kept by the side of mine. He got up lazily when he saw me walk in and I picked him up and smelled him and sat him down on the bed next to me. I felt empty. Blank. It was so quiet. All night long I'd fallen in and out of sleep to the sounds of revelers, the wind through the tall branches of the trees, cars going past every few minutes, the chipboard gates creaking, birds twitching. Every time I fell asleep, I'd dream that the fox was there, licking my face, breathing into my ear, and I'd wake up and find myself alone. It was electric; it was cold; I was alive out there in the black of night.

Now I stared at the dirty white of my bedroom ceiling, the pink paper shade with the cutout heart shapes that I'd chosen when I was eight years old from Homebase. It came with a matching duvet set and table lamp. I didn't know who that child was or the person she might have been if Harrison John hadn't done what he'd done to her when she was ten years old.

It was silent apart from the thrum of the sleeping building. I thought, I don't belong here. I belong out there. And once again the other part of me, the part that does her homework and paints her nails and watches *The Great British Bake Off,* that part of me whispered in my ear and said: "Are you sure you're not mad?" But I knew I was not mad. I knew I was changing. Becoming. Unfurling.

I took my things again that night, and slept across the street from Roan Fours. I told Aaron I was sleeping over at Jasmin's. He just gave me a look, a look that said, "I kind of don't believe you but you're nearly an adult and you're close to breaking and I don't want to be the one to push you over the edge."

The night after that I slept at home, just for Aaron's sake, not for my own, but my soul ached at being trapped indoors. I felt swallowed up by my mattress, my duvet, the warm air swirling around me. I felt claustrophobic, anxious; the sheets were twisted around my legs when I woke up the next morning, and for a minute I thought I was paralyzed. I felt a sharp feeling of panic right in the pit of my gut. I untwisted my legs from the sheet and sat up panting. I knew I couldn't spend another night indoors. I knew then that my change was nearly complete. At night I would wait for Aaron to go to bed and then I would leave.

I didn't sleep those nights. Barely. I just lay there in the dark feeling my soul fill, my head vibrating, my blood flowing through my veins, warm and vital. I didn't need to sleep. I was operating on some other level, using some weird energy pumped into me from the moon above me, from the soil beneath.

At dawn I'd go back to the flat and get ready for school. Aaron had no idea and if he did, he never said anything. He probably thought I had a boyfriend. He treated me like blown glass, like he couldn't say anything to me. It worked in my favor.

Then, halfway through January, it happened. It was a moment, I think, that I'd known would happen one day. A moment that had sat just out of my line of sight since I was ten years old. Because in any community, even a community set on the edges of a major arterial junction where six lanes of traffic thunder past morning, noon, and night, a community of double-decker buses and high-rise buildings and billboards and banks, there is still a small world in small streets where people's paths cross and uncross and cross again, where you know people from the schools they went to, from the places their mums shop, from walking the same lines to the same places at the same times, and you know that, even in a community like mine, at some point you will see the person who stuck their fingers inside you when you were ten years old. You just will.

And there he was, in the cold cloak of early dawn as I turned the corner from Roan's road onto the Finchley Road. There he was, dressed in black, with his hood up just like mine, a Puffa coat just like mine, a bag slung over his shoulder just like me. There was no other soul around; sodium light from the lamp in between us shone off particles of gauzy morning mist. At first I felt nervous because he was a man and it was dark and we were alone. But then I caught the shape of his face, the heavy brow, the slight dip in his nose as if someone had pressed it in with their thumb.

Harrison John.

The boy who wiped out the girl with the pink lampshades.

He looked at me. I looked at him.

I saw that he saw me. He smiled. He said, "Saffyre Maddox."

I said nothing, walked past him as fast as I could, looking for the bright lights of early-morning traffic coming down the Finchley Road.

"Saffyre Maddox!" he called after me. "Not going to say hello?"

I wanted to turn and walk back up the hill, square up to him, breathe into his face, say, "*You filthy, disgusting piece of shit, I hope you die.*"

But I didn't. I kept walking. Kept walking. My heart pounding. My stomach swirling.

I got home, and I scrambled through all the drawers in the kitchen until I found a paper clip. I untwisted it into a small hook and I rolled down my socks. I touched the tip of the hook against my skin. I pulled it back and forth until finally a bead of red appeared, and then another, and another, until finally I felt something stronger than the power of Harrison John.

41

Cate

FEBRUARY HALF-TERM IS over. The flat is quiet. Not the same quiet as when the kids are still in bed, not the spring-loaded quietness of bedroom doors yet to be opened, breakfasts and showers yet to be had, but the proper, pure silence of an empty house: coats taken from hooks, bags collected from chairs, empty beds, wet bath mats, children at school, Roan at work, a day ahead of nothing but her.

Cate should be working, but her focus is splintered.

There was another sex attack the day before. It's been all over the news because the police have taken the step of issuing safety guidelines to women in the area. The victim this time was a middle-aged woman, walking back from lunch with friends on West End Lane as dusk fell, pulled into the area behind an estate agent's office just off the main road and "subjected to a serious sexual assault." The attacker was described as white, slim, twenty to forty years old, much of his face covered by a stretchy black covering of the sort that motorcyclists wear under their helmets. The attacker said no words at all during the attack and left the woman in need of medical attention.

Dusk.

That was the word in the news article that had jumped out at her. Such a very specific word for such a fleeting part of the day. Immediately, she'd thought about dusk yesterday, when she was prowling around the building plot with her phone light on, looking for her missing son. Her missing son who'd returned moments later, starving hungry and with a story of seeing a Dwayne Johnson movie on his own.

Dusk.

She goes to the door of her son's bedroom. Her hand grips the doorknob.

She pushes the door open. The curtains are drawn, the bed is made, his pajamas are folded on the pillow. She pulls open the curtains and lets in the weak morning sun. She turns on the overhead light. You wouldn't think anyone lived in this room. Josh has no stuff. While Georgia always has three cups half filled with stale water on her bedside table, handfuls of jewelry, a book or two, numerous chargers snaked into each other, a sock, a balled-up tissue, a ChapStick with the lid missing, and a pile of coins on her bedside table, Josh has nothing. Just a coaster.

Dusk . . .

She falls to her knees and peers under his bed. There's his laptop, plugged into the wall to charge, the wires all neatly tucked away. She pulls it out and rests it on her knees; she won't sit on his bed, as she worries she won't be able to get his covers as neat as he's left them and he'll know she was in here.

She opens it and switches it on and knows already that the password he used for everything when he was small and she was allowed to know his password (donkey321) will no longer be his password and she will have to find some other way to access his computer. But she got quite good at code breaking last year when she thought Roan was having an affair. She'd even managed to access his work log-in. She waits for the screen to wake up and then she types in "donkey321." She waits for the error message but instead the computer switches screens and she is in.

She blinks in surprise and feels a surge of relief. If there was anything on his computer that he didn't want anyone to see he would for sure have changed his password to one his mum didn't know.

She clicks through his windows. Worksheets for maths, iTunes, an essay on *Animal Farm*, and a browser with ten tabs open, nearly all schoolwork related. The last tab is for Vue Cinemas and shows the films currently showing at the cinema on the Finchley Road.

She feels her heartstrings loosen a little.

There, she thinks, there. Just as he'd said. Gone to the movies.

She scrolls through the timings. *Fighting with My Family*— 3:20 p.m. That would have finished well after dusk.

Then she clicks on his browsing history (she'd done this once on Georgia's laptop a year or so ago and been flabbergasted by the eclectic range of pornography her then fourteen-year-old daughter had been watching).

The most recent search term is "vue finchley road films today." She vaguely registers the fact that he hasn't used his laptop to browse since yesterday morning. The search before that is "Owen pick arrest."

The search before that is for "Owen pick."

The search before that is for "Owen pick saffyre maddox."

The search before that is "saffyre Maddox missing."

The search before that is "saffyre Maddox missing teenager."

This is totally understandable.

Cate has been obsessed with the story of Saffyre Maddox ever since it broke. Hardly surprising, given that Saffyre is a former patient of Roan's and that the man who abducted her lives across the street from them. Cate should not be surprised in the least that her son is taking such a keen interest in the story. Her current browsing history, she is sure, would look very similar to his.

She closes the laptop and slides it carefully back under his bed. Then she goes to his cupboards. Here his clothes are folded into squares and piled neatly. This is also where he keeps schoolwork he doesn't need to take to school, and his pens and stationery for doing homework are on a table that clips flat to the wall when he's not using it. Why on earth he bothers every day to clear the desktop, clip it to the wall, and put everything back into the cupboard, Cate cannot begin to imagine. He is Roan's child, not hers, in that respect. In the bottom of the cupboard is his linen basket. She decides, while she is here, to empty it. She pulls the basket out of the cupboard and sees, tucked behind it, a carrier bag.

A scrunched-up bag is not a normal thing to find in Josh's domain, so she takes it out, unties the knot, and peers inside. Old sports gear. A strong smell of damp and something worse than damp. Not quite sweat, but something as animal as sweat. She pulls out Lycra leggings: they're Roan's. Then a shiny, long-sleeved top with neon orange stripes on the arms. Also Roan's.

She pulls out a pair of black socks and a pair of grippy gloves. And then last of all she pulls out a piece of black jersey that she cannot at first identify. She holds it out and turns it this way and that, stretches it out and puts her hand through a hole in the middle of it.

And then finally she works out what it is.

It's a balaclava.

42

Owen

EVERY BONE IN Owen's body hurts. The mattress he sleeps on at Tessie's is about a hundred years old. Its springs are gone, it sags in the middle, it's soft and flaccid, but his body has adjusted to it over the years. The bed in his cell is basically a slab of concrete with a thin mattress on top of it. He can feel his hip bones grinding against it even when he's sleeping.

He can't remember his bed at home, the home where he lived with his mum before she died. He can't remember if it was soft or hard. He remembered it was a single bed in a single room in the tiny flat that had been all that was left of the family home he'd shared with his parents until he was eleven years old, when it had been sold and split into two. It was in Manor House, a never-going-to-be-gentrified area of north London way out on the Piccadilly line. His mum had made it look really nice because she was good at that sort of thing, but it was essentially a horrible flat. She'd always said, "This is your inheritance, it's all in your name if anything happens to me." And then something had happened to her. A brain aneurism, when she was forty-eight. Owen had got home from sixth-form college and found her slumped facedown on the kitchen table.

He'd thought maybe she was drunk, which was a strange thing for him to have thought, as she, like him, drank only on very rare occasions.

The flat hadn't ended up being much of an inheritance. Once he'd paid off all his mum's credit card debts, of which there'd been a very surprising amount, there'd been nothing left. A few thousand pounds.

And then he'd ended up in Tessie's spare room with the saggy mattress, which, like everything about his tragic existence, he'd grown used to and come to accept unquestioningly.

Breakfast is brought to him in his cell: leathery toast and cheap jam, a mug of tea and a hard-boiled egg. He wolfs it down, hiding the toast crusts under the paper napkin so that the officer who takes his tray away again won't see them.

A few minutes later DI Angela Currie appears outside his cell. She is wearing a fitted dress with big patch pockets on the front, thick tights, and boots. She has her hands inside the pockets with her thumbs hanging over the top. She looks very jolly.

"Morning, Owen. How are we today?"

"I'm OK."

"Nice breakfast?"

"It was OK."

"Ready to talk some more?"

Owen shrugs and sighs. "Is there anything left to talk about?"

She smiles. "Oh yes, Owen, oh yes. Plenty."

The guard unlocks his door, and he follows DI Currie through the byzantine corridors to the interview suites. He had a shampoo last night with the things that Tessie dropped off for him. His hair is now clean and his clothes are clean, but he still has a big scab on his forehead from where he accidentally stabbed himself with the scissors, and he still has an asymmetric fringe that makes him look slightly psychotic.

In the interview room he sits himself down in front of DIs Currie and Henry. DI Henry is looking a little the worse for wear today. Apparently he has a newborn and is finding the sleepless nights quite painful. Not that Owen has been chatting to DI Henry about his personal life, but he picks things up when they're talking between themselves.

A moment later Barry arrives. He smells overwhelmingly of aftershave, not the fresh sporty sort of stuff that comes in blue glass bottles from the airport, but the heady, dark sort of stuff that comes in brown bottles from ancient shops in Mayfair backstreets. He says, "Good morning, Owen," but doesn't make eye contact with him.

The interview is set up in the way with which Owen is becoming very familiar. He clears his throat, takes a sip of water from a polystyrene cup, puts it back on the table.

"So, Owen. Today is Monday, the twenty-fifth of February. It's now been eleven days since Saffyre went missing. The blood we found on your bedroom wall—"

"It's not *my client's* bedroom wall," Barry says stiffly. He has to correct them every single time. "It's a wall that is part of a house that has lots of other people in it. It does not *belong* uniquely to my client's bedroom."

"No, sorry, let me rephrase that. The blood we found on the wall beneath your bedroom window . . . it was at least a week old."

"Possibly older," Barry says. This is all being recorded, and he's not going to let them get away with sloppy wording that might incriminate Owen. "As my client has mentioned on many occasions now, we have no idea how old that blood is, and he was aware of teenagers habitually using the plot on the other side of that wall as a place to gather to take drugs. This girl, who we now know had an association with the family opposite the plot, might well have been using the space herself to hang out in. She might have been high and behaving stupidly one night and injured herself. The blood on that wall proves nothing. Nothing at all other than that Saffyre Maddox was in the vicinity of my client's house at some point over the past couple of weeks."

DI Angela Currie sighs. "Yes," she says. "Indeed. But the fact remains that Saffyre's blood *was* found on a wall beneath your bedroom window and the fact that she was in the vicinity of your home at roughly the time of her disappearance is significant enough for us to pursue the issue, relentlessly if need be. We would not be doing our jobs properly if we didn't. So, Owen, it's been eleven days since she was last seen, by you, outside the house opposite yours."

"It wasn't her," he says. "I know that now. I keep replaying it and replaying it and the more I think about it the more I know it wasn't her. It was a boy."

He sees DIs Currie and Henry exhale heavily. "It was a person, according to your previous statement, matching the description of the missing girl."

"Yes," says Owen, "exactly. Which doesn't mean it was her. It could have been anyone matching the description of the girl. Everyone looks the same with a hood up."

DI Currie doesn't respond to this. Instead she slowly, deliberately, pulls a sheaf of papers from a folder on the table in front of her. She spends a moment looking at the papers, an act of pure, blatant theater. Owen knows this now.

"Owen," she says, showing him the papers. "Do you remember telling us that you weren't sexually attracted to teenage girls?"

He feels a flush of blood to his face. He can sense something bad coming his way. He clears his throat and says, "Yes."

"Do you remember a girl called Jessica Beer?"

"No."

"The name doesn't ring a bell?"

"No," he says again, more forcefully.

"Well, Jessica Beer remembers you, Owen. She was one of your students back in"—she refers to the paper in her hand—"back in 2012. She was seventeen years old. She's twenty-three now, and yesterday I went to see her. We chatted. And she told me about a very worrying incident."

"What? Sorry? Jessica who?" He peers at the paper but can't see anything to explain what's about to happen here.

"Jessica Beer. She claims"—DI Currie leaves a dramatic pause; she would not be winning any Oscars anytime soon—"that you forced yourself on her during a Christmas party on college premises and told her that you'd been watching her in your lessons and that she was pretty. That she was . . . *perfect*. She claims you touched her face and told her that her skin was radiant. That you breathed in her ear."

"What! No! That never happened!"

DI Currie pulls a photograph from her folder and turns it to show to him. It's a very pretty mixed-race girl with soft brown curls, a freckled nose, full rose-pink lips. She looks familiar. But Owen can't recall her entirely. It's possible she'd been a student of his, but then this was six or more years ago and he's had hundreds of students in the intervening years, hundreds of pretty girls. He might well have taught this girl, but one thing was for sure, he had never, ever said those things to her.

"This never happened," he said definitively. "I may well have taught her, and that I can't remember, but I did not talk to this girl, or any girl, ever, in such a fashion. I just wouldn't."

"Were you drunk on the night of the Christmas party in 2012, Owen?"

"Oh my God, how am I supposed to remember. It was seven years ago!"

"Just over six years ago, to be more accurate, Owen."

"Six, seven, whichever, how can I possibly be expected to remember? I do not remember this girl; I do not remember this party."

But Owen does remember this party. He remembers it very well. This party was the reason why he hadn't gone to a Christmas party for years afterward. He had got horribly drunk that year. Some boys who'd been quite friendly to him all term long had plied him with tequila shots. The room had started spinning at one point; he remembered standing in the middle of the dance floor, staring up at a rotating disco ball and then realizing that the whole room was rotating and he was rotating, and he'd run to the toilets and thrown up in a cubicle. Luckily no one had seen him or heard him, and he'd emerged half an hour later slightly gray and clammy and had immediately gone home. But there'd been no incident with a girl. There simply hadn't. He hadn't done that. He wouldn't and he didn't.

"This girl's lying," he says. "Whoever she is. She's lying. Just like those other girls."

"Looks a bit like Saffyre, doesn't she?" says DI Currie, turning the photo back to face her and pulling a really annoying face, as though this was the first time she'd noticed the similarity.

"I don't know," Owen replies. "I barely know what Saffyre looks like."

"Here." She turns a photo of Saffyre to face him.

"Similar coloring," he says. "That's about all."

"Same age. Both very pretty."

"Oh, for God's sake," says Owen, banging his hands down on the table. "I literally don't know who this girl is. I have never seen her before. I've never seen this girl before either." He touches the photo of Saffyre. "I don't like hurting people. I don't like touching people. I don't approach women sexually, ever, which is the exact reason why I'm thirty-three and I've never had sex. I can't look at women. Women terrify me. Girls terrify me. The last thing I would do is go anywhere near a pretty girl at a party and start saying slimy things to them. I wouldn't want to do it, and even if I *did* want to do it, I'd be too scared!"

"But not if you were drunk, Owen. Because that seems to be a unifying feature here, doesn't it? This incident"—DI Currie touches the photo of Jessica Beer—"at a party, while, according to Jessica's statement, not sober. Then the girls at college who complained about you—about your behavior, while at another party, again, not sober. Your unpleasant exchange with Nancy Wade on the street, when you deliberately blocked her path—"

"Or so she *claims*," Barry interjected. "We only have her word for that, remember?"

"When she *claims* you deliberately blocked her path and called her a bitch. That was on Valentine's night when you, by your own admission, were not sober. So my theory is that maybe, Owen, you are one of those people who behaves extremely out of character when they've been drinking, that in normal circumstances you are not the sort of man to approach women or flirt with young girls or touch them inappropriately or toss verbal abuse at women you pass in the street, but that maybe after a few drinks, your guard lowers and this other side of you comes out, this different personality. And that maybe that other side of you, as abhorrent as it might seem to you now, is in fact capable of taking a young girl off the street and bringing them to some kind of harm. And it's been eleven days now, Owen, eleven days since Valentine's night, and it's long enough. Don't you think? Long enough to make everyone suffer. To prevent Saffyre's family from getting some kind of closure. So, Owen, please, please just think back to that night, when you weren't sober, when you might have behaved out of character and done something you didn't mean to do, something that had some kind of momentum of its own. Please, Owen. Tell us what happened. Tell us what you did to Saffyre Maddox."

"I did not do anything to Saffyre Maddox," Owen says softly, but even as he says it, he feels something small but persistent pushing at the periphery of his consciousness. Like a tiny fruit fly, hovering by his nose. The girl, in the hood. The name *Clive*. He feels an echo in the soles of his feet. An echo of his footsteps, following the girl in the hoodie, calling to her in the darkness, heading after her into his garden.

43

Cate

CATE SPENDS THE rest of that morning with a cold shiver of dread trapped in her spine, making her shudder over and over again.

She's done nothing with the scrunched-up carrier bag and its contents, merely rolled it up and stuffed it behind the linen basket again.

Cate is supposed to be submitting a first draft of this latest manual to her publishers by the end of the month, and she's nowhere near ready. She sits at her laptop and words an email carefully, explaining that she will be late. She sighs as she presses *send*; being late is not something she makes a habit of. But she's too distracted to rush it out; every time she looks at the screen her mind goes blank.

Instead she switches to her browser and googles "sex attacks NW3." She opens a notepad and takes the cap off a pen.

The first attack in this spate now assumed to have been carried out by the same balaclava-clad man was on 4 January, on Pond Street.

A young woman of twenty-two had her breasts roughly fondled at eleven thirty in the morning by a young man dressed in black who then escaped very quickly on a hired bicycle when someone approached.

She writes: "11.30 a.m., 4 January."

The next attack was three days later. A sixty-year-old woman, who also had her breasts grabbed by a young man dressed in black. The attack had left her with bruises. It was at about four o'clock in the afternoon, near the leisure center, near the school.

She writes it down.

The next was on 16 January. This was the one that she and Roan had read about in the papers. A twenty-three-year-old woman grabbed from behind, sexually assaulted through her clothes; she never saw the man who attacked her but described him as smelling of laundry detergent and having small hands.

She writes that down too.

She knows the next two, both on roads very close to here. Both daytime. Both involving grabbing and bruising. And then the latest one, 24 February, at dusk, on the other side of the Finchley Road. Near the cinema. This one the most serious so far, a woman in hospital with injuries.

She breathes in hard and goes to her online calendar. Here she compares the dates and times with her own activities, desperately searching for something that does not correlate, for proof that nobody in this house could possibly be responsible for the terrible things that have been happening to women in the area.

She remembers the smell on Roan's running clothes she'd found in Josh's bedroom: not washing detergent at all, but sour, musky, ugly.

She thinks of the boys that Roan treats at his clinic, the boys not yet men who are already fantasizing about hurting women.

She thinks of Josh, his hugs, his unknowability, his silence.

The shiver goes down her spine again.

But they are not Josh's clothes, they are Roan's clothes, and Roan too has his empty spaces. He is out all day and makes himself un-contactable. At night he runs in black Lycra; sometimes he runs for two hours, sometimes more. He comes back electrified and gleaming. He has secrets. Even if there wasn't an affair last year, there was something. And there is the Valentine's card from the child, which is the wrong size for the envelope. And the missing girl who used to be his patient, who had been seen outside their house the night she disappeared.

There is so much. So much that is wrong. And now there is a bag full of foul-smelling Lycra. Now there is a balaclava.

But she cannot find a date that doesn't correlate with either her husband or son being the attacker. On every single occasion her husband and her son might possibly have been out of the house.

She looks at the time. It's nearly eleven. She imagines Josh at school, Roan at work. Those spaces. The cracks and the gaps where things can get in.

She picks up her phone and searches her contacts for Elona's number, Tilly's mum. She lets her finger hover over the call button for a moment but loses her nerve. She presses the message icon instead and types a text. *Dear Elona. Hope you and Tilly are both well. I just wanted to talk to you about something. Wondered if you were free for a coffee anytime soon. Let me know!*

Elona replies thirty seconds later. *Sure. I'm free now if that's any good?*

They meet at the Caffè Nero on the Finchley Road. Elona is very groomed: black hair pulled back into a sculpted ponytail, a black cape with a fur trim, black jeans, and high-heeled boots. Cate can't understand how people can be bothered to be so glamorous. The effort, every day, the attention, the time, the money. Elona hugs her, enveloping her in a miasma of honey-sweet perfume.

"It's so lovely to see you, Cate," she says in her singsong Kosovar accent. "You look well."

"Thank you," Cate says, although she knows she does not.

"Let me get you a coffee. What would you like?"

Cate doesn't have the energy to argue about who should be buying the coffee, so she just smiles and says, "A small Americano, please. With warm milk."

She settles into an armchair and glances at her phone. There's a message from Georgia. *Mum?*

Then another one: *Mum. Can I make a cake tonight? Can you buy flour? And eggs?*

Then two minutes later: *And soft brown sugar. Love u.*

Cate replies with a thumbs-up emoji and puts her phone away.

If anyone had told her a few years ago that one day Georgia would be the least of her problems, she would not have believed them.

Elona returns with an Americano for Cate and a mint tea for herself. "So," she says, "how've you been?"

"Oh, God, you know," Cate begins. "All a bit high drama. As you may know?"

Elona nods effusively. "I heard, yes."

It occurs to Cate that Elona probably cleared her diary in the thirty seconds after receiving Cate's message.

"So, what's been going on?" Elona asks.

"Well, you know they've arrested the guy? The one who lives opposite us?"

"Yes. I read that. Wow. And what do you think? Do you think it was him?"

"Well, it certainly looks that way, doesn't it? Though I read somewhere that it was him who told the police about seeing Saffyre there. Why would he have done that if he did it? If he hadn't said anything, they'd never have known she was on our street. They'd never have looked in that building plot; they'd never have found her phone case and the blood. It all seems a bit strange."

"Unless he wanted to get caught?"

"Well, yes, I guess that's possible. But still, something doesn't seem quite right to me."

"So, what's your theory?"

Cate laughs nervously. "I don't have one. I just have an anti-theory."

Elona smiles, blankly, clearly hoping for more.

Cate changes the subject. "So how's Tilly? I haven't seen her for quite a while."

"No," says Elona, her eyes dropping to the leaves in her tea. "No. She's become a bit of a homebody. Doesn't really like going out. Probably the weather. You know. The dark nights."

"When did this start?" she asks. "The not going out?"

"Gosh, I don't know. A few weeks ago, I suppose. Since the New Year. She's just . . ." She pauses. "She just seems happier at home."

"Does it seem . . . ?" Cate begins and then pauses to find the right words. "Do you think maybe it had anything to do with that night? The night she was leaving ours. When she said the man had grabbed her."

Elona looks up at Cate. "You know, the thought did occur to me."

"And?"

Elona shrugs. "She swears blind that nothing happened. That she made it up."

"It's weird, though, isn't it? The timing of it? And now it turns out that all the sex attacks in the area this year were kind of similar to what she originally said happened to her?"

"They are?"

"Yes. It was in the papers. Six since the New Year. All carried out by a young man in black. All involved rough grabbing and groping."

Elona looks vaguely appalled.

"I mean, can you see any reason why she might have taken back the claim? Maybe she was scared to go to the police?"

"I honestly don't know. I mean, we've barely spoken about it. I was so *so* cross with her for wasting everyone's time like that, for lying. I was so embarrassed by her behavior, you know, and I'm a single mum, and everything she does feels like such a reflection on me, you know, and she thinks so highly of Georgia and of you and your family."

"She does?"

"Yes. Oh God, yes. So much. She never had a real friend before Georgia. She's in awe of her. And I think both of us were just a bit, you know, thrown by what happened that night."

"Oh, honestly, no! She must never worry what we think. Or what Georgia thinks. Georgia is rock-solid. Nothing throws her. She's really thick-skinned. You must tell Tilly that whatever it was that happened that night, whether it was real or not, she can tell Georgia. Georgia would never judge her. No one in our family would judge her. I promise."

Elona smiles and puts her hand over Cate's. She has a heavy gold chain around her narrow wrist; her nails are painted taupe. "Thank you, Cate," she says. "Thank you so much. I will talk to her tonight and see if there's anything she's not telling me. You're very kind to take such an interest."

Cate smiles tightly. She's not being kind. She's being desperate and scared.

———

She walks home via the supermarket where she buys all the cake-making ingredients on Georgia's list. At the checkout she glances across the street again at the entrance to the tube station, subconsciously looking out for her husband, as if the echo of his appearance there two weeks ago might still be playing out infinitely.

She walks home circuitously, via a couple of the places the newspaper report mentioned, to the estate agent just past the cinema where she sees police tape up around the back entrance, a police car still parked on the street outside. Then to the dogleg in the next road down from her road, the place she sometimes goes to post letters. She doesn't know the precise location of this attack, but it makes her shudder nonetheless, looking at the hidden places here where a woman could easily be grabbed without anyone seeing.

She walks home quickly after that, all her nerves on end, her breathing coming slightly too hard. As she turns the next corner onto her street, she sees someone sitting on the wall outside her house. It's a young man, well built. He's wearing a gray coat with a bright green hoodie underneath. As she gets closer she sees that he is mixed race, very nice-looking. He gets to his feet when he sees Cate turning onto her pathway. He says, "Hi, do you live here?"

"Yes," she replies, thinking that she should be nervous, especially in the light of what she's just been doing, but she isn't. "Can I help you?"

"I . . . I guess. I don't know. My niece. Saffyre. She was here. I think. You know, Saffyre Maddox? She disappeared . . . I . . ." He pulls at his chin as he talks, as if trying to massage out the right words.

"You're Saffyre's uncle?" she asks.

"Yes, I am. Aaron Maddox. Are you Mrs. Fours?"

"Yes."

"Roan Fours's wife?"

She nods.

"Would it be OK if I asked you a few questions?"

She knows she should say no. She should say *I've said everything that needs to be said to the police* and send him on his way. But there's something in his body language that suggests he's carrying something with him, and not just the pain of his missing niece.

She says, "What sort of questions?"

"I've found something," he says. "In her room. And I know I should take it to the police. But I just kind of wanted to check in with you first. Because . . . I don't know. It doesn't make any sense. Could I come in?"

She looks across the street at Owen Pick's house. It's blank and quiet. She looks up at her neighbors' windows. "Sure," she says. "Of course. Come in."

———

In her kitchen, Aaron Maddox sits for a moment in his big gray coat before Cate says, "Here, let me hang that up for you."

"Thanks, that's great. Cheers."

Underneath the coat his hoodie has the Marvel logo and a picture of Spider-Man on it. She finds this strangely reassuring.

"Can I get you something to drink? Tea? Something cold?"

"Water would be great. Thank you."

She pours him a glass of water and places it in front of him.

He clears his throat and smiles awkwardly.

"You know," he begins, "I've met your husband. I was at Saffyre's first couple of sessions. Back in 2014. He's a good man."

"Yes," she agrees. "He is. He's a great clinician."

"I put my faith in him. You know, a little girl like that, hurting herself as she was, well, you know that there's something bad happening, something you don't really want to have to face. But he just got in there with her. Made her feel safe. And stopped her hurting herself."

"She was self-harming?"

She does already know this, not because Roan told her, but because of hacking into his work files and reading his reports the previous year.

"Yeah. Started when she was ten years old. So bad. She's still got the scars. Like, here." He points at the cuffs of his joggers. "But your husband. He cured her. So amazing. And then to find out that she was here, you know, outside his house, when she went missing," He shakes his head. "Unreal. And it can't just be a coincidence, can it? And, listen, I know"—he puts his hand out, palm first—"I know it's nothing to do with him. I know you were out that night; I know he was with you. But it's still weird. And I can't stop thinking about it. It spins round and round my head all the time. Because as far as I know, after she stopped her sessions with him, she never saw him again. And I don't even know how she knew where he lived. That's what gets me. How did she know where he lived?"

He leaves the question hanging, pendulously, between the two of them.

"Well, it's possible she saw it written down in his office one day, I suppose . . . ?"

Aaron nods and says, "Yeah, I guess it could have been something like that. I'm probably overthinking it all. And that guy." He gestures behind him in the direction of the street. "The one they reckon abducted her." His voice cracks slightly on the words. "What do you know about him? Did you know him at all?"

She shakes her head. "No. I only saw him in passing. Not even on nodding terms. He talked to my husband once, a few weeks back; he was drunk apparently and asked my husband if he was married. Kind of weird. But with what we know now about his internet habits . . ."

"Yeah," says Aaron. "That's some sick stuff. I didn't even know about all that, all that incel thing. God. Sad, sad men."

"Toxic masculinity," she says. "It's everywhere."

He nods. But then says, "Not in our house, it wasn't. I just want to say that. Saffyre lived in a house with two men who were both good, who put girls equal to boys. I want you to know that. Whatever happened I know she wasn't trying to get away from stuff at home. Her home was good. Is good."

Cate nods. She believes this man, completely, every word he says. "I hear you lost your father?"

"Yeah." His gaze drops to his water glass. "Back in October. She took it badly. Stopped eating. Stopped doing schoolwork. I said to her that she should come back and see Dr. Fours. I offered to set that up for her. But she said she was fine. I got someone in to talk to her from the school, a pastoral teacher. Didn't make much difference. And then early November she just sort of snapped out of it. Started eating. Got back into her studies. We had an amazing Christmas, just being together, you know, like a real family. And then, I don't know, after Christmas she just sort of . . . drifted away again."

"In what way?"

"Just wasn't at home very much. Spent a lot of time at her best friend's house. Or 'going for walks.' Did a lot of sleepovers. And I suppose I just thought, you know, she's seventeen, she'll be an adult soon, I guess she's spreading her wings. And she was a late bloomer in that way, kind of young for her age, never really had a social life, didn't do parties, boyfriends, hanging out, nothing like that. So I thought, well, you know, good, it's about time she found her feet in the world. And then . . ."

She sees a film of tears across his eyes and feels an instinctive urge to touch him, which she resists. He drags the back of his hand across them and smiles. "And yeah, so, I'm just left with all these questions. And I started going through her stuff. There wasn't much, to be honest. The police have still got her laptop, but I don't think they've found anything on there; they'd have said by now. Every night after work I just sit in her room, with her things, looking for something, anything that might explain what happened to her. Why she was here. What she was doing. And then last night, I found this in the pocket of some old joggers . . ."

He puts his hand into his back pocket and pulls out a piece of folded paper. He unfolds it and pushes it across the table to Cate.

She reads the words written on it and her blood runs cold and dark.

44

Saffyre

SCHOOL HAD STARTED back on 7 January, and I had gone back to being the "other" Saffyre Maddox, the one who showed up in the classroom every morning clean and fresh, hair neatly tied back, some mascara, some lip gloss. It wasn't so much that I actively wanted to look nice, it was more that if I didn't look nice, people would worry, they'd ask me questions, the pastoral-care woman would pull me into her office and expect me to tell her what was wrong with me. So I did my schoolwork. I traded in gossip. I smiled at boys but kept them at arms' length. It was like I was Superman or something, with my two different personas. By day I was Saffyre Maddox, aloof but popular, mild-mannered A-grade student. By night I was a kind of nocturnal animal, like the human equivalent of a fox. My superpower was invisibility. There in the playground at school, or in the sixth-form common room, all eyes were on me, but at night I did not exist, I was the Invisible Girl. Invisibility was my favorite state of existence.

The confrontation with Harrison had been horrific on many levels. The sound of my name on his lips. The same lips he'd licked while he'd done what he'd done to me when I was a child. The size of him, no longer a child, but a man, an adult. The way he appeared in the half darkness, dressed in black. The thought of him out there now, just being able to go where he wanted and do what he wanted. And that was the root of it really. That was what turned my head from self-harm to Harrison-harm. I felt like we were occupying the same territory, the same ground. We were both invisible, but we'd seen each other, like two foxes facing off in the muted streetlight. I thought, I do not want to hurt myself anymore because of what this person did to me. I thought, I want to hurt *him*.

Now, wherever I went, I looked for him.

I knew it would be only a matter of time until our paths crossed again.

———

Mid-January. Cold as cold can be. I had fallen asleep in the plot of land across from Roan that now felt very much like it was mine. I rarely slept, and when I did it was fast and immediate and hard and deep, usually for ten minutes, maybe sometimes as much as half an hour. Noises always woke me. Every noise. But this noise didn't wake me. The sound of a young man entering the empty plot at two o'clock in the morning and sitting behind the digger just out of sight of me and my little campsite.

He didn't know I was there. I didn't know he was there. And then I was wide-awake and, with that strange intake of breath that accompanies a sudden wakening, I was upright. I looked up, and I saw a face and it was a face I knew.

"Oh my fucking God." The boy clutched his heart. "What the fuck?"

I said, "Josh?"

He said. "Yes. Fuck. How do you know my name?"

And I was fuddled by sleep and not thinking straight and I said, "I know your dad." I pulled my sleeping bag high up around me, suddenly cold.

"How do you know my dad?"

"I was in therapy with him."

"Whoa," he said. "Really?"

"Yeah," I said. "More than three years."

"So why are you sleeping here?" said Josh.

"It's a long story," I said.

"Are you homeless?"

"No. I've got a home."

"So why . . . ? Is it something to do with my dad?"

Where to start with that one? I did not have a clue.

"Yeah," I began. "Kind of. Or at least, it started off being about your dad. And now it's about loads of other things. I just like being outdoors; it's like I can't breathe with a roof over my head."

"You're claustrophobic?"

"Yeah. Maybe I am. But only at night."

"Do you sleep here every night?"

"Yeah. I do now."

"So, was it you," said Josh, "here, on New Year's Eve?"

"Yeah," I said. "I was here. I was hiding. In the corner over there."

I didn't know what made me so open to his questions. There was something about him, something pure, untainted. I looked at him and I thought he would understand me.

"So you were listening to our conversation?"

"Yeah. You and your friend were going to unmask yourselves. Or something."

"Ha. Yeah. That's right. I think we were maybe a bit wasted."

"I thought maybe you were planning a school shooting."

"Er," said Josh wryly, "no."

"Good. So, what were you talking about?"

"Just how we were going to change it up. You know, stop being invisible. Make ourselves 'relevant.'"

"Fuck that," I said. "Seriously. Fuck that. Don't be seen. Stay behind the scenes. That's the place to be."

We fell silent for a moment and then Josh came around the digger and sat down with me.

"So my dad? Was he any good? I mean, was he a good therapist?"

I shrugged. "Yeah, in some ways. But in others, no. Like, I enjoyed our sessions and he did stop me from self-harming. But he left something behind. Inside me. It's still there."

"Something? Like what?"

"Like a cancer. It's like he got rid of the symptoms, but he left the tumor."

"That's shit," says Josh. Then he says, "I hate my dad."

His words stopped me in my tracks. "Really? Why?"

"Because he's having a fucking affair."

"Whoa. How do you know that?"

"Because I've seen him. He flaunts it. And my mum's too much of a soft touch to see what's right under her nose. They nearly split up last year, and I reckon that was because of an affair, too."

"What do you mean, you've seen him?"

"I mean, I've seen him. With this girl. All, like, touching her hair and stuff. Not even trying to hide it. And it's like . . . My mum is the best person in the whole world. She's so sweet and loving and kind; she'd do anything for anyone. And he just plays about like he can do whatever he wants and then come home and she'll have cooked him a nice meal and she'll listen to him moaning on about how stressful his job is. And I just wonder, you know, how someone whose job it is to look after people, to fix their minds, to nurture and cure, how they can do what he does to another human being every single day of his life. It makes me sick."

I had so much I wanted to say. But I just tucked my hands between my knees to warm them up and stayed silent.

"And that's one of the things I want to change this year. Like I was saying on New Year's Eve. No more Mr. Nice Guy."

"What are you going to do?"

His head dropped. He said, "I don't know."

"She's called Alicia Mathers," I said.

His head shot up. "What?"

"The woman your dad's having an affair with. Her name's Alicia Mathers. I know where she lives."

He blinked. "How?"

"I've been watching too. I've seen them. He met her at work. She's a psychologist, like him. They started dating in the summer. They spent the night at a hotel just before Christmas. She lives in Willesden Green. She's twenty-nine. She's got two degrees and a PhD. She's pretty smart."

He didn't speak for a moment. Then he looked at me with those eyes, so like Roan's eyes, and said, "Who are you? Are you real?"

I laughed.

"You're really pretty," he said.

I said, "Thank you."

"Am I dreaming you? I don't get this. I don't get any of this."

"We've met before."

He said, "What? When?"

"Last year. You did a couple of beginners' classes at the martial-arts place. I spoke to you in the changing room. Do you remember?"

"Yes," he said. "Yes. I do. You had pink hair then. Didn't you?"

"Yeah. That was me."

"Did you know who I was? Even then?"

"Yeah. Yeah, I did."

"Is that why you spoke to me?"

"Yup."

"I was so embarrassed. You were so pretty."

"Yeah, you can stop saying that now."

"Sorry."

I smiled. I didn't mind. There was something so easy about the boy. "It's OK," I said, "I'm only joking. Why did you stop going? To the dojo?"

He said, "I didn't. I still go. I just changed my class times. I go on Fridays now."

"Are you any good?"

He said, "Yeah. Green belt. So, you know, getting there."

"Remember you told me you wanted to be able to defend yourself? That's why you were taking lessons? You told me you'd been mugged?"

He nodded.

"What happened?"

He put his hand into his pocket and pulled out a little bag. As he talked he constructed a spliff on his thigh.

"This guy," he said, pulling out a Rizla from a paper packet. "Came up behind me. Last summer. Just down there." He pointed down the hill. "Put his arm round my throat, quite tight. Said, 'What you got?' Put his hands in all my pockets. I tried to push him off but he said, 'I've got a knife. OK?' Then he took my phone and my earbuds and my debit card and he pushed me, really hard, so I nearly fell onto my face and I grabbed hold of the wall to stop myself falling, and then he ran. And I just stood there. My heart pounding. It was, like, the scariest, scariest thing. And I didn't do anything. I just stood there and let him take my stuff. Stuff my mum and dad worked really hard to pay for. Stuff he had no right to. And it makes me so fucking angry. I just feel like now, if I saw him, I would kill him."

His words hit me hard. I drew in my breath. "I know exactly how you feel."

And then—and how weird is this, after three years of taxpayers paying for Roan to fix me in his warm room at the Portman, after all those hours and hours and hours of talking and talking and talking but never saying the one thing that really mattered?—I finally found the words to tell someone about Harrison John.

"Something like that happened to me," I said. "Someone took something from me. And I let them."

"What was it?"

I let a beat of silence pass. Then I talked.

"When I was ten years old, this boy in the year above groomed me. He was the tallest boy in the year. He had two younger sisters in the school who he was really protective of. He was naughty, but the teachers all loved him. And he kind of picked me out. When we played dodgeball at breaktime he'd tell the other year sixes to get out of my way. To let me have my turn. And he'd give me these looks like: 'Don't worry, I've got your back.' He made me feel really special. And then one day . . ." I stopped briefly to step back from a wave of emotion. "One day he beckoned me into this little section of the playground where the youngest children usually played, but they were all in their classroom or something, and he said, 'Do you want to see something magic? And I said, 'Yes, yes!' and I followed him in and he said, 'You need to squat down, like this,' and he squatted down to show me and I did what he said and I was looking up at him like, 'Yes! I'm squatting! Now show me the magic!' And then he . . . It was so quick. He inserted his fingers inside me and it hurt, it really hurt, and I said, 'Ow!' And he said, 'It's OK. It only hurts the first time. After that the magic happens.' He stroked my hair, and then he took his hand away from me and he showed it to me, and he smiled and he said, 'It'll be better next time. I promise.'"

It felt like a belt had been squeezed around my gut, and with every word I spoke, it was loosened a bit. By the time I got to the end I felt weirdly like I could breathe. Even though my eyes were full of tears and my head ached with the sadness of that little girl waiting for the magic that never ever came, I could breathe. Three times I let him do that to me. And then school finished for the summer and Harrison left, and I never saw him again. But he stayed, inside my head, inside my DNA, my marrow, my breath, my blood, in every single part of me. He stayed. My tumor.

Josh licked the Rizla and stuck it down, twisted the tip, stuck in a tiny roll of cardboard to make a filter. He reached back into his coat pocket and brought out a lighter.

"What a fucking bastard," he said. "That's just so sick. So sick."

"Yeah. It was. But guess what? I saw him the other day. I saw the boy who did that to me."

"Oh my God," said Josh. "Shit. Where?"

"There." I pointed down the hill. "He was just coming up from the Finchley Road. I was going down. He said my name. He recognized me and he said my name and it was like . . . It felt like the playground all over again. Like he had the right to me in some sort of way, like he was entitled to me, to my body, to my name. You know? And for a day or two I felt myself going backward, like I'd climbed the top of a mountain and then lost my footing and started slipping back and was trying to find something to grab hold of to stop me slipping but there was nothing there. And then I found something."

Josh looked at me wide-eyed, his face lit with orange shadows from the flame of the lighter he was using to light the spliff. "What?"

"Revenge. I found revenge."

"Oh my God. What did you do?"

"Nothing. Not yet. But I just know that that's the only way for me now. The only way to get him out of my DNA. I need to hurt him."

Josh brought the spliff to his lips and inhaled. He narrowed his eyes and he nodded. "You really do," he said.

I glanced at him quickly. I'd just put something into words that had been buried away so far inside me that I hadn't even known what it was until I'd actually said it. I needed to know what it looked like to another person.

"You think?"

"Yeah. Totally. He's probably still out there abusing people to this day. If he was doing this when he was eleven, getting away with it, then . . ."

I looked at Josh again. He offered me the spliff. I shook my head.

And then we both turned at a sound from the undergrowth. Two amber dots of light. The shimmer of red pelt. A snout held to the air. I put my hand into the outside pocket of my rucksack for the dog treats I now kept in there all the time. I opened up the packet toward the fox, and he came.

I laid the treats out around us, and we watched as he picked each one up in turn, never once looking at us.

"I want to help you," said Josh. "Help you get your revenge. Please. Can I help you?"

The fox sat down and looked at my bag expectantly. His tongue darted out and he licked his lips.

I looked at Josh.

I said, "Yes. Please."

45

Owen

"HOW MUCH LONGER can they keep me here?"

Barry shuffles some paperwork out of his briefcase. "Now that they've charged you, as long as they like."

"But they haven't found any new evidence. I mean, they can't take this to court based on what little they've got."

"No. But they can keep trying, and believe you me, Owen, they are raking up every single strand of your life, every filament, until they find the thing they're looking for. And meanwhile they're going to keep dragging you back into that room and asking you questions until you crack."

"Crack?" says Owen, incredulously. "But I'm not going to *crack*. How can I crack when I didn't do it?"

But as he says the words, a curtain of doubt falls across his consciousness. His mind keeps taking him back to a moment he's not even sure actually happened. The moment just after he saw the person across the street. The moment just before he thought he'd turned and gone indoors and gone to bed.

Because he cannot actually remember turning and going back indoors.

And since this morning's interview, Owen's turned over every night of his life when he's been out drinking and realized that frequently all he can remember are flashes of action, but none of the bits in between.

He can't remember journeys home. He can't remember folding up his clothes. He can't remember "Bill," whose phone number he found in his pocket the night after leaving drinks a couple of years ago. He can't remember buying the bottle of whiskey he'd found in a carrier bag on his bedroom floor once with a paper receipt with his card details on it, proving that he'd been into a branch of Tesco Metro and carried out the full transaction in person. He can't remember stroking girls' hair on the dance floor. Flicking sweat at them.

He can't remember telling a girl called Jessica with soft skin that she was pretty. And he definitely can't remember going to bed on Valentine's night. He knows he woke up in his bed wearing his shirt and one sock. He knows he slept late. He knows he had a hangover. He remembers the girl who'd called him a creep, he remembers the man with the white dog, and he remembers the girl in the hoodie. But he can't remember the rest.

And that picture keeps flashing in and out of his head: a figure, passing by him outside his door, heading toward the back of the house. It could have been her, the girl in the hoodie. It could have been someone else. Or it could be just a ridiculous fragment of his imagination, something his psyche has conjured up to deal with the trauma of his situation. You read about it all the time, about people confessing to things they haven't done. Is this how it happens? he wonders. Is it your own brain that does it to you, that plants things there to frame you, like a bent copper?

He stares down at his hands. They look alien to him, someone else's hands attached to his arms. He's starting to lose any sense of himself or who he should be or what he's meant to be doing or who he ever was. He tries to place himself back in that Italian restaurant with Deanna, tries to imprint the way she looked at him that night, over the way DI Currie looks at him in the interview room. If only he could hold on to that, then maybe this nightmare would end.

Barry strokes his fat silk tie and says, "There's a girl missing. You're all they've got. And you're looking like a good bet to them. It's irrelevant whether you did it at this point. They're not letting you go anywhere until they have to."

"I didn't do it, you know."

Barry doesn't reply.

"*I didn't do it.*"

Barry narrows his eyes at Owen. "Do what?" he says. "What didn't you do?"

"Hurt that girl. I did not hurt that girl."

Barry doesn't speak for a while. Then he looks Owen hard in the eye and he says, "Well, Owen, the time for you to prove that is right now. Prove it, Owen. Tell me something incontrovertible. Tell me something that'll get you out of here. Please. For both our sakes."

———

"So," says DI Currie, who is beginning to lose her fresh-faced glow as the investigation drags out. "Owen. Please, I know we've been over all of this. But it's worth going over it again. The more we talk about it the higher the chance of you regaining some kind of memory. Please, tell us again about the night of the fourteenth of February."

Owen exhales loudly. He can't go through all of this again, he simply cannot. "What about Bryn," he says. "Have you still not found him?"

She smiles crisply at him. "No," she says. "We have not."

"Well, I wish you would. He should be in here. Not me. He's the sicko. He's the weirdo. He's probably out there raping women right now, while you're sitting here asking me the same questions, over and over and over again."

DI Currie pauses. She looks at Owen through narrowed eyes, and then she says, "Fine, Owen. Fine. If you can tell us one thing about 'Bryn' that will help us to locate him, then please, do feel free to do that. Whenever you're ready. Please." She leans back in her chair and appraises him frostily.

Owen sighs. He rubs at his face and tries to recall something, anything that Bryn might have said to out himself. He thinks back to the details of that first blog post he read. Bryn sitting in a pub on a snowy day watching the Chads and Stacys. He squeezes at his consciousness to remember more. The Dickensian outline of the pub in the swirling snow, the glow of the old lamps hanging outside and the carriage driveway where the horses were once tethered and the name of the pub had been changed when it was gentrified and before that it was the . . .

The Hunters' Inn.

He grabs the edge of the table and says. "The town where he lives. It has a gastropub. A new gastropub. It used to be called the Hunters' Inn. It's on a common. Opposite a pond. With ducks. It's his local. He goes there all the time. If you could find the pub, you'll find him. He's got big, curly hair. He's really small. He wears a green jacket with a stain on the front. Ask anyone in there who he is. They'll know. He's very distinctive."

He sees DI Currie roll her eyes very slightly. She had not expected him to supply any useful information and she's annoyed that he has.

"We'll look into that, Owen. Leave that with us. But, Owen, even if we find this 'Bryn' character somehow—him having deleted his blog and his presence on every forum you claim he used to frequent—even if we find him and we ask him about the Rohypnol, what do you think he's going to say? Do you think he's likely to tell us what you want him to tell us, that he gave it to you against your will, that you had no intention of using it? Owen, if this man exists and if we find him, he will deny all knowledge of knowing you at all."

"But his fingerprints. They'll be on the jar. And have you asked the pub? The pub in Euston? Have you asked to see their CCTV yet? For that night? That will prove that he knows me. And it might show him giving me the drugs."

"Yes, but what you don't seem to understand, Owen, is that none of that makes any difference. The fact of the matter is that you had date-rape drugs hidden in your bedroom, and frankly we really don't care where you got them from or what you got them for. If you want to prove to us that you didn't abduct Saffyre Maddox and cause some harm to come to her on the night of February the fourteenth, then I'm afraid you're going to need to try another tack entirely."

Owen glances at Barry who looks at him as if to say, "What did I tell you?"

He draws in his breath and blinks. Then he looks straight at DI Currie and he says, "Please tell me what you think happened to Saffyre. I would really like to know. What do you think I did to her? How did I get this girl, this quite tall girl, to wherever it is you think I took her? Me, on my own. How did I drag her through the streets of Hampstead at midnight without being noticed? On Valentine's night, the streets full of people? I don't have a car. I'm not particularly strong. I'd really like you to share your theories with me. Because honestly, from where I'm sitting, you're grabbing at straws."

DI Currie purses her lips. "Owen," she says. "We are doing our jobs. We are exploring many, many avenues of inquiry. Trust us. And we have many theories about what happened to Saffyre, and I can assure you we would not be paying thousands of pounds of taxpayers' money to keep you here if we did not have a strong case to prove that you know what happened to Saffyre. So, Owen, once again, from the top, please talk us through the events of the night of the fourteenth of February as far as you recollect them. Starting with leaving the house to meet a woman called Deanna Wurth at a restaurant in Covent Garden."

Owen lets his head drop into his chest. Then he lifts it and says, "At around six p.m. I left the house and walked down the hill toward Finchley Road tube station . . ."

46

Cate

CATE SITS, WAITING for Roan to return. The piece of paper sits in front of her. Aaron had left it. She still wasn't sure why he hadn't taken it straight to the police. Some kind of misguided, misplaced loyalty to Roan, she suspected. It was as if he'd been hoping she'd offer him a palatable explanation.

She places it side by side with her own piece of paper, pulled from the pad she'd been making notes on earlier. Her eyes cast back and forth between them, taking in the similarities, and the one big difference. Her hands shake slightly as she smooths the pages out.

She glances at the kitchen clock—7:18. Where is he?

She's almost 100 percent sure now, almost positive that something unthinkable has been happening. She'd felt her flesh crawl slightly when her son had hugged her this afternoon when he got back from school.

"Are you OK, Mum?" he'd asked, his blue eyes full of concern.

"I'm fine. Just think I might be coming down with something. Don't want to pass my germs down to you."

He had a copy of *Metro* with him. He waved it in front of her and pointed at the headline. "Look," he said, "they still don't know what happened to Saffyre."

There was a strange intimacy, Cate noticed, in the way he said Saffyre's name.

"Did you ever meet her?" she'd asked casually.

"Who?"

"Saffyre. Did you ever meet her? I mean, she lived over the road from your school. And apparently she did classes at that martial-arts place you go to. It's possible you might have met her?"

He'd shaken his head. Said, "No. Definitely not." Then, "What's for dinner?"

Now she looks again at the piece of paper in front of her. The piece of paper with her son's name on it. Found in Saffyre's joggers. And not just her son's name, but the dates and locations of all the sex attacks in the area since the New Year. The same as the dates on her own sheet of paper. With one difference: Saffyre's list includes 21 January. The papers have not reported a sex attack on 21 January. But according to Cate's diary, 21 January was the day Tilly claimed to have been attacked outside their house.

In a neat cursive script underneath the dates are several seemingly random names.

Clive.

Roan.

Josh.

Alicia.

"I just thought," Aaron had said, "that maybe it meant something. I saw in the papers that you had a son called Josh. I mean, I know it's a popular name. But still. Would you be able to ask your son? Ask him if he knows what it means? If he knows her?"

The significance of the dates had hit her immediately. She'd said, "Sure, I'll ask him," and tried to keep the breathlessness from her voice. The moment he'd gone she'd torn the page from her notepad and compared them. Her hand had gone to her throat.

She'd walked straight into Josh's bedroom and pulled the linen basket out of his wardrobe. The plastic bag was gone. She'd taken Josh's schoolbooks from the shelves and flicked through them, frantically, with no idea what she was looking for. Who were Clive and Alicia? Why did Saffyre have Roan's and Josh's names written on a piece of paper with the dates of the sex attacks? *What was Saffyre doing outside their house on the night she disappeared?*

She'd found nothing in her son's bedroom. Nothing new on his browsing history. Georgia had got home from school first, gone straight to her room to strip off her uniform, tied an apron on over joggers and a sweatshirt, opened up a recipe on the iPad, propped it up in the kitchen, and started to bake. Cate had circled her distractedly, clearing things away, loading them into the dishwasher, interjecting occasionally into her daughter's high-octane monologue about how she wanted her bedroom decorated at the house, how maybe it should be dark, like, *dark dark*, maybe even black, or off-black, or, like, totally the other way, shades of white, like her bedroom here, but dark is cozier, isn't it?

Josh had got home an hour later and gone straight to his room after greeting Cate.

The cake is on the counter now, iced in a chocolate buttercream and decorated with crushed Flake bars. It gapes open on one side where Georgia has already cut herself a slice, showing the vanilla insides.

There's a pasta bake in the oven. The smell makes Cate feel slightly nauseous.

She glances at the clock again.

Seven thirty-one.

"Mum!" It's Georgia. "When's dinner ready?"

"Soon," she calls back. "When Dad gets back!"

She absentmindedly lays the table, tips salad leaves into a bowl, cuts a baguette into ovals. They'll eat without him if they have to.

But a minute later she hears the door bang, and then Roan is in the kitchen, glowing, radiating the heat of aerobic exercise.

"Oh," she says, "you've been for a run?"

"Yes, straight from work." He's still breathless as he pulls off his gloves, his snood, his beanie. "Had a lot of pent-up . . . stuff. Ran all the way up to the village and back. I found this place." He unzips his jacket and pulls it off. "Right up the other end of the village. Weirdest place. Like a kind of James Bond thing: crazy low-rise buildings, walkways, hidden away in this circle of trees." He drops the jacket on the back of a kitchen chair. "Anyway, I googled it, and apparently it's what remains of the most expensive council estate ever built! Some failed socialist experiment under a Labour government in the 1970s. All owned privately now, of course—worth a fortune. But honestly. The weirdest place. Like something from the future. Like a sci-fi film set . . ."

Roan is burbling and Cate is aware on some level of what he's talking about and on some level she would like to respond, would like to say, "Yes, yes, I saw that place too!" But the words stick halfway up her throat, because as he talks, her gaze goes to the angular outline of her husband's torso, the way the Lycra clings to his long, sculpted arms and to the fluorescent orange pattern that works its way from wrist to shoulder up the sleeves.

"Where did you find that top?" she interrupts him.

"What?"

"That top? Where did you find it?"

"I don't know. My drawers, I think . . . why?"

"I thought . . ."

"What?"

"Nothing. I just haven't seen it for a while."

Somehow the top that was hidden away in the back of Josh's wardrobe has been laundered and returned to Roan's drawer.

Roan shrugs. "I'm off for a shower," he says. "What's for dinner?"

"Pasta bake," says Cate, her voice coming out at an oddly high pitch. "And salad."

47

Saffyre

JOSH ASKED ME what Harrison John looked like, so I did a google search for him. My hands shook as I did it. I couldn't bear to find out anything about him, like that he had a kid, or that he'd done something good, or that he was clever or something. I was so scared that he'd have done something to redeem himself, to dilute my feelings of vengeance, because right then those feelings were the only feelings I really had; they were what got me up in the mornings, got me to school, got me to eat, got me to breathe.

I pressed the search button and held my breath.

And then there he was: his face, the squashed-down nose, the heavy brow, striking some kind of stupid gangster pose. According to the accompanying article, he was part of a community music project, something to do with the college he attended.

I turned the phone to Josh. "That's him."

"That's Harrison?"

"Yeah."

"Looks like a loser."

"Right," I agreed. "So much of a loser."

We were in the playground outside my flats where I'd told Josh to meet me. I was still in my school gear.

When Josh saw me, he'd said, "You look so different."

I'd said, "This is my alter ego."

"So, what's your plan?" Josh said now.

I turned off my phone. "Well, I know where he lives now."

Josh said, "How did you do that?"

I tapped my nose. I said, "I told you. I'm clever."

"Are you going to stalk him too?"

I hit Josh on the arm playfully. "I'm not a stalker!" I said.

"You kind of are," he replied.

He smiled, and I liked his smile. Like when a dog looks at you in that soulful, pure way and you think, You are too, too good for this world. That was what it was like when Joshua Fours smiled. Like he was too good for this world.

"Anyway," I replied, "I already started. I followed him to the Co-op and back this afternoon. He didn't see me."

"What did he buy?"

"Haribo. And some tobacco."

"Classy."

"Isn't it?" I said. "And now I know where he goes to college. He'll have no escape from me."

"Can I come with you?"

"You mean, be my co-stalker?"

"Yeah."

"Of course you can."

"Shall we go now?"

I checked the time on my phone. It was nearly five.

"Come on, then," I said. We jumped off the wall. "This way," I said. "Follow me."

Harrison lived up the other end of my road, toward Chalk Farm in a really ugly low-rise block of flats backing onto the railway line. We sat on a bench opposite. It was freezing cold, and I could hear Josh's teeth chattering.

"You OK?" I asked. "You can go home if you want."

He shook his head. "No. I want to see him. In the flesh."

I smiled a half smile at him. Then we both turned back to watch the flats.

And then there he was. Pushing his way through the front door of the block. He was dressed all in black again, the Puffa coat, black stretchy trousers, black trainers, a flash of bare ankle in between, a bag slung over his back. He lit a roll-up cigarette as he emerged onto the street, squinting as he inhaled. And then he turned right, headed up toward Haverstock Hill. We followed him, silently. He caught a bus up toward Hampstead, running to catch it just before its doors closed.

Josh and I looked at each other. It was a single-decker bus. We wouldn't be able to get on it without being spotted. I headed back to my flat. Josh headed back to his flat. We arranged to meet up the next day, same time, same place.

It was two days later that I saw the headline about a sex attack on Hampstead Heath. A man, in black, wearing a mask. Pulled a woman down a quiet pathway and groped her. Put his hands inside her underwear. Grabbed her breasts. And then ran.

I thought of Harrison John jumping on that bus toward Hampstead at 5:20, two days before, in his black coat, his black leggings. It was him. I knew it was.

On 21 January Josh called me. He sounded panicked. He said, "I think Harrison attacked my sister's friend. The police are here. Fuck. What shall I do?"

He explained that his sister's friend had come over after school and then left just as they were about to sit down for dinner. Then she'd come back a few minutes later saying that someone had accosted her.

"What did she say he looked like?" I asked.

There was a pause. "She said she didn't see him. But she said he was silent. That he grabbed her from behind. By the hips. That he rubbed himself against her. Tried to get hold of her breasts. But she broke free and ran back to ours. Shall I say something, Saffyre? To the police? Shall I say I think I know who it might be?"

My biggest regret is that I didn't say yes, tell them. Tell them his name. Let them track him down to his door, search his black bag, take his prints, upend his existence. Let them destroy him.

I didn't say that because I wanted to be the one. Because what if they knocked on his door and he said, 'It wasn't me'? And they believed him? And then he would close the door and his chest would puff out and he'd think he was cleverer than anyone. Or what if they went to his door and brought him in and questioned him and it wasn't him? I wanted it to be him. I needed it to be him. He was evil and he needed to be stopped.

So I said, "No, don't say anything. Just keep quiet. Leave it with me. Leave it with me."

48

Owen

BARRY WALKS INTO the interview room. Owen can recognize the sound of his leather soles on the wooden floors from a few meters away now, followed briskly by the ponderous smell of his aftershave.

"Good morning, Owen."

"Are they letting me go?"

Barry stops and closes his eyes. "No, Owen, I'm afraid not. And look, you should know—this is happening now."

He pulls a folded paper from his briefcase and throws it on the table in front of Owen. It's this morning's *Metro*: "SAFFYRE SUSPECT'S SICK PLAN TO DATE-RAPE DOZENS OF WOMEN."

Below it is the awful photo, yet again, of Owen being jammed into the police car with the fresh cut on his forehead, the wet, asymmetric hair sticking up at angles, the dead look in his eye, the hint of a snaggle tooth between his lips.

He stops and looks at Barry. "But . . . ? I don't . . . ?"

"Just read it, Owen."

Owen Pick, the disgraced college lecturer currently being held under arrest in a north London police station for the abduction and possible murder of missing teenager Saffyre Maddox, had a grand master plan, according to a friend on an incel forum he used to frequent. The friend, who wishes to remain anonymous, told us of a horrifying plan revealed to him by Pick during a pub session earlier this month. He said, "Part of the problem for the incel community is that we are being bred out of society. Women refuse to consider us as sexual partners, therefore we are not being given the opportunity to reproduce. Our genes are being phased out deliberately, by our governments, the media, and by society. This is an issue that goes very deep into the psychology of the incel community. It's something that Owen and I have discussed at great length. While I agree with the general theory and am myself active in the incel community in terms of trying to change the way we are viewed by society, I was very alarmed indeed the last time Owen Pick and I met up for a drink. He chose a shabby down-at-heel pub and I was surprised when I met him for the first time to see that he was quite well presented. He didn't, to my eye, look like a classic incel. He looked like he could pass in society. I couldn't see why he would have trouble attracting women. But there was something about him, something cold, an edge. He chilled me a little. I would say he had a lot of the traits of a psychopath. And then he told me he had a plan. He showed me a jar of pills. I had no idea what they were. He laid them on the table between us and he told me what his plan was. He was going to hook up with women on dating apps and then drug them and inseminate them while they were unconscious. He told me he was doing it for the good of the incel community, but I didn't buy it. There was something about him, a narcissism, a lack of humanity, of compassion. I would say he had a personality disorder and was using the incel community and our beliefs to legitimize a sick personal agenda. In my opinion, Owen Pick was a rapist, masquerading as an incel."

A strange noise comes from Owen. He wasn't expecting to make it. It comes from the deepest pit of his stomach, a curdled growl. He raises his fists, which had curled themselves up into rocks while he read the article, and then brings them down hard onto the table. Then he collects the newspaper between his hands, pushes it into a ball, and hurls it across the room.

"Fuck!" he yells. "Fuck this. Fuck all of it!"

He sits down heavily, drops his face into the heels of his hands, and begins to cry. When he looks up, Barry is sitting, adjusting the cuffs of his shirt. He sees Owen looking at him and passes him a handkerchief from inside his jacket.

"It's not looking good, Owen," he says quietly.

"This is bullshit—you know that, don't you? Bullshit. None of that is how it happened. He's twisted the whole thing. *He* was the one. *He* gave me the drugs. He's just pushing his agenda and throwing me under the wheels to do it. Fuck!"

Barry continues to look at him. "Well," he says. "We've still got a lot of work to do. But this"—he points at the screwed-up newspaper—"is all hearsay and should have no bearing on the investigation. Let's just put this behind us and see what our friends have got for us today, shall we?"

A few moments later DIs Currie and Henry walk into the room. Owen reads their energy. It's been slowly depleting the past couple of days as all their so-called leads take them nowhere, as their case against Owen refuses to grow. But now there is a certain bristle about the pair of them as they take their seats, arrange themselves and their paperwork.

DI Currie gets straight to the point. "Owen. Do you know a woman called Alicia Mathers?"

Owen shakes his head. "Never heard of her."

"Well, Alicia Mathers claims to know you."

Owen sighs. He's down the rabbit hole. He's in a world where people tell him that the sky is green, the grass is blue, two and two is five, black is white and white is black. And in this world, yes, of course a woman called Alicia Mathers would claim to know him.

"Does she?" he says.

"Yes. She says she saw you that night. And that you were talking to a young girl in a hoodie."

He rests his head on the table. The plastic feels cool against his forehead. His eyes are closed and he counts to five silently before raising his head again.

"And she is coming forward only now, because . . . ?"

"It's complicated," says DI Currie. "She has very good reason for not coming forward before now. Very sensitive reasons."

"And they are . . . ?"

"I'm not at liberty to share that with you."

"No," says Owen. "No. Of course you're not. So, go on, what did this *Alicia* claim to have seen?"

"Alicia says she saw you and a girl in a hoodie having a conversation. Outside your house."

A bolt of light flashes through Owen's head. It's there again, that lost moment, the moment that keeps showing itself to him in fractured shards, over and again, whenever he closes his eyes. The girl in the hoodie, not in fact walking away but walking toward him. Saying something. He thought it was false memory. But now he is being told that it wasn't.

"That might have happened," he says, feeling a surge of relief as the words leave his mouth. "I've been getting flashbacks the past day or so. It might have happened. But I have no idea what we talked about. I have no idea what she said. What I said. I have no idea."

Owen hears Barry sighing heavily to his right, and he notices the faces of the two detectives contort slightly, muscles and nerves under their skin reacting to his words.

"Owen, Alicia Mathers claims she saw the girl in the hoodie talking to you, outside your house. She claims she saw you follow her into your back garden."

"Yes," says Owen, his head swimming with blurred images, his skin tingling with the uncertain memory of a girl's hand on his arm. "Yes, that might have happened. Yes. She ran toward me. There was a woman walking toward the house opposite. The girl ran toward me. She ran across the road and she said . . ." It's there now, risen from the vaults of his mind: *Clive! Is that you, Clive?*

"She called me Clive. She wanted to see something. She . . ."

What did she do? The room is entirely silent. He can see that Angela is not breathing. He looks down at his hands. The skin on his palms tingles as he feels another memory returning. "She asked me for a leg-up. To the roof of the garage. I put my hands out, like this." He demonstrates his hands linked together into a perch. "She was heavy. I'm not very strong. She almost fell back onto me, but she managed to grab hold of something. A gutter. Something. And pull herself up. And then . . ."

He pinches the bridge of his nose. Where had this been? All these days?

He continues: "I don't know. I stood guard. I don't know how long. I didn't talk to her. Then she jumped down. She jumped down. She said, 'Ow.' And that—!" He starts as something occurs to him. "That must have been when she cut herself! On my wall. And dropped her phone. She dropped her phone and then she picked it up again. And she ran. She said, 'Thanks, Clive,' and she ran."

"Clive?" says Angela.

"Yes. I don't know. I don't know why she called me Clive. She must have thought I was someone else."

He sees DI's Currie and Henry exchange a look.

"She ran?" says DI Currie.

"Yes!" he says, his voice full of elation. "She jumped down. She said, 'Ow.' She dropped her phone. She picked it up. She said, 'Thanks, Clive.' And she ran."

He feels a burst of euphoria at recovering the weird chunk of time missing between seeing her outside Lycra Man's house and seeing her run down the street, the sound of her rubber soles against the cold, dry pavement.

"And the woman across the street?"

"I don't remember. I don't . . . She was . . ."

And there it was, retrieved like an old photo dropped down the back of a sofa: the missing piece.

"She was talking to the man across the road. The man who goes running. The, you know, the psychologist. She was talking to him. She was shouting. She was crying. And that's it," he says. "That's as much as I remember."

The room falls silent. DI Currie writes something on a piece of paper. She clears her throat.

"Well, thank you for remembering, Owen. I must say, it strikes me as rather odd, after all these days, all this time."

"It was when you said about the woman. I knew—I kind of knew there'd been something missing. But I couldn't find the memories until you said about that other woman."

"It's called a fragmentary blackout," says Barry, sitting upright. "Common after episodes of heavy drinking. And the lost memories can be triggered by someone filling in a missing detail."

Owen throws a look at Barry. There's something different about him. About his demeanor, the tone of his voice. A new softness. A new care. It's almost, Owen thinks, as if Barry believes him.

DI Currie is going through her paperwork. "Did we send someone up onto the garage roof?" she asks DI Henry.

DI Henry consults his own paperwork, flicks through it blindly. "I'm not sure," he says. "I'll check it out."

DI Currie slowly rests her hands on top of her paperwork and looks at Owen. She says, "Excuse us, please, we'll be right back."

As they leave the room Barry turns to Owen and, for the first time since Owen was brought in on Friday morning, he smiles.

"Good work," he says. "Very good work. Now let's see what they come back with."

49

Cate

CATE'S PHONE VIBRATES on the kitchen table. She picks it up and looks at the screen. It's Elona, Tilly's mum.

"Cate?"

"Yes," she answers. "Hi!"

"Hi. It's Elona. I wondered if you had time to talk?"

"Yes," she replies. "Yes. Totally."

"I spoke to Tilly. Last night. About the thing that happened. She got very upset. I think she was shocked, in a way, that I was mentioning it again. I think she thought it was over. She kept saying, 'Why are you asking me this, why are you asking?' But Cate, she started to cry, and then she said, 'I can't tell you, I can't tell you.' And I said, 'What?' And she said, 'It's bad. I can't.' She said—and here I am reading between the lines somewhat because she was not making much sense—but I think she was telling me that it did happen, that it happened and that she knows the person who did it, but she seemed scared, Cate, too scared to tell me who it was."

Cate's thoughts spiral dizzyingly back to the night of the twenty-first. Tilly in the kitchen. Curry on the stove. Josh saying, *I'm in the mood for something spicy*. Tilly leaving. The four of them sitting down to eat. It had been four, hadn't it? She squints to bring the image into focus: curry, table, Georgia, Roan, Josh. Had they sat down to eat when Tilly came back? No, it was too soon. She must still have been laying the table or serving up the food. She can't remember who was in the kitchen then. She knows Georgia was there. And Roan and Josh must have been there too. She's quite sure.

But even as she thinks this, she feels doubts crawl in and start to cloud her memory.

"Right," she says briskly to Elona. "Well, thank you for letting me know."

"But who?" says Elona, her voice tinged with desperation. "If it happened? If it did, and she's too scared to say? Who might it have been?"

"I have no idea, Elona. I'm so sorry."

"Should I go back to the police, do you think?"

"Gosh, I really don't know. It doesn't sound like Tilly's ready to talk about it . . ."

"But if they're investigating this guy, the one who attacked the woman behind the estate agent, this could be . . . it might be the same guy, yes? And they should know?"

"I really don't know, I really . . ."

"I'm scared, Cate. What if this guy, what if he's still out there and he's following Tilly? If she knows the attacker then he might know where she lives, where we live? What shall I do, Cate? What shall I do?"

Cate's stomach roils. She pulls the phone away from her ear and catches her breath. She puts it back a second later and says, "I'm sorry, Elona. I really am, but I have to go now. I'm really sorry."

And then she ends the call.

50

Owen

LUNCH IS A thin ham sandwich, raw carrots, orange squash, a blueberry muffin. Such a shame about the blueberries. Owen picks them out and leaves them on the side of the tray.

The atmosphere has changed since this morning, since he recalled the missing section of the night of the fourteenth. He's pretty sure he's being seen less as a twisted child killer and more as someone who might not actually have done it after all. But then his thoughts go back to the morning's papers, to the fake story planted by Bryn. Whatever happens here, inside these walls, however soon he is allowed to go home, charges dropped, maybe with a pair of apologetic handshakes from DIs Currie and Henry, regardless of anything that happens here before he gets to go home, he will still be the man on the front page of the papers, with the bloody forehead and the incel associations and the underwear drawer full of date-rape drugs. He will always be the guy who called a strange woman a bitch and who had a girl's blood on the wall outside his bedroom, who was sacked for sweating on a girl at a disco. He will always be Owen Pick, the weird, creepy guy who maybe hadn't killed Saffyre Maddox but sure as dammit had done *something*.

The door opens and the detectives return. They sit neatly and look at Owen. DI Currie says, "Well, we sent someone up onto the garage roof. Just got their early findings back. Footprints that match Saffyre's trainers. Her fingerprints on the guttering. No evidence of you being up there. But, Owen, we can't take your word for what you say you remember happening that night. We are not ready to drop you from the investigation. Nowhere near. So. Anything you suddenly remember, please share it with us."

They straighten their files, and leave.

Owen looks at Barry and exhales.

"We're getting there," says Barry. "We're getting there."

And then he says, "Oh, by the way, Tessie just forwarded something to me. An email. Would you like to see it?"

"Erm, yes. Sure."

Barry switches on his smartphone and slides it across the table to Owen.

It's from Deanna.

Dear Tessie,

Thank you so much for your email regarding your nephew, Owen. While I had a very pleasant evening with Owen on Valentine's night, I think I have enough baggage in my life right now without taking on any more. I have no idea what to make of his arrest or of the newspaper reports about his history and background. They do not square with the man I had dinner with, who was gentle, civilised, and thoughtful. But then people can hide a lot of darkness behind carefully constructed masks, can't they? I feel sad that you are going through this, and I hope, for your sake, and for Owen's, that this all blows over and that it turns out to be a case of mistaken identity. Please do tell him that I'm thinking of him but that I cannot possibly consider taking things any further with him in the light of the current situation.

Wishing you all the best,

Yours

Deanna Wurth

Owen reads it twice. His eye settles on the words of hope. He notes that nowhere in the message does she say she believes he is capable of murder. Nowhere does she say she never wants to see him again. Nowhere does she say she hates him or is appalled by him. This, he thinks, is a chink of light. Something to hold on to.

51

Cate

JOSH GETS BACK from school late that evening. He comes, as ever, directly into the kitchen and hugs Cate, his skin still cold from outdoors. "Love you."

"Love you too." The words feel stilted as they leave her lips.

Then she says, quickly, before he leaves the room, before she loses her nerve, "Josh. Can I ask you something? A bit of a strange question?"

He turns and looks at her. He looks thin, she notes, the dips below his cheekbones pronounced and shadowed. "Yes?"

"I was in your room yesterday."

His eyes widen and bulge slightly in their sockets, barely perceptible but just enough to betray his anxiety. "Yeah?"

"I was getting your dirty laundry. And there was a bag, behind the basket. Had some of your dad's running gear in it. Any idea why?"

There's a beat of silence. Then Josh says, "I went for a run."

"You went for a run? When?"

"I dunno. A few times."

Cate closes her eyes. She thinks of the way he moves, her second-born child, so slowly. Always a few paces behind. She remembers when he was younger, the countless times she'd have to pull over on the pavement and wait for him to catch up with her. "Stop dawdling," she'd say. "Come on!" And even now, at almost six feet, he still walks like a slug. He does everything slowly. She cannot picture him running. She says, "Really? You?"

"Yeah. Why not?"

"Because . . . I don't know. You're not the running type."

"Well. People change, don't they?"

She sighs. "I suppose they do, yes. But here's a weird thing. I didn't wash it; I left it there. But now it's gone, and your dad's wearing it again and says he found it in his drawer."

Josh shrugs, moves one foot in front of the other. "Yeah. I washed it."

"You washed it?"

"Yeah."

She closes her eyes again. "So let me get this straight. You borrowed your dad's gear to go running in. Without ever telling me that you were going running. You left it in a carrier bag at the back of your wardrobe. Then you got it out, washed it, dried it, put it back in your dad's drawers?"

"Yes."

"I don't understand, Josh. It doesn't make any sense."

"What doesn't make any sense? It makes total sense."

"No, Josh. It doesn't. And you're making me feel really uncomfortable. Like there's something you're hiding from me."

And then Josh does something Josh never does. He shouts. He opens his mouth and he growls and he says, "OK. Fuck's sake. OK. I pissed myself. OK? I was out running, and I don't know why. I do not know why, OK? But I pissed myself. Like totally through everything. And I couldn't tell anyone because I was so embarrassed.

So I just shoved the kit in the bag and hid it until I had a chance to wash it. OK? Are you happy now?"

Cate sways slightly in the aftershock of her son's rage. And then she goes to him. She takes him in her arms and she holds him and she says, "I'm sorry. I didn't mean to push you. I didn't mean to embarrass you. I'm sorry. It's OK."

She feels his arms around her and his face buried into her shoulder and she realizes that he is crying. He says, "Mum. I'm so sorry. I'm so sorry. I love you so much. I really love you."

She rubs the back of his neck. She whispers in his ear. "It's OK, Josh. It's OK, whatever's going on, you can tell me. You can tell me. It's OK."

"I can't tell you," he says. "I just can't. Ever."

And then he pulls himself from her embrace and strides from the room.

52

Saffyre

I GOT A text from Josh at about eight o'clock on Valentine's Day. It said: *Shit storm brewing! Alicia's sent my dad a Valentine's card and Georgia's just opened it. No one's read it yet. Don't know what the hell to do.*

I replied: *Burn it.*

He said: *I can't. Dad knows it's here. I'm going to confront him with it.*

He sent me a photo of the writing in the card.

It read: "I can't wait any longer. I'm dying. Leave her now or I'm going to kill myself."

I thought, Jesus, what a drama queen. I thought, How do these people get jobs where they're allowed to mess with the insides of children's heads?

I replied to Josh: *Don't do anything. Just wait.*

No, he replied. *It's time.*

My heart raced. I felt weirdly sick, like it was my family in jeopardy, not somebody else's.

I didn't hear back from Josh for hours after that. It was cold and damp out and there was a light drizzle in the air and I thought, I don't fancy sleeping out tonight, so I got into my comfy joggcrs, ate lasagna out of the microwave, and watched *Shakespeare in Love* on the TV. Aaron came back about 11:00 p.m. and we chatted for a while. And then I got a message from Josh: *She's here! Alicia's here! At our house! She's going mental! Can you come over?*

I called through to Aaron in the kitchen. "I'm just popping over to a friend's place."

"Which friend?" he called back.

"Just a friend from school. Lives Hampstead way. I'll be back soon, OK?"

I got to Roan's place at about eleven fifteen. It all seemed quiet. I messaged Josh: *I'm outside. What's going on?*

He replied: *I think I got rid of her.*

What about your parents?

They're out, he replied.

I said: *I'll keep watch.*

I walked around the corner and sat on the wall. All was quiet. After about fifteen minutes I saw Roan and his wife come home. They looked tipsy and happy and were holding hands. Then it was quiet again for a while.

I messaged Josh. I said: *I think she must have gone home. No sign of her out here. I'll wait till midnight, OK?*

He replied: *You're the best.*

I replied with a smiley face and a medal emoji.

Another fifteen minutes passed. A couple walked past holding hands; she held a single rose in her other hand. A man walked past with a small white dog. A woman walked past staring at her phone.

And then I saw something, a movement in my peripheral vision. There was a woman standing right outside Roan's front door.

She had her phone in her hand. She turned slightly, and I saw that it was Alicia.

I crossed the street so I was now on the same side of the road as Roan's house.

I whispered, "Alicia!"

She turned and looked at me. I could see she'd been crying, and I could see she was drunk. She said, "Yes?"

I said, "Whatever it is you're about to do, don't do it. OK?"

She said, "Do I know you?"

"I used to be a patient at the Portman Centre. I know Roan. And I know what you and Roan have been doing."

She said, "It's none of your business."

"No," I agreed. "It isn't. But Josh is my friend. If you do what you're thinking about doing, you're going to destroy his life."

She turned away from me and back to the door.

"Don't do it, Alicia," I said. "Please."

I heard footsteps then, coming from the other way. I turned, and there was a man coming toward us. He was kind of ambling. Shuffling. As he got closer, I saw it was Clive. Or Owen. Or whatever his name was. I looked back at Alicia. I folded my arms. I stared at her. "Please, Alicia, go home!"

As I said that, the door opened and Roan appeared. I darted to the other side of the garden gate, just out of sight. I heard Alicia say something like, "You can't just do this to me, Roan," and then her voice went kind of muffled as if someone had their hand over her mouth, and then I saw Roan pulling her out of his front garden, onto the street. I wanted to see what was going on, but I couldn't from where I was standing. I turned and saw the guy called Clive or Owen or whatever, and he was standing outside his house and he was watching the drama, and I ran across. I said,

"Clive, I need your help. Get me on that roof. Quick." And God bless him, he did as he was told, hoisted me up there. And then I could see everything.

I got my phone out and I recorded it. Alicia was going insane. She was punching Roan and he was letting her and she was saying stuff about how she was going to kill herself and it would be his fault and he just kept grabbing her wrists and saying, *Shush, shush, please, Alicia, keep your voice down. Please. God.* And it was obvious that Roan cared more about his wife finding out than he cared about whether Alicia was going to kill herself. And she got louder and louder and I saw him put his hand over her mouth. I saw her bite his hand, and I saw him slap her. She tried to slap him back, but he grabbed her arms and pushed her away from him, so hard she fell. My hands shook. It was horrible. Like watching animals.

When Alicia finally left, I saw Roan just standing on the pavement, rocking back and forth. I filmed him walking back to the house.

Clive called up. He said, "I'm going in now."

"Wait, wait, help me down!" I said.

"I've got to go to bed," he said.

"No, Clive, wait."

He looked like he was about to walk away and leave me there, so I jumped down but misjudged it badly; my leg hit the wall on the way down and I felt my joggers rip. I landed hard on my bum in a knot of limbs and dropped my phone. I was winded; I could hardly breathe, and I could feel blood seeping through the hole in my joggers, but I managed to get to my feet. I felt in the grass for my dropped phone then pushed past Clive and ran after Alicia. I wanted to check she was OK.

I had almost caught up with her when I heard the click and buzz of a security camera outside a gated mansion turning to watch me. I ducked down and pulled my hoodie closer around my face, still the invisible girl.

Ahead of me Alicia was picking up speed; she knew she was being followed. I picked up my speed to match hers. But then I slowed down again as I heard muffled footsteps behind me and I saw the long black shadow of a person coming after us.

And I knew, even before I saw their face, whose shadow it was.

53

Owen

BREAKFAST THE NEXT morning is lukewarm porridge, a small banana, and some kind of unspecific juice—tropical, maybe? Owen thinks he will miss the food when it's time to go home. He likes prison food. It's like real food but with most of the challenging elements removed. He likes the way it's arranged on a tray; he likes not having to think about it. Maybe he'd like prison too, he ponders. Maybe he'd be happier in prison than out in the world having to make decisions about food, having to deal with women looking at him as if he was going to rape them, having to worry about getting a job, a girlfriend. Maybe this was, in fact, his destiny? Maybe they'd find Saffyre Maddox's body cut up in pieces underneath his bed and he'd suddenly remember that oh yes, he had indeed killed her, case closed, life in prison, no parole. Lots and lots of bland featureless food on trays forevermore. Maybe a cult following of strange women wanting to marry him now that he was the coldhearted murderer of a beautiful young girl. Maybe it would be a better outcome all round.

He passes the empty tray to the policeman on the other side of the door. His name is Willy. He's Bulgarian. He's utterly humorless, which isn't a great state of affairs for someone called Willy.

It's just turned eight o'clock. It looks like a sunny day. Is it possible, Owen wonders, to become institutionalized in under a week? He's lost any real sense of what life used to feel like. The guy in Tessie's bathroom about to trim his fringe feels like a distant memory. The guy who used to go to work every day and teach teenagers how to code also feels like a dream. The guy in the papers, the incel with a taste for impregnating comatose women, is a fictional version of himself. The only version of himself that feels real is this one, here, sitting alone in his cell in Kentish Town. He sits for a few moments, staring at the sunny angles painted into the walls of his cell. He feels a strange moment of hopefulness. Deanna doesn't think he's a monster. That's enough. That's all he needs to go about the rest of his life.

His thoughts begin to curl back on themselves, beyond the sunny cell, beyond cutting his fringe in Tessie's bathroom, beyond the steamed-up windows of his classroom at Ealing College, beyond Tessie's hand on his shoulder at his mother's funeral, beyond his mother slumped over the kitchen table, looking as though she was drunk but actually being dead. They curl back to the other version of himself: the pretty little boy who wouldn't smile for the camera in the modeling agency studio. Who was that little fellow? he wonders now. Who was he and how did he end up here?

He tries to remember moments of pain that might have brought him to this point. He thinks about the build-up to his parents' divorce when he was eleven years old. Divorce, he thinks, is damaging for children; everyone knows that. But was there something in particular about the way his parents broke apart that might have led to, of all the myriad possible versions of himself, this one?

He thinks of the house they once lived in, in Winchmore Hill. A postwar thing with pebble-dashed walls and small windows, a porch full of spider plants, a dark dresser with a phone on it and notepad, a small chandelier. His mother had a thing about chandeliers. He remembers his mother on the bottom step, the phone in her hand, talking to a friend, a crumpled tissue at her nose, saying, "I think it's over this time, Jen, I really do."

He remembers the smell of cigarette smoke curling up the stairs to where he sat on the landing. He remembers coming down a minute after the phone call ended and saying, "What's over, Mum?" and her smiling and stubbing out her cigarette and saying, "Nothing, Owen. Nothing at all. Now get back to bed. School tomorrow."

But he'd been on high alert after that, watching his parents like a hawk for the thing that would show him what was really happening.

Suddenly Owen's flesh crawls as a memory returns to him, something he used to think about all the time but hasn't thought about for years, not since his mother died, because it sickens him so much.

He remembers his father coming home from work one night, late, the smell of London pubs about him. Owen sees him from the top of the landing, dropping his keys onto the dark dresser. Unzipping his jacket. He sees him sigh and then pull back his shoulders as if bracing himself for something.

"Ricky?" His mother's voice from the front room. "Ricky?"

His father sighing again and then moving toward the door. "Hi, love."

And then the sound, as his father opens the door of the front room, of music, not TV music, but strange, dreamy music, an American man singing something about a wicked game. His mother saying, "Hello, darling, come into my boudoir." And Owen tiptoeing down the stairs and peering through the banisters and seeing his mother standing in a room full of candles wearing strange items: underwear with holes cut out, something around her neck, heels four inches high, lips painted red, and Owen's father walking in, his mother grabbing his tie and pulling him toward her saying, "I want you to fuck me like I'm a whore."

And then the door closing and noises—grunts, bangs, muffled wails—before they stop, very suddenly, and his mother is sobbing and his father walks out of the room, doing up his trousers, his face red, and says, "Act like a whore, I'll treat you like a whore."

His mother crying, "Ricky. Please. Please. I want you. I need you. Please. I'll do anything!"

Her mascara running down her cheeks. One breast loose of the cutout bra. Drooping. Puckered.

"Ricky. Please."

His father picking up his coat in the hallway. Picking up his keys. Leaving.

The man singing about his wicked game.

The front door shutting.

Two weeks later Owen's father left for good. The house was sold. The flat was bought. His mother died. His father hated him. His father's wife hated him. His aunt hated him. Girls hated him. He lost his job. He got arrested for killing a girl. He developed a taste for prison food.

Could it be that simple? he wonders. The sight of his mother whoring herself to his father? The rejection by his father of his mother? Was that at the root of everything that had gone wrong since? His fear of women? Of rejection? And if it was that simple, then surely it could be blotted out? Redacted from the story of his life? And then it could start over again. But how? How can he excise that moment? He realizes there's only one way to erase it and that's to go to the heart of it. To his father.

He goes to the door of his cell, and he bangs on it.

Willy opens the window flap. "Yes."

"I need to make a phone call," he says. "Please. It's very urgent."

Willy blinks slowly. "I will have to find out."

"Please. I haven't made a call yet. I'm allowed one call. And I haven't had one yet."

Willy lets the window flap close and says, "I'll find out. Wait."

A moment later Willy is back. He says, "Pick up your things."

"What things?"

"Your clothing and your toiletries. Apparently you are being allowed to leave."

"What? I don't . . . ?"

"I don't know either; I'm just saying what I've been told. Please pack up your things. Now. It's time to go."

"I don't understand. What's happened? Have they found her?"

"Now."

Owen packs up his things. He looks at the golden shadows on the cell wall, the dent in the mattress, the neatly folded blanket. He looks at the square of blue sky through the cell window. He thinks of the hours he has spent in this room that feels so much like the only place he has ever known. And yet now, somehow, he is free of it.

But he knows one thing with a blinding certainty: he is not going back to the other life. He is not going back to Tessie's flat with the locked doors. He is not going back to being the sort of person that people would think capable of rape and murder. He's not going back to the incel forums and seedy drinks with raging women-haters.

Willy opens the door and Owen silently follows him through the corridors, through rooms of people who return things to him and ask him to sign things. Then he is out. On a pavement in Kentish Town. The sun is bright today, a warm sun, a portent of spring, a portent of new beginnings.

He checks his wallet for a debit card and cash, then puts out his arm and hails a taxi.

54

Cate

CATE IS AT Kentish Town police station with Josh. She hasn't told Roan that they are here. She hasn't told Georgia. She phoned Josh's school this morning and told them that he had an emergency medical appointment.

She perches her bag on her lap and clears her throat nervously, watching the swinging doors in front of her open and shut every few seconds, uniformed and nonuniformed police passing through holding files, bags, coffees, phones.

She turns to Josh. "Are you OK?"

He nods nervously. He looks like every fiber of his being is resisting the urge to jump to his feet and run.

Finally, fifteen minutes after they arrive, DI Currie appears.

"Hi, Mrs. Fours," she says. "Thank you so much for coming in. And you are Josh?"

Josh nods and shakes her hand.

"Follow me this way, if you would. I think I've managed to get us an interview room, fingers crossed; we're crazy busy in here today for some reason."

They follow her through a corridor to a door. She knocks and someone answers. "This is my partner, DI Jack Henry. We've been working together on the Saffyre Maddox case. Please, take a seat. Coffee? Tea?"

Someone goes to get them water, and then DI Currie smiles at them each in turn and says, "So, Josh. Your mum says you might have some information about the whereabouts of Saffyre Maddox."

Cate looks at Josh. He shakes his head, then nods. He says, "I don't know where she is. I just know what happened. That's all."

"What happened?"

"Yeah. On Valentine's night. And I know it was nothing to do with that guy over the road. I know that. But I don't know where she is. I don't know where Saffyre is."

Cate sees the two detectives exchange a look. DI Currie turns and smiles kindly at Josh. "So, were you there? On Valentine's night?"

Cate catches her breath because Josh has already told her this and she knows what is coming and it will be worse, she thinks, the second time round.

He'd come to her this morning, in her room. He'd perched on the end of her bed and said, "I have to tell you something. Something really bad."

She'd dropped the facecloth she'd just squeezed out to wash her face with and sat down next to him on the bed.

"Tell me," she'd said.

And then he'd told her.

And her world had fallen into shreds.

DI Currie continues: "And what did you see happen?"

Josh looks up at her. "I didn't just see it," he says. "I was part of it. Me and Saffyre. We were trying to stop something happening. And it all went wrong. And then she just ran. She ran away. And I don't know where she went. And she won't reply to my messages, and I'm scared something bad's happened to her. I'm so scared."

DI Currie inhales slowly. She smiles that slightly wooden smile again and she says, "OK, Josh, I think we're getting ahead of ourselves here. I think it might be best if you start from the very beginning. From when you first met Saffyre. How you knew her. That kind of thing."

Josh throws Cate a quick look and places his hands carefully on top of the table. "She was sleeping in the building plot. Across the way. I used to go in there sometimes. Just for some privacy. For some space. You know. And there was a fox."

"A fox?"

"Yeah. A semi-tame fox. I used to like to sit with it. And then one night I went in there to see the fox and she was there. Saffyre. And she told me she was a former patient of my dad's."

"Did she tell you why she was there?"

Josh looks at Cate. She squeezes his hand encouragingly.

"She was there because she'd been watching my dad. Watching my family. I don't really know why. And I think she had issues. Like, claustrophobia, or something? She couldn't sleep in her own bed. So she slept outdoors, under the stars."

"And why the fascination with your father, do you think?"

Cate squeezes his hand once more.

"I think, at first, it was because she felt abandoned by him? She was in his care for, like, three years or something? From when she was a child? And then she felt like he let her go before he'd fixed her. And she wasn't ready to let go. So she kind of followed him about a bit, and watched him. Wanted to still be part of his life. And then, while she was watching him, she worked out that he was . . ." Josh gulps. "He was having an affair."

Cate feels the encouraging smile fix hard on her face.

She remembers the sickening thump of it to her chest when Josh had told her earlier this morning. Followed rapidly by the sickening draining-away feeling of the inevitability of it. Of course Roan was having an affair. Roan had probably always been having an affair. For all three decades of their lives together. A continuous succession of interleaving affairs, from Marie right through to Alicia. Of course, she'd thought. Of course.

"And then," Josh continues, "I think she became fixated on him, on what he was doing, and on us, on his family. I think it was almost like she was watching over all of us. But that night, the first night we met, we got talking. It was really weird. We just kind of opened up to each other. We talked for ages. She had all these issues, about something that happened to her when she was a child. And she had this idea of how she could cure herself. And I said I'd help her. And that was when it all started kind of . . . going wrong . . ."

"Going wrong?"

"Yes. Kind of really wrong."

55

Owen

OWEN'S DAD'S HOUSE looks just like the house they lived in in Winchmore Hill: postwar, small leaded windows, a front garden, a porch, a stained glass sunray above the front door. Owen's never been here before. Just written the address on birthday cards and Christmas cards. He pays the taxi driver, and he heads up the path. His dad used to work in the civil service but is retired now.

The doorbell chimes electronically when he presses it. He clears his throat and he waits. A shadow appears through the dimpled glass of the front door. Owen breathes in, hoping it's his dad and not his dad's wife. The door opens, and yes, it's his dad. He watches his face splinter into a hundred different pieces, sees it go from surprise, to fear, to horror.

"Owen, my God, what are you doing here?"

His dad looks older than he remembers. He only retired last year, but he seems to have aged five years since then. His hair had once been a mass of different shades of brown and silver and white, but now it's nearly all white.

"They let me go," he says.

"The police?"

"Yes. Just now. They let me go."

"So . . . what? You didn't do it, then?"

"No, Dad. No. God. Of course I didn't do it." Owen peers over his father's shoulder. "Can I come in?"

His dad sighs. "It's not really a good time, Owen, to be honest."

"Dad, let's face it, it's never a good time for you. It never, ever is. But I tell you what, I've just spent nearly a week in a police holding cell being interrogated about a crime I had nothing to do with. I've had my face slapped all across the front pages of all the papers and been defamed by people who don't even know me. And now I've been exonerated, been told I'm a free man, that I've done nothing wrong and allowed out into the world to get on with my life. So maybe, just maybe, now is a good time for *me*."

His dad drops his head slightly. When he lifts it again, his eyes look watery. He says, "Come on then. But I don't have long. I'm really very sorry."

The house is warm. Every wall is painted a different color. There are neon signs on the walls: GIN THIS WAY, LOVE, OUR HOUSE. A rainbow. A rearing unicorn that changes color as it rears.

"Gina loves her color," says his dad, leading him into the front room. This has a small bow window, plantation shutters, pink velvet sofas scattered with cushions embroidered with jungle animals and more slogans. "Sit down," he says. "Please."

He doesn't offer Owen a drink. But Owen doesn't care.

"Dad," he says. "I've been doing a lot of thinking while I've been locked up. About how I got myself into that position. How I am the way I am. You know?"

His dad shrugs. He's wearing a gray sweater and navy trousers and with his silver hair he looks like a glitch in the relentless color of the room.

"You know what I'm talking about, Dad. You know I've never been quite right. Since being a little boy. But I'm not a little boy anymore. I'm a man. I'm thirty-three. Nearly thirty-four. The worst thing that could ever happen to an innocent man just happened to me, because of the way I am. And you abandoned me. You let me leave your flat that night, eighteen years old, just buried my mother, you let me leave. Why did you let me leave?"

His father shuffles slightly on the pink velvet. "It seemed for the best," he said. "You know. That flat was too small for all of us. We had a young child. You weren't happy there . . ."

"I wasn't happy there because I was made to feel unwelcome. So unwelcome."

"Well, there might be a shred of truth in that. But it wasn't personal. It was the situation we all found ourselves in. And when Tessie said she'd take you—"

"You know what Tessie's like though, Dad. You know she never liked me. She doesn't let me in her living room. Did you know that? I'm not allowed in her living room. And I'm her nephew. Why? Why didn't you want me?"

"I told you, Owen. It was nothing personal."

"Yes, Dad, yes, it was. It's all been personal. All of it. Everything that ever happened to me has been personal. Because people don't like me."

"Oh, now, Owen, that's nonsense. I like you. I like you every much."

"Dad. Tell me what happened between you and Mum. Why did you split up? Was it because of me?"

"What? No! Goodness, no. Nothing to do with you. We were just . . . we were mismatched. That was all. She wasn't . . . enough. In some ways. She was too much in others. She wanted another baby. But it didn't happen. She went very into herself. Very deeply into herself."

"You know," Owen begins slowly, "I saw something once. When I was about eleven. I saw Mum, in the living room, wearing sexy lingerie. There were candles. She pulled you in. And then . . ."

Owen's dad sighs. "Yes," he said. "I did tell her. I told her you might walk in. I told her it was stupid."

"You called her a whore. And then you split up after that. Was she a whore? My mum? Is that why you left us?" He knows the answer, of course he does, but he needs to hear his dad say it.

"Your mother? Oh, God, no, of course not!"

"So why did you call her a whore?"

"Oh, Owen. God. I don't even remember saying it."

"You said, 'Act like a whore, I'll treat you like a whore.'"

Owen feels a muscle twitch in his cheek as he waits for his dad to respond.

"Did I say that?"

"Yes. You did."

"Well. It was a bad time for us. You know. We were drifting apart. She knew I'd met someone. She was . . . I suppose she was desperate. Trying anything to keep me. And there's something so dreadful about a desperate woman, Owen. So dreadful."

They both fall silent for a moment. Then his dad says, "You know I loved your mum, Owen. I loved her very much. And you."

"Me?"

"Yes. Leaving you behind killed me."

"Did it?"

"Of course it did. You were my boy. Just on the cusp of it all. Just about to blossom. But I was under pressure. Gina wasn't getting any younger. She wanted to start trying for a family immediately.

She pulled me, really pulled me very hard, away from you both. And I can see now that that wasn't easy for you."

"So you didn't leave because Mum was a whore. You left because Gina wanted you all to herself."

His dad nods. "Essentially. Yes."

Owen pauses to absorb this.

"And you let me leave when I was eighteen because Gina wanted her family to herself?"

"Again, there were other factors at play. But yes. There was some . . . pressure there."

Another silence falls; then Owen says, "Dad. What do you think about women? Do you like them?"

"Like them?"

"Yes."

"Of course I like them! Goodness. Yes. Women are remarkable. And I've been blessed that two of them have let me share their lives with them. I mean, look at me . . ." He gestures at himself. "I'm not exactly catch of the day, am I? I've been punching above my weight all my life. And I wouldn't have it any other way."

There's a sound at the door and Owen turns and there's Gina. She's wearing a black satin blouse with dark flowers printed on it and tight blue jeans. Her hair is dyed a shiny mahogany and up in a ponytail. She's pushing sixty but still looks youthful.

"Oh," she says. "I thought I heard voices. Ricky"—she looks at Owen's dad—"what's going on?"

"They let him out, Gina. This morning. Dropped all charges. He's a free man."

"Oh." She clearly doesn't know what to say. "That's good, then?"

"Of course it's good! It's wonderful."

"And everything else?" she asks, still standing in the doorway. "The girls at college? The date-rape drugs . . . ?"

"Gina—"

"No, Ricky. It's important. Sorry, Owen, but it is. Look. I don't know you very well, and I'm sorry about that. I've—we've—had a lot on our plates over the years with Jackson, as you know. But there's no smoke without fire, Owen. And even if you've been cleared of that girl's disappearance, there is still an awful lot of smoke around you. An awful lot."

Owen feels a familiar tug of anger in his chest. But he quells it, breathes in hard. He turns and he engages Gina properly, in a way in which he has rarely engaged a woman, with clear eyes and an open heart, and he says, "You're right, Gina. I totally understand what you're saying. I've been far from the best version of myself over the years, and I take my share of the blame for everything that's happened to me. But this, what I've just been through, it's changed me. I don't want to be that person anymore. I'm going to work on myself."

He sees a chink in Gina's defenses. A slight tip of her chin.

"Well, that's good," she says. "And you could probably start by apologizing to those girls. The ones you made feel uncomfortable at the college disco."

"Yes," he says. "Yes. I'm going to sort it all out. All of it. I swear."

Gina nods and says, "Good boy." Then she looks serious for a moment. "But if it wasn't you who abducted that girl, then who was it?"

Owen blinks. He didn't ask. He'd been so shell-shocked by the unexpected sequence of events that he'd just walked out without even wondering.

56

Cate

"MY DAD GOT a Valentine's card," Josh explains to DI Currie. "My sister opened it; my mum snatched it away from her, told her it was private and that she wasn't to open it. And there was a bit of a row between my mum and my sister, my sister telling my mum that she should want to know who was sending Valentine's cards to my dad. And then my mum hid it away in a drawer. I snuck in when she wasn't looking and read it. It was from her. The woman. Alicia."

"And what did it say?" asks DI Henry.

"Oh, just all this desperate stuff. Like how she needed him and couldn't live without him."

"So it looked like he was going to leave your mother for her?"

Josh shrugs. "Yeah, I guess. And I just . . . I was so angry with my dad when I saw that card, that what he was doing with that woman had somehow found its way into my home. And I ended up confronting him."

"When was this?"

"That night. Valentine's night. He went out for a run, and I ran out after him and stopped him on the corner. I had the card in my hand. I said, 'Dad, what the fuck are you doing? You're going to kill mum if you do this. You're going to kill her!'

"But then Dad told me he'd taken Alicia out for lunch that day, to tell her that he wasn't going to leave Mum for her. That their affair was over. And me and Dad hugged and I was crying and he said he was sorry, he was so, so sorry. I said, 'What are we going to do about this card?' I said, 'We can't get rid of it because Mum knows it's in the house. If it disappears, she'll know there was something fishy going on. She'll know.' He said, 'Leave it with me. I'll sort it out. Leave it with me.' And then he and Mum went out for dinner, and me and Georgia were at home, and at about eleven o'clock the doorbell rang and I thought it was going to be Mum and Dad, forgotten their keys, but it wasn't, it was her. It was Alicia. And she was really drunk. Crying, saying, 'Let me in, let me in. I want to see him. Let me in!' And I said, 'He's not here. He's out with Mum.' I told her to fuck off. To leave us alone."

"And where was your sister when all of this was happening?"

"She was in her room, it's at the other end of the hallway and she was watching a movie with her AirPods in so she didn't hear anything."

DI Currie writes this down and then nods at Josh to continue.

"I called Saffyre then, to tell her what was happening. She said she'd come over."

"Why did she say that?"

Josh shrugs. "Like I said, we just kind of look out for each other. We're friends. I was helping her. She was helping me." He picks up his water cup and puts it down again. "She got to our street at about eleven fifteen. She messaged me to say that she was outside and the coast was clear, no sign of Alicia. She said she'd stay and keep an eye on the place. And then I heard Mum and Dad get back about fifteen minutes later and I thought that was it. That it was all over. But a few minutes later I heard voices outside my bedroom window, and I saw Dad in the front garden and then I saw him pulling someone out onto the pavement. Her. Alicia.

"I didn't know where Saffyre was then. I thought maybe she'd just gone home. A few seconds later I saw Alicia running past our house; she looked like she was crying. And then out of nowhere I saw Saffyre, running behind her. And that was the last time I saw Saffyre. Running after Alicia."

Josh clears his throat and takes a sip of his water.

"And where did Saffyre and Alicia go? Do you know?" asks DI Currie.

Josh shakes his head. "I have no idea. But Saffyre called me later that night, about one in the morning. She said she couldn't tell me where she was but that she'd done something, something really bad, and that she needed to go into hiding for a while because she was scared. She told me not to tell anyone, not the police, not even her uncle. She turned her phone off after that. I couldn't contact her. But . . ." Josh wrings his hands together, and Cate strokes them. "Saffyre was hunting someone. She was hunting a guy who did something to her when she was a child. She'd found out where he lived and had been following him, and she was convinced— we were both convinced that he had something to do with all the sex attacks in the area. You know, the guy who's been grabbing women?"

DI Currie looks at Josh in surprise. "Oh," she says. "OK. And do you have any idea who that might have been?"

"She told me never to tell anyone. She told me not to. But now I'm really worried he's done something to her. Because she should be back by now. If she was safe, she'd be back, wouldn't she?"

"Who, Joshua? Who do you and Saffyre think has been attacking women in the area?" DI Currie asks gently.

Josh sighs and there is a moment of weighty silence while he forms his response.

Cate stares at him.

Finally he replies. "It's a guy called Harrison John. He lives on Alfred Road, up the Chalk Farm end. He's about eighteen. He hurt Saffyre when she was a child, and now she thinks he's hurting other women."

The two DIs exchange a look. The male DI leaves the room and DI Currie turns back to Josh. She says, "Thank you, Josh. Thank you so much. DI Henry's going to follow that up right now."

"But there's another thing. Just"—Josh pulls his hands down his face—"one more thing." He looks up at DI Currie. "I've been following him too."

He glances at Cate. Cate widens her eyes at him. He hadn't told her this earlier.

"That was what Saffyre said to me when she called me at one o'clock that night. She said she couldn't come back until the police had got him, Harrison John. She said she was scared he was going to kill her. She told me to keep watching him until I caught him in the act, until I had some definite evidence that it was him who'd been carrying out the attacks. So I've been out at night just following him about. Waiting for him to do something. Anything."

Cate swallows hard. She's overwhelmed by mixed emotions: pride, fear, horror, love; she feels as though she might drown in them all.

"Then a few days ago I heard him on his phone telling someone he was meeting a girl on Sunday afternoon, that he was taking her to the O2 Centre to watch a movie. So I went along, and I sat through the movie with them and watched him and he was all over this girl, and I could tell she was finding him really annoying, she kept pushing him away, and then they left, and I saw him pulling this girl along the road, toward the back end of the cinema and he was trying to make out like he was playfighting with her but I could tell she wasn't enjoying herself, and so I stayed really close. Really, really close. Too close. Because he saw me and he got me against a wall like this." Josh mimes a fist around a collar. "He said he didn't know who I was or what I wanted but if he saw me hanging around anywhere near him ever again, he'd shank me. He said, 'I've seen your face now, faggot, I've seen your face. Next time I see you, you're dead.'"

Josh pauses. He licks his lips. He turns to Cate. "And that was when I wet myself."

Cate's eyes fill with tears. The thought of her beautiful boy being held against a wall. The terrible, inevitable heat of a bladder emptied in fear. His shaking hands forcing the damp, stinking clothes into a carrier bag, shoving it into the corner of his wardrobe.

"I said, 'What did you do to Saffyre?' He said, 'Don't mention that whore's name to me. She's a dirty little skank.' I said, 'Where is she? Where the fuck is she?' He said, 'I don't fucking know. Getting whatever's due to her, I hope. Now fuck off, stalker faggot.'"

Josh's shoulders slump. Then he looks up at the detective and he says, "I never caught him doing anything, Harrison John. I tried so, so hard. But can you get him anyway? Get him off the streets, please? So that Saffyre can come back. Please."

57

Saffyre

EVERY MUSCLE IN my body went hard, every sinew tensed, every hair stood on end. My heart, which was already thumping, started to race. I could see him closing in on Alicia, his pace picking up.

I thought, Oh no you don't, Harrison John, *oh no you don't*.

I stayed back in the shadows waiting for him to pass, and then I ran up behind him, hooked my arm around his neck and brought him down onto the ground. His body made a satisfying cracking noise as it hit the pavement. I kept him pinned there for a while with his face pressed into the pavement so he couldn't see me.

"What do you want?" he said.

I brought my mouth close to his ear, close enough to smell his aftershave, the lingering aroma of a recently smoked cigarette.

I hissed into his ear. I said, "Want to see something magic, Harrison John?"

I took off my beanie hat and shoved it in his mouth to muffle his screams. And then I reached down for his hand.

His right hand.

I bent it back and brought it up to his face.

Then very slowly I took each of the three fingers he'd put inside me when I was ten years old and I snapped each one in turn.

Every time he cried out in pain I said, "It only hurts the first time, Harrison. It only hurts the first time. The next time it will be *magic.*"

I loosened my hold on him and he rolled over on top of me.

"Agh," he said, cupping his broken fingers, his face contorted with pain, "argh, fuck's sake. What the fuck!" He raised his arm as if he was going to hit me with it but then his vision seem to blur and he slumped on top of me in a dead faint.

I looked up and there was the face of an angel, backlit by a street lamp, a halo of red hair. It was Alicia.

"Are you OK?" she said. I saw the beginnings of a bruise on the edge of her cheekbone where Roan had hit her.

I pushed Harrison off me, and he started to stir, clutching his broken fingers, moaning.

I looked at Alicia and said, "Are *you* OK?"

She looked at me blankly. "Who are you?"

I said, "Let's get out of here. You got Uber?"

She nodded and pulled her phone out of her bag. Her hands were shaking.

Harrison was trying to get to his feet. He started to lumber after me but I grabbed Alicia's hand and together we ran down the hill.

"I'm going to kill you, Saffyre Maddox," I heard him yell after me. "Next time I see you, you're fucking dead. Do you fucking hear me? *Dead.*"

———

The Uber took us to Alicia's flat. I thought about telling her that I'd seen her apartment block before, that I knew she lived on the fourth floor. But I thought, upon reflection, that the night had already been weird enough for both of us without adding that into the mix.

Her flat was really cute. Mint-green sofas with buttons on the backs and squat wooden feet, funky art in white frames, a lot of plants, a lot of books.

Alicia made us tea and opened some chocolate biscuits. As I picked up my mug I saw that my hands were shaking. I put the mug down again and breathed in hard. In my head I replayed the feeling of Harrison John's bones snapping, the weird noise they made, like the noise when Angelo crunched his cat biscuits. And then I pictured him lumbering home to his flat on Alfred Road overlooking the railway track, clutching his broken fingers. I saw him sitting in the emergency room at the Royal Free Hospital, and I pictured him leaving a while later with some kind of plastic covering over his hand, splints and bandages and whatnot holding his hand in place while it healed. I thought, How will he explain this to the world? And then I thought, Will he go to the police? I imagined him telling some fresh-faced, straight-out-of-Hendon cop that a girl called Saffyre had felled him in one blow and broken his fingers on a pavement in the dark for no good reason, and I could not see that happening.

"Are you going to tell me who you are now?" Alicia asked me.

"I'm Saffyre Maddox," I said.

"And you used to be a patient of Roan's?"

"Uh-huh."

I watched everything processing through Alicia's head, saw her big clever brain trying to compute everything, and failing.

"And that guy?"

"I used to know him. He hurt me. Now I've hurt him."

"He said he was going to kill you if he saw you again."

"Yeah," I said. And that was the problem. That was why my hands were shaking. I'd finally purged the childhood event that had destroyed me by inflicting pain on the perpetrator, but in doing so I'd opened myself up to yet more pain, more fear, more hurt.

"Have you got anywhere you can stay?"

I stared at my fingers. "I live with my uncle," I said.

"Are you safe there?"

"Not really," I said. "It's very close to where that guy lives. My school is just around the corner from his flat."

"You can stay here tonight, if you want?"

I glanced up at Alicia. Her eyes were still red from crying, and the scuff on her cheek from where Roan had hit her was swelling up now. I thought, She needs me as much as I need her right now. So I nodded and said, "Thank you. I really appreciate that."

———

I ended up staying at Alicia's for a fortnight.

And for a fortnight I resisted the urge to contact Aaron. I can't really explain it, how I could have done that to him. To someone who loved me and cared about me the way I knew he did. I knew he would be suffering, but each day that dawned I thought, Not today, not yet, he'll be OK for a few more hours, I'll go home soon. Each day I thought would be my last day in hiding. Each day felt like it was the day that Josh would track down Harrison John, that he would be detained by the police and that I would be safe.

Time didn't have much form during those days. Without the punctuation of being the version of myself that puts on eyeliner and goes to school every day, I just stayed in a kind of sleep mode.

My instincts didn't work properly: Alicia had to remind me to eat; I would wake up at three in the morning and think it was daytime and that I was blind.

Alicia called in sick for the first few days, and she did her best to keep me safe and sane. In weird, disjointed streams of consciousness I ended up telling her everything, everything I'd never told Roan about the real reasons why I'd been self-harming.

Alicia was twelve years older than me, but for those days we spent together, she felt more like a friend than a therapist. The sort of friend, I thought, that I'd managed to keep at arm's length almost my entire life. Then Alicia went back to work, and I was in her flat all day by myself. I could barely remember my name sometimes. Shards of my existence flashed through my mind like a psychedelic slideshow; I'd see the fox in the corner of the room sometimes. Other times I'd hear Josh's voice coming from Alicia's TV, the mewl of a tiny kitten outside the front door, Jasmin's mad laugh coming from the flat upstairs. And every time I closed my eyes, there was Harrison John, looming at me from every direction with a claw for a hand, threatening to kill me.

———

It took the shock of seeing Owen Pick's face on the front page of the paper that Alicia brought back with her from work to wake me up out of my weird fugue. I thought, Oh no, oh no, this can't be happening. Not Clive. Not that poor bastard with his crappy single bed and his evil landlady. I felt sick with guilt.

I nearly went, that day, nearly walked into Kentish Town police station to tell them the truth and get that poor bastard out of there. But something stopped me. The same thing that stopped me from contacting Aaron. A sense that I needed to let the game play itself out, that there was a different ending, just out of sight, and that it was the right one, somehow.

And then over the next few days I read about Owen Pick being an incel, about how they'd found Rohypnol in his underwear drawer, how he was planning to go around date-raping ladies in revenge for no one wanting to have sex with him and I thought maybe this was a good thing? I thought of all the women Owen Pick wouldn't get to date-rape now and thought perhaps it was good that I'd disappeared because it meant that a bad man was going to be taken off the streets.

Alicia pointed at the photo and she said, "Totally looks the type, doesn't he? When you think about it?"

I nodded and said, "He really does," and I tried not to think of him that night, all cross-eyed with Valentine's wine, helping me up onto the roof, the solid feel of his shoulders through his smart jacket, the way he kept flicking his fringe out of his eyes so he could see what he was doing, the innocence of him, the guilelessness.

And I tried not to think too much about the time we'd passed each other on the hill all those weeks earlier when he was drunk and how we'd had that pleasant exchange and I'd told him my name was Jane and he'd said, "Night night, Jane." Sweet as can be. I tried really hard not to think about any of that.

On Tuesday I woke up in a cold sweat from a nightmare. The details of the nightmare fled as consciousness returned, but the main elements remained: Aaron had died in this dream, and so had my kitten.

I knew without a doubt that it was a shout from my deepest self, telling me to end this thing, to end it now. I walked into Alicia's bedroom. It was nearly 7:00 a.m. and I figured her alarm would be about to go off so I sat at the foot of her bed and I wiggled her feet. She woke with a start.

I said, "Can you call the police today? Can you tell them you were there? That you saw me. That Owen Pick didn't hurt me. Can you tell them you saw me running away? You don't have to tell them you know where I am. I don't want you getting into trouble. But just tell them what you saw. Tell them Owen Pick didn't kill me. Please."

———

The following day Alicia brought home a copy of the *Evening Standard*. The headline read, "SAFFYRE SUSPECT FREED."

I flattened it out hard on her coffee table and read it superfast.

North London police have today released the prime suspect in their hunt for the abductor of 17-year-old schoolgirl Saffyre Maddox. Former college lecturer Owen Pick, 33, was sent home without charge after fresh evidence was brought to the case from a new witness who claims to have proof that Saffyre is safe and well in hiding. The reasons for her disappearance have not been revealed. As a result of this new evidence, police today arrested an 18-year-old man, Harrison John, from Chalk Farm, on suspicion of various sex attacks in the local area. John, who has been arrested before for crimes including mugging and petty theft, is currently being held for questioning.

I looked at Alicia, and I said, "You told them about Harrison John?"

She shook her head. "Not me."

I threw back my head and I gasped. "Josh!" I said. And then I laughed.

And then, this morning, Alicia called me from work. She said, "They've charged Harrison John. It's all over the news. A young girl came forward to say that he'd attacked her and then threatened to kill her and her mother if she ever said anything to the police. It's over, Saffyre," she said, and I could hear a smile pouring out of her so real and so good that I felt like it might drown me. "It's over. You can go home."

58

AARON IS SITTING in his car opposite Alicia's flat. I don't see him at first as I push my way through the doors, shading my eyes from the sun. But he sees me and opens his car door. He walks fast up the path to meet me halfway and almost knocks me over as he throws himself at me, locks his arms around my shoulders, buries his face into my hair.

I put my arms around him too, and I hold him hard, hard, hard; harder than I've ever held on to anything or anyone before, and I feel his love for me, I feel that he loves me, I know that I am loved.

He's crying and I realize that I'm crying too.

"I'm so sorry," I say, feeling my tears seeping into the cloth of his coat. "For everything. For the worry. For the lies. For hurting you. I'm so, so sorry."

"It's OK," he says. "It's OK."

"I didn't mean to . . . ," I begin, with no idea what it is that I want to say.

"It doesn't matter," he says. "It doesn't matter. It's done now. It's done."

We pull apart, and Aaron looks at me, looks hard into my eyes. "I knew it," he says, "I knew all along that you were safe. I could feel it." He touches his chest with his fist. "I could feel it in here. A connection. With you. With your soul. We're family," he says. "Whatever. Forever. Yeah?"

I wipe the tears from my face with the ends of my sleeves, and I look up at my uncle, this good, good man, and I smile, and I say, "I really want to see my kitten."

"He's grown big, man, since you left. He's, like, almost a cat now."

"Did he miss me?"

"'Course he missed you! We both missed you!"

We climb into his crappy car, and I pull on my seat belt.

"Can I explain, Aaron? Can I explain what happened?"

"In your own time," he says. "We have loads of time. All the time in the world. But first, let's just get you home. OK?"

"OK," I reply. "OK."

PART THREE

Now

59

Owen

OWEN LEAVES THE unit in Hammersmith where he's spent every day for the past two weeks. It's late March. It's sunny. It's his thirty-fourth birthday. He turns to say goodbye to a woman behind him. Her name is Liz. She was in the same course as him. The course was called Sexual Conduct Training and Rehabilitation for Employees and Management. Liz is an HR manager for Ealing libraries. She handled a sexual harassment case earlier this year on behalf of two female employees and did everything wrong. They all know an awful lot about each other after two weeks of role-playing and debating and videos and first-person testimonials. And of course, everyone already knew who Owen was the minute he walked through the door on the very first morning. A surge of energy had gone through the room. An almost audible gasp. It was him, the man who'd been arrested for killing that girl. The incel. The pervert. The weirdo. The creep. He'd seen all the women in the room recoil slightly.

It didn't matter that he'd been exonerated. It didn't matter that the girl had been found and reunited with her family. Her smiling face on the front pages of the newspapers had not, for some reason, canceled out his grimacing face from the front pages of the papers. There was still a potency about the image of his face, about his name. It would take weeks, months, possibly years for him to lose the terrible associations of his time as one of the most reviled men in the country.

The police had found Bryn. They'd brought him in for questioning as he left his local pub opposite the duck pond in the leafy commuter town. It was the same day they'd let Owen go home. His name was not Bryn, of course. It was Jonathan. They found more date-rape drugs in his flat. Reams of incel literature. Violent pornography. Drafts of his blog posts on his laptop. They took his prints and matched them to those on the pot of pills he'd given Owen. He's on their watch list now, as a terrorist threat. That made Owen happy.

Liz smiles at him as she passes him and says, "Bye, Owen. It's been great getting to know you. I really wish you all the best, all the very, very best. I hope you can put everything behind you. You're a good man, and I've really enjoyed getting to know you." She kisses him quickly on the cheek, squeezes the top of his arm.

He watches her dash across the street to someone waiting for her in a parked car. She waves at him from the window and he waves back.

The training course has been a revelation. Not just in terms of what it's taught him about how to behave in the workplace, but what it's taught him about how to behave, full stop; how women's minds work, what makes them feel safe, what makes them feel unsafe, what's banter, what's creepy.

Earlier in the week a woman had come in to talk to them about the sexual harassment she'd experienced from a former employer, how he had seemed so nice at first, but after a while she'd realized that every single second of every single encounter, whatever they were doing, whatever they were talking about, he was seeing her as a woman, not a human being. That had really hit Owen dead center. He'd been doing that all his life, he realized. He had never, ever had a conversation, an interlude, an encounter with a woman without the primary thought in his head being that she was a woman. Not once, not ever.

He'd put up his hand and he'd asked her how to stop doing it.

The woman said, "You can't simply stop doing it; if you consciously try to stop doing it, you'll still be putting the woman's gender at the top of your encounter. The only way," she'd said, "to stop doing it is to acknowledge to yourself when it's happening, to *own* your reaction. To work around it. Think about something else. Say to yourself, 'This is a human being wearing a red jacket.' Or, 'This is a human being with a northern accent.' Or, 'This is a human being with a nice smile.' Or, 'This is a human being with a problem who needs my help.' Own your reaction. Work round it." She'd smiled at him encouragingly, and he'd put her advice into action immediately. He turned his sensation of talking to a young, reasonably attractive woman into the sensation of talking to a human being with brown shoes on. It had worked. It broke the spell. He'd smiled at her and he'd said, "Thank you. Thank you so much."

And so now, pending confirmation from the course directors that he has passed the assessment criteria, Owen will have his job back at the college. He has written to Monique and Maisy, explained, without expecting pity or even understanding, that he suffers from fragmentary blackouts when he's drunk even a small amount of alcohol, that his recollection of the night in question is very different to their recollection, but that he wholeheartedly believes and accepts their version of events. That he is abject with regret and sadness that he made them feel uncomfortable and that he chose to disbelieve them when they had the courage to tell the truth. It was a wordy missive, but from the heart and worth doing properly, he'd thought, so that no one could ever accuse him of just doing it for the sake of getting his job back. He wants to be able to face them in the classroom next week and for there to be a bond between them, not a divide.

Owen no longer lives with Tessie. He's renting a studio flat in West Hampstead, just for now. He'll make proper plans soon. But in the short term it was important that he escape from her and her poisoned view of him. She tried to pretend she was sad that he was going. But she wasn't. Owen has a sofa now, not an armchair, a double bed, not a single, and he keeps his home as warm as he wants it to be.

He heads toward the tube to take the Piccadilly line to Covent Garden. Just before he descends the escalator, he gets out his phone, finds Deanna's number, and sends her a text. *Just getting on the tube*, it says. *Be there in twenty minutes.*

He waits a beat to see if she'll reply. Then there it is: *See you in twenty minutes, birthday boy!*

He switches off his phone, smiles, and heads into the underground, toward dinner, with his girlfriend, on his birthday.

60

Cate

CATE PUTS THE key in the shiny new lock on the front door of their house in Kilburn. She looks behind her at the children. Georgia gives her a little push and says, "Go on. Get on with it!"

She turns the key and pushes the door and there it is. Their house. It's a lovely April morning, halfway through the Easter holidays. The removals men are on their way from the flat in Hampstead and finally, 456 days after the builders first arrived, Cate's house is hers again.

The sun plays off immaculate pastel-gray walls and leaves pools of golden light on the newly sanded and waxed floorboards. There's not a fleck of dust, dirty mark, or piece of clutter anywhere. It's a beautiful blank canvas, just right for new beginnings.

Georgia gasps. "It looks so awesome!" she says, before running up the stairs to check out her bedroom.

Cate goes to the kitchen and runs her hands over the pale wood of the work surfaces, the dove-gray tongue-and-groove cabinet doors, the gleaming black ceramic stove. She can barely remember what her kitchen looked like before; too much has happened in between.

Cate has finally said goodbye to Roan. After Josh had come to her that morning back in February and told her about his father's affair, Cate had numbly thought she might still be able to make it work. She'd done it before, she figured, she could do it again, keep the marriage artificially alive for a few more years, until the children were gone. But once the drama of Saffyre's disappearance had settled and life had returned to its normal proportions, she'd woken up very early one morning, looked down at her sleeping husband's face, always so peaceful in sleep, his skin still unlined and fresh, a vaguely smug smile on his lips, and she'd thought, Everything about you is an illusion. You have conned me for thirty years and I can never trust you again.

He'd cried when she told him she wanted him to leave. Cried and said he couldn't live without her. Of course he had. That was Roan's MO. But she'd enjoyed the feeling of the power tipping back her way again after so long being made to feel the unhinged wife. He's taken a sabbatical from work to get over the trauma of finally being made to feel the consequences of his actions. He's back in Rye, in the spare bedroom of his parents' cottage. He phones a lot and talks about how much he can change. But Cate doesn't want him to change. She just wants him to leave her alone to get on with the rest of her life.

And what is the rest of Cate's life going to be? Last week she put down a deposit on a treatment room at a clinic in Neasden and once Georgia's finished her GCSEs she's going to start practicing physiotherapy again, full time. The children are mainly self-sufficient these days. Josh has blossomed since becoming friends with Saffyre and Cate no longer feels the innate need to be at home for him all the time. She will remortgage the house to pay Roan his share and will need an income for the repayments. She also needs an existence beyond her kitchen table, the stimulation of interaction with people she's not related to; doing the grocery shopping can no longer be the sole focus of her days.

So many things had dropped into place in the aftermath of Josh's interview with the police. Everything had been oddly connected.

It turned out that Tilly had in fact been attacked outside their house and that the attacker was Harrison John, the same boy that Josh and Saffyre had been hunting down. Tilly had recognized Harrison halfway through the assault; he'd been at her school for a couple of years, before being expelled for disruptive behavior and moved to a special unit. Everyone at the school knew his name; he was infamous for his bad behavior. Harrison had seen the recognition in her eyes and realized that he knew Tilly too, that he was friends with someone who lived on the same floor in her apartment block. Apparently when he saw that he'd been recognized, he'd grabbed her wrists, hard, and whispered into her ear, "I know where you live, OK, remember that. *I know where you live,*" before quoting her address at her and disappearing into the night.

And there'd been a weird and rather unsettling postscript to the Harrison John story; it emerged, once he was under arrest for Tilly's attack, that Roan had treated him at his clinic for a few weeks, back when he was eleven years old. In a strangely sickening quirk of fate, it turned out that Harrison John was the little boy who'd written the violent rape fantasies, the boy Roan had mentioned in passing only a few weeks before. The connectivity was unnerving.

Once Harrison had been charged by the police for his attack on Tilly and held on remand, just as Josh predicted, Saffyre reappeared. She never fully explained where she'd been, just told police that she'd been in fear for her life after being threatened by Harrison John and that she'd been "with a friend." The day after Cate took Josh to the police station, Saffyre returned to her flat on the eighth floor of the apartment block on Alfred Road, to her uncle and her kitten. That was the photo that accompanied all the articles in the papers, a smiling Saffyre Maddox and her kitten, Angelo. A happy ending.

Except of course it wasn't.

Nothing is perfect. Even this house, she thinks, her eyes casting about the clean lines of it, is not perfect. Even now, she sees, in this newly plastered and painted room, that there is a large crack running from the point where the corners meet. And the builders only left yesterday.

Nothing can ever be perfect. And that's fine. Cate doesn't want perfect. She just wants now, this, here, this moment as they walk around their empty, shiny, paint-smelling home, summer on its way, the garden furniture she ordered from IKEA in cardboard boxes waiting to be assembled, the barbecue party she dreamed of back in the winter months so close now she can almost smell the sweet hickory smoke.

61

Saffyre

THERE'RE NO SUCH things as happy endings; we all know that.

You know, here I am safe back home with Aaron. I got over my claustrophobia and I sleep in my bed now, under a duvet, with my kitten. When I wake up in the mornings, my sheets are still attached to the bed and not knotted around my legs. I'm predicted to do really well in my mock A levels in spite of missing two weeks of school. Oh, and I have a sort of boyfriend. Someone who's been in love with me for years. It's not quite the real deal, but it's nice, you know. And it's just good that I can finally imagine letting someone in, you know, letting someone get close.

Alicia works in a different clinic now and has no idea what she ever saw in Roan. We're still good friends, and I go over once a week or so for a cup of tea and a chat.

I stayed in touch with Josh too. He told me that his parents split up, which doesn't surprise me too much. I'm glad for his mum; she looked like the sort of woman whose whole life had been molded around a man and now she was free to find what shape she really wanted to be. Roan had some kind of mental breakdown and is currently on sabbatical from work and living with his parents down in Sussex somewhere.

And Harrison John is on remand for what he did to that little girl.

He's also on remand for two of the other attacks on that list I made all those weeks ago. The victims came forward when they saw his photo in the papers and identified him as their attacker. CCTV footage showed him to be on the vicinity of the attacks and his fingerprints matched a print taken from one victim's handbag. So, there, I got what I wanted; I got justice. I got a disgusting human being put away, and now the whole country knows what he is.

And then there's Owen Pick. Weirdly I bumped into him the other day. He was just coming out of the tube station; I was going in. We stopped for a little while, and I finally got the chance to apologize to him properly for not going to the police earlier to let them know he had nothing to do with my disappearance. I said, "My head was all over the place back then. I didn't know right from wrong."

He said, "Yeah, I know what you mean. My head was in the same place, too." He told me he'd asked for his job back at the college and they'd agreed. He told me he no longer lived in the house next to the building site, that he had his own place now, for the first time in his life. And he told me that he had a girlfriend. "Early days," he'd said. "But so far, so good."

We hugged as we said goodbye, and it felt like the last piece of the puzzle falling into place. I walked away from him thinking, There. It's all done now. Everything's back in one piece.

But.

Something doesn't sit right. Something to do with Valentine's night when I was sitting outside Roan's old place.

That first night at Alicia's I looked at the footage on my phone that I'd filmed from the top of Owen's garage roof. I watched it over and over. I zoomed in on the look on Roan's face as his hand came into contact with Alicia's porcelain skin. The engorged rage of it. The fury. The darkness.

I know how the world works.

Men hit women.

Women hit men.

Girls break boys' fingers in revenge for childhood abuse.

But there was something stone-cold terrifying about the look on Roan's face as he hit Alicia, this man whose job it was to cure people. Just like Josh had said that night when we first got chatting: How did a man with a job like his reconcile himself to causing pain to people he loved on a daily basis?

I showed the footage to Alicia that night. She had a packet of peas held to the bruise on her cheekbone. She flinched when I showed it to her. I said, "Fuck, Alicia, what sort of man is this?"

She said, "I don't want to dwell on that."

I said, "What do you mean?"

She let the bag of peas drop to her lap. "It's like he goes through life wearing a mask. Tonight, I saw it come off, and I didn't like it. It made me wonder," she said. "It made me wonder about things."

"What sort of things?"

"Just things he'd talk about. Things he wanted to do in bed. Things he'd say."

"Like what?"

She brought the peas back to her cheek and shook her head lightly. "I caught him once," she said, her breath catching slightly on the words, "I caught him in his office. He was . . . pleasuring himself. I teased him, asked if he was thinking about me. He laughed it off, said of course he was thinking about me. But I saw, out of the corner of my eye, Saffyre, I saw an essay one of his patients had written. A rape fantasy?"

My eyes opened wide.

"Look," she said. "He's one of those guys, you know? One of those guys that nothing would surprise you about, not really, if you actually stopped and thought about it. If you looked behind the mask. That he might actually be the bad guy, not the good guy. That he might not be the savior." She paused and looked up at me. "He might be the predator."

For a moment after she said that, I kind of stopped breathing.

_____

I went back to visit my little plot of land opposite Roan's old place the other day, just for old times' sake. Looks like the flats are finally going to be built. The foundations are being filled. The girders are ready to put in place. There are people there all day long, the gates are open, vehicles driving in and out.

My little place has gone now, and with it the peace and the stillness, and the little red fox.

And I sit on my bed now, on this bright April evening, and I stare up at my pink paper lampshade with the heart-shape cutouts and I feel better about the eight-year-old girl who chose it, because she grew up to be a kick-ass, finger-breaking girl who got her revenge on the person who hurt her. I look down at Angelo, not a scrap anymore, a proper little cat, my little bit of wild outdoors indoors, and I should be happy, but something's buzzing and buzzing through my head. Despite Harrison being on remand for three of the sex attacks, he has alibis for all the others, and it looks like maybe there was more than one predator at large all along.

I uncross my legs and go to my window and stare down into the plaza. And then I remember a night, earlier this year, one of the nights when Josh and I went out looking for Harrison John.

And the truth hits me like a dart in the chest.

"Try and make yourself invisible," I'd said to him.

The next time we met up he'd arrived in Lycra running gear, a zip-up jacket, a black beanie hat. I didn't know it was him at first because his face was covered by a balaclava. As he approached, he pulled it down and I saw his smiling face emerge.

He said, "What do you think? Invisible enough?"

I pointed at the balaclava and laughed and said, "Where'd you get that scary-assed shit from?"

He shrugged. "Found it in my dad's drawer."

He smiled again. "Come on," he said. "Let's go hunting."

Acknowledgments

ACKNOWLEDGMENTS ARE THEORETICALLY for thanking the people who helped you to write the book in which they are published. So in that case I mainly need to thank me, myself, and I! I do write without input or advice for the majority of the year, just me and my (three) typing fingers and my weird imaginary world. I get to the end and put in place the final full stop without anyone's assistance. I don't do research, even when I should, because it puts me off my stride (so apologies for all the bloopers), and I don't like editorial input when I'm still working it out for myself.

But from the moment that final full stop is typed, all these magical people appear over the brow of the hill and silently walk into the imaginary world you've created to fix it for you and make it look pretty, to design covers for it, and to talk to people in bookshops and ask them to sell it, and to take it to foreign publishers and ask them to publish it, to make it look appealing on bookshelves so that people will notice it and buy it and read it, and to write nice things about it to encourage other people to read it. They bring you to bookshops and libiaries to talk to readers about it, and they urge friends to read it, and they write to you to say nice things about how the book made them feel.

So of course it's not all down to me. If it were all down to me this would be a rather rough-around-the-edges, vaguely nonsensical document on my laptop full of errors and typos and you would not have it in your hands right now.

So thank you to everyone, from the ground up. To Selina, my UK editor; Lindsay, my US editor; and Jonny and Deborah, my agents, for the early-doors editing notes. To Richenda Todd for skillfully copyediting it; Luke, Anna, and the film and TV team at Curtis Brown for putting it in front of people who make films and TV; and Jody and the foreign-rights team for getting it out across the globe. To the sales teams across the world for making sure it gets into the shops, to Sarah and her marketing team and Laura and her publicity team in the UK and to Ariele and Meriah in the US for making sure everyone knows about it. To booksellers, librarians, readers, and reviewers.

Thank you.

A note on the character name "Angela Currie"

A wide selection of the UK's most well-known authors have supported the Get in Character campaign from CLIC Sargent, the UK's leading cancer charity for children and young people, since the campaign started to run in 2014. To date more than £40,000 has been raised.

I have been very happy to support this campaign over the years, and one of this year's winners is featured in this book as the character Angela Currie.

The campaign will launch again on eBay in March 2021. Further details will be available at www.clicsargent.org.uk in the build-up to the auction.